# WIDOWMAKER
## JONES

# WIDOWMAKER
# JONES

## BRETT
## COGBURN

**PINNACLE BOOKS**
Kensington Publishing Corp.
www.kensingtonbooks.com

PINNACLE BOOKS are published by

Kensington Publishing Corp.
119 West 40th Street
New York, NY 10018

All Kensington titles, imprints, and distributed lines are available at
special quantity discounts for bulk purchases for sales promotions,
premiums, fund-raising, educational, or institutional use. Special book
excerpts or customized printings can also be created to fit specific
needs. For details, write or phone the office of the Kensington
sales manager: Kensington Publishing Corp., 119 West 40th Street,
New York, NY 10018, attn: Sales Department; phone 1-800-221-2647.

PINNACLE BOOKS and the Pinnacle logo are Reg. U.S. Pat. &
TM Off.

ISBN-13: 978-0-7860-3671-4
ISBN-10: 0-7860-3671-0

First printing: August 2016

10  9  8  7  6  5  4  3  2  1

Printed in the United States of America

First electronic edition: August 2016

ISBN-13: 978-0-7860-3672-1
ISBN-10: 0-7860-3672-9

# Chapter One

The night was so pitch-black that not a single star shone overhead, and the wind howled like a banshee through the mesquite brush. Maybe that was what had Newt Jones feeling so edgy, or maybe it was the poke of gold tucked away in his saddlebags.

Either way, he was a careful man, and the sound of what he thought was a horse coming was enough to give him pause. He held the coffee to his lips and squinted through the steam lifting from the mug, cocking his head one way and then the other, trying to hear again whatever it was that was out there. The hissing, whipping flames of his campfire lit his pale blue eyes above the scarred knots of his cheekbones, and he set his coffee aside and took up his rifle, his thumb hooking over the Winchester's hammer, and the walnut forearm fitting into his other palm as comfortably as an old friend.

Behind him on their picket line, his horse and pack mule lifted their heads and cocked their ears forward in the direction of the sound of shod hooves clattering over the caliche rock ledge that banked the near side of the river crossing. Whoever it was, they were making no attempt to be sneaky.

When the horseman finally appeared in the edge of the firelight, he was a tall, broad Mexican; almost as tall as Newt, but wearing a wide-brimmed sombrero and with a set of pearly white teeth shining beneath his thick mustache.

"*Buenas noches.* May I warm myself at your fire?"

It was the middle of summer and far from a cold night. Newt's eyes searched the blackness beyond for signs of anyone else. When he was semiconfident that the Mexican was alone, he motioned with a lifting of his chin for him to dismount.

The Mexican noticed the rifle in Newt's hands and the careful watch he kept on him. He chuckled and nodded slightly as if he approved, and made a point to turn his horse and dismount where Newt could see him plainly, loosening his cinch and dropping his reins on the ground. "*¿Un hombre cauteloso, eh?*"

"Hmm?" Newt was so focused on the Mexican's every move that he only half heard him.

"You gonna take no chances."

"Always cost me when I did."

The Mexican's horse was well trained to ground tie, and even in the poor light, Newt could see that it was a good horse—big and strong, and a better mount than any he had ever owned. But that was nothing. The fancy saddle on its back was worth more than Newt had ever sunk into a piece of horseflesh. He grunted to himself and hunkered down again on the far side of the fire with his rifle laid across his thighs.

"*¿Con su permiso?*" The Mexican gestured at the coffeepot sitting on top of some hot ashes raked out of the flames.

"Help yourself."

The Mexican pulled his own enamel coffee mug from the long saddlebags behind his saddle and walked to the fire with his spur rowels rattling and raking the ground. They were the big Chihuahua kind, with the wide, heavy bands overlaid with silver and rowel spokes half a finger long. They left lines in the sand where they dragged, like tiny snake tracks.

"*Muchas gracias, amigo.*" The Mexican took up the coffeepot and poured himself some. "I have far to go tonight, and some coffee will help."

Newt merely nodded while he noticed the clean white shirt underneath the Mexican's embroidered and brocaded vest, and the row of silver conchos laced with ribbon that ran down each leg of his pants. A real dude, a man of means, or a man who cared a lot about how he looked and spent everything he could on his outfit.

"You wonder where I go?" the Mexican asked.

Newt wondered nothing of the sort, more concerned with where the Mexican had come from and whether or not he was alone.

The Mexican shrugged when Newt didn't reply, and sipped at the hot coffee. "I have a rancho to the east, but my sister, she lives in Socorro and is very sick."

Newt waited long to answer him, while the mesquite wood in the fire popped and crackled between them and the Mexican's dark eyes watched him. "Hope she gets well."

The Mexican nodded gravely, shrugged his shoulders, and made the sign of the Trinity in the air before him. "Maybe I don't get there in time. Maybe she die. Maybe I go there, and she already well. *Sólo Dios sabe.*"

Only God knows. It was a term Newt had heard many times since he had gone west. It was a perfect excuse for anything and everything in a hard country. Something bad happened and you blamed it on God. Some miraculous bit of luck came your way, and you counted it a blessing. More good than bad for most, but Newt couldn't complain. He'd finally had a bit of luck. What did they used to say back home? Even a blind hog finds an acorn every now and then? *Sólo Dios sabe*, sure enough.

It was a hundred miles up or down the river to anything that resembled civilization—nothing but burnt grass and scrub brush as far as you could see in any direction. If there was such a place as "nowhere," then he had found it. And yet, the Mexican's horse didn't look like it had come far, nor did the Mexican.

The Mexican uncurled a finger from the handle of his coffee mug and pointed at the jackrabbit carcass hanging over the coals on a leaning stick jabbed in the ground. "Your dinner?"

"It's not much, but I won't turn you away if you're hungry."

"You are very generous." The Mexican rubbed his belly and smiled again, as if to demonstrate how hungry he was. He jerked a leg off the rabbit and made a show of picking delicately at the meat and smacking in delight, as if it were the most exquisite thing he had ever eaten.

Newt grunted again, but with a little humor. A touch of a smile hinted at one corner of his mouth. Tough, stringy jackrabbit wasn't much, but it was better than nothing. And he was one to know, for until the rabbit darted from under the shade of a mesquite tree and ran in front of his rifle sights, he hadn't had anything to eat in a day and a half.

"I was considering eating my pack mule before that rabbit showed up." Newt didn't know why he said that, but he found himself relaxing his guard. That wasn't a good thing for a man camped alone on the Pecos. He cast a quick glance at his saddlebags out of the corner of his left eye and then looked back at the Mexican just as quickly.

"Your stock, they look tired." The Mexican pitched the rabbit bones aside after he finished picking them clean, and pointed to Newt's picket line.

Newt couldn't argue with that. Not that his saddle horse and the little pack mule had come so far or so hard, but neither of them were particularly good animals to begin with. But that's what a man got on short notice when he left in the middle of the night and in a hurry. Every miner in White Oaks knew that you risked your poke and maybe your life riding in any direction out of town. There were some that made a living breaking their backs digging in the hard New Mexico ground, and some that made a living waiting beside the trail for some unsuspecting, prosperous sort to come along.

And that was why he had saddled up in the wee hours and rode like hell. Not north to the railroad at Las Vegas like most would expect, but south along the Pecos, hoping to strike the Texas Pacific line and catch a ride back East with his fortune intact and some crook wondering how he had gotten away.

"You look familiar," the Mexican said. "Do I know you?"

"Never saw you before." Newt ignored the hint and opportunity to introduce himself.

"You got one of those faces that makes me think I see you somewhere before. Maybe that's it," the Mexican said.

Newt didn't take offense, but there was a time when any mention of his battered face made him self-conscious enough to want to run his fingers over the knot of his oft-broken nose or trace the buckshot and gristle texture of the lump that was one cauliflower ear. Or it might make him want to hit that person in the worst way. A good, solid lick planted right on some unfriendly's nose always did short-term wonders for his temperament. But he told himself those days were long past and he had learned to dismiss the looks strangers gave him. He had fought for every one of those scars, and he'd be damned if he would be ashamed of them. Let them think what they wanted.

The Mexican continued to study Newt across the fire. The two of them stayed like that for a long while, staring while the mesquite wood crackled and the wind pelted them with sand. Newt found it odd to be at such a test of wills with a man he had only recently met, and a smiling, overly friendly man at that.

"Now I know," the Mexican finally said. "You fight that Irishman at Silver City a couple of years ago. What his name?"

"The Butcher."

"Yeah, that was him. You pretty tough. Thought you gonna win a time or two."

Newt let a hiss of air out between his teeth that was meant as a scoff. "He broke two of my ribs, my nose, and I couldn't close my left fist for a month."

"*¿Cuántos vueltas?* Thirty rounds?"

"Forty-five. That Mick bastard knocked me down nine times."

The Mexican remained squatting, but shadow-boxed and offered phantom punches over the flames. "That was a good fight. You never imagine some people you will run across. Like you, right here. *Sólo Dios sabe.* Widowmaker Jones in the flesh."

Newt frowned. It was a silly name, and not of his choosing. Seemed like all of his life he had been ending up with things he couldn't do anything about, trying to do things folks said he couldn't, and wanting what was always out of his reach. It wasn't some fight fan or newspaper editor that gave him the name— only a dumb Welshman popping it out of his mouth over a mug of beer in the midst of a victory celebration years before. Such a name shouldn't have lasted with only a half-dozen, not-so-smart pick-handle men and hired muscle in the saloon, and most of them too drunk or too battered to hear anything. But it did. Some things you're stuck with, like it or not.

"What you make for that fight?"

"Not a dime. It was a hundred dollars, winner take all."

"You like that kind of work?"

"What do you mean?"

"Beating people. Getting beat on."

"Money's hard to come by. Worked for the railroad some, dug graves one winter after that, and worked with a blacksmith that following spring. Ended up in a mining camp after that. Fought for prize money here and there when I could and worked as a mine guard and payroll escort when I wasn't swinging a pick or handling a muck stick. You know, whatever it took."

The Mexican nodded and pointed at where Newt's hands were draped over the Winchester cradled in his lap. "Big hands. *Manos de piedra* . . . How do you say? A puncher's hands, no? All scarred from the men you've hit."

Newt glanced at his battered knuckles. He'd always had big hands. All those years ago, when he left the mountains, his mother had stopped him on the porch and taken hold of those hands. She looked at them and then looked at him with that wise old look in her eyes.

"Newt," she said, "God gives every one of us something—some talent. Some he gives smarts and some he gives beauty or the knack to make money or build things. You, he gave hands made for fighting and a head as thick as a Missouri mule. Some would tell a hot-tempered man like you to ride easy out there where you're going, and I'll say the same. It's a far land and no telling what you'll run into. But I'll also tell you, when it comes to a pinch, you use what God gave you. Smite them that vex you to and fro, and lay about you with them hands. Samson didn't have much else but muscle and bone, and he did all right."

Newt laughed to himself and savored the old memory a bit before he answered the Mexican. "I've smote a few that vexed me sorely, and been knocked around myself more than once. You take your licks same as you give 'em."

"How did you come to that line of work? This pugilist business?" the Mexican asked.

"It just happened."

"You were fast when you fight the Butcher. Most big men aren't so fast as you."

"I've always had fast hands."

The Mexican nodded and clucked his tongue, as

if it were something he already knew, and as if it confirmed something he already suspected—like a doctor adding up symptoms to make a diagnosis.

"You ask a lot of questions," Newt said.

"*Perdóneme.* I no properly introduced myself. *Me llamo Javier . . .* Javier Cortina."

Newt immediately recognized the name and started to raise his rifle, but it was too late. The pistol appeared in the Mexican's hand as if by magic, cocked and pointed leisurely across the fire at him with the nickel plating on the steel shining in the firelight like some kind of talisman.

Cortina laughed. "A good fist is something, gringo, but it don't reach so far as a bullet."

Newt's hand crawled up the stock of his rifle toward the trigger guard.

The Mexican extended the pistol and pointed it at Newt's forehead. "Don't try it. You fast, but not fast as me."

Newt cursed under his breath. Damned Cortina sitting there smiling like he was doing him a favor holding a pistol on him. The thievingest bandit on the border, they said he never met a horse he couldn't steal, a woman he couldn't bed, a priest that he couldn't make cross himself, or a man that could run him down or best him with a gun. Of all the people to ride into his camp, and him stupid enough to let his guard down.

"I should have known you right off."

"Don't take it so hard," Cortina said. "Maybe you come through this alive. I get your gold, you know, and you get to keep your life. Fair trade."

"I don't have any gold."

Cortina clucked his tongue and shook his head.

"I follow you all the way from White Oaks. Maybe if you wanted to keep it a secret you shouldn't have a drunk for a partner. That Yaqui Jim, he buy everyone in the house rounds and pay for it with gold. All the people, they know Yaqui Jim made a strike."

"You kill Jim?"

"That Jim, he don't listen to reason good."

Newt had always worried that Jim couldn't keep things quiet, despite all the promises he made when they found the pay streak. Nobody would have ever believed the two of them would find anything when they quit their mine guard jobs and headed up the side of the mountain to do a little prospecting. What did a barroom thumper and a half-breed, drunk Indian know about ore? Everybody expected to strike it rich, but few ever did.

But Newt and Yaqui Jim had—a little pocket on the side of the mountain not yet claimed by the company and with a little ledge laced with gold. It was only a small find, and it had been their plan to high-grade it and get gone before the bushwhackers or company men snooping around found out about it. They were so close to getting away with it, but Jim always loved a bottle and wanted to celebrate and show off a little.

There were more riders coming through the brush—a lot of them. Cortina heard them but, smiling smugly, didn't even look their way.

"What say you lay down that rifle and get your poke for me? Save me the trouble of digging through your things," Cortina said.

"Go to hell."

"You first, señor."

Cortina's pistol roared, and that was the last thing Newt remembered until he wasn't dead anymore.

# Chapter Two

**B**ullets hurt like hell going in, but they can hurt worse later. A lot worse, until you can't think and until you don't know where the hurt begins and ends and you would rather be dead than suffer so. But then again, the only good thing about that kind of pain is that it lets you know you aren't dead. If you're a stubborn sort, hurting like that will make you mad enough to fight through it, if only because getting to your feet is the only way you can find the son of a bitch that did it to you and do worse to him.

Newt Jones woke with his face in the dirt, and it was a long time before he could recall how he came to be in such shape. There was a bullet hole through his chest, still intermittently and slowly seeping blood. There was a lot of blood—some wet and sticky and heavy, and other blood, older, dried and matted and mixing with the sand and forming a pasteboard crust of the front of his shirt. Yet, he was still alive. Cortina's bullet had passed through him like a hot knife, but somehow it hadn't killed him.

Cortina and his men had taken everything he

owned: his livestock, his gun, his gold. Made a fool of him. The damned gold. The most money he ever had. Blood and sweat and backbreaking work. The thought of losing it hurt almost as bad as the hole in him.

At least Cortina had left his boots on his feet. There was that, even if he was too weak to walk. As it was, it took him half an hour to crawl the fifty yards to the river's edge. Most times, he would have complained about the bitter Pecos water, but it tasted like heaven. He drank and drank and then dunked his head under until his mind was clearer.

It took him most of the afternoon to rebuild his fire from the feeble coals left from his previous one, and to bathe his wounds. The second day he smashed a rattlesnake's head with a rock. There were plenty of snakes.

The third and fourth day he ate more snake and took stock of his situation. He had nothing but a sheath knife and the clothes on his back, and it was a long way to anywhere from where he was. The closest settlements were a few little Mexican sheepherder villages back up the river to the north. And then there were Fort Stockton and Comanche Springs somewhere south of him, and the old mail road, running west to El Paso or southeast to Del Rio. Cortina's gang's tracks were headed due south.

He was no scout, but from the sign they left behind, he guessed there were at least five or six of them riding with Cortina. Most likely, every one of them was as salty as Cortina. A man in Newt's condition wouldn't stand much of a chance against them. The smart thing would be to walk north and count himself lucky that he might live. A smart man would do that, no doubt.

On the fifth day he started south, following the river and walking in the tracks of the man he swore to kill. He was in no shape to walk fast, but he walked as best he could. Every step he took was a challenge in itself, and his chest ached like he had been beaten with a sledgehammer. He wasn't a praying man, but more than once he scowled at the sun and asked that if he had one thing left granted to him, then let him come face-to-face with Javier Cortina one more time. Revenge and getting his gold back was the way it should be, but if it came to that, he would gladly settle for nothing but revenge. Cortina should have known that if you're going to kill a man, you better make sure he is dead.

# Chapter Three

It wasn't much of a tent, as circus tents go—a round thing with the brightly colored panels long since faded to dull pastels, and tears here and there sewn over with mildew-stained patches. One of the stakes had pulled loose from the sandy ground, and the Arabic-styled top that should have formed a needle spire at the center support pole instead sagged deeply. Still, it was perhaps the only circus to ever visit the little Mexican village, and the people who filed inside stared at it admiringly.

Kizzy Grey peeked out of a crack between the wall of the tent and the wagon tarp draped over a stretched rope that served as a screen and a dressing room. Some two dozen Mexican families were crowded together on the small section of bleachers on the far side of the tent from her, their eyes dark beneath the flickering lantern light, and their expressions almost somber, as if they weren't sure what to expect. Some of the children tugged at their parents' sleeves and pointed at the murals of African elephants, crocodiles, immense snakes, sword-swallowers, fire-breathers, and other exotic circus themes painted on plank signs scattered around. Most of the peasant farmers and villagers had likely never seen anything approaching an elephant, nor were they apt to. Billed as a circus or not, the Greys had never owned an elephant, no matter what was on the signs. Although they had once owned a monkey and used it in the show until it bit a customer one night in Kansas City and the drunken Italian track layer pulled a club out of his coat pocket and killed the poor, ill-tempered thing.

The signs were what they were. "Ambience" was what her father used to call his painted flights of fancy—creating hope and setting mood—rather than false advertising. In Kizzy's mind they were an outright lie, but a harmless one if a lie could be such.

There had been a time when the Incredible Grey Family Circus had played before the big crowds in the big towns. But everything fell apart. Since then, it was more of the same, traveling the roads and settling for anyplace that would have them and doing their acts for whatever the local citizenry had to shell out, which of late hadn't been much.

Kizzy turned and stared at the rusted little money box on the table behind her. The night's take for the gate wasn't more than a handful of pesos and not near enough to feed their animals or to keep up with repairs. She shrugged her thin shoulders without realizing she did it. It wasn't all bad. One old woman had bought her family's way into the show with a chicken. At least they would eat well for a meal.

Kizzy double-checked herself in the mirror, dabbing at a stray strand of black hair before tugging on her hat. She smoothed the front of her dress, frowning at a stain on it and wondering if she had made the best selection from the open chest full of costumes beside her. Her father had claimed that he paid a genuine Indian maiden to tan and sew the buckskin together. The snow-white, fringed dress was a pretty thing, with embroidery and fancy stitching across the chest and beadwork at the sleeve cuffs and on the hem of the skirt. She loved the dress, even though her father hadn't really gotten it from any Indian maiden. She had known that, even when she was only ten. He had really paid a Jewish seamstress in Chicago fifty dollars to make it. The buckskin wasn't really buckskin, and the cheap suede was worn smooth in places from the days when her mother wore it.

No matter, it was still an impressive costume. She took both of her pistols by the butts and lifted them a little in their holsters, adjusting the gun belt cinched around her narrow waist until it felt comfortable. She looked into the mirror one last time and pressed her lips together to smooth the red lipstick on them, blowing a kiss at herself before she walked out before the crowd.

"Ladies and gentleman, lords and ladies," her voice rose to the sagging tent top. "Perhaps since mankind first captured fire or mastered the art of shaping flint, there has been no greater moment than when he first sat astride a horse. Until then, his spirit was incomplete; until then, the horse's spirit was incomplete. In that moment, when the horse first moved beneath him, the partnership was forged. Man and beast racing over the plains, swift and sure, stronger for one another. Nothing so mighty, they became like the wind."

She paused dramatically, noting that none of the

crowd seemed to speak enough English to understand everything she said, but her tone obviously had their attention. Half of pandering to any crowd was always about the showmanship, anyway, rather than the words.

"And in time, many men came to ride the noblest of the beasts, but every once in a generation there was born a special rider and a horseman like no other. And ever more rarely a horse was born to match him. And once every century, or two or three, that special horseman and that special horse came together and magic was the result. Man and horse working together, until the giant, beating heart throbbing beneath the rider's legs flowed into him and they breathed and lived as one."

Fonzo timed his entrance perfectly. All six of the horses loped through the open tent door in a perfect line, side by side, with their long manes dancing with each stride and Fonzo standing with a foot each on the backs of the middle two, riding standing up, Roman style, with a long set of reins attached to the halters on those two horses.

Two times, he took them around the ring, and then on the third revolution he steered to a low jump made of a small log resting on end braces some two feet off the ground. All six of the horses sailed over the jump with their front legs folded under them and their nostrils flared. Fonzo stayed standing, even through the jump, and the crowd clapped when he landed without a hint of losing his balance and his knees absorbing the shock.

Kizzy smiled. No matter how many times she saw them, the six snow-white horses were truly beautiful. If her father had done one thing for the family show—for her and Fonzo—it was that. Ten years he had spent searching for matched animals, so alike in size and looks that anyone not a horseman might not recognize a difference in them at a glance. Every spare coin her father had ever been able to put together, he spent on those horses: Bucephalus, Herod, Mithridates, Sheba, Solomon, and Hercules. Blood and sweat and tears, and all the years putting the show together, making it something, all represented in horseflesh.

Her attention switched to her brother. Fonzo was as nimble as a cat, slight and wiry and athletic, with grace and balance oozing from him as effortlessly as quicksilver sliding over glass. For all the trouble he often caused her, she would still be the first to admit that he could ride like no other, as if he were born on a horse, or as if he were once a part of the horse and some appendage that had been removed and found its proper working once returned to the body from whence it was taken.

Fonzo guided the horses around the ring one more time, the horses keeping perfect pace and spacing, and their noses even, like they were bound together with invisible harnesses. The second pass over the jump, Fonzo floated up, his feet losing contact with the horses' backs. The crowd gasped, thinking he was about to be thrown to the ground, but to their amazement, he landed on two different horses and rode around the ring smiling and waving one hand at the crowd as if it were nothing.

The somber faces of the crowd turned to smiles and they pointed to him and laughed in wonderment. Fonzo leapt to the ground without even stopping the horses. They continued to circle him until he picked up a braided, long-handled buggy whip and whistled to them and cued them with some motion of the whip that only he and the horses understood. As one, they shifted into a single-file line, and with a second signal they stopped and faced inward to him at the center of the ring, like wagon spokes surrounding him. He raised both arms high overhead, and all six horses reared on their hind legs and pawed playfully at the air.

While the other five waited, one of the horses then came slowly forward and bowed to Fonzo with one of its front legs stretched out before it and the other bent beneath it. Fonzo swung onto its back and led the other horses around the ring again at a fast lope.

Riding bareback, Fonzo took a double handful of mane and swung off as if he were going to dismount on the run. The instant his feet hit the ground he bounced back up and landed again on the animal's back. The second time he did it he twisted and con- torted his body so that he landed facing backward.

Once the crowd had quieted, Kizzy stretched one arm toward her brother in a dramatic pose. "Another round of applause for Fonzo the Great and his mag- nificent horses."

Fonzo leapt from his horse and joined Kizzy in the center of the ring, the horses still revolving around at his bidding. He motioned for the crowd to quiet.

Fonzo's voice rose high and clear in the confines of the tent, only slightly deeper than his sister's. "And man soon found that the horse was good for war, and the mighty men of old broke themselves against each other in one wild charge after another, sword in hand and a swift warhorse beneath them, until empires were made, and a time came when a warrior was no warrior at all unless there was a four-legged brother beneath him and carrying him into battle.

"Weapons of steel, sword and mace, required a strong arm, and the mighty usurped the weak, and giants ruled the world until here, on the frontier of the New World, an invention was made—a weapon so great, so cunning and minuscule, yet deadly, that history would be changed. The American cowboy likes to say that Samuel Colt made all men equal, but it is not only men that can handle a gun." Fonzo turned and bowed to Kizzy. "I give you Buckshot Annie, at the same time the prettiest woman west of anywhere, and the finest marksman to ever lift a firearm."

Kizzy bowed deeply in an imitation of the courtly dip of someone paying homage, as if the crowds were kings and queens instead of dirt-poor peasants and subsistence farmers. When she raised her head again to face them, she smiled and blew another kiss.

Fonzo went back to the circling horses and swung up on one on the fly. As soon as he was astride, she began to pitch him a series of red, shiny glass balls, one at a time. He caught them on the run, one-handed, stuffing them into a leather bag at his waist.

Kizzy stood with her back to the crowd and slowly drew the pearl-handled Colt revolvers at the same time. She let them dangle at arm's length beside her thighs, standing unmoving except for her eyes tracking her brother as he went around her. The next time Fonzo passed before her he tossed one of the glass balls high above him and she shattered it with one shot from her right-hand pistol. On his second pass he tossed two balls simultaneously and she busted those, too, with a shot from each gun.

The crowd had grown deathly quiet, but she was

used to that. She suppressed the smile building on her lips and holstered her left-hand gun and waited for Fonzo's next pass. That time, he launched four balls into the air, and she shot from the hip without even taking aim with the pistol sights. She worked the trigger on the double-action Colt Lightning so fast that the four shots almost sounded as one. All four balls shattered, and brightly colored bits of glass showered down like falling stars.

Fonzo dismounted again and the horses raced out the open door and left the tent. He ran to her side and they gave the crowd another bow. As if it had taken the farmers and goat herders that long to get over seeing such a slip of a young girl shoot so, they finally erupted into a round of applause.

"Pretty good stuff when you can impress anyone on the border with your shooting prowess," Fonzo said under his breath as they bowed again.

Kizzy smiled demurely at the crowd, and her eyes strained upward toward the ceiling of the canvas tent. She was a far better than average shot, but none of the spectators ever seemed to notice the tiny holes all over the roof of the tent or the unusually quiet pop her .38s made. Busting such glass balls out of the air with regular bullets and black powder charges would have been a feat of marksmanship, indeed, but the lead birdshot and reduced loads she reloaded her cartridges with, much like small shotgun loads, made it a far easier thing. And the less powerful shot loads were much safer for work inside the tent or around crowds, rather than sending stray bullets speeding to who-knows-where to hit who-knows-what. However, the scattering of the pellets over the last year since they had added her act had pinpricked the tent with holes to the point it leaked like a sieve on a rainy day, and the tent was getting in pitiful condition as it was.

They shook hands with the villagers as they filtered out of the tent, and Kizzy did a few more trick shots with real bullets under the open sky, where she could pick a safe direction in which to shoot. Normally, Fonzo would have mingled through the crowd to find one or more men with enough faith in their own marksmanship to think that they could best a girl in a shooting match, but there wasn't enough money in the village for anyone to make any kind of a wager.

Fonzo let the children pet his horses, and even gave a few of them a ride, smiling even though not many months ago he would have charged four bits per person to have their photo taken sitting on one of the horses. But the camera was ruined when one of the wagons overturned crossing the Rio Grande a month before, and there might not be four bits left in the entire village.

The sun was going down when their guests finally filtered back to their village of mud-daubed picket huts, eroded adobe walls, and bleating goats. Fonzo traded a stained and frayed red velvet jacket that his father had once worn as ringmaster, along with four pesos, for the services of two of the village men to help dismantle and pack the tent. It was long after midnight before the tent was loaded into one of their wagons, and it cost them two more pesos to buy some hay for the horses.

The more elaborate of their two wagons was a gaudy thing, with high wheels, a bright red paint job, and gold pinstriping on every edge. It was what Kizzy's people called a *vardo*. It had plank sides and a shingled roof, and inside it was their living quarters—a narrow bed on each side, cabinets for storage, and a small kitchen area and stove for cooking when the weather was too bad to build a fire outside.

The night was too hot to light the stove, and Kizzy butchered the hen and baked it in a Dutch oven at a fire she built beside the wagon. She had already finished her portion of the chicken and carried water to the horses from the river to their picket line by the time Fonzo and his helpers were through packing up the show. He joined her at the fire, and she noticed the weary way he walked.

He nodded at the money box she had set on the camp table beside their fire. "How much?"

"After the cost of the hay and what you paid the men to help take down the tent?"

"How much?"

She pointed at the half-picked carcass of the hen grown cold on the plate she left out for him. "You get half a chicken."

He shrugged. "Oh well, but please tell me we have a little wine left."

She lifted a pottery jug and held it close to her ear while she shook it. "There's a swallow left. Maybe we can find someone down the road that might have a little fruit to sell so that you can make us some more."

He picked at the cold chicken, brooding and lost in his own thoughts. She noticed the way his eyebrows tilted in together above his nose, like their father's had when he was deep in thought. After a while he stood and paced around the fire.

When he spoke again he switched to the Roma tongue without thinking. Although they had both been born on American soil and were as comfortable with English as any language, it was an old habit when they were alone with each other. When their parents were alive they all had spoken the language of their people among family settings. And it had other advantages when strangers were around, as it was often of benefit to them to converse where the *gadje* couldn't understand what was being said. In addition to the Gypsy language, both of them spoke a smattering of French, a thing rarely used, but their mother had insisted on it, as it was the land of her birth. To add to the confusion of their multilingual skills, there was the bit of Spanish picked up during their time below the border. Without either of them realizing it, they often mixed words of many languages in the same breath, or hopped from one to another at whim.

"Homemade wine not fit for human consumption, and a bit of cold chicken. What's happened to us?" He lifted both arms wide and then let them drop with a slap against his hips.

"You know what happened."

"I think we ought to go back to the States. There's no money down here."

"And who in the States wants us, and what money were we making north of the border?" she asked, cocking one eyebrow.

"What about the invite to Monterrey?"

She picked up the money box and rattled the few coins in it as she had shaken the almost empty bottle of wine. "I don't think there's enough here to get us there."

He walked to the edge of the firelight where his white horses stood watching him from their picket line. He picked up a brush and began to rub it over the back of one of them—a gelding slightly larger and heavier than the rest of them.

"Hercules looks like he's lost a little weight," she said.

"They've all lost weight, and I fed them the last of the corn this morning."

"We'll get by like we always do."

He whirled and threw the brush across the camp. "It isn't fair."

"Nothing is fair."

"How many people will be at that bullring in Monterrey?"

"I'm told that it can seat a thousand people, and the crowds are always large," she said. "I can get you the letter from the promoter if you want to read it again."

"How much up front did he offer us?"

"Only a cut of the gate after each show. Ten percent. We perform two acts a day in between bullfights. No guarantees of any kind."

"Getting there is a week's trip, at least."

"President Díaz is supposed to be at the fights, and the U.S. ambassador to Mexico and other dignitaries, also. I imagine it will be a big crowd," she said. "Maybe the kind of crowd that could put us back on the map."

He paced more, and she suppressed a smile the sight of him brought on. He had both arms folded behind his back and was bent at the waist, his face turned down to the ground and his brow furrowed in thought. A pacing general on the night before a battle wouldn't have looked more serious.

In an instant, his demeanor changed and he stopped in his tracks and turned to her with an impish, boyish smile lighting him like a candle. "We'll give them a real show. I'll break out the new acts I've been practicing and some special stuff for the bigger arena.

And we can think up some new things for you. Maybe you'll rethink some of my suggestions."

She couldn't help but sigh. For almost a year since their parents had passed on, Fonzo had been trying to get her to add what he called some "William Tell" parts to her portion of the show—shoot an apple off his head or a coin out of his hand, much like some of the other traveling sharpshooter acts did. He had persisted so in his arguments that she had finally agreed to practice such. Their second day of practice with her shooting a silver dollar out of his outstretched hand, she took the tip off his right index finger. The sight of him bleeding and the scarred nub of that finger, minus its last joint, was more than she could take. She knew she was an exceptional shot, but it felt foolishly dangerous to risk his health. He was the last of any kind of kin or family she had on the earth, unless she counted some distant cousins, equally as nomadic as she and Fonzo, and long since out of contact.

The shadows of two dogs crept into the edge of the firelight. Both of them were big and hairy with broad heads, outsized feet, and jaws like bears. The smaller of the two was brown and the larger one was white. They lay down at her feet on either side of her, and one of them, the white dog, carried a dead rabbit clamped in its jaws.

"Look at that," Fonzo said. "Even the dogs eat better than we do."

She reached down and stroked both the dogs' heads. "Did you ever think of giving up this life?"

"And do what?"

"I don't know. Maybe live like normal people and stay in one place."

He laughed. "We're Roma."

"There are Gypsies that don't live on the road. You've met them like I have."

"What would we do to make a living?"

"I wouldn't call what we make now a living."

"I like performing, and you do, too."

"That's not what I mean. Don't you ever think what it would be like to have a real house? Maybe something solid for once. A place to winter, at the very least."

"Sounds boring."

"Maybe."

"And what about the first time someone accuses us of some petty theft, or places blame on us whether we're guilty or not? Don't you know? We Romani are supposed to be a shifty lot. Witches, thieves, and fortune-tellers. I think I'll go find some children to kidnap."

"Don't be so dramatic." She took up her little squeeze-box accordion and began to play a wistful tune that her mother had taught her.

"Quit that. It's bad enough without you playing that stuff."

"I like that tune. It makes me think of Mama."

He sat down on a campstool and listened to her a play awhile. "Look at us. We're everything Gypsies are supposed to be. You playing that thing, and both of us without a penny to our names and wondering where we can go to snatch a little coin from someone's purse."

"We'll get by."

He jumped to his feet, the passion in his voice raising it half an octave. "We're going to Monterrey. I won't take no for an answer."

She watched him storm off into the night, smiling

to herself. Fonzo liked to announce everything, as if he made all the decisions. But in truth, she had intended to point the wagons that way in the morning anyway. Maybe Monterrey would turn out like they hoped, but that was the thing about being Roma and circus people. The next place down the road was always the same thing as hope.

# Chapter Four

It felt like he had been walking forever across a flat expanse that never changed and never ended. By the time the Comanche found him, Newt's fevered brain barely recognized what they were, and he wasn't in much of a condition to do anything about it when he literally stumbled right up to them. There were four of them, all warriors, and they were leading two spare horses with a dead antelope tied on the back of one.

One of their horses stamped at a fly, and Newt put a hand against its shoulder to steady himself. The whole world was spinning, but he willed his blurred vision to focus when he looked up at the wild Indians.

They stared back at him out of their dark eyes, their faces stoic and unreadable, and as fierce as anything ever born—nothing to greet him but fistfuls of sharp weapons and the kind of looks a hawk gives a field rat when looking down on him from above. One of them pointed a lance at him with a wicked length of ground-down cavalry saber for a head and a handle so long that the needle tip of the blade nearly brushed his chest. The Comanche with the lance said something in his native tongue and it made the others laugh. Their laugh didn't sound friendly at all. He knew only enough about Comanche to know that they would certainly kill him, and his dying would take a long time.

And Cortina was going to get away with his gold.

"I'll be damned," he said right before he fell.


When he awoke it was the second time he came back from the dead. At least it felt that way.

He was lying inside a tepee on a pallet made of a few tattered wool army blankets. The bone-white buffalo hide sides of the conical lodge had been rolled up some two feet off the ground to keep it cool. Despite the breeze blowing through the shade of the lodge, he was covered in sour-smelling sweat. A groan escaped his lips when he tried to move, and it was as if every muscle and joint in his body protested. He was bare to the waist, and someone had covered the bullet hole in his chest with some kind of mud and moss poultice. By the time he had struggled to a sitting position, some of the poultice had cracked and fallen away, but the wound wasn't bleeding.

A pack of camp dogs trotted by while he sat there getting his bearings, and one of them hiked a leg on one of the peeled lodge poles and then growled at him before it trotted off. Shortly, there came the sound of moccasins scuffing the ground, and a young Comanche woman stuck her head between the flaps of the doorway. She took quick stock of him, her eyes growing large at the sight of him awake, and then quickly disappeared.

Sometime later, he heard more footsteps coming.

This time, the warrior with the nasty scars down one side of his face who had held the lance to his chest entered the lodge, followed by another warrior. Both of them sat on the ground across from him and nodded in greeting.

They were well past middle age, although the scar-faced warrior seemed the younger of the two. One side of his head was decorated with a crow's wing tied into the top of one braid of his hair, and a bear claw necklace stood out against the brown of his throat and bare chest. Neither of the men wore any clothing except for breechcloths covering their nether parts and moccasins on their feet. They bore no weapons other than the knives on their belts.

The elder of the two said something that Newt couldn't understand. When he shook his head to let them know he didn't speak their language, the scarred one spoke.

"¿Habla español?" he asked.

Newt recognized that he was being asked if he could speak Spanish, but that was almost the limit of his bilingual skills. "No."

The two warriors glanced at each other and then the scarred warrior began to make a series of hand symbols, at first so silly as to seem like children making shapes and playing shadow games, but Newt was surprised at how easy it was for him to understand the gist of the story being told. He had heard that many Indians used hand talk as a means to trade and communicate with other tribes, but he had never witnessed it.

In short, the men had been out hunting and found him staggering and half-dead on the trail. When the scarred warrior pointed at his counterpart and made a motion of slicing the edge of his hand across his hairline, Newt understood that it had been the wish of most of them to take his scalp and leave him where he fell. Apparently, the scarred warrior had talked them out of it for reasons that Newt couldn't understand. There was a whole flurry of hand symbols that weren't clear to him, but it was plain that they brought him to their camp and tended his wounds. Also, the older of the two before him seemed to be some kind of shaman or medicine man. He had a hide rattle on the end of a short shaft of wood and occasionally shook it and said something loudly, looking up at the ceiling as if he were talking to the spirits or the sky itself.

More people began to gather outside the lodge while the scarred one was still making hand talk. From the bare calves and the bottom edge of the buckskin dresses that Newt could see revealed beneath the rolled-up bottom of the lodge, he knew it was more Comanche women, and it was quickly apparent that they were dismantling the lodge.

The scarred Comanche pointed a finger at the wound in Newt's chest and asked something.

Newt thought a moment and then made a pistol shape with his right hand and mocked the hammer fall with his thumb and the muzzle forefinger rising with recoil as he did a childish imitation of a gun sound. "Bad man. *Mal hombre.*"

The two Comanche passed a look between them, and then the scarred warrior pitched Newt's knife on the ground in front of him. Newt picked up the knife and drew it from its sheath. Neither of the Comanche so much as flinched, and Newt couldn't tell if they were daring or expecting him to do something.

Newt pointed to the wound in his chest again and then stabbed the knife into the ground. "Enemy."

The two Comanche glanced at each other again, grunted, and then stood. The shaman shook the hide rattle at Newt and said something that made the scarred warrior smile.

The squaws had the hide walls removed by the time Newt had managed to pull into his boots. Someone had cleaned and patched his tattered shirt, and he tucked it into his pants while he stood and stared at the other lodges being taking down. It was a small camp, from the looks of it, and maybe only six or seven dwellings. The pole A-frames of travois were being lashed to horses' backs, and luggage and home items were being loaded on them. A large herd of loose horses was already started east with some young boys driving them. Apparently, the whole camp was about to move elsewhere.

Newt's wound may have closed and the poultice taken the inflammation out, but he was still weak. His heart was racing and his legs shaky in the short trip it took him to get out of the tepee. He took up the water bag they had left him and sat down a few feet out of the way of the working squaws. The bag was made from the bladder of a buffalo, or some other organ, with a horn stopper and a length of rawhide for a carrying strap. His thirst was incredible, and he drank half the bag over the course of the next half hour. By that time, the lodge he had been in was torn down, loaded on a travois, and the whole camp was leaving. Nobody waved at him or came to talk to him, only looking at him in passing and saying things to one another about him that he couldn't understand.

Soon, he was alone, sitting on the ground with his

water bag and a buckskin sack full of food that they had left him. The scarred warrior and the shaman were the last to go. The scarred one was leading a spare horse and he pitched its lead rope to Newt.

Newt studied the horse. It was a short-coupled, brown horse with a light brown nose and not a white mark on it. Despite the plain coloring, the animal was exceptional-looking. It was stockier and better muscled than most of the Indian ponies, with big, good bones and dark hooves. Unlike many of the jug-headed ponies Newt had seen in the camp, the brown had a broad forehead beneath short, foxlike ears, bulldog jaws, and large, intelligent eyes.

The scarred Comanche pointed at the horse and then at Newt. By the time Newt got to his feet and took up the brown's lead rope the two Comanche were already riding away.

Newt ran a hand down the brown's neck and noticed for the first time the brand on its left hip. It was a circle with a single dot in its center. As far as he knew, Indians didn't brand their horses to mark them for ownership like Americans or Mexicans did. Odds were, the gelding had probably been stolen during a raid, but Newt wasn't going to look a gift horse in the mouth.

Actually, he did, and the brown's teeth were fine.

Newt couldn't figure why the Comanche hadn't killed him, much less doctored his wounds and left him with supplies and a horse. They had a reputation as a fierce lot and rarely gave any enemy quarter or mercy. You didn't have to know anything about Comanche to have heard all the horror stories about the cruel atrocities they committed on white folks they captured.

He would have liked to rest awhile—days, if truth were told—but he wasn't about to give the Comanche a chance to change their minds. The squaws had also left a couple of the army blankets he had lain on in the lodge. He rolled the bag of food up in them and cinched the bundle together with his belt and laid it across the brown's withers. The water bag he hung over his shoulders and across his chest, and he secured his sheath knife in his boot top. The sun was already working its way high above to the midday mark, and he wished he had his hat. He couldn't remember where he had lost it.

There was no saddle for the brown, and he was going to have to ride bareback. Normally, it would have been no feat at all for him to swing up on the horse's back without a saddle or stirrup. However, considering the shape he was in, mounting up presented a problem, even though the brown wasn't very tall.

The answer to his problem showed itself when he spotted the shallow, dry gully not far away and leading down to the river. He led the brown into the bottom of the wash, and the animal stood calmly while he climbed up on the high bank. Indian pony or not, the horse seemed smart and calm enough and obviously had some training. Newt eased onto the brown's back from above, took up the looped rein tied to some kind of halter or bosal around the horse's nose, smiled to himself at the accomplishment with so little pain to his wound, and then gently bumped the brown's belly with his heels.

The brown promptly threw him into a cluster of prickly pear.

# Chapter Five

The Circle Dot horse, as he soon came to think of the brown, was full of tricks, although he didn't buck again. Newt plucked the worst of the tiny cactus needles from his tender parts and started walking after the horse. He was not normally a man given to profanity, but the heat of the day and both his wounded body and wounded pride resulted in an exceptionally creative string of vile oaths and death threats aimed at one particular horse.

The last he saw of the horse it was still bawling and bucking and zigzagging out of sight like a mustang bronc. He followed in the general direction it had been headed, assuming it would go after the band of Comanche in order to be with the other horses. However, after a long walk he found the gelding standing three-legged with its head drooped as if it were half-asleep or waiting on him.

Newt caught hold of his rope rein once again and debated on what to do next. The nearby Pecos offered water, but it was still no country to be afoot in. It was a long way to anywhere from where he stood, and even farther if he had to trust to his own legs. He guessed that he might be three days from Fort Stockton, if not farther. What's more, the next bunch of Comanche he ran into might not be so friendly, and without a horse he was going to play hob outrunning them.

And Cortina was getting farther away by the minute.

A bronc rider was the last thing he was. Oh, he could handle a mule team or plow a decently straight furrow through rocky hill country ground, but a cowboy or horseman he was not. But it didn't matter, for he had little choice. He laid his blanket roll across the Circle Dot horse's withers again, gritted his teeth, took a double handful of mane, and swung up on its back expecting the worst.

The horse stood calmly and even bent its head around to look back at him as if to say, "What's the big deal?"

The sudden movement of swinging on the horse took the air out of Newt, and he had to sit awhile until the worst of the pain went away. He half expected the horse to throw him again when he kicked it forward, but it moved off as easy as you please and as if its former actions had never happened.

After a mile or two at a calm, ground-eating walk, Newt decided that the horse was probably decent enough and had only been startled by him appearing above it on the high bank and landing on its back.

Cortina had a big lead on him, and Newt was anxious to close the gap. He tried to stick to a trot at first, thinking it would cover the most miles without burning out his mount, but the jarring stride was too much for his wound and throughout the rest of the day he alternated their pace between a walk and a long, rocking-chair lope. When he finally made camp at sundown he guessed that he had managed thirty miles in less than half a day. Yet, the Circle Dot horse looked no worse for the wear.

Despite their rough start, he was growing more confident in the horse. It responded lightly to the slightest movement of his reins and legs, stood still when he asked, and seemed as eager to travel as he was. In fact, Newt couldn't remember ever having such a horse and had about decided that he was lucky that the Comanche gave it to him. Luck could be an iffy thing, but maybe his had turned for the better.

On the second day the horse balked in its tracks and refused to move an inch. It stopped so quickly and so hard that Newt almost fell over its neck. Nothing seemed to be wrong with it, other than it had decided to stop and couldn't be convinced to do otherwise. Newt kicked it, slapped it on the hip with his hand, and generally encouraged it in ways both kind and not so kind.

It was in the middle of this difficulty that Newt saw the white top of the wagon on the horizon. He quickly decided it was best to dismount and not provide such a tall profile on the horizon. When he stepped to the ground and moved behind a clump of bushes near the edge of the river canyon the horse followed behind him willingly enough.

"Crazy horse," Newt said. He wondered if his fever had come back or if the sun was getting to him to be talking to an animal.

The wagon was still a good mile away, but he had already spotted the woman out to one side of it. She had a shovel and seemed busy digging a hole. From the mound of earth beside it, he was pretty certain it was a grave.

# Chapter Six

There wasn't a good tree in sight, nor so much as a rock to make a decent shade, and the sun was at its midday worst. It was a country to make you sweat, if nothing else. Accordingly, the woman was sweating profusely and paused to rest against her shovel handle when Newt got close. She was old and thin, but not so old that she hadn't made good work of the hole she was digging. It was already knee-deep.

Letting one hand go from the shovel handle, she placed it on the small of her back as if to stretch the kinks out of it. "If you've come to rob me, get on with it and go ahead and shoot me now."

Her voice was heavily laden with country twang, but there was also a certain ladylike poise to her bearing. Her straightforward manner and gaze were a little disconcerting, especially for a woman alone out in that wild country. He stopped several feet short of the grave and was at a loss as to how to reply to such a statement.

She brushed a strand of gray hair out from in front of her eyes where it had come untucked from the

bonnet she wore, and her sweaty leather glove left a
streak of dirt across her forehead. "Well then, if you
aren't going to shoot me you can lend a hand with
this grave."

She pitched him the shovel and reached down in
the hole for something. When she climbed out she
was holding a Sharps big-bore rifle. The gun was as
long as she was, with an octagonal barrel and one of
those fancy, brass-tubed German scopes mounted on
it. It must have weighed fifteen pounds, but she held
it as if she knew how to handle it. Where a woman had
come by such a thing was beyond him, for such guns
hadn't been used since there were still any buffalo left
to shoot with them.

Her eyes twinkled and the crow's-feet at the corners
of her eyes folded deeply. "Are you deaf, or has the sun
got to your head? You dig and I'll see if I can fix you
something to eat. You look like you've come far."

"Yes, ma'am," was all he managed to say before she
went to her wagon and left him alone.

He dropped the Circle Dot horse's reins and
stepped down into the hole. The gelding stood where
he left it, seemingly well trained to ground tie and
content to rest while he worked. After a few shovelfuls
of earth, Newt took another look at the woman's
wagon. It was one of the big Conestoga kind rarely
seen anymore. A matched foursome of gray, medium-
sized draft horses were tied to one side, and a spotted
Guernsey milk cow with a bell tied around its neck
roamed free and followed the woman around while
she rustled her cookware beside a chip fire she had
stoked up.

There was something white on the ground that the

woman and the cow both avoided, and it was about man-sized. Newt guessed the tarp-covered form belonged to whoever he was digging the grave for.

He continued to dig through the afternoon, until she brought him a plate of beans, some fresh ear corn, and two tiny rolls of white bread. He sat on the mound of dirt beside the grave and alternated between the food and his water bag.

"You're a slow digger," she said.

He pointed at his shirt. The Comanche squaws, despite their mending and washing, hadn't been able to get the bloodstain out of it where the cloth lay over the bullet wound in his chest. "I'm not up to snuff today, but I'd say the grave's about deep enough."

"Who did that to you?"

"A Mexican bandit. He's riding with about five or six others of his kind."

Her face took on a strained look. "Was them that shot my Amos. He had ridden down to the river to water his horse and they caught him there. Would have done for me, too, but I heard them shoot him. They were still far enough out that I had time to take up Amos's gun and get off a shot."

"You hit one?"

"No, but it was enough to make them keep their distance. Amos used to say that Sharps will shoot as far as you can see, and I didn't intend to let them get close enough to make out I was a woman alone."

"You're lucky." He regretted the words as soon as he said them, and his eyes drifted to the tarp-wrapped body of her man. "That's a bad bunch. I'm sorry for your loss."

"Don't be. Me and Amos had a lot of good years.

Come to Texas from Missouri back during the war years. Had some good days, but this spring we decided to head west. Amos said it wasn't ever going to rain again here and thought it would be better in the Arizona Territory. Although, from what I've seen, the farther we went the less rainy things looked."

It came to Newt's mind unbidden. "They say it rains on the just and the unjust alike. But out here, it doesn't rain much on anyone."

"That's scripture you're quoting, young man."

"Yes, ma'am. Not that I'm a righteous man, but back where I come from we didn't have much else to read. Ma had a big, black Bible she used to read to us from, by and by, time to time."

Her eyes drifted to the bloodstain on his shirt again, and then she cast a close inspection over his scarred face. "Maybe not all of that listening took, from the look of you."

"I've seen the elephant, if that's what you mean."

"You after those Mexicans?"

"I am."

She lifted her chin and motioned for him to look behind him. "For a man with far to go you have a strange choice in horses."

Newt twisted around and saw that the Circle Dot horse was lying down, full out on its side with its eyes closed. Only the heave of its belly showed that it was alive.

"That gelding looks in good flesh and not too hard used," she added.

"I guess he's tired," he said. "And I'm coming to think he's a bit peculiar."

"How did you come by him?"

"Indians gave him to me."

"Indians?"

"Comanche, I think."

"Your guardian angel must really be something. I never heard of them doing anyone a good deed."

He helped her drag her husband's body to the grave. It was something on the order of a miracle that she had managed to get it from the river to the wagon, given how petite she was.

As if she read his thoughts, she said, "I rolled him in that tarp and drug him behind one of the horses. Broke my heart to treat him that way. He was always good to me."

A bit of the tarp came unfolded, revealing her husband's head. Newt was pretty sure the man was past caring about how he was treated, by his wife or otherwise. One of Cortina's bunch had put a bullet above his left eyebrow and a second one right through his teeth. He quickly covered the man's head before the woman had to take another look at him. It was best that she remembered him as he had been and not how Cortina had left him.

Digging the grave had sapped what little strength Newt had left, and he and the old woman took turns at the shovel, covering the body. She was a scrappy worker.

"Sorry, ma'am. Usually I'm more of a hand than this."

She nodded. "You've got the shoulders for it. Not bad-looking, either, once you look past all those scars you're packing."

"Thank you, I guess."

He took a close look at her again. His first impression was that she was old, but it was hard to tell if she was a well-preserved sixty or a hard-used fifty. She had the mannerisms of a lady, but the sharp, up-front talk of the frontier. His own mother had been a woman like that.

"What's your trade when you're not manhunting?" she asked.

He shrugged.

She laughed, but no matter how she tried, she couldn't hide the sadness in her voice. "One of those, huh? Knock-around man. Jack-of-all-trades?"

"Whatever it takes to put food in my belly and some cover over my head."

"Speaking of cover. You're going to boil your brains if you don't get a hat." She reached down on the ground where her husband's hat had fallen when they were dragging him over. "Take this if it fits you. Amos wasn't half your size, but he had a head like a watermelon."

Newt tried on the hat, and it fit him like he had picked it out himself. It was an odd hat to have belonged to an emigrant farmer—black and broad brimmed with a hitched horsehair hatband. He took the hat off and turned it in his hands, examining it more closely.

"Speaking of occupations," Newt said, "what was it that your husband did?"

"Kind of a rounder himself. Trying his hand at farming was a recent thing and only because I was tired of him being gone all the time. He was a lawman by calling and trade, you might say. He was a city marshal here and there. We lived most everyplace in Texas you can imagine. Then he was a U.S. Deputy Marshal and later he worked for those Rangers some. One of his friends out in Tucson already had him a job as deputy sheriff there if he wanted it. You know, to give us something to help get by until we settled in and found a farm."

"Sounds like a good man."

"There isn't a lawman in Texas that didn't know my Amos. He was a well-liked and respected man, even if I sound like I'm bragging." She dabbed quickly at a tear at the corner of her eye.

Newt wondered if Cortina knew he had shot a lawman, even if a former one. Probably didn't matter one damned lick to that Mexican stickup man.

Newt had to bump the Circle Dot horse in the back with the toe of his boot several times to make him get up once the woman's husband was buried. He followed the old woman to her camp, leading the horse. He and the woman took opposite sides of the little fire.

"What are you going to do?" he asked.

"I'll head to Tucson. That was where I started for, and I don't like changing my mind before I've seen a thing through."

"I'm kind of that way myself," he said. "But you might think it over again. I don't know the trail, but I wouldn't recommend it."

"Because I'm a woman?"

"Tough for anyone, I hear, and the Apache are off the reservations again. Some say they're worse than Comanche. Maybe you can sell that wagon and catch a train west. I don't imagine Apache would attack a train."

"I tried to tell Amos not to take the southern route, but he never was one to listen. And we would have taken the train in the first place, but he always liked to see some new country from the back of a horse."

"I can go on with you to Fort Stockton. Shouldn't

be too far from here. I've never been there, but I reckon I can find it."

"I'd be obliged," she said. "When I first saw you coming I didn't know what to think. If you don't mind my saying it, you look like the devil. Walking dead man if I ever saw one."

He chuckled. "I don't mind you saying it at all, but don't hold it against me if I don't give up the ghost right here and now. I've got a few more miles to cover, yet."

She looked around them at the expanse of nothing, as if she thought finding anything in it might be a miraculous feat. "What are you going to do after you help me to Fort Stockton?"

"I'm going to find the one that shot me and your Amos."

"And then what?"

"I'm going to have a serious talk with him and get back what he took from me."

"You don't even have a gun."

"I'll get one. Make do if I can't."

She rose and went to her wagon, reappearing after climbing in it and rummaging around. When she came back to the fire she was carrying a revolver with the gun belt rolled around it. She pitched the gun to him and he caught it in his lap.

It was a Smith & Wesson No. 3 in a high-cut, double-loop holster. Both the gun and the holster were well oiled, and it was plain that her man had been one who appreciated a good firearm and fine leather. The belt was an ordinary one, but had a double row of cartridge loops along its length, with every one of them stuffed full of short, fat S&W .44 Russian brass and round-nosed, heavy lead bullets. No matter the well-kept nature of the rig, the only thing unusual about it was the little blue crosses inlaid into each of the walnut grip panels. The inlaid crosses were made of some kind of agate or other shiny stone as blue as a jaybird's feathers. Gun oil and time had darkened the walnut until the grips were almost black, and the tiny stone crosses stood out like gems.

She saw him looking at the pistol grips. "My Amos was usually a plain man, except when it came to that pistol and his hat. I asked him once why he decorated his gun so, and he said that a Franciscan friar gave him the idea. He said that maybe those crosses would absolve him of some of the men he sent to hell with it."

"You believe that?"

"My Amos never shot except when he had to," she said. "But even so, I don't think there's anything that can wipe the slate clean when you kill a man, no matter what your reasons. My Amos killed men in the line of duty, and he never forgot that. It wore on him so that he even dreamed of it sometimes."

"If you intend to make it to Arizona alone, you might ought to keep this for yourself." He hefted the gun before her.

"I'm thinking you'll be needing it more than me," she said. "You know how to use one of those?"

"I've shot one a time or two."

"If you're going to carry that, you'd best learn."

"I aim to."

A sad look passed across her face that he thought was pointed more at him than it was a reflection on the loss of her husband. She washed the dishes while he sat by the fire, and when she was through she petted her milk cow, obviously lost in thought. After a while, she put her hands to the small of her back, arching and stretching against the sore muscles the hard shovel work had likely given her. Newt couldn't help but notice that for an old woman, her breasts were especially upright and prominent where the front of her dress pulled tight against them. He averted his eyes, ashamed at himself, but it was already too late.

"I'm going to my wagon alone, so don't you be getting any ideas," she said.

"I don't know what you mean."

"I saw you looking at me. Might be you're a good man, and Lord knows I'm twice your age. But I saw you looking like that just the same."

"I never."

"Might be that I'll have to take another husband one of these days, but don't go getting notions that you can take advantage of me. My Amos was a good man. I'll be a long time forgetting him."

"Yes, ma'am, but I never . . ."

"Oh, don't blubber and dodge around it. I saw the urge building in you. My Amos was a man of urges himself. There were times when Amos was younger that I felt like I was married to a rutting billy goat."

Again, Newt didn't know what to say and felt his face and neck growing warm with embarrassment. No woman he had ever met talked like that.

She stared at him, as if weighing a solemn matter. "I'm about half a mind to take you to my wagon, as sinful and horrible as that sounds. It's going to be a long night, and I don't relish being alone."

"Ma'am . . ."

"Oh, don't go to stuttering again. You come in my

wagon on the sneak, and I'll show you the business end of my Sharps."

"I'll stand guard. You rest assured that me or nothing else will bother you tonight."

"Don't mind me. I guess I've gotten so old that I'm not embarrassed to be thinking aloud," she said. "My mother used to say that I was too forward for a proper lady, but I found it was helpful to keep men off guard. A man off guard is easier to get to do what you want him to and less likely to bother you. A sharp tongue will vex many a man."

"You're the vexingest woman I ever met."

Her laugh was as dry and crackly as the wind through the grass. "Oh, you'll meet some young thing that will vex you worse. That'll be how you know she's the one to marry."

She went to her wagon without another word to him. He led her team and the Circle Dot horse on a long walk to the river to water them, and all the time while he was going out of camp he was expecting her to hear him and think he was stealing her horses. He believed her when she said she knew how to use that Sharps rifle.

She didn't raise any protest, so he assumed she didn't hear him leave. But unknown to him, she did hear him and sat up waiting for him to come back to see if she had been right about him. She was peering out of a slit in the wagon cover when he finally returned an hour later.

"What's your name? I never asked it," she whispered from inside the wagon.

"Newt Jones." He rigged some hobbles out of a length of rope he found lying on the ground and hobbled her horses and turned them loose to pick at whatever grazing they might find.

"Somehow, I thought you would have more name than that."

"How do you mean?"

"I expected you to have a name worth remembering."

"A name is what you make it."

"It is at that. My name is Matilda Redding."

"Good to meet you." He kept the Circle Dot horse on the end of a long rope, one hand holding it while he lay down on his thin army blankets. The horse could move about a bit, but he intended to keep it handy.

"Same here." She sounded like she might have been crying.

"You get you some sleep," he said. "We'd best head out at first light."

"Good night, Mr. Jones."

Sometime in the night he awoke with the fire burned down to only a thin bed of coals. It took him a moment to realize what had pried him from his sleep, and that the Circle Dot horse was standing astraddle of him with its belly blocking out the stars overhead. The horse was asleep with its neck sagging and one hind leg cocked. The thought of the horse accidentally stepping on him wasn't a pleasant one, but he was too tired to scoot out from under it and seek a new place for his blankets. He couldn't for the life of him imagine why the horse had decided to stand over him, and fell back asleep before he came up with any theories. The horse was truly odd, but everything had been peculiar the last few days.

# Chapter Seven

Three days later he stood with Matilda Redding alongside her wagon on the parade ground at Fort Stockton—not much of a fort or a parade ground at all, and only a U-shaped cluster of adobe buildings strung together around a patch of dusty ground, beaten bare by the continual comings and goings of horses and the close-order drills of infantrymen.

There was a little wagon train there of freighters headed to El Paso, and they said she could travel that far west with them. The army offered to escort her to the train tracks at the new railroad town of Sanderson, but she wouldn't hear of selling her outfit to ride the rails.

"Me and my Amos set out to reach Arizona by wagon, and that's what I'll do," she told them.

To say that she was a woman of strong opinions was putting it lightly. She bought him a used stock saddle for the Circle Dot horse and a new set of clothes at the sutler's post store. She smiled when she first saw him shaved, washed, and wearing his new clothes.

"You don't look like the same man," she said. "You clean up pretty good."

"You didn't have to do that."

"No, nobody ever made me do anything, but I wanted to. You did me a good turn out there, and this is the least I could do to return the favor." She glanced at her former husband's pistol hanging on his hip. "At least you'll make a better-dressed corpse if you're still determined to go after those Mexican outlaws."

For the better part of a day he had wandered around the post and through the nearby town of hardscrabble farmers. Nobody he had questioned knew anything about Cortina, although the owner of a saloon said that a man matching the bandit's description and five other Mexicans had spent a day in his establishment almost a week before, drinking whiskey and telling stories. They hadn't spent any gold, and they hadn't stayed the night. The six of them rode south toward Sanderson at sundown instead of taking the old mail route east or west.

Two rough-looking men came walking across the parade ground in their direction while Newt and Matilda were talking. One was a bearded, stooped man in a sweat-stained, sagging hat, and the handle of a big knife shoved inside his waistband the only thing keeping a portion of his flopping shirt tucked in. He was carrying a Springfield trapdoor carbine in one hand and a bottle of whiskey in the other.

The second of the pair was a half-breed Indian. Moccasins stuck out the end of his frayed canvas pants, and he wore no hat on his head and no shirt under his surplus army vest. A yellow lanyard ran from the butt of his flap-holstered pistol and draped across his chest.

From the look of them, Newt guessed them to be army scouts. And from the smell of them and their unsteady swagger, it was plain that they had been off post at one of the hog wallows sampling the whiskey at two bits a shot. Neither of them was taking any pains to hide the leering looks they cast at Mrs. Matilda, but most of their interest seemed to be aimed at him.

"Where'd you get that horse?" The white scout pointed at the Circle Dot horse standing behind Newt.

"None of your business." Newt reached for Matilda's arm.

"The Comanche gave it to him," she butted in.

"Like hell," the white scout said. His hat was cocked crooked on his head, as if it might be some gauge of his drunkenness—the drunker he became, the more it tilted. Besides the whiskey, he smelled liked horse sweat and manure. "Pardon the language, ma'am, but I think this man is telling tall tales. Comanche don't give anyone anything except a sharp stab in the guts. I said to Wildcat here when this man first rode in here, that he looked like one of those Comanchero traders."

"Let's go," Newt said to Matilda.

"That you, boy?" the scout continued, spittle spraying from his whiskered face while he swayed in place. "Anything I hate worse than a Comanche is those that deal with them. Trading guns and whiskey to them red heathens."

The breed hadn't said anything while his partner talked, but his coal chunk eyes took in everything. Newt had heard that a band of Kickapoo, Delaware, and Seminole renegades had fled down south of the border, sometimes hiring out as scouts to the Mexican army and sometimes selling the same services to the Americans.

"Not another word out of you," Newt said. "I'm not looking for trouble."

"Ride easy, Mr. Jones," Matilda said quietly. "Your wound has got you on edge."

The white scout turned slightly to look at his comrade and then jerked a thumb in Newt's direction. "He talks like he's plumb tough. Might be he needs a lesson."

The white scout smiled at the breed with his head turned away from Newt, hoping to relax him and put him off guard. He started a punch way down by his right hip, but it was a lazy, slow punch, and it never got halfway home. The sound of Newt's fist impacting on the man's chin sounded like the crack of an ax in a cured mesquite stump.

"Hold up there!" someone shouted.

Newt stood over the downed man with his eyes on the breed, daring him to make a move. The half-breed scout didn't flinch, but held his ground. Newt finally turned to see who was yelling at him.

It was a young cavalry lieutenant and his sergeant, and neither of them looked too happy.

"What happened here?" the lieutenant asked.

"Ask him." Newt pointed at the man he had downed.

The breed stepped forward and booted his partner in the ribs. "He don't talk for a while. He's out cold, and I think his jaw is broken."

"Lieutenant, these men were giving Mr. Jones here a hard time. They're drunk and accused him of being a Comanchero," Matilda said.

The officer scowled at the breed. "I don't doubt that. Both of these men have a penchant for the bottle."

For the first time, Newt noticed that a crowd had gathered. Soldiers stood in small groups around the parade ground watching him, and more civilians and enlisted alike watched from under the shade of the porch verandas fronting the buildings.

"You pack quite a wallop, Mr. Jones," the lieutenant said.

"I didn't like what they had to say."

"Just like that?" The lieutenant twisted at one end of his half-grown, wispy mustache. "Kind of sudden, aren't you?"

"I warned them twice, and that's twice more than I'm used to."

The breed spoke again. "No Comancheros anymore. Not enough Comanche left to trade with. No money in it."

The lieutenant turned and surveyed the crowd watching them, weighing some decision. "Normally, I wouldn't tolerate fighting on this post, but as it happens I saw the whole thing from a distance, and this isn't the first time these two have caused me trouble. If Wildcat here wasn't such a good tracker I would run them both off."

"I only drank a little whiskey," the breed said, trying his best to stand steady and appear to the lieutenant to be more sober than he was.

The sergeant kicked the bottle that had fallen from the white scout's hand when Newt knocked him down, and passed his lieutenant a look. "Only a little whiskey."

The lieutenant frowned. "Mrs. Redding, I'm sorry if these men bothered you."

"Then I'll be on my way," Newt said.

The lieutenant held up a hand. "Hold on there.

Everyone on the post is talking about you and how you claim to have come by that horse."

Newt frowned at Matilda. He hadn't said a thing to anyone about how he came by the horse.

She gave him a sheepish look. "Maybe I let it slip to a few people."

"Maybe?"

"You say some Comanche gave you that horse?" the lieutenant asked.

"It was Indians. Might have been Comanche, but I wouldn't know one for sure even if I met them. Hunting party found me after I was shot and half-dead. Nursed me some and left me with nothing but this horse."

"Unusual."

"Well, it was an unusual situation and he's an unusual horse."

"What did he look like? The one that gave you the horse."

"Short and stocky. Ugly scar down the side of his face. Two bullet scars here and here." Newt pointed to two places on his own torso. "Was another one that was with him talking to me—older man and some kind of shaman. Acted like he could talk to spirits."

"No offense, but that makes your story even more incredible," the lieutenant said. "That scarred buck could be none other than Dog. Half the soldiers in the state are after him. He's got a special hate for Texans."

"Could be that's it. I ain't from Texas."

"Yes, sir, that's quite a story. The only Comanche left running wild are a handful of scattered renegade camps mixed up with outlaw Kiowa and a few other tribes. The army put the rest of them on the reservation years ago, but those left are some of the worst.

They would as soon kill a white man as look at him. Hard to believe they let you live."

"I don't claim to know anything about them. Believe me when I say I was as perplexed as you."

The lieutenant held up both palms. "Go easy. I believe you. There's no figuring any kind of Indian. The same one that invites you into his camp one day, might meet you out on the prairie the next and take your scalp."

"I'll take your word for it."

"Which way were those Comanche headed? I received a telegram three days ago that a Mexican village was raided down south of the railroad on our side of the river. We thought it might have been Mexican banditos from across the border, but the rumor is that it was an Indian raid."

"I don't remember which way they were headed."

"You realize that those are hostiles we're talking about? Dog and his band have raped and killed and stolen livestock for years."

"Maybe so, but he treated me square. Wouldn't feel right leading you to him."

"You're a stubborn man."

"That's been said before. I don't have many principles, but I try to stick to the few I have."

"Wouldn't matter anyway, probably. Hostiles are hard to run down, even when you know where they're headed."

"Are we finished?"

Before the lieutenant could answer him, the sergeant leaned close to relay something else in the officer's ear. He had been glaring at Newt the entire time, and obviously if it had been his decision, he wouldn't have let Newt off so easily for smacking an army scout.

"I should have known it the moment I saw that punch of yours," the lieutenant said.

"What's that?"

"Are you a pugilist, Mr. Jones? A professional?"

"I'm a man that minds his manners and expects the same from others."

"Sergeant Fagan here says he recognizes you. Said he saw you fight in Denver."

"No offense to the sarge there, but could be he's mistaken."

"Widowmaker Jones," the sergeant said. "That's what they called you. I saw you knock out a big Swede twice your size that they called Rocky Mountain Jim. Lost a month's pay betting against you."

"You're a well-known man. Are you the same one that broke up that riot in Shakespeare?" the lieutenant asked. "They say that's where you got your name."

"You can hear all kinds of rumors." Newt went to the Circle Dot horse and stepped up in the saddle.

"You should be careful with that horse," the breed said.

"I'm careful with any kind of horse."

"I know that horse, and he's bad medicine. I know Dog, too. He likes his jokes and probably thought it was funny to give that horse to you."

Newt ignored the breed and looked down at Matilda. "So long, ma'am."

"Cortina has you outnumbered. Best thing you can do is to forget about what they did to you and what they took from you. Get on with your life," she said.

"This is my life. Feels like trouble is my middle name."

"I intend to move on. What's done is done, and there's no fixing it," she said.

"To each their own."

"You ever hear of turning the other cheek?"

"My own ma used to remind me of that. Wasn't too many years before she gave up and went to reminding me to lead with my left and keep my guard up."

"Widowmaker. I knew there was more name to you than you let on."

"It's a silly name. Them that gave it to me never asked if I wanted it."

"Like you said last night, a name is what a man makes it. There's lightning in that right hand of yours, but that won't be enough. Those Mexicans killed my Amos and he was as tough as they come. They'll kill you just as quick."

She went to her wagon and came back carrying her buffalo gun and a sack of cartridges. "You take this."

"You've already done enough for me."

"You take it, and don't say another word about it. It's too heavy for me, besides. Giving you guns that I don't need and that are liable to get you killed is no favor at all." She also held out a handful of money. "You take this, too. It's not much more than a few dollars, but it might feed you for a while."

"I've fought and scratched for what little I can lay hand to for most of my life, and I don't take gifts lightly."

"It's nothing."

"I'm obliged. Maybe someday I can repay you."

"You ride careful, Mr. Jones."

"I will."

"Don't you start lying to me now. I'm guessing there isn't a careful bone in your body." She stood with one hand shading her eyes and watched him ride off, going south across the barrens. She waited and watched until he disappeared, and when she was sure he was gone a sigh escaped her.

"What did you mean about that horse?" the lieutenant asked the breed.

"Bad horse. Bad medicine for anyone that rides him."

The lieutenant huffed. "Wildcat, you're a superstitious heathen and you're drunk to boot."

"Yes, I'm drunk, but that's a spirit horse. Everyone that owns him don't come out so good. Bad luck."

"How so?"

"First time I knew about that horse it was Spotted Hand from my own camp who found him wandering the riverbed with a saddle slipped under his belly and the bones of a dead man's leg and a boot hung in the stirrup."

"White man?"

The breed shrugged. "Nothing left but the leg bone, but the boot and the spur on it looked Mexican. Whoever it was, they don't tell no stories no more."

"Go on."

"Good-looking horse, so Spotted Hand took him home. He gave the horse to his daughter because it acted gentle. The first time she rode the horse a storm came up and lightning struck. The horse was fine but the girl was dead." The breed crossed his arms over his chest, as if he had proved something.

"However true that may be, it's only more superstition," the lieutenant said. "Coincidence."

"Spotted Hand thought like you. He wanted to keep the horse, even though some days it wouldn't let him ride it and some days it would. The horse is fast, and Spotted Hand raced him against some Mexicans and won. Everyone in our village talked about what a fast horse he was, and that made Spotted Hand proud. The second time Spotted Hand raced him that horse tripped and fell and broke Spotted Hand's leg. We looked but could find no prairie dog hole or anything that could have caused him to fall. One morning one of the old women was up early carrying water and saw a crow roosting on the horse's back and the horse was looking at the crow as if the two were talking. That same day Spotted Hand tried to give the horse to his brother, Jumps the River, but when Jumps the River went to catch the horse it reared and pawed him on the shoulder and made his arm no good for a long time. Dog came to the camp a few days later. He has a weakness for good-looking horses and traded Spotted Hand a new rifle for him. Spotted Hand needed a new rifle to shoot Apaches for the Mexicans, and was glad to see that horse go."

"That Widowmaker Jones didn't seem to have any problem with him."

"Laugh if you want to. White men don't know nothing about things you can't see without looking close and thinking on them. Bad things happen to those that ride that horse."

The lieutenant went to stand beside Matilda, shading his own eyes and trying to see what she was looking at. He must have had better eyesight than her, for he spotted Newt even though she had lost sight of him.

"I hear that man is after Cortina," the officer said. "It's all over the post and town that he was asking about him."

"That's right," she said.

"He's asking for trouble, then. Cortina is as good with a gun as they come, and twice as mean."

She turned to the officer and smiled. "You're young.

That man is anything but a fool. Hardheaded, maybe, and too quick to fight, but a fool, no."

The lieutenant gave her a look that the young often give their elders when they think they are secretly coddling them—patronizing, yet polite. "Cortina is said to have killed twenty-two men with a gun or a knife."

"Maybe so, Lieutenant, but Cortina ought to be worried."

# Chapter Eight

Kizzy had never known a real home, and her life was one "moving on" after another. She, like her brother, was born on the road and the road was home, if anywhere was. There weren't that many of the Roma in America or Mexico, but some of those that were had begun to settle down and grow roots and give up the old, roving lifestyle. But the Greys weren't such. Although their father and mother often talked of closing the family circus, it never happened. Both of them loved the road too much to quit it, and were natural born sightseers and show people.

There had been a time when Kizzy loved the road, too, and when it was something exciting when the wagons popped over the last hill or rounded the last curve and a new town appeared. That time was past, although she didn't know for certain when she'd started feeling different. Her nomad heart had disappeared without her noticing the moment of its passing.

But nothing was the same, not with her parents gone. Not with her and Fonzo fending for themselves and not always knowing what to do. That was why she didn't love the road as much as she used to—because the "how it once was" had been replaced with the bitter reality of the "here and now."

The town of Piedras Negras was only another dusty border town along the Rio Grande, that very same river the Mexicans called the Rio Bravo. Eagle Pass, Piedras Negras's gringo twin, lay on the American side of the river directly across from it with a bridge connecting the two. However, it was the Mexican side of the river that looked more prosperous.

The town's streets were filled with men coming in from a shift at the coal mines, or farmers returning from their irrigated fields along the river. A new railroad line from the south was almost within reach of the town, and a tent camp of construction workers lay on the southern outskirts. Among the tents, men called out to one another playfully after a hard day's work, and woodsmoke lifted from beehive adobe ovens where women prepared evening meals. The smell of hot corn tortillas, chili peppers, and other spices wafted through the air. Many people stopped what they were doing or walked to the edge of the street to watch Kizzy and Fonzo pass, with children darting through their ranks or waving at the Gypsies and running alongside the circus wagons.

One of the local liverymen let them park their wagons in his barnyard beneath an immense oak tree. After pitching camp, Fonzo left to see if he could trade something for a bucket of axle grease, for one of the equipment wagon's wheel hubs had screeched and squalled the last mile of road. He had barely left before several townspeople wandered over to their camp on the livery grounds.

The liveryman had allowed them the use of a corral to hold the six white show horses, and the people looked through the corral planks or took a perch on top to admire them. Kizzy kept a close watch, admonishing her visitors not to go into the corral and not to try and feed the horses any treats. Once, in another city, some well-meaning soul in such a crowd had fed Sheba, the only mare in the set, some watermelon rinds, and by the time Fonzo noticed and put a stop to it, the horse had already eaten a healthy share. Later, Sheba had coliced—the horseman's word for a dangerous digestive pain and intestinal spasms or blockage—and they feared that she would die. Since then, it was their policy to keep some distance between crowds and the horses, and at the moment all six of them were too intent on the stack of loose hay mounded in the center of the corral to wander over to the fence and visit with their admirers.

The matched pair of feathery-legged, black draft horses that pulled their living quarters wagon were tied to a picket line strung between two trees, and proved to be almost as much of a draw as Fonzo's white show horses. Although Kizzy let the children pet the draft team, she kept them away from the six-up team of little brown mules that pulled their equipment wagon. They were untrustworthy at best and often wicked, and Fonzo was the only one who could handle them. She feared that one of them might kick a child, and kept the mules tied to a picket line on the back side of the wagons.

After an hour or so, the crowd fizzled out and filtered away, and Kizzy went about starting a pot of beans to soak and shucking some fresh ears of corn they had stolen from a field they had passed on the way to the town. The irrigated rows of corn were so heavily laden that neither of them felt too guilty about procuring a few ears for a night's meal.

She was still in the middle of cooking dinner when the men walked up. She had tethered both the dogs to the wagon wheels, and it was their growling that alerted her.

When she glanced up from her cook fire she saw that it was five men of a look and bearing that immediately put her on guard as much as the dogs were. There wasn't a single one of the men who didn't have at least one pistol somewhere on his waist and a knife or two showing elsewhere on his person. All of them wore the large sombreros and black mustaches indigenous to the country.

They passed a bottle among them while the cleanest cut and tallest stepped closer to her fire. He was a handsome man, in spite of the dust of the road covering him and several days' worth of black whisker stubble on his jaws. The vest he wore caught her eye, being made of some kind of spotted cat hide—golden yellow with black spots and rosettes like that of a leopard or something.

But it wasn't the odd, fancy vest that left the greatest impression on her. He twirled the end of his gold watch fob in his left hand, while the other rested on the ivory butt of the nickel-plated pistol holstered on his hip. She could tell when he smiled and doffed his broad hat to her that he was a man used to women fawning over him, but for some reason, that smile made her more leery of him than enamored.

"*Hola, señorita,*" he said with his voice as silky smooth

as hot butter, but with more than a hint of slyness. *"Buenas tardes. ¿Cómo está?"*

She tried to reply in halting Spanish, but he held up a hand and waved her off.

"No need. I speak good English," he said.

In truth, his English was decent, although laden with a heavy accent.

One of the men behind him burped and snickered, and the man talking to her threw him a warning glance. The one so rude frowned back at him, but nodded an apology at her and mumbled something in Spanish.

"Please forgive Miguelito," the tall one said. "His people are nothing but goat herders, and his manners are atrocious. That is the word, no? Atrocious?"

Miguelito frowned at the tall one again, but didn't say anything. She wondered why they called him Miguelito, for he was anything but small. Although shorter than the one who seemed to be their ringleader, he was as wide as any two of them, and so fat that his three chins made it look as if his head sat directly on his shoulders with no neck at all.

"Fine horses you have," the tall one said. "I think it took you a long time to find such a matched set."

"It did."

"You are circus people, no?"

"We are."

"Will you put on a show here?"

"No, we're only staying one night and then moving on."

"What do you do in this circus?"

"Trick riding and a little shooting." She looked past

the men, hoping to spy Fonzo on his way back. He should have returned long since.

"Who does this?"

"My brother rides and I shoot."

"You?" The tall one turned to his friends and all of them laughed. He turned back to her. "What do you know of guns?"

"I assure you, I'm a very good shot."

"Is that you?" The tall one pointed at the signage painted on the side of their living quarters wagon. "Buckshot Annie?"

All of the men snickered at what he said, while Kizzy hid her surprise that he could read, and in English, no less. Miguelito handed the tall one the bottle, and Kizzy watched as he turned it up and took a long pull of the tequila, with his brown throat exposed and shining with sweat and the sharp knot of his Adam's apple pumping in slow strokes as he swallowed. They were all obviously drunk, and though she was young, her life had been spent among strangers and she carefully considered the risk they represented.

A pretty girl learned some things about men quickly, and she had known that she was pretty since she was but a girl. Perhaps she was petite to the point of tininess, but she knew that men found her attractive, and almost everywhere they went there was at least a man or two who made an effort to meet her after a show. It had been that way since she was barely twelve.

When it came to how to fend off unwelcome advances, she had a good teacher, for her mother had been a beautiful woman and a veritable expert on the subject. That was all a part of the life. There was a subtle art to appearing friendly while politely handling the harmless, flirty ones. You didn't want to offend someone who might come back and pay their admission fees for a second show. And occasionally there might be a handsome one worth talking to, but then again, there was the other, more dangerous kind altogether. The men before her were that other kind— men you didn't want to be alone with. And the tall one in the spotted catskin vest? Every sense told her that he was another kind even worse than those with him.

The tall Mexican stepped past her to the livery corral where Fonzo's white horses stood gathered around the pile of hay. He ducked through the fence rails and went to Mithridates and ran his hand down his neck and across his back. "Very fine horses. *Muy bonita.* I don't think I ever see better."

She didn't like him inside the corral with their horses, but was unwilling to turn her back on his friends. She stood uncertainly between them, wishing either Fonzo would come back or that someone else would wander by.

"Come out of there," she said.

He patted the horse's neck and smiled at her. "I mean him no harm. You act like I might steal him."

Fonzo appeared behind the tall Mexican's friends and quickly stepped past them. "Come out of there and leave our horses alone."

The tall one walked slowly to the corral fence. "And who are you?"

"Those are my horses."

The man ducked through the fence and when he straightened back up he pointed to the painted words on the side of the living quarters wagon with that same smirk on his mouth. "Is that you? Fonzo the Great?"

Fonzo stood straight and met the man's gaze. Kizzy realized that he was trying to seem taller than he was.

"Go to the wagon and get the shotgun," he whispered to Kizzy.

The tall one made a show of slowly looking Fonzo up and down. "I said, 'Is that you?' *¿Quién es, chico?*"

Fonzo was a proud young man, and always a little too aware of his small stature. Kizzy could tell that his scant Spanish skills were enough that he understood the tall Mexican had called him a boy.

"I am Fonzo," he said. "And who might you be?"

The tall one rested his hand on his pistol butt again and pointed at Fonzo while looking at his friends. "He is proud for a little one, no?"

"*Un niñito afeminado,*" one of the others said.

Kizzy didn't understand what the man had said about Fonzo, but from the way they all laughed she knew it wasn't nice. She glanced at Fonzo and could tell he was frustrated that she wouldn't go after the shotgun in the wagon. But she was afraid to leave his side.

"What did he call me?" Fonzo turned slightly so that he could see both the tall one and his friends at the same time.

"He said that you are almost as pretty as your sister," the tall one said.

The Mexicans laughed again and one of them flung the empty tequila bottle across the road.

"You are all drunk. If you don't leave I shall be forced to call the local constable," Fonzo said, and managed to keep most of the quaver of temper out of his voice.

The tall one looked down the street, making a show of acting like he was searching for someone. "I don't think the constable is around. I think maybe he went somewhere else and won't be back until tomorrow. He don't like us much."

The drunken men snickered again and a couple of them moved closer to Kizzy and Fonzo. Fonzo pulled a small knife from his waistband. He held it out toward them with the cutting edge turned up, wavering back and forth between them and the tall one on his other side.

"There is no need for that. Put away your *cuchillo.*" The tall one took his hand off his pistol butt and held up both hands. "We only came to see your horses, and maybe to see this Buckshot Annie who is written on the side of your wagon. What does it say there? The world's best crack shot?"

"I've already told you to leave," Fonzo said.

The tall one glanced at his friends as if they were a jury. "She says she is this Buckshot Annie, but I don't think what you write on your wagon is true."

"Kizzy, go to the wagon," Fonzo said, making a fake thrust at one of the men who came too close to him."

"*Muchachos*, do you think this *gringo* can outshoot me?" the tall one asked.

More laughing. Kizzy noticed one of the men had drawn his own knife—a rather large one—and was holding it hidden behind his thigh.

"How about we have a shooting contest? Me and you," the tall one said with his eyes on her and his thumbs hooked in the armholes of his catskin vest.

"Maybe another time," Fonzo said, still brandishing the knife. Without thinking, he had taken a step sideways to place himself in front of his sister.

Kizzy shoved past him. "What do we shoot for?"

The tall one looked confused. "For?"

"You think you can outshoot me. I don't think so," she said.

"That is why we will shoot . . . to see who is best. A winner and a loser. *Primero y segundo.*"

"And what do I get for my troubles?"

It dawned on him what she meant, and that caused another of his smirks. "Do you mean a wager? You want to bet with me?"

"Call it a small bet. Let's keep it friendly." She put a hand gently on Fonzo's forearm and pushed his knife down.

The tall one's friends obviously didn't speak English as fluently as he did and were looking questions at him. He spoke to them in their native tongue, and when they understood what she was proposing they seemed to find it the most hilarious thing they had ever heard.

"Six shots at a peso a shot," she said.

"And what will we shoot at?" the tall one asked.

Kizzy looked at her brother. "Fonzo, would you go get us some targets?"

Fonzo looked at her and the Mexicans uncertainly.

"It will be all right. Go get them. I will be fine here."

Fonzo gave them one last glance and went to the wagon at a brisk walk. When he came back he was carrying a sack containing the glass balls she used in their show and had her gun belt draped over one shoulder. She took her pistols from him and wrapped the belt around her waist.

The tall one looked at the rig she was strapping on and shoved his hat farther back on his head. "¿*Dos pistolas?*"

"I shoot with either hand."

"But do you shoot well, señorita?"

"We shall see. Fonzo, will you throw for us?"

Fonzo gave a smirk of his own to the tall one. "I'd be glad to."

"Where shall we shoot?" she asked. While she buckled her gun belt she noticed that several people on the streets had taken notice of them and had stopped what they were doing to see what was going on.

Fonzo stepped through the tall one's friends and walked farther up the road away from town. "Follow me."

The tall one made a graceful half bow and pointed for Kizzy to go next. She stepped in behind Fonzo, all too aware that the Mexican toughs were following close behind her.

Fonzo stopped at the freshly graded railroad bed, on the edge of a small, freshly plowed field with nothing beyond it but the river. "This should work."

The tall one nodded in agreement. "I like to shoot toward the American side. Maybe we accidentally knock some gringo off his horse over there."

"Would you like the first shot?" Kizzy asked the tall one. She already had her right-hand pistol out.

He looked down at her gun with a grunt and drew his own. "Ladies first."

Kizzy nodded at Fonzo and he pulled a red glass ball from his sack and threw it overhand high in the air and about twenty yards out in front of her. She raised her pistol to arm's length and tracked her target for a brief instant on its arc. The boom of the Colt and the shattering of the ball into tiny bits of glass seemed to happen all at once.

A couple of the men said something that sounded like approval and astonishment, but stopped when the tall one glared at them. He cocked his own pistol and nodded at Fonzo.

The tall one didn't even try to aim at the flying ball and simply held his pistol with his elbow bent at the waist. He missed and the ball fell into the corn stubble.

"That's one you owe me," Kizzy said, and gave Fonzo the signal to throw again.

She busted the second ball so quickly out of the air that it hadn't time to reach the apex of its flight.

"May I see your gun?" The tall Mexican held out his hand.

She hesitated but finally handed him her pistol butt first. He opened the loading gate and pushed out a loaded cartridge, examining it.

"No trick loads," she said.

"I thought maybe you use shot shells."

"I use them in the tent, but don't really need them to hit anything. It isn't that hard."

He put the cartridge back in her pistol and examined the pink pearl grips. "Pretty like a child's toy. A woman's gun."

"A gun that shoots better than yours."

He handed it back to her, frowning. The gunshots were beginning to draw more of a crowd, and he looked over his shoulder at the latest arrivals, frowning more.

"Are you ready?" Fonzo asked.

The tall one cocked his pistol. "Throw."

This time, he stretched his pistol out to arm's length, squinting down the barrel and trying to find the flying ball in his sights, but missing again.

"That's two pesos," Kizzy said.

Fonzo gave her a look that she knew was meant to tell her without words that she should miss her third shot on purpose. The tall Mexican and his friends were bound to be sore losers, and it might be trouble to rub it in too much.

But Kizzy had also taken note of the growing crowd, and she smiled at them before turning back to the business at hand and busting the third ball with her pistol in her left hand. The crowd clapped, and she was sure that the tall Mexican and his companions wouldn't try anything rough with so many witnesses looking on. It would serve the bunch of drunks and thugs right to learn a little humility.

The tall one cocked his pistol for a third time and, to his credit, managed to hit his target. His friends yipped and shouted high-pitched cheers.

Some of his cockiness returned and he smiled at her again. "This gun, I think it shoots a little high, but I'm getting used to it."

She shattered all of her last three targets, while he never hit another. Among the clapping and cheers of the crowd, she also heard some whispering.

The tall one reloaded his pistol while he stared at her, and there was no hiding the coldness upon his face. "You are a good shot."

She held out an open palm. "I believe you owe me five pesos."

He reached in his vest and pulled out a handful of coins and counted out five of them into her hand. "Maybe we shoot again sometime and I have a better gun."

She forced herself to smile at him. "Would you like to trade guns and shoot again? Double the wager?"

If he had attempted to hide his anger before, he did no longer. His voice was icy when he leaned closer to her. "You like to play with guns? You like to play games with men? Do you know who I am?"

"No, but I've seen enough to tell that you are an awful sport, a drunkard, and a man of atrocious manners. Isn't that how you say it? Atrocious?" She thought for an instant that he was going to strike her.

"I considered a kiss from you when I first saw you, but now I don't think so. I think maybe you are a child."

Kizzy was still thinking about what to say to that when he turned quickly on his heels and shoved through the crowd. His friends mumbled a few things, but followed him away.

Many of the people gathered came to congratulate her, and she talked with a few of them and said her thanks before they trickled back to wherever they came from. The last of them to go was an old man with sad eyes and a face like wrinkled leather beneath his straw sombrero.

"You watch out for that one," he said to her. "He's bad."

"Who is he?" she asked.

The old man looked surprised. "You did not know?"

"Know what?"

He nodded as if her answer explained something,

and then he clucked his tongue sadly. "If I was you I would be careful tonight. That man is Javier Cortina."

"And who is that?"

"He has killed many men. Stolen many things."

"He looks like an outlaw. If he's so well known, why doesn't the law arrest him?"

The old man clucked his tongue again. "The *alcalde* is his cousin, and because Cortina is dangerous, the rurales stationed here look the other way and act like they don't see him. Maybe if Cortina was by himself they would try, but not with men to help him."

"We'll be careful," Fonzo said.

"Thank you," Kizzy added.

The old man nodded. "If I was you I would keep a close guard on my horses. There is nothing Cortina likes better than a good horse, and he doesn't pay for them."

Before she could ask any more questions the old man left.

"Maybe we should wait until dark and then try to slip out of town," Fonzo said later beside their fire. "I don't like the sound of what that old man had to say."

"Whatever we do, I think he was right," she said. "At the very least, one of us had better stay up and keep an eye on things. We can take turns sleeping and keep the fire built up high."

Fonzo went to the wagon and procured a pistol and their father's long shotgun. "I would have felt better if I had these when that Cortina and his men were here."

"You are a terrible shot."

"They were close enough it wouldn't have mattered,"

he said. "And what were you doing hitting every one of your targets? Were you trying to make trouble?"

"I didn't like him."

"So you make him mad on purpose? We don't need any more trouble."

She held out the five coins. "I made this."

"And what were you going to do if he tried something? Do you think Cortina carries a gun only to shoot glass balls?"

"He was a poor shot. I outdid him easily."

Fonzo shook his head again. "And you call me the foolish one of us. For someone so smart, sometimes you don't get it."

"Get what?"

"Yes, you outshot him, but you didn't have anyone shooting back at you while you did it."

"Don't be so dramatic. We'll leave this place and never see him again."

# Chapter Nine

**A** day later they were resting the wagon teams and taking a midday siesta on the side of the road to Monterrey. Fonzo took a nap under one of the wagons, but Kizzy was too hot to sleep. The river paralleling the road looked invitingly cool and too tempting to miss. Kicking off her sandals and hiking her skirt to her knees, she waded into the shallows and made her way along the willow-shaded bank, liking the cool mud bottom against her bare feet and bending over to cup an occasional handful of water and rub it against the back of her neck. Up the hill closer to the road, her dogs were busy trying to dig an armadillo out of its den, wagging their tails happily and sending dirt flying.

She remembered the times when they were a whole family, and her father used to stop at such places as this and all of them would swim in the river, laughing and splashing one another and him always the one to start the roughhousing. He had been a playful, mischievous man: quick to laugh, never met a stranger, and talkative to the point that he was silent only when sleeping or when he was daydreaming about one of his grand schemes. Who would have thought such a kind man would end as he had?

She pushed away the harsh images that crowded in on the good memories and found a seat in a patch of grass with her feet still in the river. Good things were the only things worth spending your time on. That's what he had always said. Waste no time with what is done. Move on and leave it behind.

They hadn't even buried him, and left him like that. She and Fonzo had to take him down, carrying him away in the early light of morning while his tormenters slept after a night of so much evil, peacefully as if they felt no guilt or would ever realize the good man they had done so wrong.

You move on. Dig your graves, bury the hurt, and move on. One last look behind you and that is all. But some things follow you.

She waited for the silt in the river water to settle and studied her face in the mirror of it. Amber, almond-shaped eyes stared back at her, slightly distorted in the current, and looking older and sadder than she would have expected. She didn't feel sad. Most times she felt happy, except when it came to her how alone she and Fonzo really were. Nothing but each other in the whole wide world—each other and the road. Lots of people, but all strangers and nothing more than an audience to stand before, to pass before, clapping or leering. Gypsies, Roma, didn't mingle with the *gadje*, the outsiders.

She brushed her hair with her mother's mother-of-pearl brush, the feel of the heirloom soothing as it moved slowly through her long black locks, lost in thought while dragonflies dipped and darted out over the water.

The dogs barking jerked her from her reverie. At first she thought they were only barking in excitement or frustration over the armadillo they had cornered, but then she realized that they had left their game and were farther away. The sound of running horses on the road above her caused her to stand and turn back toward camp.

The willows between her position and the wagons were too thick to see through, but loud voices carried to her, and among them was her brother's. She had slipped back into her sandals and was washing her hands when the first of the gunshots cracked through the trees, so loud that she flinched as if struck by a bullet. She ran for the wagons with her heart racing in her chest.

She barely reached the road in time to see the men come flying past her. They were the same ones who had bothered her and Fonzo back in Piedras Negras, and they had Fonzo's white horses roped together and leading behind them. All five of them laughed at her when they saw her on the edge of the road, and one of them tried to stop his horse, but it was poorly trained and ill broke and took the bit in its teeth and threw a runaway with him jerking cruelly on his bridle reins and cursing in Spanish.

The tall one in the spotted vest, Cortina, loped leisurely along behind the rest of them. She thought he would stop when he reached her, but he merely gave her a tip of his sombrero brim and a smirking smile. He veered his horse around the body of one of her dogs, dead in the road, and loped away.

She knelt over the dog. It was the smaller of the

two—Bullsar, the brown one. His body was bloodied with multiple bullet wounds, and the tears were already brimming in her eyes when she looked up to watch Cortina and his men disappear into the dust. Her fingers lingered in the dog's wet fur while she took note that Fonzo was nowhere in sight. She ran again for the wagons and feared that they had killed him also.

The first thing she saw was the white dog, Vlad, with its hackles raised, teeth bared, and growling deeply where it stood at the end of the living quarters wagon. And then she noticed one of their draft horses was dead in its harness, its mate standing trembling beside it. Fonzo must have been hitching them to the living quarters wagon when Cortina showed up.

The mules were scattered in a meadow on the edge of the road not far away, grazing calmly as if nothing had happened. Nothing seemed much disturbed other than the dead horse and the growling dog. Not a thing overturned or ransacked, and the pot of soup over their midday fire bubbling and steaming.

And then she saw the bullet holes in the side of the living quarters wagon. She traced that line of holes, punctured through the painted circus scenes and revealing the white, splintered pine beneath. One of the bullets had punched dead center through the depiction of her mother's crystal ball. Kizzy had always thought it was a horrible and corny portrayal of a fortune-teller, and her mother had never worn a veil over her head or such gaudy bangles, and the dress more fitting to a harem girl. But you gave the crowd what they wanted if you intended to make a profit, and such was the way most *gadje* imagined a Gypsy fortune-teller to look.

She spoke to the dog, letting it hear her voice and comforting it. It took two steps forward, its head dropping and wagging its tail uncertainly, almost as if it were ashamed of what had happened and thought it was to blame.

Something stirred in the wagon, and she tensed until Fonzo stumbled down the steps at the tailgate, holding his head and groaning.

"Are you hurt?" she asked.

"Ran my head into something diving in the wagon. They almost got me." He rubbed the bloody knot above one eyebrow and grimaced.

"They took your horses."

"They came up so fast I couldn't do anything. I ran for the wagon and a gun, but they were all shooting at me. I lay down in the floor and I think they emptied their guns at me. I don't know how they didn't hit me."

She looked again at the bullet-riddled wagon. It did seem a miracle that Fonzo wasn't hit. The sides of the wagon were one-inch pine planks, and little shelter from the storm of bullets he had obviously endured.

Before they could bemoan their misfortune any more, the sound of running horses came again and another dust cloud rose up from a bend in the road to the north, in the opposite direction from where the bandits had fled. Both of them scrambled for the wagon, running into each other in their haste to arm themselves. By the time Fonzo shoved his shotgun out of the back door their newest arrivals had already pulled up their lathered horses in the middle of the road facing their camp.

"Maybe these men are why Cortina didn't stay longer," she said.

"It's all right." Fonzo stepped down to the ground. "They're rurales."

Kizzy stood on the tailgate that served as a rear porch for the wagon and surveyed the dozen men sitting their horses before her. She was less comforted than her brother by their arrival, but she had to admit that she had never seen their like.

All of them were dressed in the charro style with wide sombreros upon their heads and wearing gray uniform blouses draped with rifle bandoliers, red neckties, pinstriped pants, and leather leggings that reached from their ankles to their knees. The big spurs they wore on their boots rattled as their horses stamped and shook bridle chains.

Despite the matching dress, no two of them were armed alike. A few of them had sabers hanging from their waists or from their saddle swells, and in their hands were everything from Winchesters to muskets. Some wore as many as two and three pistols—everything from muzzle-loaders to modern cartridge revolvers.

They looked more like wild vaqueros, revolutionaries, or brigands than policemen. True, Porfirio Díaz had increased the number of such lawmen since he had taken over the country once again, but their reputation in many parts of Mexico was little better than that of the renegade Indians and bandits they were supposed to pursue.

She kept the pistol she had managed to grab hidden in her skirt and studied the rurales with her other hand shading her eyes. Vlad growled beside her, and she commanded him to lie down. He did, but the hair on his back was standing straight up again.

"Thank goodness you've come," Fonzo said.

The man who must have been their officer rode his

horse a couple of steps out from his men. He looked at the dead horse and then back to Fonzo. His eyes last landed on Kizzy.

He asked something in Spanish, and though both she and Fonzo had picked up a smattering of the language in their time on the border, she couldn't understand what he said, for he spoke too fast.

"What happened here?" the rurale officer asked again in broken English.

"Brigands," Fonzo replied. "They stole six of our horses and likely would have killed us if you hadn't come along. They must have seen your dust or known you were behind them."

The officer grunted and looked up the road to the north.

"His name was Cortina," Fonzo said. "He followed us from Piedras Negras."

"Yes, it was Cortina," the officer said. "He was seen this morning and we hoped to catch him on the road."

"Well, go after him."

The officer said something to one of his men and that man started his horse in the direction that Cortina had fled. The others waited.

"*¿Cuántos hombres?*" the officer asked.

"There were six of them," Fonzo said, his voice growing impatient. "You can catch them if you hurry."

"*¿Cómo?*"

"Hurry. *Pronto. Vamonos.*"

"We will catch Cortina in time." The officer sat slumped in the saddle with his posture as languid as the tone of his voice. To hurry was obviously the last thing he intended, as if his body had taken on the tempo of the hot day. "Are you alone?"

Fonzo gave Kizzy an uncertain look. "It is only us."

The officer grunted again and nodded at Kizzy. "Your woman?"

"My sister."

The rurales exchanged looks, all of them smirking and saying things too low and fast for her to understand. The officer gave orders and four of the rurales broke off and loped their horses to the meadow where the mules grazed. They circled the mules and began loose herding them toward the road. The mules, so calm before, went back to their usual, difficult antics when it was plain that the lawmen were intent on capturing them or taking them someplace other than the lush grass of the river bottom.

"Thank you for the help. I could use some help hitching those mules. We only traded for them recently, and they can be difficult to handle," Fonzo said. "And maybe some of your men could help me roll this dead horse out of its harness."

The officer continued to stare while the men he had sent after the mules finally managed to rope all but one of them. They gave up on catching the last one, the most crafty of the team, as it made it to the timber along the river, where pursuing it on horseback was futile. When they returned with the mules in tow the officer waved them past him and down the road back in the direction of Piedras Negras.

"Where are they going with our mules?" Fonzo asked.

Another of the rurales dismounted and shoved past Fonzo and sampled the stew from the kettle over the fire. The broth was scalding hot and he cursed and spat it out before kicking the pot over and spilling what remained. Vlad growled and crept forward on his belly, his dark eyes focused on the man at the cook pot.

Kizzy snapped her fingers at the dog and shushed him. And then her pistol came out from behind her skirt, pointing at the man beside the fire. "Stop!"

Fonzo retreated, leveling his shotgun on them from the hip. "You are supposed to help us."

The officer looked into Fonzo's shotgun as if it weren't there at all. "Do you own the field where your mules grazed?"

"No, but it was only grass and an hour's grazing wasn't going to hurt it."

"The man who owns the field might not see it that way. You can pay for damages? For the use of his land and his grass?"

Kizzy instantly knew that he was fishing with his question, and had she any money, he would be the last man she would tell. There was about these men the same air that Cortina and his compadres had possessed, and the same look in their eyes, no matter the uniforms and badges.

"We have nothing to pay with," she said.

"Then you will have to settle any fines other ways." The officer made no attempt to hide the look he aimed at her.

"Fines?" Fonzo asked.

"The *juzgado* will decide your penalty. You should put down your gun. You don't want to shoot at us and get yourself in more trouble."

"Don't put down your gun," Kizzy said. "Don't listen to him."

"Maybe we find things in your wagons that will settle this matter. Then maybe we don't have to take you back to Piedras Negras."

Two more of the rurales dismounted and started toward the equipment wagon parked beneath a huge cottonwood tree. One of them climbed up on the wagon and started tossing things out on the ground, while the other examined what he threw out more closely.

"Tell him to stop." Fonzo eared back one hammer on his shotgun.

The mounted rurales shouldered their rifles as one, all pointing at him and Kizzy.

"I don't think you want to do that," the officer said.

Vlad was almost beside himself, alternating between growling and whimpering, but thus far obeying Kizzy's command to stay where he was.

"I will shoot your dog if he growls again," the officer said.

Kizzy kept her pistol pointed in the general direction of the rurales, but knelt over Vlad and took hold of his collar. The two rurales from the equipment wagon came back shaking their heads, as if they had found nothing worth their troubles. They stopped before the officer, casting glances at the living quarters wagon as if waiting for his permission to search it, too.

"Are you smugglers?" the officer asked Fonzo.

"We are circus people," Fonzo replied.

"Circus? ¿*Payasos*?"

"What?" Fonzo didn't understand the word.

"I think you are clowns."

"You're no better than Cortina."

"This police business, it don't pay so good. My men need food for their bellies and cartridges for their guns. These things we must get if the roads are to be safe."

"Tell your men to come back with our mules."

The officer looked up the road. His men and the mules were already a quarter of a mile away. "They don't hear me. You come back to Piedras Negras. We settle this there. The court will decide, if you want."

"You've left us nothing to get there."

The officer's demeanor changed and his speech became slower and more filled with malice. "We've left you everything when we could have taken all. Go back across the river and be glad we were kind to you. Consider this a lesson."

The officer gave another order and rode away with his men in double file behind him. Fonzo stepped out into the road behind them.

"They can't do that," he said.

"I'm afraid they can."

"We should have fought them. I should have fought them. I am sorry that I am a coward."

"You are no coward, no more than I. They would have killed us, as sure as the world."

"I don't know what to do."

"What we always have done. Make do."

Fonzo turned and went to the one horse remaining to them, standing in the traces beside its dead teammate. "I will go after them."

"There were too many, and they are the law."

"Not the rurales. Cortina," he said. "He can't go far before night, and I can catch him if I ride hard."

"And what then? Will you fight him and his men? Will you go wandering off like *vadni ratsa* and get yourself killed and leave me alone?"

He calmed slightly at the mention of the old Romani legend of the wild, wandering goose. "I will ask for help in Piedras Negras."

"You saw how Cortina walked openly there. Who will help when he is feared? The rurales? They just robbed us."

"Yes, they have no honor, but what would you have me do? I am the man of this clan."

"We are but a clan of two. Listen to me and go catch that mule while I bury Bullsar. And then we will hitch it to the wagon with our last horse."

"What about the equipment wagon?"

"We will leave it for now. Maybe we will pass someone who can watch it for us while we are gone. Perhaps we can hide it by the river and cover it with brush."

"Someone will find it and steal it while we are gone. I think everyone in Mexico must be a thief."

"And who will not tell you the same about Gypsies?"

"True, that, but must we always suffer such bad luck?"

"The droppings of the flying bird never fall in the same spot."

"Father may have said that, but they have landed on us too much of late for me to believe it."

"As I said, we make do. Maybe the wagon will be okay if we aren't gone long."

"Gone to where? Back to Piedras Negras? And after who? The rurales or Cortina? What if they go different ways?"

"We might make it without the mules and perhaps sell the living quarters wagon or trade it for a team to replace them, but we have no show without your horses."

"I want to kill them all."

"That is your temper speaking. You have a temper like Mother, but you aren't a killer. We must be smart. Think this through and get your horses back."

"And what else, all-knowing, all-wise sister of mine? Will you tell me how this ends happily?"

"A story is no story until it has an ending." Her face changed to a look not at all like the wistful, lip-biting expression she had borne while she was thinking things over.

# Chapter Ten

**H**e practiced with the unloaded pistol every night—standing before the campfire and drawing it from his holster slowly and methodically and cocking it and dry firing it at targets he picked at random; learning the feel of it balanced in the hard heel of his fist and the long barrel of it a slight counterweight to the snap of the trigger and fall of the hammer. In the quiet, alone, he held the revolver close to his ear and cocked and recocked it in order to listen to the internal working of its springs and notches clicking into place, and the cylinder rotating with paw and ratchet meshing and locking together with precise perfection and an order that was at odds with the rest of the world around him.

His second day out from Fort Stockton he crossed the Texas Pacific Railroad tracks at Sanderson, Texas. The painted sign nailed to one end of the depot house was the only reason he knew where he was. Nobody greeted him, and only a few of the town's hardy patrons paused in their tasks to watch him go by or stood in their doorways with shaded eyes and took his measure.

He had heard that a year before there had been two thousand booted men camped on the site, grading roadbed, laying iron, and raising hell on payroll days. But the railroad crews were gone, and nothing was left but the rubbish of where their tent city had lain and dust devils dancing in and out of the handful of buildings scattered along the tracks.

The next thing he saw was his former horse tied to the rail in front of the Cottage Bar and hitched to a wagonload of wool. The horse's new owner was a Basque sheepherder who had bought the horse from Cortina six days earlier. He had also bought Newt's pack mule, but claimed that it had fallen in a ditch and broken its neck.

No matter. Newt lacked the money to repurchase his old horse, or the mule, either one, even if he had've been of a mind to buy a dead mule. He spent a half-dollar from the stake Matilda Redding had given him on a pair of cold, grease-soaked tamales and a mug of beer in the Cottage Bar. By high noon, he was riding again, following the railroad tracks east in the direction the sheepherder claimed Cortina had ridden.

The railroad tracks lay in the bottom of a narrow valley rimmed with low ridges and buttes to the north and south. In places the cactus-riddled and rocky floor of the valley gave way to patches of drift sand, and it had blown until it almost buried the iron rails. The Circle Dot horse was so marked with streaks of sweat salt and caked in the dust of the land that it appeared a pale, gaunt ghost of itself.

Where the land along the Pecos to the north had

been relatively flat, the farther southeast he went from Sanderson the more broken it became. Low, bald mountains, buttes, and twisted, deep canyons and arroyos lay for miles and miles and for as far as he could see, with desolate stretches of short-grass plains in between. The only trees to be found were a few scattered mesquites and some occasional cottonwoods, willows, and elms in the bottom of some shady canyon. It was a devil's maze that the railroad cut through, and Cortina was somewhere ahead of him. It was as fitting a country for a bad man as Newt had ever laid eyes on. You could have hidden a whole horde of killers and thieves in one of those cuts, along with the bones of those without the good sense to ride wary, and none of them might ever be found.

Langtry, Texas, almost two days down the track, was as unimpressive as Sanderson had been, unless one were to consider that it had two saloons instead of one. The Circle Dot horse walked up to an empty hitching rail in front of the first one and stopped without being asked. Newt sat still in the saddle, contemplating, while the horse let out a sigh, lowered its head, and took a resting stance beneath him.

Apparently, the saloon the horse chose was the more popular of the two, for although it was yet morning, there were already four horses standing at the hitching rail in front of it. One of the horses had a blanket-wrapped corpse tied on its saddle.

Newt dismounted, slipped his cinch, and walked over to the horse bearing the corpse. He folded back the blanket to reveal the dead man's head and lifted it gently to take a look at the face to see if it might be

Cortina. The bloated, pale face staring back at him was that of a young Chinese man. Newt covered the head again and stepped up on the saloon porch.

To his surprise, a small black bear was chained to a few steps off one end of the porch. It wore a wide leather collar and sat on its haunches leaning against the post and staring at him. It batted at the flies swarming around its head and rubbed one of its matted eyes. The poor animal's hair was tangled and worn away in some places, as if it had the mange or some other skin affliction.

The Circle Dot horse opened his eyes long enough to glance at the bear and pin one ear, but then closed his eyes again, to all appearances intending to nap. The first thing Newt had come to learn about the horse was that it never missed a chance to rest. In fact, it slept more than any horse he had ever known.

Whoever had built the saloon was obviously not as much a carpenter as they were a bear lover. Not a single board was sawn to fit correctly or cut square, the bungalow roof sagged, and one wall of the building was well out of plumb, as if the wind had given it a permanent lean. The whole ramshackle affair was cobbled together out of weather-dried scrap lumber haphazardly nailed together and rusty sheet iron the owner had probably been able to salvage from the railroad construction crews, but it did have a pleasing sign nailed to one porch post. ICE BEER TEN CENTS.

Newt dismounted and slipped his cinch. The thought of a cold beer to wash the dust out of his mouth was enough to make him ignore the voices from inside the saloon, obviously in a heated argument of some kind. He trudged up the steps and through the open door.

The argument ceased immediately when he entered. The four men leaning against the bar turned as one to face him, and the bartender they had been talking to earlier placed both hands on the bar top and squinted at him out of one eye without turning his head, as if looking through a set of rifle sights.

"Welcome," the bartender said.

Newt found a place at the near end of the bar. "That sign out there true?"

"Which sign, and who you calling a liar? I wouldn't nail anything up on my property that wasn't true," the bartender said. He was a stocky man of barrel chest and a hint of a belly held back and kept in check by his belt. A neatly trimmed and heavy beard covered his face beneath his derby hat, and one of his shaggy eyebrows sagged down over his eye like a wilted leaf, giving him the appearance that he was always facing the sun or giving a conspiratorial wink.

"I'll take one of those cold beers, then," Newt said.

The bartender reached under the bar and brought out a brown bottle that he wiped the dust off with a dirty rag and uncapped and stood before Newt. "That'll be ten cents."

Newt wrapped his left hand around the bottle and found it warm to the touch. "Sign says 'ice beer.'"

"Some days, but we're out of ice."

One of the men at the bar laughed. "You don't ever have any ice. You're too cheap for that."

The bartender scowled at the man, but turned his attention back to Newt. "I was going to build an ice-house, but I can't find anyone in town willing to work. All they want to do is stand at my bar and sass their betters. You expecting a discount because we're out of ice? I won't sell on the cheap. This here is a cash-and-carry business."

Newt took a sip of the lukewarm beer and noticed that the men down the bar from him had nothing but empties in front of them. He pulled the last of his money from his pocket and counted it. Three dollars.

"How about a round for these men?" He laid fifty cents on the bar.

The bartender picked up one coin and examined it, as if it might be counterfeit. "Big-spender, eh? First you insult my beer and now you want to buy a round. You're contradicting yourself."

One of the men at the bar sauntered to the door and looked down the street. "Look there. Your competitor must have seen the horses tied in front of your place and decided to open early so he doesn't miss a chance at business."

"What?" The bartender scowled again and strode quickly across the room to stand in the doorway and watch a little Mexican man pass before him on the far side of the street, heading toward the settlement's only other saloon.

"By God, I'll show him." The bartender jerked a Colt pistol out of his waistband, and after he fumbled with it a bit, leveled it on the little Mexican outside. But the man beside him knocked his gun arm down.

"Go easy, Judge. You can't shoot Torrez, no matter how cranky you are this morning." The man kept his hold on the bartender's gun arm and gently and slowly pried the pistol free.

"He's breaking the law. I done told him several times, but he won't listen."

"What law?"

"Opening his saloon before noon without a permit."

The man beside him kept a smile on his face. For the first time, Newt noticed the badge pinned on his vest—a round badge with a star cut out in the center. Texas Ranger. He looked at the other men and noted that they, too, were wearing the same badges.

"You're open before noon," the Ranger said, coming back across the room and laying the bartender's pistol on the bar.

"I got a permit," the bartender said, remaining in the doorway.

"And who issued it?"

"Me. I'm the by God justice of the peace. If it weren't for me, that Mexican would have this place run to hell. You've got to have a little law and order or you bring the tone of a place down in no time. That's civilization—somebody making rules and somebody else following them. You should have let me shot him, and spare us the trouble of trying him."

"You stay sore at Torrez because he steals your customers. Could be because he actually sweeps up every now and then." The Ranger scuffed one boot in the litter of peanut hulls, cigarette butts, dead flies, and filthy sawdust on the floor.

"I hear he's running against you in the next election," another of the Rangers said, acting as if he were studying his beer bottle but watching the bartender out of the corner of his eye.

"He doesn't have the sense God gave a goose," the bartender said. "Might help my business if you Rangers didn't leave dead men out in the sun in front of my place. That corpse is beginning to stink, and the train's due in a little while."

"Gives off the impression that folks are dying to get into your saloon," said the Ranger.

"Who is it?"

"I don't know. Some Chinaman," the Ranger said. "Found him about three miles down the river, shot in the back. Thought you might want to look him over and hold an inquest."

The bartender reared back his head and sneezed loudly. "Son of a bitch," he said as soon as he finished.

"Bless you," said the Ranger who had taken away his pistol.

*"Gracias."* The judge wiped at his nose with his bar towel. He took a big breath and then let it out in a grunt. "Quite a horse you have there, mister."

Newt realized that the bartender was talking to him, and walked to the doorway with his beer in hand. The Circle Dot horse had lain down on his side and was asleep, even though the rein was tied short to the hitching rail, and his neck was bent and contorted and suspended off the ground.

"Did you ride him to death, or is that horse some kind of contortionist?" the bartender asked.

"He likes his siestas."

"I'm partial to them myself, but don't look comfortable. Does he always do that?"

"I've quit guessing about him."

"You ought to kick him until he gets up. I wouldn't tolerate such out of a horse. Seems like he's spoiled. What if you needed him in a hurry, and he was lying there sleeping like that?"

"That horse and I have a deal. I don't kick him and he doesn't kick me."

"How's that deal working out?"

"It's worked so far."

The bartender grunted again and went back behind

his bar. He gathered Newt's empty beer bottle and those of the others. "Another round?"

Newt nodded and reached in his pocket for more money. The bartender shook his head.

"Pay up when you leave." The bartender lined up the empties at the far end of the bar. "I'll count the bottles when it's time to settle your account."

Newt took a second beer and propped one boot on the rail at the foot of the bar. He adjusted the Smith on his hip until it was at a more comfortable location, and one of the Rangers glanced down at it. He turned to the men beside him and said something so low that Newt couldn't make it out. All of them looked at his pistol and then leveled their eyes on him.

"That's a fancy set of grips you've got," the nearest Ranger said.

Newt took a slug of beer instead of answering.

"Judge, you see this man's fancy shooting iron?" the same Ranger asked.

The bartender tiptoed and leaned out over the bar so that he could see. "Yep, that's Amos Redding's gun. Know it anywhere."

The Ranger nodded. "And I remember Amos wearing a fancy hatband like that one."

Newt took careful note of the fact that the Ranger speaking had his hand resting on his pistol butt and that the other Rangers were spreading out and stepping away from the bar. He could already see what was coming.

"What's the problem?" he asked, stalling for time.

The bartender smiled coolly. "The problem is, son, you ain't Amos Redding."

# Chapter Eleven

"**T**he hat and the pistol were given to me," Newt said, straightening and taking a step back from the bar.

"Amos Redding never gave his gun to anyone," the same Ranger who had taken the bartender's pistol away said.

"He's dead."

The bartender jerked a sawed-off shotgun out from under the bar as quick as a cat and laid it on the bar top with the twin barrels aimed at Newt and the muzzles not six inches from his belly. "You don't say? How about you lift them hands high and wide and let these Rangers here pluck that shooter off you? Seems like today's court session is going to be a busy one."

"I assure you that this isn't what it seems."

"And I assure you that you're a trigger pull away from a quick trip to hell. Lift those hands away from that smoke wagon. *Manos arriba, pendejo.*"

Newt raised his hands slowly. "Bandits killed him north of Horsehead Crossing, and Matilda Redding gave me his gun."

"Save your defense for the official record." The

bartender waved his free hand to dismiss any talk. "You'll have your case heard in time."

One of the Rangers lifted Newt's pistol from its holster and stepped away.

"When?" New asked.

"The judge will hear your case as soon as he's ready," the same Ranger said.

"What judge?"

"Me," the bartender said.

"And who the hell are you?"

"Judge Roy Bean, law west of the Pecos, at your service. Thought you read the signs. It was all there in clear, bold letters if you had cared to read instead of complaining about the temperature of my beer."

"Thought it was only the saloon name."

"No, that's on another sign, but now you know different. How about you buy another round while we wait for court to get in session? Noon train ain't run yet, and I don't like to hang a man with the strangers around. Upsets their trade. Makes them think we aren't civilized in these parts."

Newt stepped back to the bar. "Give me another one."

"What about another round for the boys here?" The judge jerked his head at the Rangers.

"Let them buy their own damned beer."

"No sense turning hostile," the judge said. "You're in enough trouble as it is."

The judge gave up his shotgun, but one of the Rangers took a chair in the corner of the room and leaned back against the wall with the same scattergun laid across his thighs. The air in the saloon grew increasingly hotter, and Newt nursed another lukewarm beer and thought while he sweated and listened to a big blue blowfly buzzing around the room.

The judge sneezed again. "Damnation!"

"Bless you," one of the Rangers said.

Several people began to show up, some of them travelers apparently deciding to wait for the train in the saloon instead of the depot house, or because they had spotted the dead man on the horse out front and wanted to gawk. All of them walked wide around Newt and congregated at the end of the bar when they noticed the guard on him.

"Did he kill that one out front?" a drummer in a suit and derby hat asked the judge behind the bar, as if Newt couldn't hear him. "He looks like a desperate man."

"No, two separate cases," the judge said. "State of Texas is going to be busy this afternoon."

"Wish I could stick around, but I've got to catch the westbound," the drummer said. "Always like to see you at work, Judge."

The so-called judge sauntered down to Newt's end of the bar. "Care for another one? Going to be a hot one today."

"I believe I'll pass."

"Well, if you ain't thirsty, maybe you want to buy Bruno a drink? Lots of the tenderfoots do. They pay a dollar a beer to see him drink one."

"Buy who a drink?"

"My bear. Ever seen one drink a beer? Loves the stuff. Drinks it straight out of the bottle like a man," the judge said. "Seein's how you ain't no tenderfoot tourist, I'll let you have the beer at regular price."

"Still believe I'll pass. Let the bear buy his own beer."

"Your attitude is beginning to bother me. Bears don't have money. No need to be a smart aleck just because you committed a crime and had the misfortune or poor sense to walk into a house of the law."

"I didn't murder anybody, and this court looks more like a saloon to me."

"Amos Redding was a well-liked man in these parts. We don't tolerate dry-gulchers nor man killers. No, sir, we don't."

Newt turned his back to the bar and leaned against it, staring at the Ranger with the shotgun who stared back at him as if standing guard was old hat to him. Newt walked slowly to the front door, wondering how far the Ranger would let him get.

"Don't take any notions about running," the Ranger finally said when Newt was almost to the door. "I'd hate to have to shoot you."

"I'd hate for you to have to shoot me. I was only checking on my horse."

"Sergeant Pridgen, why don't one of your men take this man's horse and throw him in the lot out back?" the judge asked the Ranger standing guard.

"Want we should bring that Chinaman's body inside so that it don't scare the train folks?" the sergeant asked.

"No, I've had second thoughts. Might be good for business, in fact," the judge said. "Nothing gets folks in more trouble than their curiosity. Man I knew used to have a two-headed calf stuffed and mounted in his bar. People would come in his place to look at it. Maybe that Chinaman carcass will drum up a little business."

Two of the Rangers went outside to take care of Newt's horse, and then the lot of them played poker for the next hour until the westbound train pulled into the station. The conductor's voice could be plainly heard inside the saloon, and the drummer grabbed up his valise and reached in his vest pocket for the money to pay his bar bill. He gave the judge a ten-dollar silver piece.

"That all you got? I'm about out of change, and I'll have to go in back and dig out some money," the judge said.

"Hurry. I've got a train to catch."

"No hurry. They'll be topping off with water, so you've got a bit."

The judge went through a back door into a room that must have been his sleeping quarters. Newt could hear him rummaging around in there while the drummer tapped one foot impatiently and stared out the front door.

"That conductor just gave his last call," one of the Rangers said. "You better get gone if you want to catch that train."

The judge came out of the back room shaking his head. "Can't find my money bag. Will you wait here while I go down to the street and get this coin changed?"

"How about I pay you next time through?"

"No, you might come on hard times by then and not be able to pay your bill."

"I only owe you for three beers."

"Thirty cents might not seem like much, but if I let everyone stiff me like that I'd be a pauper in short order."

"I want my change."

"Okay, wait for me or go down to the store and get Pete to make change out of his register."

"I don't have time."

"You had time to drink three beers. You shouldn't begin a purchase if you don't have time to follow it through. I waited for you to drink your beer. Didn't rush you at all."

The drummer hefted his valise and started for the door in a trot. "You owe me. Don't you forget the next time I'm come back through."

The judge waved at the drummer and shoved the coin in his vest pocket. "See ya next time."

"Hey, Judge," a big man in bib overalls and a leather shop apron said. "Let me pay out. My woman is going to throw a fit if I'm in here all day and not working."

The judge reached under the bar and brought out a small metal money box. He counted out the man's change, grinning while he did it.

"How many times are you going to pull that change bit on the train folks?" the man asked. "I can't believe that drummer went for that. I would have had my change or bent a shop hammer over your head."

"You tend to your blacksmithing and I'll tend to my bar business," the judge said. "And you be ready in case I need you for jury duty. And don't be pounding on that damned anvil of yours when court gets in session. It disturbs my thinking."

The judge caught Newt looking at him, and the smirk on his face faded.

"Doesn't seem like a judge thing to do," Newt said.

"I'll pay that drummer if he comes back. And speaking of bills, what say you pay your tab? I've been generous with credit, even though I had my doubts about you the moment you walked in." The judge pointed to the line of beer bottles at the end of the bar.

Newt made a quick count. There were fifteen empties, but he had only drunk three himself, plus two rounds of four for the Rangers. The bartender claiming to be some kind of judge had obviously slipped a few extras into the group to increase the bill.

"I think you stuck someone else's beer in on my tab by mistake," Newt said.

"No, I'm careful that way," the judge said. "You owe me a dollar fifty."

"I already paid for the first five. Gave you a fifty-cent piece."

"Oh, that's right. Another dollar ought to square us."

"I don't owe you but sixty cents."

"Sergeant, are you hearing this? Man here can't pay his bill."

"Tend to your saloon business yourself," the Ranger with the shotgun said. "The state ain't paying me to settle beer squabbles."

Newt slapped sixty cents on the bar and turned to watch the noon train huff and puff and clank out of the station, visible and framed through the open door as it passed before the saloon. A cinder from the smokestack caught a clump of dry grass on fire, and one of the Rangers ran out of the saloon and stomped it out.

"Should have let it burn," one of the customers at the end of the bar said. "A good fire would be fitting. What was it old General Sheridan said? If he owned Texas and Hell he would rent out Texas and live in Hell."

"Shut up, Rex, and order another drink, or get out if all you're going to do is disparage my town," the judge said. "Little Phil Sheridan was a damned Yankee who didn't know anything."

"Sorry, Judge. I forgot you wore the gray," the man mumbled into his empty whiskey glass, and avoided looking the judge in the eye.

"That's right. Rode with Colonel Baylor at Mesilla,

until that damned fool Sibley come and took over."
The judge pointed to an old Confederate cavalry
saber hanging beside the bar mirror. "Best you bite
your tongue and remember the Stars and Bars before
you go quoting Yankees in my saloon."

The judge watched the last of the train cars pass
and then took off his derby hat and exchanged it for
a black John Bull felt. Next, he lifted a brown frock
coat from a peg on the wall and shrugged into it.
Either the coat once belonged to another man or
he had grown in girth since he purchased it, for he
quickly gave up buttoning it across his middle. He
tucked a pencil behind one ear and came out from
behind his bar carrying a thick book under one arm
and a bottle of tequila in his other hand.

"Time for legal business," he called out as he went
out the front door. "What say we hold court out on the
porch where we can have a little breeze."

The Rangers and the few leftover customers filed
out behind him. The Ranger with the shotgun gestured with it in the direction of the door, and Newt
marched out in front of him.

The judge was sitting in a wicker-bottomed chair at
a little round card table, pouring tequila in a clay cup.
The Rangers took the last of the remaining chairs or
leaned against the porch posts, some of them still
nursing bottles of beer. The rest of the crowd leaned
against the wall or sat on the edges of the porch.
Several chickens clucked and scratched at the dusty
street and peered for grasshoppers in the weeds growing against the walls of the saloon.

"Sergeant, bring this court to order," the judge said.
The Ranger with the shotgun turned it up and
pounded the judge's table with the butt of it. As soon

as he did, one barrel went off, punching a ragged hole in the low porch roof and raining down bits of wood and dust. Two white hens were so startled that they cackled and fluttered their wings and took brief flight.

"Damn it, Sergeant!" the judge yelled, rubbing one ear. "What in the hell were you thinking?"

"You usually whack your pistol butt on the table to start the proceedings." The Ranger was looking rather sheepishly at the hole in the roof.

"I don't do it with a hair-triggered street howitzer," the judge said. "Watch where you point that thing. I don't want to take the second barrel the next time you decide to let it go off."

Newt walked to the porch steps while the judge cussed and rubbed at his ringing ear.

"Hold on there," the Ranger sergeant with the shotgun said. "You aren't going anywhere."

Newt turned and leaned against a vacant porch post. He tried not to notice the same hair-triggered shotgun pointing casually his way. "Can I say my piece now, Judge?"

"Huh?" The judge twisted one finger in his ear and leaned closer.

"I said, will you listen to what I have to say now that court is going?"

"You'll talk when I say you can talk." The judge nodded at the Ranger sergeant.

The sergeant made sure the shotgun was pointed in a safe direction and cleared his throat. "Hear ye, hear ye. Order in the court. We're now in session. Justice of the peace, the Honorable Roy Bean presiding."

"First order of business, we're going to have an inquest over the body you boys brought in." The judge looked to the Rangers scattered around him. "Where did you find him?"

"We didn't find him," a short, scrawny Ranger in a pair of suspenders and a floppy-brimmed hat said. "That boy of yours told us where he was at, and we went and fetched him."

"Sam? How did he happen across him?"

The Ranger looked at his fellow officers before answering. "We were talking to Sam when somebody rode up and said they had found a Chinaman dead right outside of town. Our horses were worn out, and we asked Sam if he would go look and see if there was really someone dead."

"Sam's a good boy like that."

The Ranger cleared his throat. "Funny thing was, Sam didn't even wait to ask where the body was. He rode out lickety-split and come right back with the body."

The judge leaned back in his chair and turned his clay cup up. He knocked down the tequila in one swallow and smacked his lips and set the cup upside down on the table, all the while staring hard at the Ranger.

"What are you implying?"

"Everyone knows that your Sam don't like a China-man. Takes after you in that regard," the sergeant with the shotgun threw in. He looked away as soon as he said it, his eyes finding something down the street of more interest and less uncomfortable than the return look the judge gave him.

"Sam is a good boy," the judge repeated.

"That he is," the first Ranger to give his account said. "But he's wild, too. If he was drunk and that

Chinaman said something that he took wrong, he might have taken a shot at him."

"Sam never shot anybody in the back. Bring that body up on the porch, and one of you go get Sam."

"Too late, Judge," the sergeant said. "We already looked for Sam after it dawned on us that he knew where the body was without us telling him. He's already run off, and that looks even worse on him."

"I sent Sam to check on my hog farm. That Italian I partnered with has been claiming small litters, and I think he's cheating me."

A red rooster walked across the porch boards cockily, almost strutting, and the bold bird leapt onto the judge's table. It was a scrawny, long-legged rooster, with curled spurs on its legs, the comb on its head pecked and scarred and fallen over from many fights, but with an impressive plume of glossy red tail feathers arched out behind it. Newt watched the bird and surmised it was the tail that gave the bird such a vain and bold posture.

The judge shooed the rooster back away from his law book, but otherwise ignored it and let it remain on the table. Two of the Rangers went and untied the body and carried it to the porch.

"Well, let me see it," the judge said. "Your dawdling is holding up the course of justice."

They unwound the body with a couple of sharp tugs like it was a roll of carpet. The Chinese man was tiny, even bloated and swollen like he was. The body stopped rolling, faceup at the judge's feet. There was blood and bits of bone and gut all over the chest of the dead man's white shirt where the bullet had come out.

"Like we said. Somebody shot him in the back," the Ranger sergeant said.

"What was this Chinaman doing in Langtry?" the judge asked.

"Maybe he worked on one of the railroad crews and decided to hang around when the work was finished, or maybe he was passing through."

"What would a Chinaman want here? There aren't any other Chinamen around for him to talk to." The judge scanned the street as if he expected more Chinese to show up any second.

"Who knows?" the sergeant said. "There was that Chinaman that fell off the high trestle over at the Roost and died year before last."

"I doubt even a Chinaman would come here to fall off a trestle. Hurry up and make some sense. You're dawdling again."

"We asked around some, but nobody knows a thing about him except that Jesús Torrez said he had seen him around a time or two. Maybe he has been working on that new bridge over the river."

"What would that crooked Mexican know? But it doesn't shock me that he knew this Chinaman. Leads me to believe this fellow was up to no good. Vagrant. Probably sneaking around town looking for something to steal. You ever notice how shifty those slant eyes of theirs look?"

"The man ain't even wearing a gun or a knife," the Ranger said, working a chew of tobacco in one cheek. He leaned over to spit, his lips puckered.

"You spit on my porch, Sergeant, and I'll have to fine you for contempt of court. What kind of lawman spits on the courtroom floor while court's in session? Don't you have any respect for the law?"

"Pardon me," the Ranger said with his head tilted back and sounding like he was gargling or about to choke on his tobacco juice. He twisted his head and let his spit fly onto the dusty ground off the edge of the porch.

"Did you search his body?" the judge asked.

The sergeant looked at the rest of his men, but none of them had anything to say. "It was hot and the flies were getting bad on him, so we decided to wait and examine him in the shade."

"Well, do it now."

The sergeant leaned over and went through the dead man's pockets. He laid his findings on the judge's table. Among them were a little money and a small, over-and-under, two-shot Remington pocket derringer.

The judge picked the derringer up and held it before the sergeant in his open palm. "What did I tell you? A sneak gun."

"Many a man carries a pistol hid out for insurance in a tight situation. That don't mean they're a sneak."

"Look in his shoe tops. I bet he had a knife stashed," the judge said. "Chinamen are like Mexicans and prefer a knife."

"There were a whole passel of them west of here when the railroad was being laid. I never knew one of them to knife anyone."

"How many Chinamen did you ever know?" the judge asked.

"Just those I saw working on the railroad. Didn't really know any of them. They come out from California laying track this way."

The judge nodded. "I once lived in California. Did you ever?"

"No, I never."

"Well then, I guess I'm the expert here if that's

where Chinamen congregate in the greatest measure. And you don't have to live in California to know they can't be trusted. A child has that much sense. Always jabbering in Chinese so you can't understand what they're complaining about. I once left my clothes in a Chinese laundry and forgot I left money in my pocket. You think my money was there when I got my laundry back? Why do you think the Texas Pacific didn't work those yellow-skinned bastards on their leg of the line? Only that damned Southern Pacific bunch did, because they could get them on the cheap."

"Be that as it may, it still stands that somebody shot this man in the back. We'd best round up Sam and take him and the body up to Fort Stockton for trial."

"You don't have any evidence that points to Sam shooting him."

"We all know that Sam doesn't like Chinamen."

"That's the second time you've said that. I don't like them, either, but I sure didn't kill him. Want to make me a suspect?" The judge pulled his pistol out of his waist and turned it butt forward and whacked the table. "Wake up, Slim! No more drinks for you if you can't stay awake in court."

The Ranger in a chair who had been caught napping straightened his back and his hat and tried to look attentive.

"Any of you ever heard of Sam shooting anyone, much less in the back?" the judge asked.

"No, but he shot at Little Frank Mendez last year."

"He missed. What makes you think such a poor shot could have downed this Chinaman?"

"Maybe he got lucky or maybe he was up close. Poor marksmanship shouldn't rule him out."

"His marksmanship is what is called circumstantial

evidence. You wouldn't know that because you ain't trained in the law," the judge said. "We all know, my son or not, Sam can't shoot worth a shit."

"That's a fact, Judge, but . . ."

"Damned right it's a fact," the judge said. "Won't be a trial unless this inquest says the case merits one, and so far I don't see anything suspicious or duly warranting further trouble on our part."

"Judge, a man's been killed. I'd say that was highly suspicious."

"No, it was a Chinaman. You stand corrected, Sergeant. Nothing suspicious about someone shooting one pilfering around where he doesn't belong."

"Judge . . ."

"You hold on while I consult the law."

The judge opened the big book on the table before him, and Newt saw that it was the *Revised Statutes of Texas*, 1879 edition, five years out of date. The judge wet a finger and flipped through page after page, grunting occasionally when it seemed he found something of interest. The rooster jumped off the table and began to peck at one of the corpse's eyes.

After making a show of serious study, the judge slammed the book closed. "It's what I thought. I can't find anything that specifically says it's against the law to kill a Chinaman."

"Sam's our best suspect," the Ranger sergeant said.

The judge kicked at the rooster halfheartedly, but the fowl dodged easily, as if it were an old game between the two of them.

"Get away from that body, Shanghai," the judge said to the rooster. He flipped his cigarette butt off the porch and the bird's keen eye caught the motion. It immediately ran off the porch and began to peck at the cigarette butt as if it were a bug or something worth eating.

The judge cleared his throat and levered his attention away from the rooster to the Ranger sergeant. "Do you have any witnesses?"

"No."

"Then your whole case is circumstantial."

"The circumstances make me believe Sam might have done it."

"The circumstances are that Sam can't shoot for shit, nobody saw him do it, and nothing in this law book says it's against the law to shoot a Chinaman."

"This ain't right, Judge."

"If Sam shot this Chinaman, as you suppose, what crime did the Chinaman do to provoke Sam?"

"He might not have done anything."

"No, Sam's hot tempered, but he wouldn't shoot a Chinaman without cause. You can't tell me what no good this Chinaman was up to, so I say you don't have any motive. Motive is important when you accuse a man of premeditated murder."

"Maybe it wasn't premeditated."

"No, Sam's a slow aim and would have to think on it some to make sure he didn't miss."

"I still say this isn't right."

"Well, haul that body up to Fort Stockton if you think you can get a different verdict. Waste your time if you want to instead of doing your duly appointed duty to look out for the well-being of real Texans and Americans instead of foreigners."

"That's a long ride up to Stockton," the sergeant said. "And the body's already smelling some."

"Well then, I've given my ruling here in Langtry. If it ain't good enough for you, have a five-day trip and try and get another one in Stockton." The judge whacked the table with his pistol butt again. "I see no grounds for the state of Texas pursuing this matter further."

The sergeant saw the judge shoving the deceased's money and derringer in his pocket, and the judge squinted back at him.

The judge whacked the table again with his pistol, harder and louder this time. "I dismiss this case due to a lack of evidence and sufficient motive, plus there ain't nothing in the books that says it's against the law to shoot a Chinaman. Furthermore, I fine this Chinaman"—the judge paused and pulled the coins back out of his pocket and counted them—"six dollars and forty-three cents for carrying a concealed firearm. Get that body off my porch."

"The governor and the state attorney are still complaining about you not turning in all your fines," the sergeant said.

"Let the governor run things up in Austin, and I'll run things here. I'm the law in Langtry."

Two of the Rangers rolled the body back up, with one at each end, and disappeared around the corner.

The judge shifted in his chair and turned to Newt. "And now to you."

# Chapter Twelve

"What's your legal name?" the judge asked.

"Newt Jones."

The judge took up a stub of a pencil and squinted over a notebook before him, making slow work of entering Newt's name. "Any aliases?"

"No."

The judge looked up from the notebook and gave Newt's face a closer look. "You've got a rough look about you. My experience is that most men with your kind of scarred-up mug are likely to have more than one name, and it wouldn't surprise me if these Rangers had paper on you. You on the scout?"

"I'm not wanted anywhere."

"Where you from?"

"Rode down here from New Mexico Territory."

"I mean, where were you born? I hear some mountain in that accent of yours. You one of those hill boys?"

"East Tennessee."

The judge let out an indignant huff of air. "Tennessee? Never had much use for the state. I'm a Kentucky man myself."

"Davy Crockett was a Tennessean," one of the Rangers said.

"And Kentucky had Daniel Boone. He was a heap better fighter than that Crockett and had better sense than to let himself get cornered by a Mexican army and killed. Old Daniel would have laid low in the woods and picked them off one or two at a time. Kentuckians have sense that way."

"Judge, you ought not go disparaging Tennesseans," the same Ranger said.

"Oh, I know. I think half of Texas is made up of you Tennessee boys. You all ought to wear coonskin caps to save me the trouble of having to pick you out in a crowd," the judge said, and pointed a finger at Newt. "How plead you? Did you kill Amos Redding or not?"

"Innocent," Newt said.

"How come you're wearing his gun?"

"His widow gave it to me for burying him."

"Big, fat woman with red hair? Don't talk much?"

"Skinny woman with yellow hair." Newt couldn't help but chuckle. "And she says plenty."

The judge looked at the Rangers for a moment, and then back to Newt. "Sounds like you know Matilda. Talkin'est woman on God's green earth. But that don't mean you didn't kill Amos."

"I was chasing after a Mexican and his gang and found her in a bind with her man dead. Helped her bury him and then took her on to Fort Stockton."

The judge's expression changed, and he leaned back in his chair, as if to see Newt better. "Chasing a Mexican?"

"Man named Cortina. He shot me and stole my stock and a peck of gold I was carrying. Then he killed Amos Redding a few days later."

"You don't look prosperous enough to be carrying gold."

"I've been less prosperous since I met Cortina."

"That's Cortina's trade—making people less prosperous. He's a pocket lightener, for sure," the judge said. "How do I know you aren't making all this up?"

Newt untucked his shirt and pulled it up until all of them could see the scabbed-over bullet wound on his chest. "That's where he shot me."

"For God's sake, dress yourself. There might be womenfolk walking about." The judge scanned the street again and then poured himself another tequila. "What are you doing in my town if all this is true?"

"I come through here riding after Cortina. Sheepherder up the tracks in Sanderson said Cortina sold him my old horse and was headed this way."

The judge slammed his cup down, sloshing tequila over its side. "Damn right he came through here! First thing you've said with a ring of truth to it."

"I've told you the truth. Every bit of it."

The judge shooed a fly away from his face with a wave of his hand while he thought for a bit. "You know anything about spotted cats?"

"Bobcats? I've seen a few of them. Trapped a couple when I was a boy."

"Big cats. Big enough to down a man or a horse."

"Might steal a chicken or two, but a bobcat won't bother anyone."

"I'm not talking about bobcats," the judge hissed. "For once I'd like to have a defendant come through here that was smart enough to make me feel sorry for his predicament. Obviously you aren't that man. I'm talking about a jaguar. Big, spotted, Mexican devils. Size of a mountain lion or so."

"I thought they were supposed to live way down in Mexico. Jungle sorts. Never heard of such in Texas."

"No, they're here, too. People see them from time to time, although it's a rare occasion. I had me a tanned hide from one of those cats nailed up behind the bar for a conversation piece. Eight foot long from its nose to the tip of its tail."

"No offense, but what's that got to do with my case?"

"Nothing, but you're the one got me to thinking about Cortina again. People saw him come through here two nights ago, and then my cat hide turns up missing the next morning. I gave fifty dollars for that hide, and I was partial to it."

"Sounds like you had almost the same kind of trouble I had with him."

"No, our kinds of trouble are far different. I ain't under arrest. You've got worse troubles by far."

Newt took a few deep, slow breaths, trying to keep his calm. "You've heard my story now. No reason for you to keep me. I'd appreciate it if you'll let me have my gun and my horse back, and I'll be riding on."

The judge whacked the table again. "Court's in recess. Sergeant, confine this man while I ponder on his judgment. It's grown too hot, and even justice needs a nap now and again."

The sergeant motioned Newt off the porch with a jerk of his shotgun barrel. "You heard the judge."

Newt glared at the judge one last time before he went down the porch steps. When he reached the ground he turned and looked back at the big sign above the porch roof: JUDGE ROY BEAN, LAW WEST OF THE PECOS.

There was no jail in Langtry, as Newt soon came to find out. The judge's orders to confine him resulted in Newt being handcuffed and fasted to a short length of chain secured to one end of the porch.

"That's a joke for a court if I ever saw one," Newt said. "And if that JP is a real judge I'll kiss your backside."

The Ranger sergeant put one boot up on the porch and leaned on that knee. "Don't take Judge Roy lightly. I admit he's not usual in any sense, but he gets it done."

"No, nothing about him is usual. How does a man like that get a seat on the bench?"

The Ranger laughed. "He came down from San Antonio to these parts when the railroad was being built. Started a tent saloon at Strobridge, or what they're calling Sanderson now. Got in a little scrape with the competition there and moved his outfit to Vinegarroon over by the river. Can't tell you how he got to be a JP, but Vinegarroon was wild then and eating a man a day. Every tough, cardsharp, and would-be badman knew there wasn't any law closer than Fort Stockton over a hundred miles away. Judge Roy set up court and claimed he was brave enough to try them if we were brave enough to bring them in. And by God, we done it. Held court every day and cleaned up that end-of-the-tracks hell town."

"I don't think he knows a lick of law."

The Ranger shook his head. "Judge Roy tends to make it up as he goes sometimes, but out here regular laws don't always fit. Common sense goes a long way."

"You call fining a dead man so that you can rifle his pockets common sense?"

"I admit Judge Roy is a little crooked, but his antics like that are usually harmless, and they provide a little entertainment for folks. Keeps us laughing on days when there might not be a lot to laugh about."

"I don't know how the Rangers aren't ashamed to bring their prisoners to him."

"If you had to haul prisoners all the way to Fort Stockton, you might think different. Judge Roy is handy, if nothing else, and most of those we drag in here don't deserve any better, and not many of them are important cases. Mostly it's pretty cut-and-dry and we just need someone with an official stamp."

Newt held up his shackled wrists. "I didn't shoot Amos Redding, but he's got me chained up like a dog."

"Don't worry, the judge ain't ruled a hanging more than once or twice that I can remember."

"You're not a comforting man."

The Ranger headed for the inside of the saloon. "The judge will get to you in time."

Newt listened to the sergeant's boots thumping on the porch boards, and when he was gone he dug one heel into the dirt and watched the little dust cloud it caused at the end of his outstretched legs.

The bear was chained only ten feet or so from the end of the porch, and it ambled to the end of its chain with its ears pinned like a mad horse. The chain stopped it barely short of Newt, but it reached out with one paw and made a swipe at him.

Newt crawled up on the end of the porch, giving him a little more distance from the bear, and kicked another cloud of dust at it. "Get out of here."

"Don't go accosting my bear," the judge's voice said from behind him. "I can't stand an animal beater."

Newt twisted and saw the judge standing behind him, holding two beers by the bottle necks.

"I told you I wasn't buying any more beer."

"They ain't for you." The judge stepped past him

and off the end of the porch. "You don't pay your bills, nohow."

The bear gave the judge the same mad look and ducked its head and threatened to paw at him. The judge ignored the threat and held out a beer to his unruly pet. The bruin immediately swiped at the bottle, but the judge jerked it away and produced a foot-long scrap of one-by-four plank from his back pocket. He struck the bear a resounding blow on the top of its head with the piece of board, and the bear whimpered like a little kid and cowed down before the judge.

"That's better," the judge said.

"Thought you didn't like cruelty to animals," Newt said.

"We've all got to learn our lessons. Spare the rod and spoil the bear." The judge held the beer out again, and this time the bear squatted on its rump and reached gingerly for the bottle with both paws. It jammed the bottle in its mouth, holding it like a sucking baby. "Ever see the likes of that?"

"I didn't come down here to watch bears drink beer," Newt said.

"You're a surly sort."

"You ain't seen surly yet."

The judge handed the bear another beer and watched it go to work. "Are you really after Cortina?"

"I was till I run into you."

"Cortina won't be easy to catch, and not a man most would like to corner if they did."

"You turn me loose, and I'll handle him."

"Think you're tough, don't you? I've seen plenty of others who thought the same." The judge rubbed his beard in thought. "Think those scars of yours give you an edge?"

"I've got it to do. That man took from me."

"How much gold did he take from you?"

"Better than four thousand, give or take an ounce or two."

The judge let out a low whistle. "That's a pretty good stake, but you must put a pretty cheap price on your skin to go traipsing after more trouble with Cortina."

"He tried once and didn't get it done. We'll see how it goes the next time."

"Talk's cheap."

"You let me loose and I'll quit talking."

The judge stood. "No, I'm going to have to think on you some. I'm still not sure you didn't kill Amos Redding. Might be I should send one of those Rangers back up the trail and make sure you're telling the truth."

"You don't think I killed him, but I'm not sure what your game is."

"When a man gets to be my age, he gets to really disliking surprises. I let you ride off free, what's it going to look like on me when some posse comes riding up the next day looking for you because you really did shoot Amos? I've got my good name to look out for."

"Your good name?" Newt scoffed and wanted to spit.

The judge looked down at him and his face turned hard with the red coming to his cheeks. He pointed to the roof. "Yes, my good name. You read that sign up there. I'm the law here, and the only law in these parts. You'd do well to remember that."

# Chapter Thirteen

Come morning, Newt woke with a crick in his neck and a sour taste in his mouth. The plank porch was too hard to sleep on, and the bare-beaten ground he had chosen for his bed was little softer. He rose and dusted himself off as best he could with his hands shackled and the chain rattling around his knees.

It was the sound of a crowbar punching the earth and grating on the gritty sand and rock that woke him. He rubbed at the sleep in his eyes and tried to make out the fellow digging a hole on the edge of the street in front of the saloon. He was a young, wiry lad with a black mustache and sweat already soaking through his shirt. A skinny cow pony stood three-legged nearby, with its head sagging and one rein draped on the ground. Tied to its saddle horn on the end of a rope was a heavy cedar post about fifteen feet long.

The young cowboy continued to beat out his hole, without consideration for those who still might be sleeping so early in the morning. No matter the racket, the bear was curled up asleep and didn't stir.

Newt barely had time to take a seat on the end of the porch before the four Rangers trooped out of the saloon carrying their bedrolls on their shoulders. Last he remembered before he gave in to fitful sleep was the Rangers' voices coming through the walls, still telling stories and swapping jokes until the wee hours. Every one of them looked sour and hungover after their long night of the judge's hospitality and cheap whiskey.

Three of the Rangers went around the corner toward the horse corral in back, but the sergeant took the time to set a graniteware plate containing some chili and beans and a soggy corn tortilla on the porch beside Newt.

"Much obliged," Newt said.

"Don't thank me until you've tried it. The judge claims he makes his chili con carne out of goat meat, but from the taste of it I suspect he isn't above slipping a little rattlesnake or armadillo in the pot when goat prices get too high to suit him."

"I've eaten snake. Wouldn't recommend it, but a man can live on it in a pinch."

"You and the judge ought to make a pair then, if you're so open-minded and tolerant of culinary deficiencies."

"Where is that highbinder of a judge?"

The sergeant ignored him and went after his comrades, leaving Newt to sample the judge's cooking. The first bite confirmed the Ranger sergeant's opinion of the judge's cooking skills, but Newt was too hungry to be picky and made do with what was offered.

No less than the judge himself finally came out the front door, rubbing his jowls with one hand and scratching at the seat of his pants with the other. He was wearing a sugarloaf sombrero, which was the third hat Newt had seen him in. Obviously, the judge was a man of many hats: one for bartending, one for court, and one for whatever the morning held in store.

On stiff knees the judge stumbled over to the end of the porch and handed Newt a tin dipper of water. "I imagine this prisoner bit has left you thirsty."

"Where are those Rangers going?" Newt asked.

"Back on patrol." The judge waved a hand in several vague directions at once, as if that accurately identified their heading. "They've promised to check into your story once they make it up to Fort Stockton."

"And how long will that be? I don't relish the thought of being chained to your porch for much longer."

"Could be a week or two."

Newt set down his plate and looked the judge in the eye. "I'm about to decide I don't care for you."

The judge grunted like a straining old bull. "They're leaving you in my custody. Got a chore you might help me with."

"You've got a lot of gall to suggest I help you with anything."

The judge pointed at the cowboy digging the hole. "That's my boy, Sam. See that post there he drug up? Know what I'm going to do with that post?"

"You tell me."

"Sam is a slow worker, but he'll have that tall post set in the ground by the time we're back."

"What do you mean when *we're* back?"

"He's going to nail a good stout cross member to that post before he raises it, and I'm going to hang Cortina from it, or I ain't a Bean from Mason County.

A Bean always means what he says and says what he means."

"You still haven't said what you meant by 'we.'"

"You're going to ride down into Mexico and help me catch that saucy Mexican bandit. I'd send the Rangers, but they don't have jurisdiction down there. Law don't go far in Mexico, anyway."

"I don't need any partners."

"You can rot here chained to this post while I'm gone or go with me. I'm doing you a favor. You're under suspicion of committing murder and have already refused to pay your bar bill. I'm giving you a chance at a suspended sentence and something to work off your debt."

"Are you still trying to get me to pay for beer I didn't drink?"

"Needless to say, your record in my town doesn't put you in a good light so far, and a less likely man for the mercy of the court I probably couldn't find if I searched for a long while."

"Yet you would trust me to go after Cortina with you?"

"I didn't say I trusted you."

"You ought not. I'm building a pretty good grudge."

"You've got to promise me one thing if you want me to turn you loose."

"What's that?"

"Promise you won't kill Cortina when we catch him, no matter what he did to you."

"You're asking a lot."

"I don't want Cortina shot down below the border by any old fellow like yourself. I want him brought here and hung by yours truly. If I let him get off with my jaguar hide folks are going to start saying old

Judge Roy has lost his mettle, and just any fool bandit with some guts can ride in here and take from him," the judge said with the gravel and the crankiness coming back into his voice. "I won't have anyone laughing at me and my court."

"Say I went with you. How do you know I won't waylay you or run off the first chance I get?"

The judge pointed to the four Rangers riding around the corner leading the Circle Dot horse and another saddled spare. "Those boys yonder might not look like much, but they're tougher than whang leather and would as soon quit a criminal's trail as would a bloodhound with six legs and three noses. They owe me a few favors. Might be I've kept my mouth shut when they delivered a little vigilante justice without the court's blessing and wrote them up some papers to make things look legal for them."

"What are you getting at? Quit beating around the bush."

"You run off on me, or cross me in any way, and you won't come back to Texas without them after you. I'll write up all kinds of charges against you. Might be if they caught you they might be tempted to be a little prompt and enthusiastic in their duties."

"Thought this all out, have you?"

"Your choice. You do what you think is best, but I don't have time to wait around. I won't be the laughingstock of the border. No, sir, I'm going to have the last laugh when I stretch Cortina's neck. Make an example out of him."

Newt calculated the head start Cortina had on him—one that was growing by the second—and weighed that against the bad feeling he had about any deal with the judge. In the end, he held up his shackled hands. "Let me loose."

The judge pulled a key from his pocket and unlocked the handcuffs. He didn't wait around but stepped off the porch and went to the horse the Rangers held for him. For a man who appeared well past his prime, he put a boot in the stirrup and stepped up easily enough, although he sat a saddle slumped over like a sagging sack of grain.

Newt went to the Circle Dot horse, checked his rig, and then mounted. The sergeant held out his Smith pistol, and he took it from him and shoved it into his holster.

"Don't you disappoint the judge," the sergeant said. "He's a friend of ours."

The Rangers spurred off before Newt could say a word to them. He was left alone with the judge.

The same red rooster from the day before flew up and landed on the back of the judge's saddle skirt. The judge held out something to it, and the rooster pecked it from his hand.

"You going to haul that bird with you?" Newt asked.

"Old Shanghai is a good friend of mine," the judge said. "Won me many a peso fighting him when he was younger. He can go where he pleases."

"Just thought it was odd, that's all."

"Daylight's a-wasting." The judge started his horse off with the red rooster riding calmly on the back of the saddle.

Newt pulled in behind him and they followed the railroad tracks out of town at a slow walk with the rising sun in their eyes. The judge rode a pencil-necked gray gelding with its mane rubbed out and weeds tangled in its tail. Other than a long-barreled

Colt shoved behind his belt buckle, the judge had no other firearm, despite their intention to go man-hunting.

"Where are we headed?" Newt asked. "You know something I don't?"

"I know that Cortina's got himself a sweetheart," the judge said, filling one cheek with a wad of chewing tobacco. "Young, pretty little thing. Her daddy's got a fine rancho and hacienda a day's ride west of Piedras Negras. A hacendado like him don't have any use for the likes of Cortina, but that girl don't have his judgment. She's been meeting that thief on the sly when he's in the country. Like I said, she's unusually pretty, and he'll go to her like a fly to sugar. You can bet your last dollar on that."

"You can't be sure he's headed that way."

The judge pulled up his gray nag and twisted his head away from the sun and squinted at Newt. "I brought you along for muscle and not your wits. We're going down below the border. You ever been down there?"

"No, I never."

"Then you'll do well to listen to me. It's a whole nother world. Hard country. Easy to lose your bearings. Many a gringo goes over the line and can't find his way back. Been down there several times myself, and I like to have not got back every time."

"What's that Jersey Lily bit back there on your porch?"

"You're a slow reader of signs. It's taken you two days to get a handle on them all."

"You have a lot of signs."

"You've never heard of the Jersey Lily? Miss Lillie Langtry?"

Newt shook his head.

"Finest-looking woman on God's green earth. Saw her in person once, but an angel like her don't even recognize the likes of me or you in a crowd. She had a voice like you never heard. Named my saloon in her honor, and then the town."

"She must have made quite an impression on you."

"Don't speak slightingly about her. You ain't worthy to lick the dust from her dainty little high-button shoes. If I close my eyes and listen close, I can still hear her sing. Makes me feel kind of floaty when I do, and makes me want to sing myself." The judge cleared the phlegm from his throat, hacking and spitting, and then began to sing loudly and mostly off key. "Oh, do you remember sweet Betsy from Pike? She crossed the high mountains with her lover Ike. With two yoke of oxen and a big yellow dog. And a tall Shanghai rooster and one spotted hog. Too-ra-li-oo-ra-li-oo-ra-li-ay."

Newt hoped the song didn't have many verses.

"You feel free to sing along if you have the voice for it. I find that a good bass goes well with my fine Irish tenor," the judge said, and cleared his throat again in preparation for another verse.

Newt resisted the urge to reach out and knock the old highbinder out of his saddle, feeling the irritation crawl up his spine and settle like a heavy weight on his chest. The devil on one shoulder argued with the angel on his other. Behind him, the sound of the cowboy digging the posthole for Cortina's hanging post rang like a church bell in his head. Hard country, indeed. Hell and Texas.

# Chapter Fourteen

It took Kizzy and Fonzo the better part of the afternoon to bury the dog and to wrestle and roll the dead horse out of its harness. And it took them even longer to capture the wily mule and to get their equipment wagon off the road and to cover it with cut brush. They were still two miles out from Piedras Negras, and it was near dark when they met the southbound stagecoach.

It was traveling at a high clip, and Kizzy felt in danger of being run down and barely managed to pull the living quarters wagon to the side of the road before the stagecoach came flying past with the driver up in the seat and hauling on his ribbons in a unsuccessful attempt to slow his runaway team. Through the cloud of choking dust both of them noticed that the stage was pulled mostly by the mules formerly belonging to them.

"Those mules never did mind well," Fonzo said. "I'm almost glad the rurales stole them."

"Knotheads or not, they were our knotheads," Kizzy said. "We'd have to rob a bank to buy more mules."

"Those rurales must have sold them to the stage company as soon as they hit town."

Kizzy nodded.

"They won't suspect that we will do anything about it," Fonzo added.

"There's nothing we can do about it. Best thing is for us to keep a low profile and take a look around for Cortina and your horses."

"It wasn't right, what those rurales did."

"No, but if you get us in trouble with them we won't ever get the horses back. Who's going to believe us? Those rurales are the law. It's our word against theirs."

"I don't want to let it lie. I can't."

"Do you want to end up like Father? Listen to me."

Fonzo looked at her, his jaw trembling with passion and his eyes wet with tears and anger. "Are you scared, sister?"

"Yes, but we will see this thing through and have your horses back. Promise me you will not try to make trouble with the rurales if we meet them again."

He hesitated long before he nodded agreement. "It's going to get worse. This thing we do will not be easy."

"I know. That's what scares me."

They recognized some of the rurales' horses tied in front of a seedy cantina on the southern outskirts of town. It was already dark enough that lamplight was spilling out of the open door into the street, and from the raucous laughter and banter coming from inside Kizzy guessed that the rurales had chosen their bivouac for the night.

Kizzy made sure they camped on the opposite side

of town, fearing what Fonzo might do. Fonzo woke her up the next morning, knocking loudly on the side of the wagon. It was a little past sunup, but there he was, standing with his arms crossed over his chest and an impatient set to his face. He looked wide awake and as if he had been up for a long time.

She rubbed the sleep out of her eyes and gathered her sleeping gown and went down the steps and took a seat on a campstool beside the smoking ashes of the night's fire.

"I found the *alcalde* this morning, and then the local judge," he said in a quick spurt.

"At this hour?"

"I woke them."

"I bet they appreciated that."

"They won't do anything. The rurales already let it be known that they captured our mules in a raid on an Indian village."

She took a deep breath. "You're going to make trouble for us that we can't afford. The horses are our priority."

"I think the judge is somehow kin to the rurale captain."

"Things often work like that. We can file a grievance with the court if you want to, but it sounds like that wouldn't work. I think we had best find out if Cortina came through here with the horses and where he was headed if he did."

"I talked to a Mexican lawyer, too. He wants fifty pesos to take our case."

"You've been busy this morning."

He began to pace back and forth. "Is there no justice in this country?"

"This is our reality."

He stopped abruptly several steps from her and arched one eyebrow. "It seems I'm not the only one who got up early."

She only then noticed Vlad lying beneath the wagon, wagging his tail and avoiding her gaze. The dead chicken clamped in his jaws didn't hide the shameful grin behind his revealed teeth.

"Why didn't you tie him up last night?" Fonzo asked. "You know he is bad to kill chickens. He's gotten us in trouble for that more than once."

She rose and went to the dog and took the chicken from him. It was a nice, fat young hen. "That was the very reason I didn't tie him up. We were short of anything for breakfast."

"And you tell me not to take chances."

"Good Vlad." She patted the dog and held the chicken up by its legs. "Will you refuse some hot chicken and dumplings this morning? Should he come around, I doubt the hen's owner will recognize his bird in a bowl."

He took the dead hen from her. "I will pluck it."

"Maybe the hen belonged to one of the rurales. Think positive."

"I'll keep that in mind, but it still doesn't make up for the fact that it's wrong. We are circus people and artists, not chicken thieves."

"The dog stole the chicken. We are only keeping it from going to waste."

He cast a glance at the dog, unable to hide the growing grin on his face. "At the bare minimum we are conspirators."

"We are hungry. Troubled times call for difficult measures."

She rolled out some dumplings from the last of

their flour while he plucked the chicken and cut it up. Later, with an empty bowl and a full belly, he said, "That's twice in one week that we've had chicken. I must say that it's better than our usual fare."

She smiled. "Things must be looking up. How many people do you think are sitting down right now to such fine dining?"

# Chapter Fifteen

**A**pparently, nobody in Del Rio, Texas, found it odd that the judge rode with a red rooster perched on the back of his saddle skirts. Either it was nothing out of the normal, or the judge was known there, for several people stopped to wave at him or to call out greetings. Once, the rooster spied another little white rooster with a small harem of hens and wanted to go make a challenge, but the judge enticed him to stay mounted by reaching in his pocket and offering something to peck from his palm. Newt finally realized that the judge was carrying corn and using it to keep the fowl's company. The man obviously thought a lot of his pet.

No matter that his pet rode with him, the judge had been in a cranky mood, probably stemming from the fact that his boots had become wet swimming the Pecos River the evening before. When dried in front of a campfire, the boots had shrunk to the point that they pinched his feet badly—something that he continually complained about, no matter that Newt had taken his boots off to keep them dry while swimming the river and had suggested that the judge do the same. The judge hadn't listened, but the warm welcome he received in Del Rio seemed to lift his spirits, pinching boots or not.

"It appears you're a known man in these parts," Newt said.

"I admit I have somewhat of a good name along the border," the judge said. "Remind me tonight, and I'll show you an article that the San Antonio newspaper wrote about me last year. Called me a staunch advocate for law and order."

Newt had no wish to read anything about the judge, but kept that to himself. They crossed the Rio Grande midmorning, after the judge took the time to consort with some of his contacts. He said little of whatever he found out, but seemed confident that where he was taking them would lead to Cortina. Newt wasn't sure of that, but whether he liked to admit it or not, the judge was the best lead he had.

They camped on the side of a bare, rocky ridge overlooking the river below and the stage road that paralleled it. Anybody going south to Piedras Negras couldn't pass without being seen from their high perch.

The red rooster immediately began to scratch around in the sand and search the rock crevices for something to eat, clucking its strange chicken language, as if holding its own conversation. But the judge didn't let him get too far away, and held out a bit of the corn from his pocket.

"Come here, Shanghai," he said.

The rooster's head rose at the sound of his name, and his sharp vision immediately spied the yellow kernels in the judge's open palm. It didn't hesitate and darted through the rocks at high speed with its neck outstretched and its wings held away from its body. The judge smiled while the rooster pecked the corn from his hand.

"Smart bird, old Shanghai here. Don't miss much, and he's got a set of eyes as sharp as a buzzard."

Newt was only half paying attention, for the judge never unsaddled his horse, it seemed, at least not for the two times they had made camp. Newt felt sorry for the animal and slipped its bridle, removed the saddle from its sweaty back, and rubbed it down with a handful of dead grass. There was nothing to graze on in the rock pile the judge had chosen for their campsite, so Newt gave his and the judge's horse some of the corn from his own saddlebags, pouring it out on a flat rock.

"You dote on that animal too much," the judge said.

"That horse won't carry you long without something to eat. Can't say I appreciate having to feed your horse from my own stores."

"These Western horses know how to make do. We can stop and let them graze a bit in the morning when we get back down on the flats."

Newt started to tell him that he wasn't going to take care of his damned horse anymore and hadn't hired on as his groom, but what the judge did then startled him too much and he lost his train of thought.

The judge grabbed the red rooster by the neck and snapped it with one twist of his fists. He let go of the bird and studied its twitching body for a moment. "Old Shanghai had a good run. Took him in trade from a Mexican fighting rooster man that owed me a dollar for a tooth I pulled for him."

"Why did you kill him if you thought so much of him?"

The judge looked up. "Why did you think I brought

him along? I don't favor posse work on an empty stomach, and old Shanghai was long past his prime."

"He's liable to be tough eating, at that."

"You got anything against eating something besides frijoles and beef? I'll not share my commissary with you if you do."

"No, I don't get chicken often," Newt said. "I thought you were partial to that bird."

"Not as partial as I am to not going hungry. I remember when I first come west. I bet it was two years before I ate another egg or drank a cold glass of buttermilk. Man, did I ever get to missing buttermilk."

Newt took a seat on a rock and watched the judge do a poor job of plucking the bird. "You ought to heat up some water to pluck that bird."

"You pluck it, or let me do it my way."

"Did you come out after the war?"

"War?" The judge jerked at a handful of feathers and grunted. "I never served in the war."

"But I thought you said you were with Baylor at Mesilla. That sword in your saloon . . ."

"You never heard me say that. Only time I was ever at Mesilla was when I was still hauling freight on the Santa Fe and Chihuahua Trail."

The judge was making sloppy work of the bird. He pitched it on the ground and with a frown on his face rubbed his palms together, trying to get clean of the feathers stuck to them. "I never was much good at picking feathers. My daddy whupped me once 'cause I was too slow when we were killing fryers. Whupped me like a dog, and I left out of there and come west."

Newt could tell that the judge wasn't going to finish the bird, and picked it up and went to work on it as best he could. "Kentucky?"

"I never said I was from Kentucky. You got to get your facts straight."

Newt knew good and well that the judge had claimed earlier to be from Kentucky, but he let it alone and worked at plucking the bird. "I tell you, some hot water would help things."

"I ain't emptying my canteen. Go down to the river and fetch some if that's your wish. I say we gut it and hang it over the fire. The worst of those feathers will burn off."

"I don't favor feathers with my chicken."

"Suit yourself. I mind the time I was up on the Santa Fe Trail. I was a young buck then, fresh on the plains and out to prove I was tough as any of them. Was driving a six-up span of oxen. They paid me to break them to pull before we set out from Missouri. Big, old longhorn steers they bought off some Texan; mean as rattlesnakes and never had a rope or yoke on them."

"I've got a little lard in my saddlebags. I don't have any flour, but what say I quarter this bird up and we fry it?"

"Like I said, suit yourself." The judge lit a cigar and leaned back against a rock. "I mind the time when I would have eaten the ass-end out of a week-old dead buffalo. You ever been hungry? I don't mean just your usual hungry, but really hungry. So hungry that you can't think about anything else and would do anything to get a bite?"

Newt didn't answer, knowing that the judge didn't need a reply to keep on with his story, whether he wanted to hear it or not.

"It was back when I was whacking that bull train. Late in the year, and we got caught in a blizzard and lost the trail. We were out of supplies and had been for three days. Captain Cleveland, he offered to go ahead and find our way. Said if we tried to wait it out we would starve before the snow broke. Took his nigger, Sam, with him. Sam had been with the captain many a year and they were close.

"Well, Captain went out ahead and we didn't see him for a whole day. The snow was flying so thick you couldn't see fifty foot in front of you, and we thought we had lost him. Didn't make more than four miles or so, but we seen his fire right before dark and went to it. There he was, sitting beside it warming himself and he had a stewpot going. The smell of it like to have drove us crazy.

"He said he had stumbled across a snowbound buck antelope and killed it. We didn't even unyoke our teams, and tore into that stew like it was manna from heaven. Never tasted anything so good."

Newt laid the plucked bird out on the ground and gutted it, careful to save the heart, liver, and gizzard from its craw. The grease in the cast-iron skillet over the fire was already melting before the judge went on with his story.

"We were already through with that antelope stew and leaned back and rubbing our bellies before any of us thought to ask where old Sam was. Captain Cleveland, he went to stuttering and wouldn't look us in the eye.

"We questioned him hard, and he admitted that he had killed old Sam and cooked him up in a stew."

Newt fed a dead yucca stalk into the fire beneath the skillet and looked up at the judge. "You mean to tell me you ate a man?"

"Don't sound so judgmental. You weren't there."

The judge rubbed his cigar butt out and leaned forward. "I thought a lot of old Sam. Hell, we all did. Me and him got along fine. He might have belonged to Captain Cleveland, but he cooked my breakfast and made sure I had enough blankets when it was cold.

"Yes, sir, he saved my life that day. Won't say it didn't bother me some, later, but it was what it was. We thought about killing Captain Cleveland, but we were all guilty the same. Every one of us had eaten a bit of Sam."

"I think you're pulling my leg."

"You think what you will. Ain't that chicken cooked enough yet? The smell of it won't let me quit thinking about Sam." The judge reached out and plucked his rooster's back from the skillet, tossing the hot morsel back and forth from hand to hand to keep it from burning him.

"I think that's still half-raw."

The judge blew on it and tore off a piece and stuck it in his mouth. "Mmm. No, just right. Not as good as old Sam was, but it'll do in a pinch."

"I'm beginning to think you're full of it."

The judge squinted his sagging eyebrow, and Newt wasn't sure, but thought the judge winked. "You questioning the word of a justice of the peace in good standing and repute with the state of Texas?"

Newt set the skillet aside and took a leg from it. He picked gently at the hot flesh while he studied the judge over it. "I'm questioning the word of a windy fat man on the side of a Mexican mountain, with nothing better to do than to tell me tall stories to pass the time."

"You ever ate nigger? Until you have, you aren't

one to judge the merits of this case. My story stands until you qualify yourself as a subject expert."

Newt worried at the gristle on the end of the leg bone he'd picked clean, frowning over it.

The judge grunted, as he was wont to do. "Did I offend you? You Tennessee boys are a mixed-up lot. Some were for the North and some for the South. Abolitionists some, and some for the slavers."

"How about you quit treating me like a tenderfoot and tell me where we're headed?"

"You hand me that last leg and I'll tell you."

Newt nodded at the skillet. By the time he had finished a wing, the judge had managed to eat the rest of the rooster.

The judge wiped his greasy hands on his pants leg, adjusted the Colt pistol stuffed behind his belt to a more comfortable place under the overhang of his belly, and sucked at his teeth. "We'll find Cortina with his sweetheart, exactly like I told you. No hurry. You can't rush this manhunting business."

"If you're so certain he's there, why not catch him sooner rather than later?"

"Cortina's got friends. We go racing around after him and he'll get word," the judge said. "We'll let him get settled in and his mind on other things. We want him surprised when we show up."

"I don't care how we find him."

The judge scoffed. "Do you know anything about Cortina? I can tell you don't, or you wouldn't be so careless. Cortina's used to being hunted. Has been since he popped out of his mama squalling. They say he took hold of her teat and his first pistol at the same time."

"Seems like he's a known man."

"Not as much as his daddy was, but he's cut a little swath of his own since then."

"Who was his daddy?"

"You ever hear of Red Cortina?"

"I never."

"You must be new to Texas. He was a Mexican army officer, politico, and big-shot *grande* at one time. Hated Texans worse than anything and formed himself a bandit army and raised hell with the Anglos on the American side of the river, stealing cattle and killing at will. The Rangers tried to bring him to bay for years, but he was a crafty cuss."

"What happened to him?"

"His problem was that he was overly ambitious and always swapping sides with one government faction or another. Styled himself the power around Matamoros. Díaz finally had him locked up in prison."

"And the Cortina we're looking for is his son?"

"Yep, back when Red was playing up to that Frenchy government and Maximilian he got hooked up with a young lady in Maximilian's court. I've heard that she was Maximilian's niece, but I don't know. Sometime later she had herself a bastard, but by that time Red had already double-crossed the French and swapped sides to fight against them. No matter, the whole thing was swept under the rug. At least that's what the rumors say, and what Javier tells his amigos sometimes when he's in his cups. Maybe it's true, or maybe Javier wants to sound more important than he is. Red Cortina had quite a following on the border. Came across the river once and took over the town of Brownsville. Like to give the Texans a fit until the Rangers pried him out."

"You act like you know Cortina good. The young one, I mean."

"Oh sure. I know that young devil well. He's been down here on the border long as I have. Comes by my place from time to time, though I haven't seen him in a long while. Usually he has the good sense not to thwart me, but he's been growing bolder as of late. Probably thinks poking a finger in my eye will make him a name," the judge said. "He ain't a patch on the seat of his daddy's pants, but he's a nervy one."

"How far is it to where his sweetheart lives?"

"Maybe two days."

"I still think we ought to get there quick as we can. Maybe he won't be there long."

"Young Cortina had him a little book learning somewhere. Speaks Mex, English, and a smattering of French. That learning has given him the big head, and that's why we'll catch him."

Newt remembered the confident, almost mocking way that Cortina carried himself. "I'd think a smart man would be harder to catch."

"Should work like that, but it don't always," the judge said. "The reason Cortina is so cocky is that he thinks he's smarter than the rest of us. A man don't ever want to underestimate his enemies, but young Cortina will be lying down there with his sweetheart laughing about how he stole my jaguar hide and me not knowing how to catch him or where he's at. He'll have his guard down."

"There were several men with him back in Texas."

"And that's why we'll have to ride careful. His numbers change from time to time, but he's always got a handful of no-goods riding with him."

"Won't be easy."

The judge shook his head. "He won't want his amigos with him on this romance business. I'm thinking he'll leave them somewhere close while he goes off courting. That girl's pretty enough to make him stingy, and he's every bit as careless as he is bold."

"Be easier to kill him on the spot than to try to get him back to your place," Newt said. "I imagine those men of his will come after us when they get wind we have him."

"I've thought of that, and don't get me wrong. I'd enjoy putting a bullet in young Cortina's brainpan, but it's a rare occasion to get a chance to hang such a sassy bandit. Folks down here on the border will get the message that you don't mess with a Bean. No, sir. We stick to my plan."

"Gonna be a long ride back to the border, even if we can catch him."

"You let me do the worrying. Best we get some sleep."

Newt rose from the fire and chose a bare spot of ground between three boulders, picking up the smaller chunks of rock and gravel before spreading his blanket. The judge had no bedroll, nor did he seem inclined to have one or to be bothered by it. He simply lay down on his back as close to the fire as he could, wiggling a depression for his shoulders, legs outstretched, and crossing one ankle over the other. He cocked the pistol tucked behind his belt but left it there with his hand resting on it. Shoving his hat brim down over his face with the other hand was the last of his bedtime preparations.

"Doesn't it worry you to sleep with the pistol cocked in your drawers?" Newt asked.

"I like to be prepared in case some bandit sneaks up on us in the night and wishes a fight."

"What if you get to having a bad dream? You might blow off your parts."

"I don't have nothing but good dreams, and old though I may be, I still value my parts as much as the next man."

"Suit yourself."

"Like I said, you let me do the thinking. I'll lead us to young Cortina, and then you can take him by the lip and hold him for me. I'm thinking that's all you might be good for."

"I'll try not to let you down."

"Good. Hush up now. You talk too much, and I'm a light sleeper."

Newt rolled over on his side with his back to the fire and the judge and with his blanket pulled up to his ears. He hoped he would get to sleep before the judge, for the old man snored horribly.

"I'm going to miss Shanghai. I counted him as a good friend, and he served me loyally," the judge said at the perfect, annoying moment when Newt was about to succumb to sleep.

Newt rolled over and looked across the fire, but the judge was already snoring.

# Chapter Sixteen

There was no sense in leaving Piedras Negras without knowing which direction Cortina had fled. Surely someone had seen him if he had, indeed, come through the town. The six white horses in his possession were a thing to catch people's eyes.

Yet, it took Kizzy most of the day to find a baker woman who had seen the outlaw and his gang. Cortina and his men had spent the night at the hotel, leaving the horses in the livery barn across the street. The livery man told much the same tale, adding that the horses were so beautiful that many had come to his barn the night before to see them. Cortina explained his possession of such fine mounts as the result of a trip far to the north to purchase them from an American horse breeder. Everyone believed him, except for those who had seen the horses when Kizzy and Fonzo had come through town the first time. But nobody contradicted Cortina's story, in part because he was a known ruffian and his men had many guns, and in part because all there knew that the Americans possessed many fine horses and should be a little more generous by sharing them with their poorer neighbors south of the Rio Grande.

Kizzy scolded herself for not making a careful search of the town the night before while Cortina was still there. At worst, at least she knew that Cortina had headed west with the horses, even if he had almost a day's head start on her.

She wiped at the corners of her eyes, mad that she was crying. Fonzo paced when he was upset, and she cried.

The baker woman was watching her when she came out of the livery barn, and motioned her back over. She took one look at Kizzy's wet eyes and clucked her tongue and shook her head.

"You are very upset, no?" the woman asked.

"Those horses are all my brother and I have. We are supposed to do a show with them in Monterrey at the end of the month. President Díaz will be there."

"Díaz." The woman spit on the ground. "Benito Juárez should have killed the tyrant years ago when he had the chance."

When the woman noticed that Kizzy had no opinions on the politics of the land, she put a hand on her shoulder. "You should not go after Cortina. No good will come of it."

"We have no one else to help us. We must go after him."

"Well then, many know that he has a woman near Zaragoza. Her father and his vaqueros came here not too long ago, looking for Cortina and wanting to kill him. He is a rich man and will not tolerate a poor outlaw casting a bad name on his daughter."

Kizzy wiped at her eyes again. "And this girl lives in Zaragoza?"

"Her father's rancho lies north of there on the Rio de San Antonio. Ask for the hacienda of Don Alvarez. All the people in that country work for him and will point the way for you."

"*Gracias.*"

"*De nada.* You owe me no thanks. I should be ashamed for telling you and perhaps sending you to your death."

"Would Cortina kill a woman?"

"He does not have such a reputation, but for horses like those I would think his kind might. And some of those that ride with him would not need the excuse of the horses. Their hearts are black and they kill for the fun of it. No woman is safe with them. I hear one of them raped a farm girl at Nava no more than a month ago."

"I'll do what I must."

"We all must die, but none of us should hurry to death. It will find us without seeking it out."

It was dusk before Kizzy made it back to their wagon. Fonzo was waiting for her.

"Where have you been?" he asked.

"Cortina was here last night."

"I know. Everyone knows, but he is gone now. Gone to the west, but where? We aren't trackers."

Kizzy handed him a half loaf of bread wrapped in a bit of cheesecloth. "The baker woman gave me this."

Fonzo tore off a chunk of the bread and spoke with

his mouth full. "The bread is good, but what do we do next?"

"The baker woman said that Cortina has a girlfriend in Zaragoza. She gave me the girl's name and where she lives. She thinks he is on his way there."

Fonzo stood quickly. "I will hitch the team."

"No, we don't know the road to Zaragoza and we should travel it in the daylight."

"He's getting away."

"We can't run him down with the wagon, but if he is going to see this girl we can find him there," she said. "I'm told her father is rich and does not like Cortina seeing her. He has many riders on his ranch, and maybe he will hear our story and help us get back our horses."

Fonzo nodded, thinking it out himself. "What if this rich man won't help us?"

"We will get some sleep tonight and then go to Zaragoza tomorrow. We will see then if he will help. If not, we will think of something else."

"It's hard to sit here and wait when I know Cortina is so close."

"Patience. Stay calm and do as I ask."

"I will stay calm."

The thing happened the moment he said it. The rurale captain came up the street by himself and tied his horse in front of a cantina across from where their wagon was parked. He paused before going inside, noticing Kizzy and Fonzo watching him, and lifted a hand in a mock wave and with a cruel grin on his mouth.

Kizzy put a hand on Fonzo's shoulder, as if she could hold him in place. "Forget him for now. It's Cortina that must come first."

"Did you see how he mocked us?"

"I saw, but you must be smart. Don't do anything that will put the rurales after us. We can't have that. Not now."

"I won't."

"Good. How about I cook you some supper?"

"More beans?"

"I kept Vlad tied up today, so you wouldn't feel like a chicken thief."

"Maybe I need to rethink my position on that."

# Chapter Seventeen

**S**omething woke Kizzy, and it took her a while to come fully awake and realize what it was. She had fallen asleep on her campstool, leaned back against the side of the wagon with Vlad curled up at her feet. The big, white dog hadn't growled, nor was he awake.

Fonzo was gone. The fire had died down to nothing, and she searched the dark around the wagon and then inside the wagon, yet there was no sign of him. Fearing the worst, she checked inside the rear door of the wagon for the shotgun they kept on wall pegs there. When she lit a lantern she saw the shotgun was where it was supposed to be, but her gun rig that hung beside it had one empty holster.

She ran down the steps and strained to make out the cantina in the distance. There were still lights burning inside, but the rurale captain's horse was gone.

She went back in the wagon and took up the shotgun and then untied Vlad. Together, they set out. For some reason, something was telling her to head out of town, and she followed that hunch. They walked for what seemed like a long while, but in reality, they were only a quarter of a mile outside town. The river bridge and the border guards' lanterns were visible from where she stood.

Vlad growled, and she reached down and felt him to see where he was pointed and where his attention was focused. To their left, the river made a sharp bend, doubling back far enough to the south that it came near the road for a short stretch. Something was moving in the wild growth along its banks. She could hear the limbs breaking and someone breathing hard.

She eared back one hammer on the shotgun and waited. The shadowed form coming toward her was already visible. Whoever was coming was leading a horse.

Vlad growled again, and the person stopped.

"Don't come any farther." Kizzy felt silly warning somebody who might only be coming from the river for a perfectly good reason and meaning her no harm.

"Sister, is that you?"

"Fonzo?"

"Help me."

"What have you done?"

He came to her and fell against her. Something hard bumped her leg, and when she reached down she found her pistol clutched in his hand. The barrel was still hot.

"Whose horse is that?" she asked, already fearing what he was about to say.

"I followed him out of town."

"Where is he?"

"I put rocks in his clothes and shoved him in the river."

"Oh, you didn't."

"I didn't intend to kill him, but he laughed at me and then he came at me with a knife."

"Why didn't you listen to me?"

"He was drunk and wouldn't stop when I told him to." Fonzo was shaking and his voice sounded lost. "He said when he was finished with me he was going to find you and do awful things."

"We can't be caught with his horse."

"What can we do with it?"

"We can hide the saddle and send the horse across the river. It might be a while before anyone finds it."

"I'm sorry."

"What's done is done. Go to the wagon and hitch the team. I'll be along as quick as I can."

"I will stay and help you."

"No, I need to you to hook up the wagon and pack our things. We need to get out of here in a hurry."

She took the horse from him and waited until he was headed toward their camp before starting for the river. She took the saddle off and hid it in the shallows beneath the eroded roots of a giant tree leaning over the river. Then she led the horse out until she was thigh deep and slipped the bridle off and slapped the horse on the hip. The animal threatened to turn back, but she splashed and stumbled to keep between it and the near bank, waving her arms trying to spook it in the direction she wished. The dog helped, and its barking made her afraid that the guards at the river crossing or the entire town would hear him and come to investigate. After much effort, the horse finally headed for the far bank, swimming in the faint moonlight with only its head showing above water.

She watched until it went out of sight, and then listened longer to make sure that it had not doubled back. When she heard it splash out on the far side she walked along the riverbank, looking for any sign of the rurale captain's body. She wished she had a lantern. There was no telling what evidence of his crime Fonzo might have left.

After she tripped twice and scratched herself in the heavy growth, she gave up and headed back to town, glad that Vlad was with her. Her heart was beating as if she had run a race, and her ears kept telling her that there was someone else's footstep on the road behind her. She looked over her shoulder often, and was in a run by the time she reached the wagon. Fonzo had their team already hitched to it and was loading the last of their things.

She helped him and then climbed up onto the wagon seat with the shotgun propped up on the dashboard. Fonzo was soon beside her. He wasn't shaking anymore, and his breathing was so quiet she couldn't hear it.

"They'll come after us if they find him," he said. "There's no way we can outrun them in this."

"Maybe they will take the wrong road. That will buy us time." She slapped the slack reins on the team's backs, and they lunged forward in the traces. The wagon creaked and the dry wheel and axle squeaked.

"I thought you greased that axle two days ago," she said.

"I forgot. Loud, isn't it?"

Any moment, she expected the screeching wheel hub to wake someone and bring them out of their home to see the wagon passing by. She urged the team to a trot, pointing them toward the middle of town.

"Where are you headed?" he asked. "Maybe we

should cross the river to the American side and wait there and see what happens."

"You want those horses back, don't you?"

"Yes."

"There's supposed to be a road that goes southwest to Zaragoza. That's where we'll find Cortina."

"If the rurales don't catch us first."

"Yeah, if the rurales don't catch us first."

# Chapter Eighteen

**T**he horsemen passed below their camp right after sunup. The judge was still nursing his mug of coffee and carried it with him to a better vantage point. Newt leaned against a boulder beside him and peered over it at the road along the river.

"That white horse is easy to spot," the judge said. "Fine-looking horse, but I wouldn't have him. Pick him out of the brush a mile away."

The other of the two travelers rode a normal-colored bay, and they were going down the road at a high lope. Newt wished he had a set of binoculars or a spyglass, for it was at least three hundred yards to the road. But apparently, the judge had wonderful eyesight.

"That fat one on the white horse is Miguelito," the judge said. "I'd know him anywhere."

"Is he one of Cortina's gang?"

"Yep, and he's going somewhere in a hurry."

"You figure?"

"He never bought a horse like that. I'd imagine he

stole it and is headed as fast as he can away from its rightful owner."

"Who's that other one?"

"Can't tell, but if he's with Miguelito he's bound to be bad."

Newt ran for his horse, but the judge seemed content to watch the bandits ride away.

"Come on," Newt said.

"No hurry. They'll hit Piedras Negras in a couple of miles. We can have a talk with them then."

"I don't share your calm."

"Patience. I don't have any use for Miguelito, and he's too fat to haul all the way back to Langtry to hang," the judge said. "You can kill him when I'm through talking to him."

The white horse, along with its bay counterpart, was tied in front of the first cantina they came to when they reached Piedras Negras. The town was busy and full of people on the street, and that made Newt nervous for what it was they had to do. He was a foreigner in a strange land, and could only guess how the native citizens would look on a gringo accosting one of their own.

The cantina was no more than a picket jacal—slim wooden posts set butt-end in the ground with adobe dobbed over the outside of it. The roof wasn't seven feet off the ground, and a sow and her litter of little pigs were resting in the mud hole off to one side of the door.

"This Miguelito isn't picky about where he drinks," Newt said, pulling up his horse.

"No. Being picky will get you nowhere in Mexico,"

the judge said. "How about you ride around back in case there's a back door? I'll go in the front and see if I can talk to these boys."

"Why don't I go in the front with you?"

The judge rubbed out his cigar on the cap of his saddle horn and put it in his vest pocket. He then took out his watch and checked the time, as if it mattered for what he had planned. "No, Miguelito's dumb as a box of rocks, but that doesn't mean he won't be edgy. He sees me come in the door and he's liable to start shooting and ask questions later. Especially if you're with me. Your looks don't exactly inspire trust."

"I could say the same about you."

The judge cleared his throat and spat in the road. "I'll go easy and try not to spook him and his compadre. They come out the back, don't ask any questions. Open up on them."

"I'm no lawman, and you don't have jurisdiction down here."

"They know me down here. This is close enough to the border that folks get on both sides of the line regularly. They won't want to incur the wrath of my court should they ever get north."

"Sounds like a sure way to a hanging to go shooting people in a country that ain't ours."

"Ride around back and keep a lookout. I'll handle this. It isn't Miguelito we want, but maybe he'll tell us the whereabouts of young Cortina."

"He might have been one of them that was with Cortina when they robbed me and left me for dead."

"Maybe. We'll ask him if you'll do like I say," the judge said. "If I had known you were so hardheaded I would have left you back in Langtry. I must say, now that I know you better, it's no wonder you found yourself in trouble with the law."

Before Newt could say anything else, the judge kicked his gray forward and went to the hitching rail in front of the cantina. Two of the little suckling piglets got under his feet while he was dismounting, causing him to stumble.

"Get out of here, you pigs," he shouted and waved his arms to shoo them away. "I would never have hogs in front of my saloon."

Newt rode around to the back of the cantina, circling around what had once been a hog pen but was in too poor of a state to hold anything anymore. He sat his horse under a cedar tree where he could see the back door to the place.

He grew impatient after what must have been five minutes, and dismounted and headed for the back door, hoping he might take a peek inside or hear what was going on. He was almost to the door when one of the bandits came running out of it. It wasn't the fat one, a little man no less, but he was going fast enough to almost knock Newt down when they collided.

The bandit did go down, but by the time Newt had regained his balance the little Mexican was up on his feet and clawing at the holstered pistol on his hip.

Without thinking, Newt let go with a right hand brought from way back behind him. The blow struck the bandit square on the side of the chin, dropping him again. Newt barely had time to catch his breath before a gunshot sounded from within the cantina, and then two, three more. He could hear the judge cursing even before he charged into the room.

The bartender had taken cover behind his bar, and a few other customers were under tables or sucked back against the walls of the room with their eyes big and so startled they appeared afraid to breathe. The judge was down on the floor at the end of the bar nearest the front door. His pistol was in his hand and pointed outside. The sound of a running horse was plain and the dust it stirred floated inside in a cloud.

"Are you hit?" Newt asked.

"No, he didn't get me, but I missed him, too," the judge said, and then went to coughing. "Help me up. I think I twisted my knee in the fight."

Newt helped him up. "What happened?"

"Miguelito was edgy like I said, and must have recognized me for the law. I barely had time to ask a single question before he pulled on me."

"You're lucky."

"I'm lucky Miguelito was slow and a damned poor shot," the judge said. "I got my feet tangled and fell down, and then I missed a snap shot at him as he ran out the door."

Newt glanced at the rusty Colt the judge held. The firearm was so poorly kept that it was a wonder it had fired at all.

The judge sneezed loudly. "Shit."

"Bless you."

"Thank you kindly. What about the other one that ran out the back?"

"I tended to him. He's lying outside."

"Dead?"

"No, but you might say he's indisposed at the moment."

"Well, let's go have a talk with him."

"What about Miguelito?"

"We won't catch him. Did you get a good look at that

white horse he was riding? We don't have anything that will outrun it."

The judge shoved past him, and Newt followed him out the back door. The bandit Newt had punched was conscious and had dragged himself up against the wall and was clutching his jaw with both hands. Blood trickled out between his fingers.

"Did you shoot him in the head?"

"No, I punched him. He was going for his gun."

"Punched him? Why didn't you pull your own gun?"

"I didn't have time to think about it."

The judge eyed the groaning bandit and then took a look at Newt's right fist. "If God had meant for us to fight like animals he would have given us claws and sharper teeth. If you're going to wear that pistol you'd best learn how to use it. Somebody might not let you get close enough to use those fists of yours, and besides, clobbering a man like that isn't gentlemanlike."

The judge squatted down beside the wounded bandit. He asked a question in Spanish that Newt couldn't follow. The bandit's eyes fluttered, and Newt wasn't sure that he still had his wits.

"Answer me," the judge said, and shook the bandit by the shoulder.

"What did you ask him?"

"What do you think I asked him? I asked him where Miguelito was headed, and is Cortina with his sweetheart," the judge replied. "You want to do the questioning, or leave me to it?"

"No, I don't speak Spanish."

The judge asked the bandit another question, or maybe two. When the bandit didn't answer him the judge jerked the man's hands away from his face. The bandit's jaw immediately sagged and more blood ran from his mouth. A bit of broken tooth was stuck to his lower lip.

"What did you hit him with?" the judge asked.

"Nothing but my fist."

"Lord, man, I think you busted his jaw."

The judge asked the same questions again and the bandit blubbered something.

"I can't understand you. Talk plain."

The bandit opened his mouth, tears running from his eyes at the strain and pain of it. He pointed inside his mouth and slurred something again.

"Look at that. He almost bit his tongue in two," the judge said. "How am I going to interrogate him now?"

"He came at me quick. It was him or me."

The judge pulled out his pistol again and put the barrel against the bandit's temple. "I won't ask you again, messed-up tongue or not."

The bandit slobbered blood and tried again. Newt was sure that even if he had spoken Spanish he wouldn't have been able to understand the man.

"Say that again," the judge said.

The bandit repeated his performance before he choked and gagged on his own blood and slobber.

"He said Cortina went to Zaragoza, and that Miguelito will likely go after him."

"Ask him if he was with Cortina when they robbed me."

The judge rattled off the question in Spanish, and the bandit did his best to answer him while he strained to keep watch on the Colt held against his temple, his pupils so far to one side that mostly the whites of his eyes showed.

"Said he's never seen you before and didn't join up with Cortina until a few days ago, but he's probably lying," the judge said.

"Ask him if he knows where my gold is."

"Already did. He claims he doesn't know a thing. Said they robbed a circus and stole a set of white horses," the judge said. "Apparently there was some kind of falling-out with the gang and they split ways with Cortina, and his favorites took a horse apiece to settle things."

"I don't care about circus horses. It's my gold I'm worried about."

"They've likely already spent it. Money doesn't last long when you're riding the owl hoot." The judge stood and holstered his pistol. "What do you want to do with him?"

Newt shrugged. "I don't want him if he wasn't with them that robbed me."

"Thought you were a hard man."

"I'm a fair man."

"I counted on you being a hard case."

"I'm after Cortina."

The judge asked the bandit another question.

"What did you ask him that time?"

"I asked if he knows where my jaguar hide is."

"And?"

"That damned Cortina had a vest made out of it."

"Miguelito is going to tell Cortina we're after him."

"He doesn't know we're after Cortina."

"You said yourself you're a known man, and don't you think that Cortina is bragging about where he got that cat hide, even if Miguelito wasn't with him when he stole it from your saloon? It won't take much thinking to figure you're down here after him."

"Hmph. Stands to reason."

"Best we ride hard and see if we can run down

Miguelito before he gets to Zaragoza. Might be he'll camp come dark and give us a chance to catch up."

"Odds are against it, but it's worth a try."

Newt turned and went for his horse, expecting the judge to do the same. The sound of the cocking pistol turned him in time to see the judge put the Colt against the bandit's temple again and pull the trigger. The report of the gun and splatter of gore against the wall were one and the same.

"He might have come hunting us when he healed," the judge said, studying the effect of his bullet on the bandit's skull.

"We'll be long out of Mexico before he could have healed."

The judge shrugged and took a fresh cartridge out of his vest pocket and exchanged it for the empty hull he thumbed from his pistol cylinder. "These Mexican outlaws don't have any respect for borders. He could have come waylaid us one night when we weren't expecting it."

"What about the Mexican law? All these gunshots, and they're bound to already be on their way down here."

"Don't worry about them. I had long enough before Miguelito started shooting at me to learn that the company of rurales stationed here left about an hour ago. Seems they found their captain's body floating in the river this morning."

"You hang around if you want to, but I'm riding right now."

"Think you're leaving me, do ya? May I remind you that you're in my custody?"

"You want to keep it that way, you'd best get on your horse and ride. I'm headed to Zaragoza."

The judge lingered a moment over the corpse while Newt ran for his horse.

"Damned Mexico," the judge said. "Been like this every time I was down here."

# Chapter Nineteen

It was only thirty miles or so to Zaragoza, and the road was level and easy where it was carved out of the low brush or wound through various farm fields or open stretches of poor grassland. Newt had little hope that they would catch up to Miguelito before he reached Cortina.

They alternated the pace of their horses between a long lope and a trot, and Newt wondered if the judge, at his age, could hold up to the rigor. Yet, come night-fall, the judge was still riding beside him, slouched in the saddle as if his spine were a sagging spring, but uncomplaining as if he could go like that all day long.

Having come about twenty miles, somewhere near midnight they gave up overtaking Cortina's hench-man and staked the horses on a bit of lush grass on the edge of a large, spring-fed marsh and lake— what the Mexicans called a *ciénega*. They built no fire nor did they eat anything, being too tired to give the effort.

"Didn't think we could catch him." The judge lay down on the ground on the flat of his back, as usual, without so much as a blanket to lie on or cover himself with.

"Maybe he took another road," Newt said while he spread his bedroll.

"My guess is he's already with Cortina," the judge said.

"What next?"

"Nothing changes."

"They'll be ready for us."

"If I had known you were soft I wouldn't have brought you along."

"Do you mean because I didn't kill that man back in Piedras Negras?"

"You said you wanted justice, but maybe you don't have the stomach for it," the judge said, grunting and trying to find a more comfortable spot on the ground.

"He said he wasn't with them when they robbed me."

"You trust the word of an outlaw with a pistol held to his head? That man would have cut your guts out for a half-dollar if you gave him the chance. I know his kind."

"I never got a look at any of them, except Cortina. He was the one that followed me out of White Oaks and put a bullet in me, and he's who I want."

"Be careful what you wish for. You keep wearing that gun and somebody will come along and make you use it."

That the old judge was a killer, Newt had no doubt. Crafty to the point of comedy at times, he hadn't hesitated to execute the bandit back in Piedras Negras. He'd murdered that man with no more compunction than stomping a spider or twisting the neck on that rooster. Newt knew himself to be a man of black moods, but the judge was the kind that had lost any guilt over laying low those who opposed him. Most men like that tended to look after their own hide first and foremost, and justified whatever they felt they needed to do, no matter what it was. He'd bear watching, and Newt knew he should have cut loose from him the second he was turned loose back in Langtry. He couldn't say why he was still riding with him.

"What are you going to do if you actually get your gold back?" the judge asked.

The question threw Newt off guard. Some things were best kept to oneself, at least in his opinion. Things that seemed special often seemed not so special anymore when you had to talk about them. Vague ideas that excited him when still only thoughts sounded silly when he tried to put them to words. He was put out that the judge had asked such, but knew that if he didn't answer the judge would keep on talking.

"I was going to Houston or maybe farther east. Thought maybe I would set myself up in a shop."

"What kind of shop?"

The judge's tone made Newt even more reluctant to discuss the matter. He didn't have the whole thing worked out. When he gave an answer it was a quiet one.

"A wagon shop. Maybe some cabinet and furniture work, too." Not only did his words sound silly to his own ears, but they came out as if he were hearing his own ideas for the first time.

"Never would have taken you for a craftsman," the judge replied. "I've guessed some things about you, but never that. Where did you learn the trade?"

"Never did."

"You what?"

"I said I never did."

The judge propped himself up on one elbow. "And what makes you think you would be good at it?"

"I like wood and I've always been good with things I can do with my hands."

"Well, I've always liked whores, but I never thought I would make a good pimp. Whores are like liquor, and a man who can't keep from sampling too much of his wares won't last long in business."

Newt made a fuss over making his bed, hoping the judge would let it go. But he didn't.

"There's no telling the ideas some men have rattling around in their heads," the judge said as if Newt weren't even there, and as if he were talking to himself.

"Pa worked wood a little. Not fancy woodwork— only some carving and scrapping together a few pieces of furniture or mending someone's wagon," Newt said. "And then I was apprenticed to a wheelwright down in the low country, but that fell through before I was with him a month or two."

"That's not enough time to learn anything."

Newt only half heard him, with his mind wandering back to the way fresh wood shavings smelled piled up beneath his father's feet while he turned a table leg on an old foot-powered lathe he had built himself. And he could still remember the first fancy coach he had seen passing along the road, and he and his father had stood hand in hand on the side of the road and watched it pass, with its high red wheels, varnished wood, and brass lanterns as shiny as gold. He had thought then what a fine thing it would be to ride in something like that or to build such a wonderful coach—something shiny and something that could take you places.

The judge pointed at Newt's battered and knocked-down knuckles and then at his face. "A man should stick to what he's good at."

"I've had my fill of getting my skull busted or getting paid to bust someone else's skull," Newt said. "Never has gotten me anything but headaches."

"How'd you get in the skull-busting business?"

Newt shrugged. He hadn't said so much all at once in a long, long time, but there he was telling things to an old, worn-out killer like the judge. "I don't know. I was trying my hand on a little placer claim and having no luck. The whole camp was having trouble with claim jumpers, and a couple of men approached me and said they would pay me fifty dollars in gold if I would guard their claim for a week while they went up to Denver to purchase what they needed to sink a shaft they had planned. I cut myself a big stick and sat on that claim for them for a month."

"Anybody give you any trouble?"

"Some, but I got that fifty dollars."

"Did you get those scars then?"

Newt shrugged. "There and other places. Next boom camp I was in there was a disagreement that got out of hand between some miners and the company they worked for. The miners were a bunch of hard-rock Welshmen and Irishmen. You know the kind—stout workers and every bit as hardheaded. They picketed the gate to the mine one night and weren't letting anyone in or out. One of those company men had heard about me and came and asked if I could gather some tough men and go up the hill and convince his employees to get back to work. I was broke, so I took the job."

"That cauliflower ear of yours—most men I've seen with such are regular brawlers like yourself, or have spent time in a boxing ring."

"I fought for prizes, time to time. Seemed like a lark at first. I never was any great shakes at it."

"You said your pappy was a woodworker. How come you didn't go into the trade back there instead of coming west?"

"Pa's heart quit him when I was fourteen. Found him behind his plow mule and drug to one end of a furrow. We didn't have much of a place and never could afford any bottom ground. You know, rocky, thin mountain ground."

The judge nodded, as if he really did know.

"There were three of us boys and a baby sister for Ma to feed. My oldest brother went to work with a timber crew, sending money back home from time to time until we heard he drowned walking a log raft on the Mississippi River up in Minnesota. Things got worse after that. My younger brother was the best farmer, but no two-bit, hardscrabble farm like we had was going to grow enough to feed the family, much less turn any profit. So, I thought about it some, and one morning I left out to lighten the demands on our table."

Newt regretted having said the little he said. There was no way the judge could understand, and he was probably laughing at him the whole time he rambled on. Newt lay down and stared at the stars overhead, the sky a canopy that seemed to go on and on forever. A man could change. Because he was one thing didn't mean he couldn't be something else if he put his mind to it. He was tired of scrapping and tired of waking up every morning no farther along than he had been the day before. Always doing someone's dirty work or being done dirty.

He'd left home for the opportunity to do things, and to show them all he could find his fortune. The people going west said there were fortunes to be made out there, and all it took was a man with gumption. He had plenty of gumption, but it turned out things out West weren't much easier than back in the mountains he left. Oh yes, there were gobs of money being made in ore, timber, railroads, and cattle, but none of it fell his way. Seemed like the only thing he had to offer the world was the muscle on his stubborn bones. Every time he was down on his luck, somebody came along and offered him a fighting job. It seemed like the only thing he was good at, but he was tired of fighting and tired of living like some attack dog kept chained to a post until its owner needed to sic it on someone. And he was tired of being ashamed of what he had become. The gold he had found should have fixed all of that and given him the chance he wanted.

"Judge?"

The judge didn't answer him.

"Judge?"

The judge's breathing was already deep with sleep. Newt continued to stare at the night sky, lost in his thoughts until he finally fell asleep. He woke with someone kicking him in the sole of the foot.

"Wake up," the judge whispered. "Somebody's coming down the road."

Newt got to his feet and struggled to get his mind awake and working. "Who is it?"

"Don't know. Might be anybody or it might be somebody we're interested in."

The marsh reached almost to the edge of the road. The horseman, or horsemen, was going to be visible quite a ways off, and so was their camp to whoever was coming. A lone clump of mesquite brush and low oaks barely big enough to hide a couple of men lay on the other side of the road a few yards away.

"You take a stand in that little thicket, and I'll lead our horses out in the cattails," the judge said.

Newt finished saddling the Circle Dot horse and slapped it on the hip as the judge led it off. The judge and the horses waded into the tall water grass and cattails at the edge of the marsh.

"I'll be right back," the judge called over his shoulder.

Newt could see the rushes bending and hear them splashing through the mud and the judge's low cursing even after they disappeared totally from sight. He ran to the clump of mesquite and found the best cover he could. He could barely make out a rider in the distance, but that didn't last long. It was three men, and one of them was riding a white horse.

Newt cast another glance in the direction the judge had gone, but there was no sign of him. The riders were only a hundred yards away and closing at a long trot. They were close enough by then that Newt could tell the one in the middle on the white horse was Miguelito.

Newt gave up on the judge getting back in time to help and stepped out in the middle of the road with his pistol drawn and hanging down at the end of his arm beside his leg, turned slightly with his left foot forward so that the pistol was hidden from them. The riders saw him in an instant and slowed their horses to a walk.

"Good morning," Newt said because he couldn't think of anything else to say.

All three men looked around for signs of anyone else with Newt or evidence of how he had appeared in the road before them.

"*Buenos días*," the one to Newt's left said. He was wearing a straw farmer's sombrero with a tattered brim, and wasn't a man Newt had seen before.

All three of the Mexicans stopped their horses less than five yards in front of him. He didn't recognize the man on the other side of Miguelito, either, but it didn't set well with him that the man had a Remington rolling-block carbine laid across his saddle swells and his thumb on the hammer.

Miguelito said something in Spanish, and when Newt couldn't answer, the man in the straw hat translated.

"Did you lose your horse?" he asked.

Newt kept a close watch on Miguelito. "He broke loose last night and left me afoot," Newt said.

Miguelito edged his horse forward two steps and said something again.

"He don't believe you," the one in the straw hat said. "He thinks maybe you were with the judge back in Piedras Negras."

"Judge?"

"*El juez viejo malo.* Bean."

The men were still looking for someone else with Newt, as if they didn't trust the setup.

"We think you lie," the man in the straw hat added. "Where is the judge? We would like to talk to him."

"Kill him," Miguelito said. Apparently, he did speak a little English.

The man with the carbine was the first to get his gun up, but his horse lunged forward and shied, frightened at his quick action. He was slow getting a bead on Newt because of it. Newt cocked the Smith pistol and brought it around and leveled it on the man with the rifle. It felt like he was handling the pistol entirely too slowly and that he was going to die long before he got it into play.

His bullet struck the man with the carbine in the center of his chest and toppled him over the back of his saddle. Newt felt the Smith buck in his hand and recocked it on the downfall. The dead man's horse veered wide, but the other two bandits were charging forward straight at him. Something whipped past his right ear and another bullet kicked up dust at his feet. His second shot missed Miguelito and there was no time for a third. The two bandits were already on top of him.

Miguelito fired down at him point-blank, and although his shot missed, he lashed out with his boot at Newt's face. Newt ducked and staggered sideways, right into the path of the other rider. The horse hit him at a dead run, knocking him down. A flying hoof struck him a glancing blow in the back of the head, and he was slow to get to his feet. He expected the bandits to pull up and turn back to finish him off, but both of them were fleeing down the road.

He scrambled to find his pistol where it had been knocked from his grasp. He dug it out of the powdery roadbed, but already knew that the bandits were far out of his effective range. The judge came running

out of the marsh carrying the Sharps buffalo rifle
Matilda Redding had given Newt.

"Where were you?" Newt asked.

"Thought it was best that I hung off to the side and
covered you." The judge was breathing hoarsely from
his exertion.

"You left me alone with three of them."

The judge gave him a sheepish grin. "Wasn't sure
how many were coming, so I thought it best to look
things over before I committed to anything."

"You told me to stop them."

"I told you to take cover in that thicket. What did
you think they were going to do? Ask you to sit down
to a tea party?"

The judge went to the clump of trees and rested
the Sharps on a mesquite limb, aiming down the road.
Miguelito and the other survivor were already two
hundred yards off and rapidly increasing the distance.

"How's this gun sighted in?" The judge pitched
his sombrero on the ground and put his cheek to
the gunstock and peered through the brass tube of the
scope.

"I don't know. Never shot it."

"Have to do a little guessing then," the judge said.
"There now, a little Kentucky windage and proper elevation is all it takes."

Before Newt could say anything else the Sharps
boomed.

# Chapter Twenty

**T**he buffalo gun bellowed and the white horse staggered, took three more lumbering strides, and then flipped end over end.

"Shoots a little low at that range." The judge had the Sharps's breech open and was thumbing another finger-length cartridge in it.

Miguelito was on his feet and he moved fast for a heavy man. He swung up behind his partner on their remaining horse and they were running again by the time the judge fired his second shot. It was a clean miss; no more dead horses and no more dead men.

"Held a little high that time." The judge ejected the spent shell and slung the Sharps over his shoulder. "This Sharps kicks like a mule, but my God she'll reach out there and touch them."

Newt appraised the distance to the dead white horse. It was at least four hundred yards away.

The judge was standing over the man Newt had killed. He booted the body in the ribs. "You drilled this one center. Thought for a minute there you were going to try to talk them to death."

"Those two that got away—Cortina is going to know we're coming for sure."

The judge found the dead bandit's pistol and he jerked the gun belt from the corpse. He pitched the rig to Newt. "Take that. It might come in handy."

It was an old Remington-Beals cap-and-ball Navy converted to take brass cartridges, with the grips worn slick and the long barrel mottled and freckled with rust. A handful of .38 rimfire rounds were tucked into the dry-rotted loops on the gun belt.

The judge picked up the dead bandit's carbine. It was equally old and in the same poor condition. The judge frowned over it in a disappointed manner and then took a piece of latigo string from his pocket and tied it around the stock's straight grip so that he could hang it from his saddle horn later. "Not worth much more than five dollars."

"I would have thought a professional outlaw would have better guns," Newt said.

"Bad decisions like that probably led him to a life of crime. It's been my experience that most bandits ain't the thinkers you'd expect them to be," the judge said. "Why don't you go get the horses while I look his body over for evidence?"

"Evidence?"

The crafty look came over the judge's face like a mask. "Might have something on him that will tell us the whereabouts of young Cortina."

Newt followed the bent and broken growth to the horses, getting his boots soaking wet in the process. He led the horses back out onto dry ground in time to see the judge putting something in his pocket— something he had taken off the body.

"Looking for an extra peso or two?" Newt asked.

The judge frowned at him, but didn't reply.

Newt handed over the judge's horse and mounted his own. The dead man's horse was standing not too far off. He rode over and caught the flighty gelding with more than a little difficulty. The judge eyed the horse he was leading when he came back, and a sly grin cracked his face again.

"Looks like you came off far the best when it comes to salvage operations," the judge said. "That ain't much of a horse, but he'll still bring twenty or thirty dollars, and that saddle a few dollars more."

Newt dismounted again and hung the dead bandit's pistol belt on the Circle Dot horse's saddle horn, "Help me load the body."

The judge looked at the dead bandit. "No need to bother with him. Leave him lay. You ride into Zaragoza with that body and you're asking for trouble. He might have friends there that wouldn't take kindly to those that had done for him. Might be all kinds of trouble involved that you can't even guess at. Been my experience that associating with dead folks has all kinds of ramifications."

"It was a pure case of self-defense. Maybe the law there has papers on him," Newt said. "What about you, Judge? Thought you were the upstanding sort. Law and order every time, right?"

"Boy, you don't know anything about Mexico. It ain't civilized down here," the judge said. "We get in the wrong situation, and they won't think anything about executing two gringos. No trial or nothing."

"What if somebody comes along behind us and finds his body?"

"And what about the one we left back in Piedras Negras? We're putting together a pretty good string," the judge said. "Most down here won't mind us thinning out a few undesirables, but some won't see it that way. Been a lot of years of trouble on the border, and there are those on both sides of it that judge a man on the color of his skin."

"What do we do with him?"

"Throw him in the lake," the judge said. "And on second thought, throw his saddle in with him and turn his horse loose. I hate to lose the sale of that horse, but it might cause us more trouble than we'd make off it."

"Lend a hand—we've still got to load him."

"He doesn't look too heavy, but I've got a trick back. Goes out on me sometimes if I strain wrong."

"Come over and help me." Newt took hold of the dead man's armpits and lifted half of him off the ground.

"If we had a shovel you could bury him."

"Take hold of his legs."

"You could put a rope around his heels and drag him over there."

"Talking won't get it done. Take hold."

"That's why I went into the bar business and then into the legal business. It was to get away from such labor."

They wrestled and heaved until they had the body draped facedown over the dead bandit's horse. Newt cut a few short lengths off the riata hanging from the man's saddle horn and secured him as best he could.

"You ought not cut up a good riata like that. We could sell it for a dollar or two should we run across a man that can rope. Cowboys and vaqueros set store by a good rope."

Newt didn't say anything and mounted back up

and led the other horse behind him. He rode out into the edge of the marsh again, deep into the cattails, and drew his knife and cut the body loose. It slid off the saddle and beneath the waist-deep water and muck. Newt undid the cinch and let the bandit's saddle fall, and then rode back to where the judge waited. He pulled the bridle from the bandit's horse and cracked it across the rump with the reins. The horse bolted and ran along the road toward Piedras Negras.

"Somebody might wonder who that horse belonged to," Newt said.

"It was probably stolen in the first place, and anybody that finds it will only be glad they have a new horse."

They rode in silence to where the white horse lay far up the road where the judge had shot it. The bullet had taken it under the root of its tail, driving lengthwise into its vitals. Other than a little pool of blood on the ground, there was little evidence as to what had laid the animal low. The horse looked like it could have been struck by lightning, died of a heart attack, or been smitten down by an act of the heavens.

"That's what we down here call the old Texas one-hole shot," the judge said.

"It was a fine horse."

"Yeah, shame. Wished I had held a little higher and plucked that Miguelito off his back."

"What's that I hear?" Newt cocked his head, trying to interpret the faint sound in the distance.

"Church bells," the judge said. "We're not too far from Zaragoza."

"And this sweetheart of Cortina's lives there?"

"Her daddy's rancho is about a half-hour ride to

the north on the river." The judge dismounted and began to open the saddlebag pouch on the exposed side of the dead horse.

"You have no shame," Newt said.

"Spoils of war and the price old Miguelito's paying for thumbing his nose at the law."

"You ain't the law down here. Might be best for us if you would quit saying that."

"You don't quit being one thing just because you ride across some river or boundary. The arm of Lady Justice is long and she's blind. Ain't you ever seen the image of her? She wears a bandanna over her eyes so that she can go where she pleases without question."

"The blindfold is meant to show that justice is impartial."

"Huh?"

"Fair and square. Treats everyone the same."

"What do you know about such? Learn that in school?"

"I went to school some, although not much. Had a teacher who taught me that. He was going to teach me to read some Latin next, but spring was on and it was time to put in the crops."

"Know what you mean. I never went to school more than a month at a time without having to quit and go to work. My pappy put me to work full-time when I was ten, and I never saw a schoolhouse again."

"Get on your horse. Maybe we can get some breakfast in Zaragoza."

"Could be those pictures of Lady Justice holding up her scales with that bandanna over her eyes ain't like that teacher of yours thought," the judge said. "Maybe she was covering her face and about to rob a train."

"Are you going to stand around all day blabbing, or are you going to get on your horse?"

"This scholarly thinking has my bowels upset," the judge said. "Ride up the road a piece. My guts won't work right if I think you're watching me."

Newt rode off about fifty yards while the judge went behind a clump of cactus. He was there a long time, and Newt grew tired of waiting.

"Oh Lord," the judge said.

From the sound of it, Newt guessed that the judge had got himself a sticker from a cactus.

"Help me," the judge called out.

"What's the matter?" Newt reined his horse around and walked it nearer where the judge was.

The judge came out of the cactus clump with his pants around his ankles and the trapdoor of his long underwear down. He was holding his left hand cradled in the other.

"You snakebit?" Newt asked.

"No, but I'm poisoned."

Newt rode closer but he couldn't tell anything about the judge's hand, because the judge wouldn't let go of it and was wobbling in circles. He finally got tangled up in his pants and fell down. He had risen to a sitting position by the time Newt dismounted.

"I'll be lucky if I ain't dead before noon," the judge said.

"Let me see that hand."

The judge grimaced and let go of it and held it up for Newt to examine. "Scorpion got me."

Indeed, the judge's hand was already swelling, mostly at the base of his thumb, and his skin was red with inflammation.

"Little scorpion did that?"

"Little? I bet it's one of those big black ones," the judge said. "Oh Lord. I saw a man over in Sonora once when I was young. They got those big black ones there. One of them got in his bedroll and stung him on the nutsack. His balls turned as black as an ace of spades. There were several of us and we were discussing amputation, but it never got to that. The poison had done gone too far. It settled in his neck and choked him to where he couldn't breathe."

"Well, you're bit on the hand. Maybe it won't hit you so hard."

"That man was dead within an hour of the time he was stung. Go over there and see if you can find it. See if it's one of those big black ones."

Newt dropped his rein and went where the judge had been. Apparently, the judge was stung before he had time to do his business, but Newt did find where the ground was scuffed where the judge had squatted. He brushed a dead stick around in the rocky ground, but found nothing.

"Did you find it?" the judge asked when Newt came back. "Tell me it wasn't one of those black ones. They get longer than your finger. Got a stinger on them the size of a roofing tack."

"How do you know it was a scorpion if you didn't see it?"

"I got a glimpse of it. I think it was black."

"Maybe they don't have the black ones here. Could have been a regular brown little scorpion. Never heard of anybody dying from one of them. It will sting some, but should go away after a while."

"Oh, I don't think so. Felt like a knife going in me; like my hand was on fire," the judge said. "I don't want to lose my hand. Old Billy Bartholemew—he was a

prospector I once knew out in Arizona—he got bit
by a Gila monster. They got mouths so nasty they're
pure poison. Billy's whole hand rotted off by the time
he wandered back to where people lived."

"You're jumping the gun a little. We're talking
about scorpions here."

"You don't care because it isn't your hand. I've had
this hand a long time and grown partial to it."

The judge was sweating profusely. Newt didn't
know if it was because of the scorpion's poison or because the judge's hat had fallen off and he was sitting
in the sun. The judge put the heel of his hand to his
mouth and sucked on it and then spat. He repeated
the procedure several times.

"You getting anything out? I've heard of that for
snakebites."

"I can't tell."

"Put a chaw of tobacco on it and that will draw the
heat out."

"Would you chew some up for me?" The judge
jerked his chin down at his vest pocket.

Newt squatted and found the judge's little square
of plug tobacco and tore a chunk off it with his jaw
teeth. He wasn't a chewer, and the stuff tasted like tar.
He fought off the urge to gag, and as soon as it was
moistened a little he took it from his mouth and
placed it on the heel of the judge's thumb.

"Hold that there and get up."

"I'm feeling faint. Things are spinning."

"You'll die of heatstroke if you don't put your hat
back on and get out of the sun."

The judge got to his feet with a groan and struggled with the seat of his drawers and tugged his pants
up one-handed. He held the other hand gingerly up

to the sun as if it were a thing brittle and delicate or some kind of offering of submission.

Newt picked the judge's sugarloaf sombrero off the ground and sat it on the judge's head.

"Thank you kindly." The judge scratched at his neck with his good hand. "I'm itching all over."

Newt untied the white bandanna the judge was wearing. In doing so, he noticed the ugly scar ringing the man's neck. It was an old scar, wrinkled and a dull mahogany brown like an old burn; it was like the kind a rope makes sliding hot across your flesh.

"That must have smarted some." Newt nodded at the scar on the judge's neck while he tied the bandanna around the old man's hand to hold the chewing tobacco poultice in place.

The judge looked away.

"Somebody hung you, didn't they?"

"It was a long time ago."

"You, the upstanding judge, the belle of the ball at a necktie strangle party?"

"It was before I was old enough to have any sense. Nothing but a misunderstanding."

Newt went to his horse and climbed on.

"What are you doing?" the judge asked.

"That Miguelito might already be with Cortina now and telling him we're coming. I don't aim to lose him."

"Forget about Cortina for now. Can't you see I might be dying? I need medical attention."

"Get on your horse. There's nothing the matter with you but a little scorpion sting."

The judge made a show of having trouble getting on his horse, but finally landed in his saddle. "I tell you, I'm feeling floaty."

"You said you get to feeling floaty when you think about that singer girl you were telling me about. The one you named your saloon after."

"I do sometimes get floaty over old memories, and that's what scares me. Reliving the past is the closest thing to death. Mark my words. Getting floaty is a sure sign we're hovering on the edge of the hereafter."

Newt started his horse toward Zaragoza at a walk. The judge passed him at a hard trot, bouncing in the saddle and mumbling to himself.

"I think I've already got a fever." The judge wiped at his brow when Newt caught up to him.

"No wonder you're sweating. It's already turning hot as Hades," Newt said. "I never thought a grown man would carry on so over such a trifle as getting stung."

"Anything with a stinger bothers me something fierce. Bees, wasps, hornets, you name it. Never been stung by a scorpion. I'm always careful, but it caught me off my guard this time."

"I imagine you'll suffer through."

"My brother hit me over the head with a singletree when we were young. I couldn't see anything but black for a while, but then I saw these white spots dancing everywhere."

"I've seen a few stars myself. There's nothing unusual about feeling punchy after taking a good lick."

"Mama said those spots were angels celebrating my coming to the Kingdom of Heaven. Said if a dying man listens close he can hear them sing."

"I've never heard angels sing when I was hit. Just people shouting at me to get up or cussing me to stay down."

"You said you went to school some, didn't you?" the judge asked.

"Some."

"I was always good at my sums. Never took to the reading primer, but I was quick with my sums. You remember what a fraction is?"

"I do."

"A fraction is a thing all broke up. It's a thing that's only a part of a thing. It ain't whole."

"I could do without the lesson. I wasn't partial to math myself."

"It ain't math I'm talking about. You didn't see Billy Bartholemew with his hand rotted off. There wasn't anything left of him but a fraction—a piece of the man he was—and the thought of that scares me to no end," the judge said. "Don't tell me you aren't scared of anything."

"I guess everyone's scared of something. Some more than others."

"You're too young to understand. I'm already losing my parts and I'm not the man I used to be," the judge said. "My joints ache and my back hurts most times, and some days I can't even take a good shit. I'm losing all my powers."

"How old are you?" Newt thought he fought off the grin the judge's complaining brought on.

"I see you judging me and finding me wanting. Think you're better than me," the judge said.

"I was only thinking about how far is left until we make Zaragoza."

"Wait until you get my age and death won't seem so out of reason. Old Death's hanging around the corner for all of us and doesn't care if you're young or old. I know that much. Seen 'em come and go already."

"There'll be a doctor in Zaragoza if it's anyplace at all."

"You're not a kind man, Mr. Jones. I saw that the first time I laid eyes on you."

"That's kind of the pot calling the kettle black, isn't it?"

The judge groaned and studied his wounded hand again. "Never thought I would go this way. I've been shot at and knifed and hung, but a scorpion gets me in the end. It ain't fair."

"Nothing's fair."

The judge sighed. "No, I expect you're right. Specially in Mexico. I should have never let you talk me into coming back down here."

# Chapter Twenty-one

**L**ate in the morning and still four miles from Zaragoza, the judge's hand was already swollen to twice its size, and he was babbling nonsense and his eyes were swollen slits and his face turned lumpy. Twice he called Newt by some other name, and he held conversations with himself or with others riding along with them that only he could see.

At first, Newt found it at least something to pass the miles, but the more he thought about it the more it began to bother him. It dawned on him that the judge was talking to ghosts—people who he had known who weren't anymore. Newt had seen his own share of troubled times, and even the good times scattered in between left memories that a man can't shake and that come back to visit time to time when someone's mind is fevered or when they're clutching at anything they can lay hand to. Newt preferred to leave his ghosts in the past and shut out of his thoughts.

He was beginning to doubt that the judge would be able to ride the rest of the way to Zaragoza. He didn't know what to do for him and was considering if he

could tie him over his saddle. It also didn't go without
notice that he was going through an awful lot of trouble for an old sharper that he'd sworn to punch in the
face and leave behind the first chance he got, but he
couldn't bring himself to abandon a wounded man,
no matter how annoying he was. Maybe the scorpion
had done him a favor. If he could get the judge to a
doctor he was bound to be laid up for a while to recu-
perate. That would give Newt more than time enough
to get shed of him.

He was thinking those things when he saw the
odd-looking and brightly painted wagon. It was crawling along the road at the bottom of a long hill ahead
of him.

The judge groaned again, and Newt grimaced and
kicked his horse back up to a trot, heading straight
down the road after the wagon. The judge's gray nag
followed him like a faithful hound, picking up its pace
to match Newt's. The judge reeled in the saddle like
he was drunk.

"Onward, my good man," the judge said.

Newt shifted over to the upwind edge of the road,
trying to avoid the dust the wagon was raising. The
first thing that struck him when they had almost
caught up to the wagon was that it was pulled by a
little brown mule and a black draft horse twice its size.
The harness and collar the mule wore were obviously
made for a twin to the draft horse, and the little long-
ear looked absurd and comical in the ill-fitting gear
and walking alongside the horse. Whoever owned the
outfit wasn't one to take much pride in a matched
team, nor did they appear to give a damn for appearances.

The wagon was as odd as what pulled it—paint so

bright it almost hurt the eyes with garish scenes, and obviously advertising some kind of snake-oil show or circus. It was probably the circus performers the people back in Piedras Negras had said were robbed of their horses—the same circus people who the rurales were looking for. A big, shaggy dog trotted alongside the wagon, and it stopped in the road with its hackles up when it noticed Newt and the judge nearing it.

Newt waited until the road widened for a stretch and chose that time to speed up and ride cautiously alongside the wagon. The dog growled and scratched the ground with its back feet and then ducked in behind their horses' heels, sniffing their smell and with the hair on its back still standing almost straight up.

The young woman driving the wagon was the prettiest girl he'd ever seen, so beautiful that it was almost disconcerting. She wore a short-sleeved white blouse gathered at the waist with a broad, tooled leather belt, and a bright red skirt that ended right above her brown ankles. Her sandaled feet were propped up on the wagon's dashboard. She wore no hat, despite the fact that the sun was hitting her full in the face, and her black hair hung long and curly down to the middle of her back.

"Good morning," he said when she turned and recognized he was alongside her wagon. The rear axle was squeaking like it hadn't been greased in a long time, keeping her from hearing his approach.

He realized something else when he got a full-on look at her face. She had the damnedest eyes. Some called them almond eyes, but that didn't do hers justice. They were more like a cat's eyes, or maybe that was the way she had drawn out the outside corners with some kind of blacking or cosmetic liner. It came to him after a while that he was staring and should look away out of politeness, but he couldn't stop himself. Not with those amber cat eyes staring back at him.

The dog growled again and the woman hissed at it to shut it up. The Circle Dot horse cocked one hind leg and bluffed a kick that sent the dog scampering away.

"Hallelujah!" the judge bellowed. "Follow me, boys. There's whiskey and women in old San Gabriel tonight."

The young woman's eyes shifted slowly to consider the judge, but she said nothing. Newt could tell from the rapid fall of her chest and the purse of her full lips that she was nervous.

Her companion on the wagon seat leaned forward so that he could better see Newt and the judge. There was, of all things, a silk top hat on his head, and he leaned so far forward at the waist and placed his upper body at such an angle that it appeared that there was no way the tall hat shouldn't topple from his head. Yet, somehow it defied the laws of gravity.

He looked as young as she. Maybe the same age or older, but his features were boyish and made it hard to tell. The similarity in their looks led Newt to believe they were kin. The man/boy seemed as nervous as the girl beside him, yet there was a smile on his face.

"Good morning," the boy in the funny hat said while he took in the judge.

Newt couldn't place the young man's accent. It was like none he had ever heard. Like the girl, it had more than a hint of the exotic about it.

"My name's Newt Jones, and this here is Judge Roy Bean of Langtry, Texas."

The man/boy tipped his hat and made a bow from the waist. "Alfonzo Grey, at your service, and this is my sister, Kizzy."

"I take it you two are some kind of circus folks." Newt gestured at the paintings on the side of the wagon.

"You would be correct," Fonzo said. "The Grey Family Circus."

The apprehensive look was still on the woman's face, and Newt couldn't blame her. No doubt, she was on the lookout for the rurales following them, coupled with the fact that he and the judge probably wouldn't inspire confidence in anyone. He hadn't shaved since he left Fort Stockton many days before, his clothes were filthy, and his face was never one that warmed strangers to him. The crazed judge's babbling didn't help matters.

"We have nothing left worth taking," she said.

Maybe not rurales, but no doubt she took them for possible road agents. He assumed that the brother had killed the rurale back in Piedras Negras, but truth be known, you never could tell, and he had been wrong before.

"We're peace officers." As soon as he said it he wondered how they would react to it, being wanted by the law. He had only been around the judge a few days, and already he was taking up his lying.

The glance both she and her companion cast over him made it plain they were looking for a badge on his person and found none.

"We had a run-in this morning with some outlaws

we've been tracking and it got a little rough," Newt added.

"What are two American lawmen doing below the border?"

Her brother whispered something, but she waved him off with an oddly graceful wave of her hand.

"Texas has papers on the bunch we're after, and we pursued them across the border," Newt said. "They're as bad a gang of cutthroats as you've ever seen."

"What gang?" The look on her face changed.

"The Cortina gang."

She stopped her team, set her wagon brake, and wrapped her reins around it. She shared a look with her brother.

"Did you say Cortina?" she asked.

"That's right." Newt stopped his horse.

"How do we know you're not making this up and not outlaws yourself?"

Newt started to get the judge to chime in with his credentials, but noticed that the judge's horse had wandered off the road and stopped under a shady oak. The judge was staring at his hand and crying.

"I assure you that we aren't bandits," Newt said.

"What's wrong with that man? Is he drunk?" Fonzo said, looking at the judge.

"Scorpion stung him, and he's bad sick."

"Maybe I can help him," Kizzy said.

"I was hoping there was a doctor in Zaragoza," Newt replied. "They tell me it's not much farther up the road."

"Put him in our wagon," she said.

"I think he can make it in the saddle."

As if on cue, the judge toppled from his horse,

hitting the ground with a solid, limp thump. The dog started toward the judge, growling again.

"I'd appreciate it if you called your dog off," Newt said. "I don't want to get bitten when I get down."

She produced a pistol she had kept hidden on her off side, and Newt had no time to draw his own. When she noticed the expression on his face she shrugged and uncocked her gun and shoved it in a holster lying in the floorboard of the wagon. "How was I to know who you were? We haven't had good luck lately with those we've met on the road."

Newt looked from her to her brother. Like her, Fonzo shrugged an apology. Newt didn't think the boy looked like a killer, either. Before he could think of what to say she climbed down from the wagon and started to where the judge lay. She crouched over the fallen man and lifted his swollen eyelids and pried his mouth open.

"You two come over here and help me get him in the wagon," she said.

"Is he dead?" Newt asked.

"We would be burying him instead of putting him in the wagon if he was. Get off that horse and help me."

"Is she always like this?" Newt asked Fonzo as he swung down out of his saddle.

"Bossy?" Fonzo said as he got down from the wagon. Newt nodded.

"My sister has been accused of that."

Newt looked at the side of the wagon again. "Fonzo the Great and Buckshot Annie. I take it you're Fonzo and she would be Buckshot Annie."

"I only break her out for special occasions," she said. "Today I'm only Kizzy. Are you going to stand there like a dumb ox or are you going to help me lift him?"

Newt took hold of the judge under his armpits. "You two take his legs."

"He looks bad," Fonzo said as he took hold of one of the judge's legs.

"He never was pretty," Newt said.

"He's having trouble breathing," Kizzy said between grunts of exertion as they carried the judge to the wagon. "His throat is swollen and so is his tongue. I've seen this before, although never with a scorpion sting."

They placed the judge on one of the two beds in the wagon, and Newt stood awkwardly in the doorway while she tried to make the judge comfortable.

"Don't just stand there. We need to get to Zaragoza and find a doctor," she said.

"Will he live?" Newt asked.

"How am I supposed to know?"

Newt helped Fonzo load the steps and close the rear door, then he mounted his horse while Fonzo took the wagon seat. The sound of the judge gasping and wheezing for breath carried outside the wagon.

Fonzo started the wagon moving and Newt rode alongside it, leading the judge's gray.

"How come you're after Cortina?" Fonzo asked, even though it was hard to talk over the screeching wagon axle.

"He shot a man and stole his stake, and then he robbed the judge on his way back to Mexico."

"Shot a man?"

"Yeah, me."

"Oh."

"You sound like you know something about Cortina,

and the look on your sister's face when I mentioned him gave me the same feeling."

"He robbed us, too. Stole six of our white show horses."

"Heard about that back in Piedras Negras. You're lucky he didn't kill you."

"I know it."

"What are you two doing down here in Mexico?"

"Trying to make a living, like everyone else. We're supposed to do a show in Monterrey next week."

"You're going the wrong way."

"We don't have a show without those horses. They were everything we had—like family to us."

Newt tried to put on his best poker face and not to think of the dead white horse he and the judge had left in the middle of the road a few miles back. "You aren't following Cortina, are you?"

"We are."

"Your horses are probably long sold off by now. They will stick out too much, and Cortina won't be fool enough to keep them."

"I think he might," Fonzo said. "He strikes me as a vain sort. He's probably riding one of my horses right now and thinking how good he looks on it. He'll look like he belongs in a circus himself on a white horse with that spotted vest of his."

"Spotted vest?"

"Some kind of cat hide. He was wearing it both times we ran across him."

"The judge will love to hear that."

"Is he a real judge?"

"Depends on how finicky you are about what you call a judge. I met some Texas Rangers that thought so."

"That must be Zaragoza up ahead," Fonzo said.

"I reckon."

The town lay sprawled on a brushy flat with the church bell tower rising out of the scrubland. There was a haze in the air, probably dust, and it made the place look more like a distant, smoky painting than something real.

Fonzo leaned out around the side of the wagon to check their back trail. Newt followed suit and was quick to notice the dust cloud worming its way along the road a mile or so behind them.

"Friends of yours?" Newt asked.

"Not so you would notice."

"Folks back in Piedras Negras told us about Cortina stealing some circus people's horses."

"I've already told you about that."

"Yes, but those Piedras Negras folks also said that those same circus people killed a rurale captain and left town on the run," Newt said. "Now might be the time to be honest."

Fonzo urged his mismatched team up to a trot and the wagon screeched louder. "Have you told us the truth? About everything?"

"Mostly the truth."

"Well, I'll tell you mostly the truth. I sure hope those rurales don't get close enough to us to make out who we are before we can get this wagon hid somewhere in town."

Newt twisted in the saddle and looked at the road behind them one more time while he rubbed the whiskers on his chin. "Was it you that killed that rurale, or was it your sister?"

"I did it."

Newt noted the defiant quaver to Fonzo's voice.

"I guess there's a story that goes with that. You two don't strike me as the kind that goes around killing policemen."

"They came up on us right after Cortina robbed us. We asked them for help, but they didn't care," Fonzo said. "And then they stole our mules."

"And you killed one of them while they were at it?"

"No, that was later. We followed them to Piedras Negras. Kizzy said we should forget about the mules and go after Cortina and our horses, and I intended to listen to her. But . . ."

"But what?"

"I saw him and I couldn't help but go talk to him." Fonzo paused for a while, the look on his face making it plain that he was back in that moment. "He was drunk, and when I told him to give us our mules back he laughed at me. He laughed and then he asked where my sister was. Said that as soon as he was through with me he was going to find her and teach her a lesson, too."

Newt tried to imagine the little man facing up to any kind of bad man and couldn't wrap his head around the image. This Fonzo didn't seem made of that kind of metal. "So you shot him?"

"He had a knife. I shot him before I had time to think about it."

Newt nodded. "That rurale captain should have known better. It takes a damn fool to bring a knife to a gunfight."

"Are you going to help us? I'm afraid we're in bad trouble."

Newt ignored the question, looking back again at

the dust cloud behind them. "Where did you ever manage to find six matching white horses?"

"My father gathered them over several years."

"Where's he at?"

Fonzo looked straight up the road over the team's backs. "Some vigilantes hung him over a year ago."

Newt threw a quick look at Fonzo. "Seems like you've got the outlaw blood."

"I'm no outlaw."

"You are now."

"It's my sister that I'm worried about," Fonzo said. "She had nothing to do with me killing that rurale."

The judge cried out something Newt couldn't understand. At least he was still alive.

"You never said if you would help us," Fonzo added.

"You're asking a lot, and you don't have a clue what kind of man you're asking it of."

"Hurry, Fonzo," Kizzy said from inside the wagon. "I think he's getting worse."

Newt tried to guess how far behind them that dust trail was. The dust was big enough that it looked as if there were several riders making it. They were going to be hard-pressed to get to Zaragoza ahead of them. Yes, indeed, it was going to be close.

# Chapter Twenty-two

**T**hey parked the wagon behind the low adobe wall of a set of abandoned corrals in the middle of town, and Fonzo went to try and find a doctor while Kizzy remained with the judge. Newt rode back to the edge of town to a small cantina and took a cheap glass of some kind of Mexican brandy and a place at the bar where he could see the street through the open front door.

The proprietor of the cantina wore no hat or shirt and only a soiled and stained white apron covering his hairy chest. He looked more like some kind of butcher than a bartender and was the only occupant of the cantina besides Newt. After a few failed attempts at some conversation in Spanish, the bartender finally gave up and left Newt alone to nurse his drink and watch the street.

Newt didn't have long to wait, for the rurales—ten of them—came riding by before he could finish his drink. They were leading a horse, and he recognized it as the one belonging to the bandit he had killed. Furthermore, the same dead bandit was draped across its back.

Newt finished the drink and waved off the bartender when he paused with the clay jug poised over the empty glass. He hitched his pistol to a more comfortable position and went to the door to watch the rurales go down the street. They soon disappeared from sight around a corner. Confident that they were gone for the time being, he went back to the bartender and took the jug from his hands, slapping the last of his money down on the bar top before he took a table in the back corner of the room. It was a seat where he could still see out onto the street.

Not that he considered himself a thinking man, but he had plenty to think on. There was the dead bandit the rurales had found; there was the judge mortally sick or dying; there were the circus people with the rurales after them. And most of all, there was Cortina somewhere close by. Newt didn't like complications, and at that moment there were too many of them. He was no do-gooder, and he had plenty of troubles of his own. A man who took on the weight of others' troubles only ended up with a broken back.

The rurales would soon learn of the new gringos in town and want to question them over the dead bandit they had found. The girl's brother would likely get an impromptu firing squad for killing the rurale captain, he might get the same for killing that bandit back up the road, and Cortina was going to get away with everything he had done. Yaqui Jim had been a good man. A little wild when in his cups, but Jim hadn't deserved killing.

In Newt's opinion, few got what they deserved, not really, in the end. Maybe he hadn't deserved to find that gold. Lord knows, he wasn't a good man like Jim, but that made the gold all the more precious—when you get something that maybe you shouldn't. It was a chance to make right the things he had done wrong. He knew where he was headed and how his kind ended up—lying in some ditch with their own skull caved in or a bullet in their brainpan, and nobody to care how you came to be that way.

Cortina was somewhere nearby. The thing to do was to find him before he had a chance to run. That's what he had come to Mexico for. Keep it simple. Hard things were better done without thinking. Those that thought too much or talked too long were usually the first to take it on the nose and end up under someone's boots. Ever since he had found the gold back in New Mexico, he kept telling himself to be a winner for once.

He had been a fool to listen to the judge. Anyone who found the bandit's horse, even a blind man, could have followed the broken trail through the cat-tails and water grass to where he had dumped the body. What were the odds of those rurales taking his word that the dead man had been a bandit and that the whole matter was one of self-defense? The best thing he could do was get on his horse and ride. There was a chance he might be long gone before the ru-rales had time to put things together and come hunting for someone to blame. Go find Cortina, get the gold back, and then kill the son of a bitch. Simple. Plain. Be a winner.

She was such a pretty thing to have to face up to those rurales. What he had seen of those Mexican lawmen at a glance, they were a rough bunch. She and her fancy brother having to face up to them was like feeding mice to the house cats. It wasn't going to be pretty.

The bottle was half-finished by the time he made up his mind and got up to head for the door and his horse. He was a little surprised to find that his legs were unsteady. The sticky-sweet concoction he had been drinking tasted like some kind of kid's drink, and he had been thirsty enough to let it sneak up on him. So lost in his thoughts was he, he hadn't even realized he had sat with the bottle so long.

He put a hand out to the table to steady himself and to adjust to the feeling. He was standing that way when the riders rode up to the cantina. There were a lot of them by the sound of it. He assumed it was the rurales coming back for him, and that was more of a faith in his usual bad luck than it was a guess. The first man through the door headed straight for him and stopped a few feet away. Five vaqueros filed in behind him and lined the front wall behind him and to either side of the door. Their attention locked on to Newt.

None of them were the rurales Newt had seen earlier, and although a cleaner-cut lot, they struck him as men you wouldn't want to fool with. One of them was slapping a riding quirt on his leg while his other hand rested on his pistol. All of the men were wearing too many guns to suit a man so outnumbered as Newt was.

The man who had come through the door first was the oldest of the lot and obviously their leader; he was neatly dressed with a fancy black sombrero and a white silk scarf around his neck. His vest and his flare-bottomed charro pants were embroidered in some kind of fancy silver thread. He was the only one not wearing a gun, but the look he gave Newt was the hardest one in the room. There was steel in that look and in the stiffness of his posture.

"I get the feeling there has been some kind of mis-understanding," Newt said.

The leader shook his head. He didn't bother with

Spanish, and his English was impeccable. "I have two questions for you, señor. Were you on the road from Piedras Negras this morning, and where did you get that horse you have tied out front?"

Newt took a glance to see if the room had a back door. It did, but it was closed and too far away.

"I would suggest that you answer both my questions very carefully," the man added.

There was no way things weren't going to go from bad to worse. The liquor was working on Newt and he felt that old stubbornness working its magic inside him. He never had liked to run from anything.

"Who the hell are you?" he asked.

The vaqueros started forward, but their leader stopped them with a lifting of his hand. He smiled, but it wasn't meant to be friendly.

"I am Don Carlos Alvarez, and who might you be?"

Newt assumed that he was supposed to be impressed with the man's title. He knew just enough Spanish to know that a don was some kind of big-shot landowner down Mexico way. "I'm a man minding my own business and wanting no trouble at all."

"For a man who wants no trouble, you have an odd way of showing it."

"Why don't you get straight at whatever's eating at you?"

Don Alvarez sighed as if he were dealing with a child. "The rurales found a dead man left in the lake to the east of town. You were seen coming from that direction less than an hour ago."

"I came from Piedras Negras."

"This dead man I speak of, he was one of my vaqueros."

"He was a thief and a killer."

"My guess is that you are one who can hardly make such accusations."

"That dead man you speak of rides with an outlaw I've been after, or did until he tried to kill me out on the road this morning."

"So, you confess to killing him?"

"He and two others pulled on me. They got away, but he didn't. Simple as that."

Don Alvarez made a sweeping gesture at the men behind him. "These men live by few rules. One is that they serve me and my family without question, and the second is that they look out for their own."

Newt understood all too well, and nodded grimly. That was the way it had been back in the mountains where he came from. All wars and blood feuds were predicated on such. You hurt one of ours and we hurt one of yours. Simple as that. Eye for an eye, a tooth for a tooth, and killing to offset other killing. Showing weakness was the same as losing.

"To wrong one of my men is to wrong me," Don Alvarez said. "It is a matter of respect. You have done this thing, and I must do this other thing. Examples must be made."

"Do you know a man named Javier Cortina?" Newt tried to keep his voice level.

Don Alvarez shared a look with his men. "We know of Cortina."

"Well, your vaquero was one of Cortina's bunch and was coming here to meet him."

"What makes you think Cortina is nearby?"

Newt smiled, trying to match the man for pure sarcasm. "Why, I imagine he's with your daughter right now while you stand here bothering me over nothing."

Don Alvarez flushed, and Newt could tell that he

had struck a nerve. It was apparent that the man was aware of the rumor that Cortina had a thing for his daughter.

"Speak of my daughter again and I will have you flogged before I have you killed," Don Alvarez said, and then he said something else in Spanish to one of the vaqueros. The man he spoke to went rapidly out the door and mounted his horse and left in a run.

"You check into it and you'll find Cortina is around," Newt said. "And you'll also find I've been telling you the truth."

Don Alvarez said nothing, as if he were weighing the matter.

"I'm getting tired of standing here," Newt said. "Why don't we sit down and talk this out over a drink or two? There's plenty of time for other things later if you still don't believe me once you've heard me out."

"I'm afraid it is not so simple a matter. My men, they are very passionate, and the one you killed was well liked."

"You ride back up the road and you'll find a dead white horse," Newt said. "Cortina's bunch stole that horse and several others from a pair of circus people I came to town with. One of Cortina's men was riding that horse, and your man and another were riding with him."

"You tell a good story."

"I'm telling you the truth."

"But you have not said all, such as how you come by that horse you ride?"

"What business is that of yours? I brought that horse with me out of Texas."

Don Alvarez's look turned mean again. Not hot mean,

but the cold kind of mean, like something simmering
and building to a boil.

"That horse you ride belonged to my son. He left
here five years ago riding it, and it was the last time he
was ever seen."

Newt said nothing, and his own breath sounded
loud to his ears.

"These men will see to it that you talk. Maybe it will
take a while, or maybe it won't take so long, but you
will talk in the end," Don Alvarez said. "But, first I
would like to know your name. I have thought about
this day for a long time, and what your name might be
when I finally found you."

Newt reached over and took the jug off the table
and turned it up to his lips. He felt the mad rising up
in him and flowing through him like the liquor sliding so smoothly down his throat. It was the old anger
that had been his curse for so long. No matter how
hard he fought it, it was always there, like a tool waiting to be used. He set the empty jug down on the
table with a thump and straightened himself to his full
height, shoving the building fury down inside him.

"Newt Jones."

"Jones, it is a common name for an American criminal, no?" Don Alvarez shook his head pitifully. "But
suit yourself. Do me the courtesy of telling me where
my son's body lies, and I will see that you die quickly."

"That horse was given to me by an Indian up in
Texas. I've never laid eyes on your son that I know of,"
Newt said slowly and carefully.

Don Alvarez studied his face, as if he could read
something there. "You are an Indian trader? I don't
think so."

"Cortina left me for dead and stole something that belongs to me. I started walking after him and met some Indians. They doctored me up and gave me that horse you're talking about. We heard Cortina was headed here, and that's why I'm standing here now."

"We?"

"A judge from up in Texas. Roy Bean."

Don Alvarez seemed startled. "He is here? Hand over your gun, and we will go talk to him."

"I'm not giving you my gun. You either kill me or leave me be."

It was at that instant when someone came through the back door. And Newt knew before he even twisted around that it was more of Don Alvarez's men with guns leveled on him.

Newt let out a deep breath and tried to relax his hands. He realized that he had been clenching them into fists. He held his arms high and wide while one of the men lifted his pistol from its holster.

Don Alvarez said something to his men in Spanish, and one of them poked Newt between the shoulder blades with the barrel of a rifle. They marched him out the front door with their patron leading the way.

"Where is Judge Roy?" Don Alvarez asked.

For a moment, a little ray of hope hit Newt as squarely as the midday sun hitting him in the face. He adjusted to both of the feelings with a squint. "Are you and the judge some kind of old friends?"

Don Alvarez laughed bitterly. "Not quite. The last time he was here I tried to kill him."

Everything had to be the hard way. Always had been and always would.

# Chapter Twenty-three

**N**ewt wouldn't tell them where the judge and the circus people were, but they found the wagon anyway. A couple of the vaqueros didn't take well to his reluctance to give up the judge's whereabouts and had seen fit to club him over the head with a pistol barrel and give him the boot or two, or three, while he was down. He almost laughed at them if they thought he hadn't taken worse before.

The first thing Newt saw when they reached the wagon was that the rurales had found it first and that they had Fonzo up against its rear wheel, working him over. It looked like the rurales had been *interrogating* him for a while. A large gash above one of his eyes was already pouring blood, and his mouth was busted.

Kizzy was seated on the ground against the adobe wall in front of the wagon, with three of the rurales standing guard over her. Newt had the impression she had been thrown there. She leaned around their legs to see what was happening to her brother and screamed for them to stop.

Don Alvarez said something loudly in Spanish, and

had to say it again to get the rurales' attention. They quit hitting Fonzo, but kept him pinned against the wagon wheel while the one in charge came over to converse with the rich rancher. Whatever it was that Don Alvarez was telling him, the rurale didn't like it. After a bit, Don Alvarez went inside the wagon, but came back out quickly.

"What's wrong with him?" he asked Newt.

"Scorpion stung him," Newt answered.

Kizzy tried to get up and go to her brother, but one of the rurales shoved her back down. Newt took a threatening step forward, but was rewarded with a rifle barrel punched into his kidney.

"Fine sorts you have for lawmen down here." Newt stared at the man who had struck him while he readjusted his hat on his head.

"That boy killed a rurale captain," Don Alvarez said.

"Maybe, but what did the woman do? I wouldn't have thought a *grande* like you would tolerate such."

"You are in no position to dictate these things."

Don Alvarez glanced at Kizzy, and Newt could tell that he didn't like how she had been treated any more than he did. Don Alvarez rattled off what sounded like more orders, and whatever importance he carried was enough that the rurales begrudgingly helped Kizzy to her feet. She ran to her brother, ignoring the men surrounding him and shoving them aside. Fonzo fell to a sitting position as soon as the rurales let go of him, and she crouched beside him, examining his face and whispering things to him.

The leader of the rurales and Don Alvarez held another conversation off to the side, and when it was over one of the rurales went to his horse and gathered two sets of manacles out of his saddlebags. When he came back he gestured for Newt to hold out his hands and snapped the wristbands closed on each of Newt's wrists.

Newt looked down at the instruments of his bondage while the rurale went to Fonzo and secured him in the same manner. The handcuffs were crude iron things with two-inch bands and with the forge work and the blacksmith's hammer dimples still showing. A half a foot of heavy chain coupled them together, and crude locks functioned with a key so old it might have unlocked a castle keep or a torturer's dungeon. The steel was turned coal black with age, or maybe stove blacking, so as to appear ancient in its misery, and flecked with speckles of what might have been dried blood. Newt wondered how many men had worn the handcuffs.

Don Alvarez's vaqueros and the rurales marched them back up the street with Kizzy under their watch, but striding unbound beside her brother. The chain between Newt's hands rattled and clinked like wagon traces, except it was a far more solemn sound to Newt's ears, like a hearse rolling slow during a funeral procession.

After a long walk they came to what served as a jail, which was nothing more than a low-roofed adobe with a tiny front room containing a jailer's cot and an old office desk, and two cells in the back on either side of a narrow corridor. They threw Fonzo in one cell and Newt in the other. Despite Kizzy's protests, they wouldn't let her come inside.

The jail bars that made up the wall of the cells along the corridor were the same black as the handcuffs. Newt held out his hands to be freed of his manacles, but the rurales ignored him and locked the cell door.

Fonzo didn't ask to have his hands freed, and fell on the floor as soon as they shoved him into his cell. Newt wasn't sure that Fonzo wasn't hurt badly.

Newt's cell hadn't been used in a long while, for cobwebs spanned every corner or hung down in silky strings as white as cotton in the little sunlight pouring through the single tiny window. The floor was littered with old straw and a coating of fine dust, and from the tiny black pellets there Newt assumed that someone had once kept a goat in the cell.

Don Alvarez gave an order, and the rurales and his men strode out of the back room with purpose. Only the don remained behind.

"I will come back tonight or tomorrow, and then you will talk to me more about the horse you ride," he said.

"What did you do with the girl?" Newt asked

"She is free to go. She will not be bothered again."

"What about the judge?"

"We have no doctor here, but one of the priests is skilled in such things and will see to him as best he can. I have things to say to Judge Roy, as well. Things I have waited long to say." Don Alvarez turned to go.

"You're going to your ranch to check on your daughter, aren't you?"

Don Alvarez stopped, but kept his back to Newt. "I have warned you once not to mention my daughter. If I do not find Cortina at my home as you say he is, I will come back here and kill you myself for the insult, if nothing else."

Newt folded the single moth-eaten blanket into a pad and sat down on the rope-laced cot that was the only furniture in his cell. He listened to the sound of the horses leaving the jail at a high gallop, and then some time later Fonzo took hold of his cell bars and pulled himself up to lean against them.

"Do you think he meant what he said?" Fonzo asked.

Newt struggled to work up some moisture in his dry mouth and finally spat on the litter between his feet. He stared at the sunlight coming through the little window and listened to the horses' hoof falls fading away.

"He meant it."

# Chapter Twenty-four

It was the next morning before Don Alvarez returned. He left the rurales and his vaqueros sitting their horses in front of the jail and went inside alone. Newt was standing at his window looking out at the church bell tower in the distance, but didn't turn around when he heard the sound of the man's spurs in the corridor between the two cells.

"Face me," Don Alvarez said. "I want you looking at me."

Newt slowly turned. The morning sunlight hitting him in the back made him seem taller. "Did you catch Cortina?"

"No."

"But he had been there, hadn't he?"

Don Alvarez ignored the question and paced the corridor with his hands clasped behind his back and his head bowed. Finally, he stopped, facing Newt again. "I loved my son very much."

"I told you how I came by that horse. I don't know a thing about what happened to your son."

"There was a time when that horse you ride was

young, and every one of my vaqueros wanted him as their own. They wanted him even after we tried to break him as a four-year-old, and he threw every one of my best riders."

Newt leaned against the adobe wall, looking over the don's shoulder. Fonzo had risen to a sitting position on his cot and was listening to the story, if for no other reason than it prolonged what the young man's eyes showed he thought was coming for them when Don Alvarez stopped talking.

"My son wanted that horse, but I feared that he would be hurt. I put the horse in the string of my best vaquero. He was a man of patience and skill, and I thought maybe he could gentle the horse, train it, and then I would give it to my son." The tone of Don Alvarez's voice was a weary one. "The horse showed promise, after a time, and then one day it returned with no rider. We found that vaquero in the brush with a mesquite limb stuck through his throat. From the way the ground was torn it looked as if the horse had tried to buck him off and then thrown a runaway."

Don Alvarez seemed unaware that Fonzo was on his feet and very near to the cell bars right behind him. Newt wondered if Fonzo could grab the man through the bars, and if there was enough slack in the handcuff chains to give him the reach needed. Maybe they could bargain their way out of town if they had a hostage.

"The horse was bad luck. Everyone knew it," Don Alvarez continued.

"I doubt the horse had much to do with it," Newt answered. "Many a man has been killed on the back of a perfectly good horse."

Don Alvarez shook his head. "Coincidence, you think? I thought so, too, and then the next man to take that horse roped a bull on him. We found that man, the horse, and the bull tangled in the rope among the brush. I can only imagine the struggle. But what matters is that the man and the bull were broken and strangled to death, but the horse was fine."

"I would say the bull might have had more to do with that, or a man foolish enough to rope a grown bull alone." Newt wished Fonzo would look at him and wished there were some way he could know what Fonzo was thinking. Taking hold of the don was about the only chance left to them.

"Do you know how that horse came to wear that brand? It is not my brand. My son thought he was too fine-looking a horse to mar his flesh with a hot iron," Don Alvarez said.

"He was wearing it when I got him," Newt answered.

"He was stolen from my ranch during an Indian raid."

"Apaches?"

"No, there are other renegade Indians in the mountains to the west. Tribes with names so old that no one remembers them. You can't imagine how primitive they are. They live in tiny, remote villages and sometimes in caves high up and hard to find. Sometimes they come down and raid us. Usually they only steal our crops or kill a beef or two, but that time they took the horse. It was two years before we saw the horse again. Some soldiers found him on the road west of Ciudad Chihuahua, and one of them had worked for me and recognized him. When the soldiers brought him to me he was wearing that brand."

"It's an unusual brand. What's with the circle and the dot?"

Don Alvarez shrugged. "Some of the Indians who worked for me thought it was a medicine wheel or maybe an eye."

"An eye?"

"A power symbol. Whatever it was, they were sure it was meant to mark the horse in some way. Not for ownership, but for something else."

"How did your son finally end up with the horse?"

"Two of my vaqueros got into a fight over which one of them should have the horse in his string. The loser was cut very badly with a knife. I was going to have the horse killed, but my son took him away and hid him. We thought the horse had run off, but weeks later my son rode up to me on that horse. He said there was nothing wrong and that it was a fine horse. I could never say no to my son."

Fonzo seemed hypnotized by staring at Don Alvarez's back and wouldn't look away from it for Newt to catch his eye and pass some kind of signal. Newt wondered if Fonzo had nerve enough to take action, or if the idea of grabbing their captor had even passed through his mind. He could only hope that Fonzo was as desperate as he was. And then there was a chance that the don didn't have the cell keys. And the chances of that were high. Those men outside would shoot them down in their cells without batting an eye for laying hands on their master.

"How did your son disappear?" Newt asked.

"He rode that horse for a year, and everyone almost forgot about the things that had happened before, except for the whispers of a few of those Indians who worked for me. The rest of us soon agreed that it was the best horse on the ranch, and maybe the best horse we had ever seen." Don Alvarez swallowed and looked away. "My son rode north one morning with his saddlebags full of money to pay for a set of American bulls I had purchased in Brownsville. We searched for a month when he didn't come back, but I never saw him again."

"Someone probably knew he was carrying that money."

"Yes, that is what I thought. Maybe some banditos waited for him on the road, or maybe the Americans killed him."

"That was what, five years ago? And you think I was the one who did it, and then was foolish enough to come back here on your son's horse?"

"I never got to bury my son."

"I'm sorry for your loss." Newt tried to catch Fonzo's attention. Don Alvarez wasn't going to talk much longer.

"The rurales want to put you against a wall. This boy behind me, also."

"Those rurales stole our mules," Fonzo said. "They are no better than thieves. I killed that captain, but only after he would not give our mules back and threatened me with a knife."

Don Alvarez turned so that he could see both of them, and any chance for Fonzo to grab him was gone.

"Your sister tells the same story. She is quite persuasive."

"Cortina robbed us, and then those rurales did the same," Fonzo added. "We are only simple show people."

Don Alvarez ignored Fonzo and shifted his attention

back to Newt. "What would you do if you caught Cortina?"

Newt stepped forward and took hold of a cell bar in each hand, his face only inches from the don's. "I intend to kill him."

"What did he take from you?"

"That doesn't matter. What did he take from you?"

"My daughter. I have men out after them this moment, but a messenger came only a little while ago and said they have lost Cortina's trail."

"I could get him."

"What could you do that so many men can't?"

"They don't want him as bad as I do."

"You only beg for your life."

"How bad do you want Cortina dead?"

Don Alvarez began to pace again, casting an occasional glance at Newt in passing.

"You let us out of here, see these circus folks safely on the road, and I'll get Cortina for you."

The don stopped in front of Newt again. "There are the rurales to think of."

"You're some kind of big shot around here. I'm sure you can change their minds."

"You have killed a man with many friends."

"He wasn't much of a man."

"Favors granted require favors on my part. It can cause difficulties and complexities in the future that can't be calculated. Intrigue and politics often weave a tangled web."

"You want your daughter back, don't you? I've got a notion that some of those rurales, if not all of them, might have connections to Cortina. Are you going to trust them to run him down?"

"That rurale company is a joke. I count on them for

nothing," Don Alvarez said. "I have over fifty vaqueros that ride for me. Those are the men I count on."

"You said yourself that they've already lost Cortina's trail. I've followed him this far, and I'll follow him as long as it takes."

"I want him brought back to me alive, or I want his head in a sack."

Newt held up his shackled hands. "Let me and young Fonzo there go, and I'll get Cortina."

"The circus boy stays. I will see to it that he is looked after and that no harm comes to him or his sister while you are gone."

"I want to go with him." Fonzo grabbed his cell bars, clutching them until his knuckles were white. There was panic written all over him. "Those rurales will kill me. My sister has no one else."

"The rurales will leave you alone. I will see to it that you are turned loose if this man does as he says," Don Alvarez said. "If this man does not come back, I will leave you to whatever justice the rurales wish to inflict on you."

Newt started to ask another question, but was interrupted by two of the vaqueros busting into the corridor. One of them had a set of keys and opened Newt's cell door. Newt marched out with one in front of him and one in back, with Don Alvarez leading the way. Newt cast one look behind him at Fonzo, but the circus boy had already turned away from him.

When they stepped outside at least twenty riders were waiting for them, sitting their horses in a semicircle fronting the jail. The rurales were off to one end of the line, slightly apart from the vaqueros. The judge and the girl were standing in front of the posse.

The vaquero with the keys unlocked Newt's handcuffs,

and Newt noticed that he was the same one who had busted him in the kidney with a rifle barrel the day before.

The judge was holding Newt's gun belt and held it out to him. Newt rubbed his chafed wrists and took his gun and swung the belt around his hips. He looked from the judge to Don Alvarez.

"You already had this deal thought out before you came in the jail, didn't you?" he asked Don Alvarez.

"Judge Roy will go with you," Don Alvarez said.

"Thought you said you tried to kill the judge the last time you saw him."

"We have settled those matters."

"I don't need his help."

The judge started to bluster something, but Don Alvarez cut him off. "I set the terms. He will go with you."

Newt looked at the judge. "You seem to be on the mend."

The judge held up his hand, and most of the swelling was gone. His face almost looked normal, too. "The priest said I'm over it, but it was a close call."

Newt buckled his gun belt and scowled at the don and the judge. He didn't trust either of them.

"Where's my horse?" he asked.

"I have ordered that he be destroyed," Don Alvarez said.

"That's my horse, and I want him. If you want this done, you have him brought to me."

"I have many other horses that you can choose from, and you are in no position to bargain."

"You want Cortina, you bring me that horse."

"He is cursed."

"Then we're a pair."

Don Alvarez looked mad, but made a motion to his men. One of them took off in a run.

"You have one week to either bring me Cortina or his head," Don Alvarez said. "If you aren't back by then, I will turn the boy over to the rurales, and I will do everything in my power to hunt you down."

The rurale company looked none too happy about the deal in the making. Newt assumed that the rurales, and probably Don Alvarez's vaqueros, would hang back a little, but follow him after Cortina.

"I never even met these circus people until yesterday afternoon, and they have nothing to do with me," Newt said. "Why don't you let them go now?"

"The boy stays locked up until you return. That is our pact."

Kizzy was looking at Newt the whole time with those odd, lovely eyes. She seemed to expect him to say something else, but there was nothing more to be said. She gave him one last look and ran inside the jail.

At that same moment the vaquero came back leading the Circle Dot horse. The horse already had Newt's rig on it, with the Sharps buffalo gun tied to the saddle strings on one side and shoved under the stirrup leather.

The judge was already getting on his gray nag. Newt took one of the bridle reins offered him and tightened his cinch. He started to mount, but hesitated and turned back.

"One more thing," he said.

"What's that?" asked Don Alvarez.

"Hey, you." Newt pointed at the vaquero who had hit him in the kidney with his rifle, and waved him over.

The vaquero looked sullen, but walked up to Newt.

The rest of the men gathered around stopped talking when they noticed what was going on.

"You like hitting a man in the back?"

The vaquero didn't understand English, but he put his hand on a big knife sheathed on his belt and said something back in Spanish. Some of the men laughed, and the vaquero smiled as if it were a funny thing.

Newt smiled back, and then he drew his pistol and swung it in a slashing blow. He was aiming for the vaquero's pox-pitted nose, but was a little off and the end of the pistol barrel hit the vaquero right between the eyes. The vaquero ended up flat on his back with his eyes rolled back in his head, mumbling something, and slobber running out of one side of his mouth.

Metal rasped against leather as several guns were drawn at once. A gambler would have been hard-pressed to lay odds on which one of them was going to shoot Newt first. He ignored the guns pointing at him and shoved the Smith back in its holster. He hovered over his victim, daring the man to get up.

"Nothing I hate worse than a backbiter." Newt spat on the fallen vaquero and then headed to his horse.

Don Alvarez shouted orders and stepped between Newt and the mounted men. The vaqueros and rurales didn't put away their guns, but they did hold their fire.

"Do you have a death wish?" Don Alvarez asked. "Are you a fool?"

Newt didn't answer until he had mounted his horse. He pointed at the vaquero on the ground. "He ought to be careful who he pokes."

"You had better find Cortina. These men would like nothing better than if you didn't." Don Alvarez waved him away.

Newt reined the Circle Dot horse around and shoved his way through the crowd of men. The judge soon pulled up beside him.

"Son, you're a fool for trouble," the judge said. "What kind of crazy stunt was that, pulling your shooter in front of all of them? We're lucky you didn't get us both killed."

"Keep it to yourself. I'm not in the mood."

"You think you really did something, striking a deal with Don Alvarez, don't you?"

"What kind of deal did you make?" Newt asked. "Doesn't surprise me that you two are old chums."

"I wouldn't exactly say we're friends. Far from it," the judge said.

"What's he have against you?"

"I came through this country once when I was younger. Had a little shooting scrape over a señorita."

"What did that have to do with Alvarez?"

"The man I shot was some distant cousin of his, and Alvarez set in after me. I don't think he was close enough kin to try too hard to catch me, but I outran him to the border anyway."

"And he's letting you come with me? Just like that?"

"Alvarez would as soon have me killed as he would you, but he's a practical man. He sets store by that girl of his. The likes of Cortina even talking to her is what Alvarez would consider defiling her, and now to rub salt in the wound, that sassy bandit has run off with her. Alvarez would have his head for the insult to his family name, if nothing else."

"It was good luck on our part that Cortina did what he did," Newt said.

"You realize you struck a deal with the Devil, don't you? Don't let all those fancy manners fool you.

You ain't any more than a flea on a dog's ass to that man. He's got his own angles to work, and we looked useful to him for the time being."

"Those vaqueros are going to follow us."

The judge nodded. "Sure as the world. I'd do it that way if I were him. There's no reason he thinks we can track any better than his boys, so he must think we know something about where Cortina might go."

"Do you?"

"I don't have a clue."

"I don't trust Alvarez to keep his word. I think he still thinks I had something to do with his son's death."

"It'll be a chancy thing. Those vaqueros know the country and we don't."

"He'll hand that circus kid over to the rurales, even if I bring him Cortina's head, won't he?"

"A man like Alvarez is hard to figure. He sets store by his word, but then again, that might only hold in a gentleman-to-gentleman situation. You ain't no gentleman, and neither am I."

Newt noticed that the judge had a new gun hanging by a strap from his saddle horn. It was a short, double-barreled coach gun—a ten-gauge with stubby Damascus steel barrels and mule-ear hammers on the side locks. Those side plates were engraved, and faint traces of silverwork were barely visible. At one time it might have been some rich man's bird gun before somebody sawed it off to make it handier for shooting men. There was a handkerchief bundle knotted at the top and hanging beside the shotgun, and the brass cartridges inside it jingled occasionally with the judge's horse's stride.

"Where'd you get the street cannon?" Newt asked.

"Couldn't find any cartridges for the carbine I took off that bandit you killed, and I thought our work might be close up and better suited to a scattergun," the judge said. "Traded that carbine and the Navy Colt you took for the shotgun, straight across."

Newt hadn't even noticed that the dead bandit's pistol was gone from his gear. "Better have them close. That thing won't pattern at all at any distance."

The judge patted the shotgun's butt stock. "It's been my experience that a shotgun can save some shooting and can get a man to go easy when nothing else will. You point old Gabriel at someone, and they look into the business end of him and get afraid he's going to toot his horns."

"Old Gabriel?"

"That's what I named it. Didn't you ever read the Bible?" The judge scoffed. "I swear, I'm riding with a heathen."

They pointed their horses north following a wagon road to the Rancho Alvarez. It was two more miles before either of them spoke again.

"I don't know what kind of deal you and Alvarez made, but don't you cross me," Newt said. "I've got enough troubles without worrying about you."

The judge did his best to look offended. "Same deal as you made. We have to catch Cortina. And besides, you haven't exactly been honest with me, either."

The judge reached inside his vest pocket and pulled out a folded, badly wrinkled sheet of paper. He unfolded it and held it out, reading it. He grunted after a while and passed the paper to Newt. It was a flyer advertising a boxing match in the mining camp of Granite Gap.

"Think I didn't know who you are?" the judge asked. "You're a known man, and one of the Rangers recognized you back in Langtry."

"Where did you get this?"

"You might say I'm a bit of a boxing fan."

"I told you I fought in the ring a few times."

"You've got a name for more than that, Widow-maker Jones," the judge said. "They say you'll hire out to anyone that will pay your price. Tear a man down for fifty dollars, and don't care who it is. The company decides they want a claim, and the man that holds it disappears."

"That's a damned lie." Newt stopped his horse.

The judge yanked his pistol from his belt and leveled it on Newt. "You won't do me like you did that Mexican cowboy back there."

Newt stared into the bore of the gun. "Use it if you're going to."

The judge eared the pistol's hammer back. "You think you're some kind of good man? I saw the way you were looking at me back there in Piedras Negras, like you were better than me. Well, I judge folks for a living, and I knew you for what you were at first glance. You're a thumper for hire that hasn't done a good deed since you were weaned off sour milk. Widowmaker Jones, that's who you are."

Newt straightened in the saddle. "Don't you ever call me that again, and you use that gun or I'm going to make you eat it."

The judge uncocked the pistol and shoved it back behind his belt. "We get Cortina and you can go your merry way. Go build wagons and pick flowers and give them to old widow ladies, or kiss babies and preach sermons for all I care."

"I thought you wanted to hang Cortina. Don Alvarez wants his head."

The judge made a clicking sound with a suck of his cheek. "I admit I was looking forward to stretching that devil's neck, but maybe Don Alvarez will let me have the head. I could pickle it and keep it in a jar on my bar for a conversation piece. They did that with old Joaquin Murrieta after he killed my brother Josh out in California. I would have paid a pretty penny to have that horse thief's head. The California Rangers charged people a dollar to look at Murrieta's pickled noggin."

Newt twisted in the saddle and looked back toward town.

"You're thinking about that woman, aren't you?" the judge asked. "You're too ugly for a pretty little thing like that, but I can see you're worrying over it."

"I wasn't thinking about her."

"To hell you weren't. You'd best mind your own business. Always strikes me funny that even the most sensible men turn fool over the littlest things," the judge said. "With some it's money or gambling, and with some it's women. Wouldn't have took you for a romancer, but you never can tell."

"Those rurales are a rough bunch. They might give her trouble," Newt said. "She's a pretty little thing."

"I wouldn't have thrown any rocks at her in my younger years, I'll give you that, but Don Alvarez won't let anything happen to her. And besides, she struck me as a girl that can take care of herself."

"I can most certainly take care of myself." Kizzy

stepped her horse out of a gully on the side of the road ahead of them.

Both men noted how she parked her horse broadside in the road, as if to block them like some kind of road agent out to rob their purses. Apparently she had been waiting for them, and they had been arguing too much to notice her. Newt hoped she hadn't heard him mention that she was pretty.

She was riding the black draft horse that had been hitched with the little mule to her wagon. Her saddle looked undersized and tiny on its broad back. The big white dog stood at the horse's feet.

But it wasn't so much the horse and the huge dog that made her an odd sight. It was the way she was dressed. She was wearing some kind of buckskin dress, bone-white, with beading and fringe all over it. Where her dress ended Newt could see the lower legs of a pair of men's canvas pants tucked into fancy riding boots. Dainty, nickel-plated gal leg spurs with brass star rowels sat above their heels. The hat on her head was a high-crowned, preposterous thing, as white as her dress and with a wide brim. Newt hadn't seen anything like it except ones worn by the performers in some of those traveling Wild West shows.

"Go back to town, girl," the judge said.

The dog growled and took two threatening steps forward, causing the judge's horse to shy backward.

Kizzy shoved the front of the brim of her hat up against the crown so that she could see better. "Don Alvarez will let the rurales have my brother if you don't get Cortina."

"We can take care of that," the judge said. "Go back to your circus wagon and tend to some sewing or such."

"I can ride or shoot with any man." She patted one

of the pearl-handled pistols on the double rig she had belted over the dress.

"All right, if you don't like women's work, play some checkers and chew tobacco with your brother while he waits."

"Cortina has our horses. We need those horses," she said. "Fonzo would go with you if it was me that was locked up."

"There's no place for a woman where we're going." The judge looked to Newt to confirm his opinion. "Tell her to get her ass back to town."

The dog growled again, and the judge cursed and fumbled for his pistol. "You get that dog back, or I'll shoot the damned thing."

"Mind your language in front of the lady," Newt said.

"Lady?" the judge exclaimed. "She's nothing but a Gypsy wench. Can't you tell?"

"I won't ask you again." Newt was talking to the judge, but kept a watch on the brute of a dog. He had never seen its like. It was the size of a yearling bear cub.

"He'd better not shoot my dog," Kizzy said. "Vlad's not really mean, but he can be a little overly protective of me."

"Where did you get that outfit you're wearing?" Newt asked.

She looked bashfully down at her dress. "I use it in our show. It was the only thing I have that I thought durable enough to hold up on a long horseback trip."

"Think we're playacting here?" the judge asked. "This ain't no Wild West show."

"You can't stop me from going."

"To hell we can't," the judge said.

"What are you going to do, shoot me?" She giggled.

"I'll take that horse and put you afoot." The judge thumped his horse in the belly with his heels, intending to ride forward and snatch her reins.

She put a hand on her right-hand pistol. "I could shoot you before that fat belly of yours draws another breath."

The judge kept his horse coming, and she shucked her Colt Lightning slick and fast. She held it leveled on the judge, and he pulled up short.

"By God, but this is a pistol-pulling morning," the judge said.

"I'm going with you two," she said. "Like it or not."

The judge started to say something else and pointed a finger at her. The dog must have taken his hand movement as a threat to his owner and charged forward and grabbed the judge's gray horse by the tail. The horse threw a fit, bucking and shying while the dog was swung wildly by the horse's tail. Somehow, the judge clawed at his saddle with both hands and managed to stay on, but when the horse finally stopped it was twenty yards off to one side of the road and astraddle an agave plant. The dog was standing between the judge and Kizzy, growling and with a thick strand of the gray's tail hair hanging from its mouth. Kizzy still held the pistol steady and businesslike.

"This ain't right," the judge said. "Who in the hell gets in a gunfight with a woman? I can't win here."

The judge looked to Newt again for support, but Newt said nothing and pushed his horse past Kizzy's, not even looking her way.

Kizzy and the judge were left together while Newt was steadily putting distance on them. She kept the pistol leveled, but took a chance and made a quick look to see how far Newt was ahead of them.

"What's it going to be?" she asked.

The judge squinted at her and rubbed the gray whiskers on one sagging cheek. After a while, he kicked his gray past her, mumbling to himself while the horse shied widely around the dog.

"What's the world coming to?" she heard him say. "It ain't right, I tell you. Big grizzle dogs attacking my good horse, and Gypsy women pointing pistols at me. A judge can't get any respect down here, I tell you."

Kizzy let him get a little ways ahead of her, then turned her horse in behind him. Newt was already a hundred yards ahead of them and disappearing over the top of a hill. All three of them were soon out of sight.

Two of the vaqueros followed behind them several miles back, and the company of rurales took another trail to the west, paralleling the main road.

# Chapter Twenty-five

**K**izzy sat on the opposite side of the fire from the men. The day's ride had been a long one, but still not enough time to trust either of the pair she had set out with. The big man who called himself Newt didn't say two words all day long, while the judge—if he was really a judge—was continually chattering, making jokes, telling odd stories, insulting her dog, and filling in the rest of his time talking to himself when nobody else would listen. She found it odd that she was less bothered by the big man with the fierce face than she was by the old man. But her years on the road had taught her that bad intentions could often hide behind a glib tongue and a crafty smile.

Not that the big man didn't worry her. On first look, there was something about Newt that made her draw back. She had no doubt that he was a hard case and maybe a killer, but that wasn't all that made him seem threatening. He wasn't a bulky sort, but for a man somewhere a little over six feet tall, everything about him was outsized, from the big hands and wrists, to the spread of his shoulders. He had a broad, stout chin and jaw, and his cheekbones seemed made of stone. It might have been a handsome face, if a tad on the harsh side, but there was that nose that looked as if it had been broken more than once, the battered ear, and the lacework of little scars crisscrossing both his cheekbones and chin. One brow was scarred so badly that the eyebrow was thin and all but gone.

In contrast to the dangerous demeanor about him, when he spoke his voice was deep and soft, and his eyes appeared honest, although somewhat intense. And she hadn't failed to notice the way he slowed his pace as the day grew long and the miles began to wear on her. He didn't mention it, but he did it just the same.

Kind eyes or not, she wasn't going to be fooled or caught unawares. The last thing she had wanted was to end up with two such men. It was drilled into her from the time she was old enough to talk that you didn't trust outsiders. You didn't trust the *gadje.* If you were Roma you sometimes learned that the hard way. It had been like that in England where her father came from, and it had been like that in France, the land of her mother. It had been like that all the years and in all the lands as her people moved on. The *gadje* didn't trust Gypsies, and Gypsies didn't trust them one bit more.

And despite it all, there she was alone and with two of them—rough strangers of callous ways and crude talk, and men who didn't wash their hands regularly or before a meal. She had watched from the jail door and seen Newt beat the vaquero; she had seen him enjoy hurting that man. A part of her was satisfied to see one of the men who had accosted her and Fonzo beaten, but another part of her recognized that she

was at the mercy of barbarians and that life was cheap
in their company.

She was tired of being at the mercy of one thing or
another. She was homeless and she couldn't do anything about it. She was a Gypsy, a second-class citizen
looked down on by almost everyone she met, and she
couldn't do anything about that, either. Her brother
was locked up and in danger of being killed, and
Cortina had stolen their last means of supporting
themselves. She could do something about that, or
maybe not. But at least she could try. Because things
were one way, or a person was one way, it didn't mean
it had to stay the same. You didn't have to be at the
mercy of anything if you were smart. Her father had
always said that brains were what separated humans
from the beasts. Being smart was the trick—being
smart and being brave. She didn't know if she was
brave, but she knew she was smart.

She kept a careful watch on the two across the fire.
They paid her little attention other than an occasional
glance her way or to offer her a share of the beans
they had cooked in a little pot Newt carried tied to
one corner of his saddle skirt. She had offered to help
with the evening's cooking, but although the judge
had seemed inclined to let her help, Newt had insisted on cooking himself. The beans ended up hard
and undercooked. Manhunters, maybe, but poor
cooks, certainly.

Their day's ride had brought them to the Alvarez
hacienda on the banks of a shallow, narrow river, the
one the natives called the Rio de San Antonio. It was
a sprawling, flat-roofed adobe home with a red tile
roof and little patios and courtyard gardens walled off
throughout it. The walls extended higher than the

roof, and the gun loopholes left in the adobe bricks testified to a time when the place was as much a fortress as a home. Around it lay a score of outbuildings, barns, corrals, and small homes for the ranch's hired help. Cattle, horses, and a few sheep dotted the countryside, and a few irrigated farm fields lay along the river. Alvarez was obviously a very wealthy man.

Kizzy had hoped they would stay the night at the hacienda. The wagon horse she rode was never meant for riding and had a rough stride to him, especially at a trot. Her backside ached and the insides of her thighs were raw and stinging. It had been long since she had ridden so far, and even longer since she had ridden astride and without a sidesaddle.

But there were still two hours of daylight left, and Newt moved them on after he and the judge had a little talk with one of Don Alvarez's hired men they came across pulling weeds out of a vegetable garden in front of the main house. From him, they learned that Cortina and Alvarez's daughter had headed west along the river. What's more, there were three more men with Cortina.

Newt was anxious to be on Cortina's trail and had pushed them hard along a narrow trail that followed the river. There were occasional thickets, but the country began to open up into brown scrublands, dotted with cactus and other spiny low brush. You could see for miles and miles, and a set of high mountains loomed up to the west. They had made camp an hour after nightfall.

Somewhere in the night, she must have nodded off for a second. Newt was still awake, sitting on his saddle and staring at their little campfire. Curled up at his feet asleep was her dog. Maybe she had done more than nod off for a wink or two, for she hadn't noticed Vlad leave her. The white dog normally stayed close to her when around strangers, and it shocked her greatly to see him so contented with the big man, and in truth it hurt her feelings a little bit.

"I think Vlad likes you," she said when she could no longer take staring into the campfire flames without falling asleep again, and saying something was the only way to stay awake.

Newt reached down and touched the sleeping dog's broad head and ruffled the thick hair on its neck. "Dogs always like me. What kind is he? I've never seen his like."

"I don't know what you would call his kind, or how to translate it. But my grandfather's grandfather brought them from the Carpathian Mountains in Romania," she said. "And each succeeding generation of my father's line has bred them."

"What's he good for, besides accosting travelers and their horses?" the judge asked.

Kizzy had thought the judge was asleep, for his eyes were closed and his hat tipped down over his face to shield it from the heat of the fire.

"They are herding dogs, sometimes, and others are used to hunt or for protection," she said.

"Half bear and half alligator," the judge said. "Doesn't surprise me that he likes the Widowmaker there."

"Widowmaker?" Kizzy looked to Newt and then back to the judge, trying to catch what was meant.

"Don't mind the judge," Newt said.

"If you want my opinion, we ought to send this Gypsy girl and her attack dog back the way they came," the judge said. "We've already got enough trouble."

"I didn't ask for your opinion," Newt replied.

"You're as rude as that dog. No wonder you two get along." The judge grunted and shifted his boots away from the fire. "And you'd best remember that you're in my custody and at the whim of my goodwill."

"I must get our horses back." Kizzy noticed the tension between the two men and sought to change the course of the discussion.

"You could get you some new horses," Newt said without looking at her. "No horse, not even six of them, is worth getting killed over."

"And where would I find six more white horses, perfectly matched? And what about the time it would take to train them?" She shook her head and fought off the urge to pull her own hair and kick and scream like a little girl. "Our show is gone without those horses."

"Think up a new act," said the judge, shoving his hat back on his head to reveal his face and leaning back against the saddle he was using as a backrest, both hands clasped on his bellyful of beans.

"It's not only the act. Those horses are family to us, but you wouldn't understand."

"Speaking of horses, you'd best stake that horse out where he can graze a little," Newt said. "He won't last long if you don't take care of him."

Kizzy had eaten her meal holding her unsaddled horse by a lead rope, and it still stood close behind her. She wanted to let it graze, but feared that they would take it from her while she slept and leave her behind.

"I don't know what I'll do if we don't get our horses back. I don't know what Fonzo will do. They're everything to him," she said. "I can't quit thinking about them being mistreated or one of them harmed."

Newt and the judge glanced at each other with odd expressions on their faces and a hint of something she couldn't guess at.

"A man that will hurt a horse is pretty low-down," the judge finally said, and then cleared his throat. He and Newt shared that same look again.

"I would think you would be more worried about your brother," Newt said.

"That, most of all, but Fonzo will be set free if you find Cortina, and we might regain our horses in the same stroke."

"Best we get to sleep. I intend to be riding early," Newt said as he rolled himself in his blankets.

"Do you still intend to take this girl with us?" the judge asked. "I say we hash this out. What kind of man takes a woman when he's out after outlaws?"

"I'm not taking her anywhere, nor will I be responsible for her." Newt lay down on his side with his back to the judge. "If she comes along it will be her own choice."

"What if something happens to her?"

Newt rolled over enough that he could look at the judge over one shoulder. "Go ahead, stop her. I don't think she'll go back without shooting her."

The judge hissed and mumbled something that sounded like he was cursing again. He was going to say more, but Newt was apparently asleep or feigning it. Within a few minutes, Kizzy could tell by his breathing that he was really asleep. She badly wanted to give in to weariness herself, but waited another long while until the judge was snoring before untying her single blanket from behind the cantle of her saddle.

She added another length of rope to her horse's lead rope to give it a little more room to pick for grass, but she kept it clenched in her fist. One of her pistols was clenched in her other fist. If they thought they would wake up early, take her horse, and leave her behind, they were going to be in for a surprise.

Cortina's tracks were covered and all but obliterated by the numerous hoofprints of the vaqueros Don Alvarez had sent after him. However, all Newt and his party had to do was follow the vaqueros' sign, knowing that it would lead them in the direction Cortina had taken, at least until the point the posse had lost the trail and turned back. They found that quitting point barely an hour into the next morning.

Newt and the judge pulled up their horses and looked the torn ground over. Even Kizzy's untrained eye could tell that the vaqueros had stopped there, and that their horses had been milling and stomping around. The ground was chewed and churned, as if there had been some kind of confusion.

The judge rode a circle around the location, dismounted once, and came riding back with something in his hand. He pitched a brass shell casing to Newt, and then a couple more.

"Those vaqueros didn't turn back because they lost Cortina's trail," the judge said.

Newt studied the tip of a narrow mountain reaching down toward the river. "Are you thinking Cortina and his boys took a stand up there?"

"I am."

"I wouldn't have thought those vaqueros would quit so easy. They had Cortina outnumbered."

"When lead starts flying, a lot of men suddenly decide there's a lot of better places to be," the judge said. "They probably told Alvarez that they lost the trail to stay out of trouble with him."

"You don't think Cortina is still up there?" Newt pointed at the ridge.

"No, he would have already shot us if he was."

"You're a great comfort."

"Worrying about where he might be waiting for you is how he wants you to think. Taking to this broken country and laying up for a potshot every now and then slows down any pursuit, and gets us stopping and worrying over every point he could ambush us," the judge said. "But, no, he's moved on long ago. There's no water up there, and he'll be looking to put all the distance he can between Don Alvarez's vaqueros and himself."

They rode upriver cautiously, with Newt riding fifty yards ahead, and Kizzy in the rear. They took a detour up the ridge and found where Cortina and his men had taken their stand and fired upon the vaqueros. Amid the tracks and horse droppings they found more shell casings. Looking down from the ridge, it had been no more than a two-hundred-yard shot to the river, and from the amount of empty brass they found, Cortina and his outlaws had really made it hot for the vaqueros.

Newt led them back to the river. They rode for another hour, and the river became nothing more than a few stagnant pools and then only a dry streambed. High, treeless, knife-edged mountains rose up unlike any Newt or Kizzy had ever seen. Some of them ran in odd curved shapes and others ran parallel to the next in an almost wavelike fashion, one after another, with narrow, steep canyons between them. At times, the trail slipped between those mountains, winding through them like navigating a maze or a labyrinth.

The judge said those mountains were the eastern-most portion of the Sierra Madres, or what some called the Sierra Madre Oriental. Twice they lost the bandit's trail in the southern fringes of those mountains, but found it again where Cortina and his men had cut back to the trail to La Babia. The third time they lost it both Newt and the judge were stumped and couldn't find it again.

"We'll wait here while you see if you can scare up some sign," Newt said.

The judge scoffed. "I'm no tracker and never claimed to be. I was counting on catching Cortina at the Alvarez hacienda. Never figured on it going farther than that."

Newt scanned around them in every direction. "You don't think he doubled back on us, do you?"

"No, Don Alvarez will have men to the east watching the Rio Grande crossings from Ciudad Acuña to Laredo. Water is easier to find to the south, but Alvarez has a lot of influence and family around Monclova, so I don't think Cortina will go that way."

"What's that leave Cortina?"

"I wish we had an Indian tracker," the judge said. "I'm reminded of a Mescalero tracker I saw work once. That Injun could see a week-old set of hoof tracks and tell you what the rider weighed, what color his skin was, and what he had for breakfast."

"Well, we don't have any Indian tracker," Newt said. "And I'd just as soon as not run into any Apaches. What I'd like to know is how we're going to keep on Cortina's tail."

"Man tracking ain't so much about reading sign," the judge observed. "A man that spends all his time trying to follow tracks is going to get way behind in a hurry. Even if we were trackers, Cortina can ride a lot faster than anyone can track."

"What are you saying?"

"I'm saying that a good hunter guesses where his quarry is going and heads that way, using the sign occasionally as a way to make sure he's guessed right," the judge said. "In dry country you can bet a man will head for the next watering hole, or in mountain country he'll be limited to certain passes or picking places that aren't too rough to ride over."

"That stands to reason."

"Okay, you two man trackers," Kizzy said from the side. "Cortina is getting farther away while you sit there and argue and philosophize over techniques."

"Mind your tongue, girl," the judge said. "This is a man's business."

"Where do you think he's headed?" Newt asked. "Best guess."

The judge thought on it for a bit. "I'd say he's headed for the pass at La Babia. He'll water at the spring and then cut through the mountains there."

"And then what?"

"That desert country to the west of the mountains is a long, dry stretch, and I think he'll turn north and skirt the west side of the mountains and head for the crossing at Las Boquillas."

"Why would he head back to Texas?"

"It's been my experience that these border outlaws will work one side of the line until things get hot, and then they'll drift across to the other side, hoping that whatever they did there in the past has had time to cool off. There's a lot of wide-open country to the west of these mountains, and I'm thinking Cortina will like staying in the roughs where he's got more cover."

"He's got that girl with him, and he might not be able to keep up the pace to outrun any posse that caught him in open country."

"Now you're thinking. You might make a manhunter, after all."

"How far to this La Babia?"

"We'll be there a little before dark, if we ride hard."

"Look here," Kizzy said. "We haven't lost their trail at all."

The men looked to her and saw that she was holding a few white mane or tail hairs in her hand. A few others were hanging from some kind of spiny bush one of the bandits' horses had rubbed against.

"They still have my horses," she said.

She was even smiling a little bit, and Newt didn't have the heart to tell her that she was never going to get one of those white horses back. A pair of low-down specimens claiming to be lawmen had already killed it with a buffalo gun.

He pointed them west without another word, leaving discussions of the chances of recovering all six of her horses to the judge. The judge was good at making up stories, although he might not tell them the same way twice.

# Chapter Twenty-six

La Babia, like other such presidios scattered over northern Mexico, had been built back in the days when Spain still ruled the country and was trying to make war on the Apaches and other tribes thwarting attempts to colonize northern Mexico. The old fort was all but in ruins, but although weathered and fallen in some places, many of the stacked rock and adobe brick walls still stood. On the west end overlooking the mountain valley stood one remaining bastion. It was a round stone tower some twenty or thirty feet high with a parapet on top of it. There were crenels, or notches, cut in the parapet walls for shooting through.

The sun was still above the mountains when they reached La Babia. The trail climbed steadily but gradually upward through a narrow pass in the high mountains. They came through a small grove of pine timber at the narrowest point of the pass, and the trail dropped gently into a small valley. It was a pretty valley with enormous bald mountains walling it to the north, and a somewhat smaller mountain dark with pine timber near its top to the south.

The presidio lay close to the pass with a small grove of scattered trees around it, and the ground nearby it was more lush and green than the valley below it to the west. Newt could see what looked like a narrow stream of water following a broad wash that began where the old fort stood at the mouth of the pass. That green contrasted greatly with the rest of the valley, and he assumed the pass and that water were why the fort was where it was.

Anyone on the remaining walls of that fort could see for miles and was likely to spot them coming out of the pass. Newt led them up the side of the bald mountain on the north side of the valley, and they dismounted in an eroded fold in the mountain at the foot of a sheer bluff of pale rock rising hundreds of feet over them. They left the horses hidden and climbed up into the scattered boulders and other debris fallen from the bluff over the years.

From their position on the side of a mountain a quarter of a mile from the fort, Newt could barely make out what looked like a man standing watch on top of the remaining watchtower. He also spotted the trickle of smoke rising from the fort.

"That's La Babia." The judge nodded his head downhill at the ruins of the fort.

"What does La Babia mean?" Kizzy asked from behind them.

"Means having your head up in the clouds, kind of dreamy like."

"Fitting, I'd say." Newt glanced at the smoky white clouds wisping against the mountaintops like the tickle of a feather.

"There's nothing dreamy about that campfire smoke," the judge said. "Down there is the reality of the matter."

"You think that's Cortina's smoke?" Newt asked.

The judge had the better eyesight, and he studied the presidio awhile longer before he answered. "Could be any kind of traveler coming through the pass, but we've got to treat it like it's Cortina. Once or twice I thought I caught something else moving down there through the breaks in those walls. Could be horses."

Kizzy's study of the presidio was as intense as theirs was, but apparently her young eyes were also no match for the judge's. "Those horses you see, are they white?"

"I keep seeing white flashes. Could be your horses, or maybe a gray. Could be an albino goat or a snow-covered pig, for that matter."

Kizzy gave the judge a dirty look, but the judge didn't seem to notice.

Newt pointed to the charred remains of a couple of buildings and what looked like a set of corrals close by the fort. "Looks like somebody had a homestead there not too long ago."

"Some American ranchers bought them a land grant down here a few years back, and that was the La Babia headquarters," the judge said. "Was until the Apaches burnt them out last year. I was assuming they had rebuilt by now, and that we might find shelter there for the night."

"Are you thinking that's Apaches down there now?"

"No, if it was Apaches they would have already spotted us and lifted our hair by now."

"How do you want to play it?"

"We could ride down there and knock on the door and say, 'Howdy do, Mr. Cortina. Would you kindly let us haul your ass to Texas and hang you?'" the judge said. "'Oh, and pardon me, Mr. Cortina, you low-life, stealing bastard, but we promised Don Alvarez we would cut off your head for rooting his daughter.'"

Newt frowned at him and jerked his head at Kizzy behind them.

"Begging your pardon, ma'am," the judge said. "I forgot you were around or I would have watched my language."

"Do you see that creek bed behind the fort?" Newt asked the judge.

"I see it."

"What do you think Cortina would do if somebody shot down on him from up here?"

"He'd shoot back."

"And then what?"

A crafty smile spread across the judge's face. "He'll likely assume he's outnumbered and use that creek bed as cover to get the hell out of there."

"Exactly," Newt said. "And what if we were waiting on the creek banks?"

"Who's going to do the shooting to make them think we're all up here?"

Newt turned and looked at Kizzy.

"Oh no, you're not," she said. "You're not leaving me alone up here."

"You said you can shoot as good as any man," the judge said.

She looked uncertain as Newt went to his horse and brought back the Sharps buffalo gun and his sack of cartridges for it.

"I don't know if I can hit anything that far away," she said.

He gently shoved the rifle into her hands. "You don't have to hit anything. Just pepper the walls as best you can."

"And what are you going to do?"

"Me and the judge are going to Indian down the side of this mountain and get behind them. You wait until you see us in position before you start shooting."

"What if I can't see you?"

"Give us until that sun is right on top of that mountain at the end of the valley. That should be long enough."

"What's going to keep them from coming up here after me?"

"Shoot a lot and from different spots. Shoot every shell in that sack if you have to. We want them to think there's more than one of us. Might not hurt to fire off a few rounds from those pistols of yours."

"I might hit a horse, and there's Don Alvarez's daughter to think of."

"You will be able to see real good through that scope. Be careful where you shoot," he said. "Do you need me to show you how to operate that rifle?"

She shook her head. "I know how to shoot."

"Then find you a place to hunker down with cover in front of you. They're liable to pop off a few shots your way, so you want to keep your head down."

She glanced at the presidio in the distance, and Newt could tell she was nervous. And she had every right to be. He wasn't calm himself.

"And keep hold of that dog," the judge said. "We don't want him following us and ruining our setup."

Kizzy glanced at Vlad lying obediently beside her. "Are you going to kill them?"

Newt thought it was a hell of a question to ask after they had come so far after Cortina, but held that in. "We'll give him the chance to surrender if he'll listen."

The judge snickered. "The price for your brother's life is Cortina's head. There are no two ways about it. It's either him or your brother, so you let us tend to our work, or those rurales will put your brother against an adobe wall and shoot him dead."

"Go easy there, Judge," Newt said, and then turned to Kizzy. "Maybe I shouldn't ask you to do this, but you'll be all right. None of them are going to be able to hit anything with you this far off and high up, not if you keep low."

She nodded and held up the buffalo gun. "What if one of them has a gun like this?"

He started to turn away, but paused and looked over his shoulder. "Like I said, keep your head down."

Newt and the judge angled down the mountain, moving fast, but keeping to the cover of the scattered brush, rocks, and every ditch, draw, and eroded crease in the mountain on their way. She lost sight of them before long, and for the first time it really dawned on her that she was alone.

She went back to the horses and slid her rifle out of its saddle scabbard. It was an old iron-framed Henry, .44 rimfire, and had been her father's gun. While it lacked a lot in power, it made up for some of that by holding seventeen rounds stuffed in its tube magazine. She left the Henry lying on a rock behind a clump of brush and moved several yards away where there were two more large rocks on a little knob that offered a perfect vantage point of the pass below. She rested the forearm of the buffalo gun between a crack in the two rocks and waited. Vlad panted beside her. The sun seemed to take forever to settle on top of the mountain Newt had told her to watch. It was going to be a long wait.

# Chapter Twenty-seven

It took them longer to cover the distance to the creek bed than Newt expected. The terrain was rough, and the all-but-bare slope at the foot of the mountain slowed them, for they feared being spotted by the guard manning the watchtower. After a half hour of careful zigzagging and sometimes crawling on their bellies, both knees were torn out of Newt's pants legs and he was cut and scraped all over. To make matters worse, there were more cactus needles in one of his forearms than he had time to pick out.

The sun was already sinking low, and Kizzy wouldn't know they weren't yet in position and could start shooting any moment. He and the judge made a dash over a slide of rock and then trotted through the brush to the north bank of the streambed, only a hundred yards to the west of the fort. He was surprised that the judge had managed to keep up.

The creek channel was deepest near the fort, with its sides some five feet tall and covered somewhat by the brush on the ground above and several scattered trees. A narrow stream of water flowed down its rocky center.

The judge pointed with a shaking hand to the head of the wash where it ran close to the fort, and where lush water grass grew as if there were some kind of pool there. "That's where the spring's at."

"I'll take the far side," Newt said.

"I won't argue with you." The judge was breathing heavily through his mouth.

"Take care you don't shoot Alvarez's daughter," Newt said.

"There won't be any time to talk this over with them. You'd best remember that," the judge said. "Let them get close, then open up."

Newt slid down the slope to the bottom of the wash and trotted across it to the other side. The stream was shallow, but enough to get his boots soaking wet. He climbed the far bank and bellied down with his pistol out and pointed toward the fort. After a while, he crawled to a better vantage point and could make out the flicker of a campfire through a break in the walls.

If he were Cortina under heavy fire, he would slip out the back of that fort and ride down the creek bed, going slow until the wash grew shallow and the cover of the trees played out. Then he would run like hell, already putting himself out of easy distance for a rifle shot. Cortina ought to come within a few yards of him and the judge. That was, if things worked out exactly as planned, which in Newt's experience, they never did.

The setting sun was turning the whole pass a weird orange, and a thundercloud the color of a purple bruise was sifting over the mountains far to the west. Newt wiped the sweat from his forehead and waited.

Although he was expecting it, Newt flinched when Kizzy's first shot came from the side of the mountain.

Kizzy had been a performer for most of her life, but never had she been so nervous when it came her time to step up and play her part. She had never regained sight of Newt and the judge, and all she could go on was the location of the setting sun as she had been instructed. She sat with her knees bent and her legs crossed Indian style, and pressed the butt stock of the buffalo gun up against her shoulder. The gun was too large for her, but she managed to crawl her cheek far enough forward on the stock to bring the scope into focus. She cocked the hammer and could see the scope's crosshairs rising and falling with every beat of her heart.

She thought she had been mad enough to kill when Cortina stole the horses and tried to kill her brother, and had sworn all kinds of oaths of revenge. However, she found herself reluctant. It was an entirely different thing to be holding a loaded gun pointed at your enemy.

And she couldn't quit thinking about the off chance she might accidentally hit Don Alvarez's daughter or one of her horses—any horse, for that matter. All she had to do was make the outlaws believe that a whole posse was up on the mountainside, and no more than that. She was no killer, and wouldn't be when it was said and done. All she wanted were her horses back and to see Fonzo freed from jail. Then the two of them would leave Mexico far behind and never look back.

At the same time she was thinking such thoughts,

she knew that no matter what Newt and the judge said about giving Cortina a chance to surrender, they were going to do nothing of the kind. They were going to wait until he and his gang came out of the back of that fort and gun them down at point-blank range. It didn't matter that she wasn't going to be pulling the trigger on them. She was helping arrange it.

How had it come to that? It was as if what had happened to her father was a sign of the misfortune to come and marked the point where their lives would never be the same again.

She closed her eyes and thought of Fonzo beaten and suffering in the squalor of his jail cell. Don Alvarez wanted Cortina in exchange for Fonzo's life. There was no one left who cared for him besides her. She had to be strong. How had the judge put it? What was the life or the head of one outlaw versus her brother's? But no matter how many ways she worked it, she found no peace.

She could see the guard on the bastion clearly in her scope, and lowered the fine crosshairs until they pointed at a spot on the tower wall two feet below him. Other than some odd ricochet, her bullet ought to have no chance of hitting the girl down there or one of the horses.

She let out half a breath and squeezed the trigger. The recoil of the gun drove her back so that she barely saw where her bullet kicked dust at the bottom of the tower barely above the ground. The guard hunkered down at the shot, but she could see him aiming his rifle out of one of the gun ports. She ignored her aching shoulder and her bruised cheekbone and worked the Sharps's lever to drop the breech block and eject the spent cartridge. She thumbed a fresh shell into the chamber, slammed the breech home, and peered down the scope once more while she eared back the hammer for another go.

She aimed higher the next time, with more of an idea how much the bullet dropped at that great distance. She was pleased to see her second shot strike the tower only a foot below the crouching sentinel. Other men were shouting from inside the fort ruins, and she saw a puff of gun smoke from somewhere behind the dilapidated walls. The shot came nowhere near her.

Setting the Sharps aside, she drew both her pistols and began to fire them straight up at the sky, alternating one and then the other. She shot until both pistols were empty and then scrambled on her hands and knees toward where she had left the Henry. More gunshots were aimed her way, many in fact, but only a couple of them came close enough for her to see or hear the bullet strikes. None of them were close calls, but they terrified her nonetheless.

Vlad wasn't with her anymore, and she had no clue where the dog had gone. He was well used to gunfire from his time with their traveling show and her continual pistol practice.

She tore her attention away from thoughts of her missing dog and lay down on her belly and aimed the Henry down the mountain, picking a chunk of broken wall as her target. It took her three shots to find the proper sight elevation to take, but she finally got close enough to kick up dust in the general vicinity. She worked the lever on the Henry as fast as she could, picking random targets.

Several tiny clouds of gun smoke puffed up at different locations along the fort's near wall, and one of those shots hit the rocks below her with an angry whine at the same moment she fired off the Henry's last round. She took the empty gun with her and crawled back to the buffalo gun, intending to make use of it again.

The gunfire from the fort had all but ceased by the time she had reloaded the Sharps. She scanned the building with the rifle scope. At only one point was the yard within the walls visible, and she could see what looked like jacales, or little huts, standing inside and against the outer wall. While she watched, several men exited one of those low-roofed huts, leading their horses behind them. Her spirits lifted when she saw that three of those horses were as white as snow.

The outlaws mounted and disappeared from her view almost as quickly as they had appeared. It looked as if Cortina was going to run, exactly as Newt and the judge had predicted he would.

Kizzy leaned the Sharps up against a rock and began to reload her pistols while she watched the scene below. It was out of her hands now—as if it had ever really been in them in the first place.

# Chapter Twenty-eight

**N**ewt didn't have time to signal the judge that they were coming. There was a clatter of shod hooves on the rocks of the creek bed, and then two riders appeared not thirty yards away, walking their horses. Neither of them was Cortina, and neither of them rode a white horse—both were sitting on plain sorrels.

Both outlaws had guns at the ready and were keeping a sharp lookout for trouble, but most of their attention was on the north bank in the direction of the mountain where Kizzy had fired from. Newt recognized neither man, and debated on letting them pass and saving his attention for Cortina. Shooting at them or alerting them in any way to his presence would warn Cortina and likely cause the wily bandit leader to detour around the ambush. Newt could hear other horses entering the wash near the fort.

Something white flashed in the corner of Newt's eye and he dared a glance to the far side of the creek. The white thing was darting in and out of the grass and low brush, and it took a bit for it to register with him that what he was seeing was Kizzy's dog coming at a run. The dog leapt off the far bank with its tongue flopping out of one side of its mouth and appearing as happy as if he were chasing a rabbit.

The outlaw nearest the dog was as startled as Newt was by the dog's appearance, especially because it came flying from directly above him like a mountain lion leaping from a high ledge. Both of the bandits' horses shied wildly, scrambling and staggering over the rocks, and the one farthest from the dog bolted down the creek.

The bandit nearest to the dog managed a shot at it while he fought to get his horse under control. The shot was a clean miss, and instead of fleeing with the same speed with which it had arrived, the crazy dog began to circle the bandit's horse, barking loudly. The other bandit with the runaway horse was almost directly between the judge and Newt and at a dead run by then.

It was happening so fast that Newt had no time to think. While the remaining bandit was aiming for another shot at the dog, the judge rose up on the far bank and let go with both barrels of his shotgun—first one barrel for the bandit tormented by the dog, and then swinging the stubby coach gun as smoothly as a duck hunter risen from a blind and tracking his prey in flight. He fired the second at the back of the bandit on the runaway horse. It was point-blank range and the rider near the dog threw up his arms and fell off the back of his horse, dead before he hit the ground. The judge must have winged the other rider, for he reeled in the saddle but managed to stay there, charging away from the ambush site clutching his side.

The judge was cursing at the top of his lungs, lost in the heat of the fight, or perhaps because he was having trouble reloading his shotgun. He was a prime target when a third bandit came down the creek at a dead run with his pistol cracking. The white horse he rode had its ears pinned and its belly low to the ground like a racehorse on the homestretch, and water and sparks from its hooves on the stones flew up beneath it. The judge dropped quickly, and Newt couldn't tell if he was hit or if he had merely dived to the ground to take cover.

Newt took a steady hold on his Smith in both hands and touched it off. The Mexican badman was turned in the saddle, laying fire at the judge's position, and Newt's bullet took him under the left shoulder blade. The bandit tried to keep in his saddle by hauling on his reins, grasping and clawing at anything to stay mounted, but all that did was to jerk his horse's head around to one side and throw it end over end.

Like the judge, the heat of battle had gotten to Newt, and he stood for a better shot at the bandit in case he should rise from his fallen horse. The instant Newt stood and skylined himself, two more riders burst into view, both of them astride white horses. Newt recognized the spotted vest the bandit was wearing before he recognized Cortina's face.

Don Alvarez's daughter rode sidesaddle beside Cortina, and her red dress atop that white horse was so out of place amid the moment that it all seemed like a dream. She lashed her horse's hip with a braided riding quirt, matching Cortina's horse stride for stride.

Newt was quick to swing his gun, but maybe it was a fear of hitting the girl that made him hesitate his aim for a fraction of a second. That tiny moment of

deliberation was enough for Cortina to see him and
to get his own gun into action.

Before Newt could pull his own trigger again,
Cortina shot a chunk out of Newt's pistol holder, and
his second shot burned Newt's left ear. The next
thing Newt knew he was falling off the edge of the
creek bank, tumbling and rolling wildly until he hit
the bottom. He rose only in time to see Cortina and
the Alvarez girl fleeing down the creek with Cortina
hanging off one side of his horse like an Indian and
snapping shots in the judge's direction. The judge's
shotgun went off again, but the range was too great
for the cut-down weapon. Cortina and the girl were
soon out of range of any kind of marksmen, disappearing with Kizzy's barking dog giving chase at their
heels.

Newt found his pistol and staggered to the middle
of the creek where the bandit he had shot lay under
his fallen horse in the ankle-deep water. When Newt
got closer he saw that the bandit appeared dead, but
his death grip on one of his reins had the horse's
head and neck bent around and kept it from rising.

The judge slid down the other bank and broke the
shotgun open and shoved two more brass ten-gauge
shells down the pipes while he walked over to Newt.
Newt reached down and yanked the left rein out of
the dead man's grip. He toed the horse gently in the
shoulder, and the animal rose, shaking itself. Regard-
less of the crash, it seemed no worse for the wear.

"Did you hear old Gabriel blow his trumpet?" The
judge patted his shotgun affectionately. "It ain't only
walls that this here scattergun will bring tumbling
down. It ain't too bad for tumbling Mexican miscre-
ants, either."

"Cortina and the girl got away, and so did another one," Newt said.

"I peppered that first one pretty good. He ought to be leaking like a sieve," the judge said. "I doubt he'll make it too far."

"Cortina was who we wanted."

"And Cortina is who we'll get in time. If we had let those first two pass we would have had them at our backs when we tried to take Cortina."

Newt studied the fort and the gap in the wall where the bandits had poured forth from. "You think there's any more of them in there?"

"We won't know for sure until we wade in there and have a look around."

Newt led the dead bandit's white horse up the creek toward the break in the wall, half expecting someone to pop up out of the ruins and take a shot at him. The judge followed several steps back, whistling, and with the shotgun thrown over one shoulder, like he was returning home from an evening squirrel hunt.

Among the piles of stone and weathered timbers they found where the bandits had taken shelter in two jacales lining a solid section of the fort's walls. They searched each one of the mud-and-stick huts, but found nothing. Nor were there any bodies to be found in the rest of the ruins.

Newt located the stairs that led up to the bastion and made his way to the top. He scanned the valley to the west for signs of Cortina, but Kizzy, leading their horses, rode into the fort before he could spot his quarry.

The Gypsy girl leapt from her horse and ran to the white gelding Newt had left tied to a charred roof beam sticking out of a pile of adobe bricks and stone.

She hugged the horse around the neck like it was a long-lost friend, and pressed one teary cheek into its hide.

When she looked up at Newt there was a smile on her face. "It's Herod."

He nodded.

"Herod is my brother's favorite," she said.

"I'm glad we got him back," Newt said. "But Cortina got away."

She led the horse in a circle, examining it to see if it was sound. The horse didn't limp or seem injured, but it was noticeably thin and matted with dried sweat. Its belly on both sides was stained with dried blood where the bandit who had ridden him had worked it over cruelly with his spurs.

"Poor Herod," Kizzy said, examining the spur marks tenderly with the tips of her fingers.

"That polecat won't be spurring any more of your horses," the judge said. "Widowmaker up there put out his lights."

She considered what the judge had said and looked up at Newt again with a measuring glance. "That's twice I've heard him call you that."

He turned away from her and looked back to the valley. He soon spotted what he was looking for. Cortina and the girl had caught up to the wounded bandit the judge had maimed with his shotgun, and the three of them were raising a dust cloud so far off they were barely in sight.

Newt turned to the east, and after a moment's glance he said, "Judge, you and Miss Grey had better get mounted. We've got other company."

Instead of mounting, the judge clambered up the

steps to join Newt atop the tower. His twinkling old
eyes searched the narrow pass above the fort.

"How many of them do you make out?" Newt asked.

"Maybe ten of them."

"Are you thinking that's who I'm thinking it is?"

"That'll be Don Alvarez and those gun-toting cow
tenders of his."

"That's what I was afraid of." Newt measured the
distance to the notch in the mountains and guessed it
at no more than two miles.

"They must have been hanging back behind us the
whole time, and then heard the shooting and thought
we had Cortina cornered." The judge spat off the
tower and watched his spittle hit the ground below.

"What do we do?"

"I imagine they heard the shots and came at a pretty
good clip to see if they could get in on the action," the
judge said. "They're going to have some awful tired
horses."

"We run like hell?" Newt couldn't help but grin.

"You got it."

The judge hobbled down the steps as fast as he
could with Newt on his heels. Newt jerked the cinch
tight on the Circle Dot horse and then swung up on
his saddle without touching a stirrup. Kizzy was getting
on the black draft horse, intending to lead her white
horse on the end of a rope.

"Swap to that white horse," Newt said.

"Herod is in no shape to ride," she answered.

"That wagon horse of yours can't run fast enough
to matter, and it looks like we're about to have to do
some running."

She looked a question at him. "Why are we running?"

"Don Alvarez is coming."

"That's good news, isn't it?"

"I think he's got it in his mind that I had something to do with the death of his son."

"Did you?"

"This is the first time I've ever stepped foot in Mexico, but that doesn't matter to him. He wants to feel like he's avenged his son after all these years, and that horse I'm riding is the first lead he's had."

"But he has a deal with you," she said. "I spoke with him and he seemed a gentleman."

"A gentleman, sure, but he's a man that doesn't forget a thing. He's got too much pride, like his kind usually do."

"He'll see what you did to Cortina's gang, and that you are keeping your deal."

"There not much left of that gang but Cortina, and Alvarez won't need my services anymore. He's got more than enough men to run down Cortina."

"Then why did he make the deal with you in the first place?"

"One more party out after Cortina was going to increase his chances of catching him, or maybe he saw me and the judge as cannon fodder. I don't know."

"I still don't think he'll break his word."

"You stay here and keep thinking that. I'm going to ride."

Newt and the judge rode out of the fort at a trot. They didn't stop until they reached the two dead bandits. Newt was the first to dismount, and he knelt over the one the judge had shot and quickly searched his vest pockets.

The judge laughed. "You're learning. Might be something there we can make a few dollars off of."

Newt ignored the judge and ran over to the other dead bandit when he was finished with the first one.

"Aren't you going to at least take their guns? That's a good Winchester rifle laying beside that 'un."

As bad as Newt hated to admit it, the judge had a point. Kizzy had likely spent most of his ammunition for the buffalo rifle, and he was going to need another long gun. When he finished a fruitless search of the second bandit's pockets he took up the Winchester. It was a relatively new '76 express model in .45-75 caliber with a fancy case-hardened receiver, a half magazine, half-round and half-octagon barrel, and multi-leaf rear sights. The rifle looked like it should have belonged to some rich prince or big game hunter instead of a poor Mexican bandit. There was no telling who it was stolen from.

Newt unbuckled the cartridge bandolero that was slung across the dead bandit's chest and secured it in the same manner on his own person. He could feel the don's posse breathing down his neck, but he took one last precious moment to snatch the woven, striped serape poncho from the dead man. He hurriedly tied it behind his saddle cantle with his bedroll and swung back on his horse.

"Didn't find a lick of your gold, did you?" the judge asked. "I told you they were likely to have spent it already."

Newt didn't answer him. Kizzy rode up as he was mounting, and from the way she looked at him and the tight set to her mouth, he could tell she disapproved of his looting of the dead. He had no time to explain himself and spun his horse around and charged down the creek at a high lope with the judge and the Gypsy girl following close behind.

The purple storm cloud blew a gust of wind and dust across the valley. They found a good place to leave the creek bed and set out along the length of the valley, riding three abreast. Kizzy led the black draft horse behind her, and the judge was turned in the saddle with a watch on their back trail and his shotgun propped on one thigh.

"I hope those vaqueros aren't riding good horses," Newt called to the judge.

"Oh, everyone knows that Don Alvarez raises the finest horses in the state of Coahuila," the judge called back.

"Great." Newt kicked the Circle Dot horse to a run.

# Chapter Twenty-nine

They had followed a well-worn mule trail over a low mesa at the western end of the valley. The mountains went on and on to the north, as far as Newt could see. It was a rough, broken, desolate landscape, with numerous game trails and steep valleys offering possible byways to Texas if a man knew his way through them. They had picked up no sign of Cortina, and were traveling west only at the judge's say-so that the bandit would head for the road to the river crossing at Las Boquillas. Newt thought it as likely that Cortina might keep to the rough country to make his way to Texas, if that was where he was going at all. They were riding on nothing more than a hunch, and Newt had learned long before that hunches often weren't worth much.

Dark caught them on the western edge of the mountains and overlooking a vast lay of open desert and low mesas and hills to the west. Weary and hungry, and with their horses played out, they made camp on a flat not far off the road north to Las Boquillas. The same thunderclouds Newt had seen earlier must have passed over their campsite, for there were a few big mud puddles in the bottom of an arroyo. That stingy offering of moisture would soon sink into the sand, but it was enough to water their horses and to fill their coffeepot, even if they had to strain the water through the judge's neckerchief to make the coffee.

They kept the fire tiny, unsure if Cortina might be nearby, and because of the judge's continual talk about bloodthirsty Apache Indians being partial to raiding the area. Newt started to handle the cooking chores, but Kizzy shouldered him aside without asking. They were down to a double handful of beans, a few stale tortillas, and a small piece of skirt steak that had grown so dry that it looked more like jerky than steak.

"I'm sorry that we're not better supplied," Newt said.

Kizzy shrugged and smiled. "I assure you, I've eaten worse meals. Now, do you have any peppers to spice these beans up? I've found the trick to not having enough to eat is to make sure that the little bit you have tastes good."

Newt went to his saddlebags and brought her a little string of dried peppers that had been in the supplies Don Alvarez had equipped them with. He watched as she ground a couple of the peppers between two rocks.

"Maybe we can resupply at Las Boquillas," he said.

She shrugged again. "We'll make do."

"Nothing at Las Boquillas but a tiny peasant village," the judge said. "We'll be lucky to find anything but goat meat and frijoles, or burro meat if we aren't lucky."

"They eat burros?" Kizzy asked.

"Sure, haven't you ever ate one? Let me tell you

about one time when I was hauling freight on the Santa Fe Trail. We got caught in a blizzard, and hadn't had a bite to eat in days. There was this . . ."

Newt cut him off. "I assure you, Miss Grey, that's a story you don't want to hear."

The judge let out a big breath of air in a grumpy harrumph. He glanced at the white dog lying not far from where Kizzy was preparing their meal. The dog had appeared shortly before nightfall, footsore and limping.

"We could always eat the dog," the judge said.

The dog growled when it noticed the judge staring at it.

"I think you're only trying to get to me," Kizzy said. "Nobody would eat a fine dog like Vlad."

The dog growled again.

"Dog is tough eating anyway." The judge gave the dog a final glare and lay back with his hat over his eyes. "Let me know when the vittles are ready."

"All your talk of Indians has me thinking we ought to take turns standing watch tonight," Newt said.

"Good idea. You and the girl take the first two watches, and I'll stand guard after that," the judge said.

In a matter of minutes the judge was snoring.

"Is he really already asleep?" Kizzy asked.

"I wouldn't put it past him to play possum to get out of standing watch, but yes, I think he's really asleep," Newt said.

"Doesn't he ever use a blanket?"

"The judge is real careful about what he puts any effort into."

"You mean he's lazy?"

"I mean he's peculiar."

"In what way?"

"In every way, and most of them irritating. Seems like everything about this trip is peculiar."

"So why do you ride with him?"

Newt thought about that before he answered. "Man like me doesn't often get to be picky."

"Why does the judge sometimes call you the Widow-maker?" She sliced up the last of the skirt steak and dropped it into the bean pot.

"Think nothing of that. You should have seen by now that the judge is a little windy."

She took a seat on her saddle. "Are you some kind of outlaw? I heard the judge say something about you being in his custody."

"You ask a lot of questions."

"I'm too tired to sleep and need something to do to keep my mind off food until the beans finish cooking."

"I'm no outlaw. A hard case, maybe, but there are many a lot worse than me."

"I know the rurales wanted you for killing a man on the road to Zaragoza."

"The rurales were looking for you and your brother, too." He watched her carefully to see how she took that.

She nodded, and shoved the hat back off her head, letting it hang against her back by the braided rawhide chin string. Without the ridiculous hat, he was reminded how pretty she really was.

"I saw you beat that vaquero with your pistol," she said.

"That man got what was coming to him. You wrong someone, you can't expect it not to come back on you. I won't be wronged. You let people run over you and there's no end to it. There'll come a time when you aren't going anywhere except backing up. I don't back up for anyone."

"You don't have to call me Miss Grey. Kizzy will do fine."

"All right, Kizzy. Seems like I've been in one kind of a fight or another since I was big enough to walk."

"You've killed two men since I've known you, and Cortina will make three if you find him again."

Newt grimaced. "Cortina and his men tried to kill me some time back, and took everything I owned. They shot me down like a dog and left me to rot."

"So you intend to kill him, and that will make up for everything he did to you?"

"It's his head that will get your brother's fat out of the fire, so don't you high-and-mighty me." Newt had let the coffee in the bottom of his cup go cold, and he pitched it in the fire in frustration. Who was she to be questioning him? She was a chatterbox like the judge, and most talkers didn't understand that there aren't words for everything.

"I didn't mean to make you mad." She checked the beans and gave him an apologetic look when she sat back down on her saddle.

"I'm not mad."

"Tell me why they call you the Widowmaker."

"It's not much of a story."

"Tell me anyway."

"Are you always this nosy?"

"Pardon me, but the one thing I enjoy about traveling is hearing people's stories. I can never lay hand to enough good books, but I've found that the truth, as they say, is often stranger than fiction."

"We'd best eat and get some sleep. We're liable to have another hard pull in front of us tomorrow."

"The beans aren't done yet." She arched one eyebrow and played with the bracelets and bangles on her wrist while she awaited his next excuse.

Newt asked himself why he was talking to the girl about such things. His business was his business, and that was the way it had always been. True, she was uncommonly pretty, especially by the firelight, but he had been around pretty women before and wasn't such a fool to think a woman of her beauty would ever look twice at a man like him. He checked to make sure the judge was still asleep before he spoke again.

"I knocked around for a long time when I first came west. I was laying track and swinging a sledgehammer for the Katy railroad through Indian Territory up north of Texas. I was the only one on the crew that wasn't an Irishman, and those Irish boys surely liked to fight." A slight smile came to Newt's mouth, but faded as quickly as it had appeared. "I got in a fight with one of them on the railbed. You know, it was hot and things weren't going well. Tempers got the best of everyone. I was the outsider, and a kid to boot, and they thought I was easy pickings. Kid or not, I was holding my own against that fellow until a couple of his friends decided to lend him a hand."

"You whipped them all?"

"No, not even close, but I made a good enough showing that they left me alone after that. And the crew boss saw the fight and came to me the next day and asked to look at my fists. He'd been a boxer back in New York City, and said I had the makings to be a prizefighter if I wanted to learn how to really fight. I spent every evening for a few months with that man schooling me. I'd fought some back in the hills where I come from and thought I knew a thing or two about fighting, but that man could make me look foolish without even breaking a sweat."

"So you turned prizefighter?"

"Not right off. The man that was training me was run over by a wagon loaded with railroad ties and killed. I went on west and did one odd job after another. Wasn't long before I took the gold fever like every other fool, and if you've ever been in one of those mining camps you know how rough they can be. Those miners liked to see a good bare-knuckle match on the holidays. I never did have a nose for picking a good claim, but I found I could make a few dollars if I was willing to step into the ring. I never fought in any kind of big match, not then. Just little rough-and-tumble bouts against other amateurs or local tough men."

"So that's where you got the name?"

"No, word got around that I wasn't afraid to fight, and before long I got other offers. You know, mine guard and such. Most times there wasn't anything to do but stand around and look mean while the big bosses told their men how things were going to be, and it was a lot easier work than busting my back in some mine shaft or freezing my feet off in some cold stream bent over a gold pan.

"I was working as a mine and payroll guard in Shakespeare up in the New Mexico Territory. It was a company town, and they ran a tight operation. You know, paid cheap wages and shook down their miners after every shift to make sure they weren't high-grading. Come payroll days at the company store most of the miners ended up owing the company money instead of having any pay left over. That didn't set well when those men saw all the ore coming out of the mines. Some that spoke up got on the wrong side of the company and were roughed up a little. The word came to me one night that the miners were down at one of the saloons putting a load on and working themselves up to a riot. Half the boys hired to handle such trouble were gone on the trail guarding a silver shipment, and that left only a handful of us to handle things in camp.

"That mob finally drank enough courage and came down the street on the warpath. It got ugly real quick. Every man jack of them was packing lengths of chain, clubs, hammers, knives, and anything else they could lay hand to. Some of the big talkers among them had them worked up to a frenzy over how the company was mistreating them, and they came down the street fifty men strong, toting torches and swearing they were going to burn the company office and kill anyone that stood in their way."

"And what did you do?" Kizzy asked.

"I had my men go inside the store and grab them each a brand-new pick handle, and then we went out on the street and waited for that mob. Like I said, that bunch was crazy drunk and slobbering mad, but I could see the main fellow egging them on was right up front. I knew him from other places, and he was always one to talk big and stir things up. By then, they were throwing bottles and rocks at us and shouting all kinds of threats, and I knew if we let things go any further there was going to be no stopping them. That's how I got my name."

"How? I don't understand."

"It wasn't much. Nothing worth the name."

"What did you do?"

"I walked right up to that one stirring them up and

put a pick handle upside his head. Then I hit the next one foolish enough to open his mouth. After that, they decided none of their complaints was worth all the trouble."

"You must be a brave man."

"No, I was young and foolish and bad to drink. The liquor always made me mean, and I hadn't figured out that the fifty dollars a month I was being paid wasn't worth one bit of it."

"So they gave you the name after that?"

"The rest of the company guards showed up right after the riot, and they dragged me inside the nearest bar to celebrate. Sometime during the night, a big Welshman I worked with stood up on a table with his beer sloshing all over him and shouted that name at me. I thought at the time that it wouldn't stick, but it did. I was a known man wherever I went, and it got worse as time went on and I fought boxing matches with some professional sorts brought into the camps to entertain the labor." Newt paused over that last word. "Labor. That's what those companies called us. Nothing but gristle and muscle and bone to use up and throw away, as long as the ore kept coming."

"My father boxed some when he was younger, back in England," she said.

"Then maybe he would understand what I'm telling you. I never had anything to work with but my two good fists. A man gets hungry enough, and he'll do about anything to feed himself. And now look at me with nothing to my name but a dead man's horse and a dead man's gun."

"People don't have to stay the same. My papa said that we write our own stories."

"No one gets to write their own stories."

"We can all change."

"It wasn't too long ago that I was thinking the same thing. I thought I might go back East and set myself up in a carriage shop."

"And who's to say you can't?"

"I know it wouldn't be easy, especially not at first. I thought I might build a place with quarters in the back, and stay there until I got the shop on its feet."

"And then what?"

He shrugged and looked down at the ground. "You know, maybe build a house and live like an honest citizen. Can you imagine a bruiser like me living like that, with the regular folks passing me on the way to church and tipping their hats and saying 'Good morning, Mr. Jones. Fine day, isn't it?'"

"Sounds like a fine dream to me. What kind of house would you build?"

"Nothing fancy, but neat and trim, you know. My ma was always partial to flowers, even though we laughed at how she fretted over them. Might be I could plant some of my own flowers. I close my eyes and sometimes I can still smell those flowers of hers."

She turned her back to him and took the bean pot off the fire.

"You're laughing at me, aren't you?" he asked.

She didn't answer immediately, but finally spoke. "No, I'm not laughing. We had a real house once, but Papa gave it up and we went back on the road full-time. It didn't bother Mama that much. She had the wandering heart more than Papa did."

"What happened to your folks?"

"Mama took ill in Louisiana. Some kind of fever. The doctors never could tell us exactly what it was, but we lost her three days later. Papa never was the same after that."

"And your papa?"

"Fonzo shouldn't have told you."

"You don't have to say."

"They hung Papa. Hung him like a common thief."

"Who hung him?"

"We did a show in Austin and camped on the roadside on our way to San Antonio. A group of men rode up in the night and dragged us from our wagon." She wiped at one eye with the back of her hand. "Somebody back in Austin had stolen a horse, and they thought Papa did it, even though we didn't have the horse."

Newt had seen more than one lynch mob, and he could easily imagine the scene. The ugliness and terror were written plain on her face as she relived it.

"They were all drunk. Papa tried to reason with them, but they wouldn't listen. All they kept saying was that the no-good thieving Gypsies were going to learn to stay out of their county. They held us while they put Papa on a horse and led him under a high tree limb. Fonzo fought them, but they only laughed and knocked him down. I told him to look away when they hung Papa, but he wouldn't."

"I'm sorry for your loss."

"They left Papa hanging. We cut him down and loaded him in the wagon. Didn't bury him until we crossed the river into Mexico. I wasn't about to bury him in Texas."

"You didn't go to the law?"

"Who's going to listen to a Gypsy? I saw how they treated my Papa, and him a gentle man who never hurt anyone. I never thought such cruel men existed, and we came to Mexico thinking things might be different."

"And they weren't, were they?"

"Not one bit."

"I . . ."

"I know you mean well, but there's nothing you can say. This whole country is filled with nothing but callous, coldhearted ruffians."

"Like me?"

"I'm sorry. I didn't mean to . . ."

"No offense taken."

"What about your parents?" She wiped at her eyes again and tried to take on a happy face.

"They're both gone. Pa went before I came west, and I got a letter two years back that said Ma had passed away."

"Any other family?"

"One brother, but I haven't seen him in years. He and I never saw eye to eye on anything. My sister married a missionary and the two of them moved off to Nicaragua, or some such jungle place. Last I heard from her was when she wrote me the letter about Ma."

"Do you miss your family?" she asked.

"Some. We had hard times, but lots of good times, too."

"Fonzo is all I have left, and those horses are all we have left of Papa."

An awkward silence settled between them. Newt tried to catch hold of something he could say, but by the time something witty came to him the judge interrupted his intentions.

"Are those beans ready?" The judge lifted his hat off

his face. "I'm nigh to famished, and all this courting talk is keeping me from my rest."

Newt stood and walked off into the dark to check the horses.

"Touchy, ain't he?" The judge propped himself up on one elbow and looked at Kizzy. "Don't you be getting any fool ideas about that fellow yonder. I've seen his kind before."

"I was only talking to him," Kizzy said.

"You listen close and you'll hear him out there—the sound of that pistol of his pulling out of leather and him practicing with it over and over. Maybe he means well and talks well sometimes, but you notice the way his eyes change when you mention Cortina. They don't call him the Widowmaker for nothing. He's mad-dog mean."

Kizzy spooned some beans on a plate and set them on Newt's saddle for him when he came back. She put some on a second plate and walked over to the judge. He rose to a sitting position and brushed a hand through his whiskers and smacked his lips expectantly.

"Be a good girl and fetch me that canteen, if you don't mind." The judge held out his hands for the plate of beans.

She turned and dropped the plate on the ground in front of the dog. The judge leaned forward, intending to snatch the plate up, but the dog was already standing over it and growling.

"Why, you no-good, spiteful varmint." The judge scooted back to his former position and glared at the dog while it ate his supper. "I swear I'm going to kill that mutt if you don't keep him away from me."

Kizzy bent over the pot and scooped out the last of the beans for herself. She sat down on her saddle and took the first mouthful while she stared into the dark and listened for the sound of Newt out there with the horses.

After a while, she looked to the dog, who was licking up the last of the judge's beans. "Good Vlad. Good boy."

# Chapter Thirty

**B**reakfast consisted of nothing but hot coffee, and Newt waited while the judge nursed a third cup and squinted up at the stars overhead. It was still two hours before sunup, but Newt already had his horse saddled. He wished the judge would hurry up. Don Alvarez was probably already gaining on them, and the night's conversation with Kizzy had him feeling awkward in her presence. She glanced his way several times, but he looked away or found something to busy himself with.

She stood beside her white horse, adjusting the cinch on her saddle. She had swapped the dead bandit's saddle to the black draft horse, and they had lashed their bedrolls and other equipment to it to lighten the load on their saddle horses.

Finally, she could find nothing else to busy herself with and needed to say something, anything. "What were you looking for on those dead outlaws back at the presidio?"

Newt didn't answer.

"He was looking for his gold," the judge said. "Didn't

you know that the Widowmaker here is a mining tycoon?"

"I was looking for what Cortina stole from me," Newt said.

She reached into the bandit's saddlebags on the black, and held up a rusty tobacco can. "I found this in his saddlebags last night."

"What's in it?" the judge asked.

She pitched the can to Newt and he caught it and pried the lid off. Inside it was a white coffee sack. It seemed empty, but Newt could feel something at the bottom in one corner. He turned the sack up and dumped a little, crudely poured gold ingot into his palm. It was roughly two inches long and quarter that thick.

The judge leaned closer and peered at what Newt held. "So that's the fortune you've been after."

"There was more than this. A lot more." Newt put the little gold bar back in the sack.

"I wouldn't be ashamed," the judge said. "Why, there must be a hundred and fifty dollars in that sack. That's well worth riding down here into Mexico and risking your life."

"I had twenty of those ingots. Me and Yaqui Jim paid a man down at the stamp mill to pour them for us on the sly."

"Well, one of them is all you've got now. Better that than a sharp poke in the eye."

"Cortina could have the rest of them."

"Or he might have spent his share already."

"That's what I aim to find out." Newt poured out the last of the coffee and tied the empty pot to the black's saddle. Then he mounted the Circle Dot horse. "You coming?"

The judge swallowed his last drink and rubbed the inside of the cup clean with a handful of sand before going to his own horse. "Reckon I will."

Newt rode past Kizzy and looked her full in the face for the first time that morning. "Thank you."

They turned into the road to Las Boquillas before daylight, with Newt riding far in the lead and none of them talking. The judge waited for the sun to come up before he rode up beside Newt. Kizzy remained well behind them, leading the black draft horse and seemingly content to have some time to herself.

The judge looked behind him to make sure she was out of earshot before he whispered, "Don Alvarez might have already let those rurales have her brother."

"I know it," Newt said. "But she doesn't know that, and don't you bring it up."

"She thinks we're going to ride back to Zaragoza and hand over Cortina's head to get that boy out of the calaboose."

"I don't see any way around it."

"We ain't riding back there. My mother didn't raise any fools," the judge said with his voice rising a little too much. He lowered his voice to a whisper again. "You help me take Cortina alive, if we can, and get him back to Langtry, and I'll pay you a hundred dollars."

"Cortina is mine."

"You gave me your word, or I wouldn't have let you loose in the first place."

Newt glanced at the dog trotting alongside his horse and then turned to the judge. "Like you gave Don Alvarez your word that you would bring Cortina or his head back to him."

"Worst thing you could do is to go back there. He

wants your head, too," the judge said. "You keep on the straight and narrow with me and don't waste your time fretting over that Gypsy girl back there, nor her brother, either. Me and you had a deal first."

"I'll figure it out. Cortina is going to get what's coming to him, one way or another."

"I done had a hanging post put up. There's the principle of the matter to think on. Cortina's head down here doesn't do me any good. I want him hanging up in Langtry for everyone to see."

"It's been my experience that we don't always get what we want." Newt took his hat off, slapped it against his thigh to knock some of the dust off it, and wiped at the sweat on his brow before setting it back on his head. "I think you're kidding yourself if you think we could take Cortina alive."

"Try is all I'm asking."

"You're asking too much."

"You cross me, Widowmaker, and I won't forget."

"Get in line with the rest of them that want my hide and wait your turn."

Newt pulled his horse up. Somebody was coming down the road from the north raising a big cloud of dust. After a short wait he recognized it was a herd of sheep driven by a man and two stock dogs.

Kizzy called Vlad over and tied a rope to his collar and secured it to her saddle horn, fearing he would fight with the two strange dogs. Newt waited beside her while the judge went up the road and conversed with the sheepherder.

Newt and Kizzy bided their time and then swung wide of the bleating sheep. The judge met them in the road on the other side.

"That sheepman said he came from Las Boquillas

yesterday morning and hasn't seen anyone on the road between here and there," the judge said. "But he did say he heard horses passing east of him last night on the foot of that mountain yonder."

"Maybe the best thing we can do is to beat Cortina to Las Boquillas and wait for him, if you're positive that's where he's going," Newt said.

"Oh, he's headed back to Texas. You can bet your hat on it. Could be he intends to cross the river into Texas elsewhere, but he's headed north," the judge said. "A lot of the Rio Grande runs in a canyon hereabouts, but leave it to him to know where he can cross."

"The trouble is going to be finding his trail again."

The judge shook his head solemnly. "We won't have to track him. That sheepherder said that there's an old trail that goes to the east of those big mountains you can see there to the north. Said that trail goes to an old logging camp and then on to Las Boquillas the back way. Said there's nothing left of that place but an old church and some ruins, but there's plenty of water there."

The mountains to the north sat alone and separate from the other mountains to the east. In places they rose straight up for a thousand feet, and their tops were shrouded in dark green timber, in sharp contrast with the brown scrubland below. From a distance, the mountains looked more like an island floating in the sky.

They cleared the herd's dust, and the judge waved his hand in front of his face. "Damned Mexicans and their stinking sheep."

"You are a prejudiced man," Kizzy said.

"Prejudiced? Hell, I'm married to a Mexican woman."

"I didn't know you were married," Newt said.

The judge grunted and tried to look insulted. "What? A fine-looking man like me, and you think some pretty woman didn't latch on to me?"

"I didn't see a wife back in Langtry," Newt added.

"She lives in San Antonio. I ride up to see her once or twice a year, and the kids stay with me sometimes."

"That doesn't seem like much of a marriage," Kizzy said.

"We have a perfect marriage, as long as we keep plenty of distance between us."

Kizzy let her dog loose, and it loped out in front of them, scouring the brush for rabbits.

The judge watched the dog work and pointed at it after a time. "Did I ever tell you about an old coonhound I had when I was a boy that could count to five?"

Newt looked at Kizzy and shook his head. The two of them spurred forward, leaving the judge behind.

"Hold on there," the judge called out. "I haven't finished my story."

The trail the sheepman had spoken of was hard to miss, as it was cut deep with ruts from the two-wheeled Mexican carts that must have traveled it in some bygone day. Those ruts followed a winding route, climbing through a narrowing valley, crossing over low foothills, and diving off into deep, narrow canyons. The higher they climbed, the more the land changed. The scrubland turned to low ridges covered in grass and scattered oaks. Higher still, they rode through stretches of piñon pines and fir trees, and the terrain became rockier and more challenging.

Dogwoods and other trees not seen on the desert below grew in the shady canyons.

Twice they flushed mule deer in front of them, and a startled black bear sent rocks rolling as it fled across a mountainside above them. A lone eagle drifted on a thermal high above them for much of their ride, and high at the top of a dizzying tower of rocks Kizzy spied some kind of animals that the judge said were bighorn sheep.

"What do they call these mountains, Judge?" Newt asked while they were taking a break to let the horses blow on a particularly steep stretch of the trail.

"Maderas del Carmen," the judge answered.

"What does that mean?" Kizzy asked.

"Timber gardens, or some such like that."

The constant weariness and worry and all the hard miles behind them weren't enough to make any of them blind to the grandeur around them.

"It's a beautiful place," Kizzy said. "Like a Garden of Eden in the middle of the desert."

"Old Adam and Eve never rode such high country," the judge said.

An hour later they found the rurales, or what was left of them. The dog stopping in the trail and growling warned them of what lay ahead, and they soon saw the bodies lying in the grass and strewn along the trail on an open stretch of ridgeline. All of them looked to have died hard, and all of them were stripped and mutilated.

"There's your Garden of Eden," the judge said after riding through the bodies. "Apaches caught them unsuspecting coming over this ridgeline, easy as pie. That's the way Apaches like their ambushes. Easy, and no trouble for the killing."

Newt didn't stop his horse, not wanting Kizzy to look on the dead men any more than she had to. He had heard stories of what the Apaches did to their victims, but he couldn't have imagined it would be like that. All of the rurales were stripped, and most of them had been slashed and cut all over their naked bodies. Body parts were removed and cast aside, like some wicked child's playthings. He was a man with a strong stomach, but what he saw was hard to look upon.

Only one of the rurales' horses was left, and it was as dead as the men. The Indians had obviously taken the rest of the horses, along with the rurales' firearms and everything else of any use.

The judge rode a wide circle around the massacre site, leaning from the saddle and searching the ground for sign.

"What do you think?" Newt asked when the judge came back.

"Don't know how many of them there were. It's hard to tell with Apaches. They'll travel different trails in little bunches, or even in singles. Then they'll meet up someplace and raise hell and filter off in their little bunches again when they're through," the judge said. "I'd guess they hit the rurales sometime yesterday evening."

Newt recognized a couple of the dead men as those who had been in Zaragoza. "How did the rurales beat us here?"

"I imagine Don Alvarez sent them through the pass to patrol the road and to block Cortina to the west."

"Can't say I'm going to miss those rurales, but I wouldn't wish that back there on any man." Newt scanned the ridgeline ahead of them, and the mountainsides above them. "Those Apaches could be up there anywhere. I don't like the thought of riding into an ambush."

"No, it's not a pleasant thought. Damned Mescaleros keep leaving their reservation up in the New Mexico Territory and raiding down here until they've raised enough dickens to suit them. Then they go back to the reservation and act like good Injuns. Those Injun lovers in Washington ought to know that you can't tame an Apache, and thinking you can make farmers of them is pure foolishness."

"How far to this old church? What did you call it?"

The judge cleared his throat. "Saint something or other. They've got more saints down here than you can shake a stick at, and they all get to running together on me so that I can't keep them straight in my head. We should reach it about midday."

Newt looked at Kizzy. "Maybe you should turn back. The judge could ride with you back to the main road and take you to Las Boquillas."

"Like hell," the judge said.

Kizzy straightened in her saddle and stared straight ahead to avoid looking back at the dead men. "No, Indians or not, I'm going on with you."

"Those Apaches won't care that you're a woman," the judge said.

"There's no need to scare her," Newt said.

The judge jerked a thumb over his shoulder at the dead men behind them. "I think it's a little too late to worry about scaring her."

Newt checked his Winchester to make sure there was a cartridge in the chamber and then started his horse along the trail. "Miss Grey, you're putting me in a hard spot. No man that's any account would drag a woman along on a trip like this. If those Apaches hit us, it will be my fault if some harm comes to you. Same with Cortina if he starts shooting our way."

"You're not dragging me anywhere. I'm an adult, and it's my right to go where I please." She rode past him, intending to put an end to any more such conversation.

"Those Apaches might have already done for Cortina," the judge said. "Killing Mexicans is an Apache's favorite sport. Apaches hate Mexicans as bad as Mexicans hate Apaches."

At midday, the trail crossed a narrow stream pouring down from high on the mountainside, and they found the tracks of three horses at the water's edge. A little farther on the trail passed through a thin stand of pines. Their horses made little sound on the bed of pine needles blanketing the ground, and there was nothing but the creak of saddle leather when they pulled up at the edge of a high meadow with the ruins of the church on the far side. The church wasn't the multistoried, adobe affair with a bell tower that Newt had come to expect in Mexico, but instead, it was a low, rambling building of stacked stone. The only thing that testified to its being a church was the weathered wooden cross mounted on its roof above the front door.

The church and the rest of the abandoned logging town butted up against a sheer rock bluff made of enormous slabs of stone that rose high above the meadow. The same stream they had crossed earlier ran through the meadow, and near the church there were the ruins of other dwellings lining its banks.

They sat their horses in the edge of the timber, watching and debating on whether to ride out of the timber. There was no way to reach the church without crossing two hundred yards of open ground. Newt debated on leaving his horse and going on foot along the foot of the bluff, but the cover there was scant enough that he was still going to be easy picking for anyone on the lookout in that old church. The meadow extended well past the church, so there was no option to come at it from behind. There was no smoke rising from the church, or any other sign of habitation, but the thought of crossing that meadow wasn't a pleasant one.

"It could be that Cortina has already moved on, if he was ever here in the first place," Kizzy said.

The judge snorted. "And it could be that he's got a rifle propped in one of those church windows waiting for some unsuspecting soul to come riding into his sights."

"We could wait until nightfall," she added uncertainly.

Newt rode out of the timber, his rifle butt resting on his right thigh and the barrel pointed at the sky.

"What's he think he's doing?" the judge asked. "Sometimes he hasn't got enough good sense to pour piss out of a boot . . . Begging your pardon, ma'am."

"Why don't you go with him?" she asked.

"I believe I'll sit here and watch."

"Coward." Kizzy trotted forward until she caught up to Newt. When she looked back she was pleased to see the judge riding from the timber and taking a course paralleling their own several yards away.

They went across the meadow at a walk. A beaver dam had turned much of the middle of the meadow into a shallow pond, and Newt and Kizzy skirted the dam and splashed through the marshy ground, starting up the far side. The judge rode up the other side of the pond, with him and Newt occasionally catching each other's eyes. It was a slow, cautious ride, where every second each of them expected the worst.

They were within fifty yards of the church when Don Alvarez's daughter called out to them. Rather, she screamed at them. *"¡Deténgase! Para sus caballos! ¡Vete!"*

Newt stopped his horse behind the stone foundation and the collapsed log walls of a cabin. "What's she yelling about?"

"She said for us to leave." The judge had dismounted behind a stone fence and was peering over the top of it.

"Yeah, I kind of guessed that," Newt called back.

The woman inside was still shouting, and they could hear what sounded like crying between the things she shouted at them.

"I'm guessing they left her behind," the judge said.

Newt had been thinking the same thing. There wasn't a horse in sight, and if there was anyone else in the building, Cortina or the other bandit, they would have long since fired on them. He stepped off his horse, dropped a rein on the ground, and started for the church.

"You be careful," the judge said. "She might have a gun, and there's nothing worse than a crazy woman with a gun."

Newt stalked toward the church. The front door was barely hanging by one hinge and propped wide open. Through the dark eye of the open doorway and behind the shuttered windows the woman's voice became more frantic. He didn't have to speak Spanish to understand that she was threatening him and warning him not to come inside.

He paused to one side of the doorway, letting his

eyes adjust to the gloom inside. The dog went in first, and drew no fire. For once, he was glad that they had the dog along. When he stepped inside he held the Winchester at hip level, cocked and pointing the way.

There was nothing in the chapel but cobwebs and a single busted church pew that someone had scavenged partially for firewood. And his boot heels sounded loud on the stone floor as he crossed the room and headed for the closed door on his left. He could hear the judge come in the room behind him, and the cocking of his shotgun hammer.

Newt pushed gently against the closed door and found it locked or barred from the other side. It was made of flat-hewn pine logs as thick as a man's leg. He raised his foot and kicked into the door as hard as he could. Something creaked and cracked, and the door gave inward slightly. Two more kicks and the bar across the doorway on the inside splintered and snapped. The door swung slowly inward, revealing the tiny room on the far side. A soot-stained fireplace was in one corner, and Don Alvarez's daughter stood before it.

She was little more than a girl. No more than thirteen at the oldest, and her fancy dress was soiled and torn from hard travel and her face was streaked where tears had muddied the grime on her face. Her hair had come free from the silver comb tucked into it at the crown her head, and a loose black strand of it hung over her face. The hand that held the knife shook badly while she kept swiping that strand of hair out of her eyes. Girl child though she may have been, and cultured rich man's daughter or not, she cursed him as vilely as a border town prostitute.

"¡Váyanse, o me cortaré sus cojones!" she threatened.

"She says if you take one more step toward her, she's going to cut off your balls," the judge said from behind him.

"Put down the knife." Newt eased the hammer down on his Winchester and let the rifle hang from one hand, pointed at the floor. "We mean you no harm."

She spat something else at him, talking far more loudly than necessary for the tight confines of the room, and jabbing at the air between them with the knife. It was a small but wicked dagger, with a double edge and a needlepoint.

"Talk to her, Judge. Ask her where Cortina went."

"She's not making sense. Seems like she's a little high-strung and upset with her recent beau."

Newt moved sideways, leaving the judge in the doorway. Don Alvarez's daughter shifted the knife from one to another of them.

"Keep her talking, and I'll see if I can get that knife away from her," Newt said.

She immediately whirled on him, crouched like a cat, with the knife leveled on his gut.

"I think you ought to know that she speaks English," the judge said.

"Now you tell me."

Kizzy stepped into the room past the judge. "Put down the knife. Your father is coming soon, and he has trusted these men to find you."

The Alvarez girl spat her disdain while Kizzy stepped closer.

"Don't fool around with her," the judge said. "She'll cut you, sure as the world."

"Please," Kizzy said in a quiet voice, holding out her hand for the knife.

Newt took a step sideways, and the knife immediately shifted to him again. Kizzy sprang and grabbed the girl's wrist, and the two of them struggled for an instant. The Alvarez girl clawed at Kizzy and jerked her arm repetitively to free her knife hand. Before Newt could close, Kizzy drew back her right fist and punched the girl squarely on the nose.

The Alvarez girl crumpled to the floor, clutching her bleeding nose with both hands and staring up at Kizzy with tear-flooded eyes. Kizzy pitched the knife to Newt and squatted beside the girl with a hand placed gently on her shoulder.

"You go tend to the horses," she said to Newt. "Judge, you stay here in case I need you to translate. She's had a hard time, but I think she's settling down now."

Newt went past the judge, and the two of them shared a look.

"That Gypsy girl packs quite a punch for a little thing, don't she?" the judge observed. "Kind of reminds me of someone else I know, 'cept she's easier to look at."

# Chapter Thirty-one

The Alvarez girl sat on the fireplace hearth glaring at them. The silver hairpin she wore had come totally loose, and her long, black hair hung free and uncombed. Her pouting, sullen expression, bloody nose, and the filthy remains of her fancy dress made her seem more of a beggar orphan than a *grande*'s daughter. Kizzy studied her, trying to decide what possessed such a girl to run off with the likes of Javier Cortina. There was no telling some women's taste in men, but considering that Cortina had taken her horse and run off and left her, her devotion was surprising.

The girl's nose looked horrible, already swollen and with dried blood crusting over both nostrils. Kizzy felt a little bad for hitting the girl so hard, but only a little. While the girl had decided to act less hysterical than when they had first found her, she still glared at them like a pouty child. Something about that look made Kizzy want to hit her again. The spoiled little fool had no clue.

"I'll ask you one more time. Is Cortina headed to Las Boquillas?" Newt stood in the doorway, leaning against one side of the jamb, his arms folded across his chest.

She spat at him. "He is going to kill you. He knows it was you at La Babia and knows it was you that killed one of his men outside Zaragoza."

"Why didn't he come to find me then, or wait for me here?"

"You think you are strong? You are nothing, *nada*. Javier is a real man." The girl went back to her native tongue and scolded Newt more. Her tone was vile and hateful.

"This little princess has got quite the filthy mouth on her. I've known river flatboatmen and Missouri bullwhackers who can't outcuss her," the judge said.

"Does Cortina have my horses?" Kizzy asked. "White horses."

The girl started to curse Kizzy like she had Newt, but flinched and quieted when Kizzy stood. One hand went to her tender nose, and the other reached out to fend Kizzy off.

"Oh, quit the dramatics," Kizzy said. "Another knock on the snoot might do you some good, but I won't be the one to do it."

"Who's with Cortina?" the judge asked. "I know I put some buckshot in his hide back at La Babia."

"I don't know him." The girl sniffled and wiped gently at her nose with the back of her fingers. "His name is Juan."

"How bad is he hurt?"

"He said no fat old judge could hurt him."

Newt reached down and grabbed a bloody shirt-sleeve from the floor. It was obvious that it had been torn off and used as a bandage or for a cloth to bathe a wound. "Looks like he was bleeding some."

"Javier said you and the judge are back shooters and too afraid of him to face up to him like a man," the girl said.

"Does he intend to cross the river at Las Boquillas?" the judge repeated.

"He didn't say."

"You're awfully loyal to a man who ran off and left you here alone with the Apaches raiding," the judge said.

The girl's expression changed somewhat, and they could all tell from her face that she didn't know anything about the Apaches.

"Javier will come back for me. He promised."

"Young Cortina ain't coming back," the judge said. "He's used you, and now he's done with you. Grow up."

"Your father is looking for you," Kizzy said to take some of the sting out of what the judge had said. "He is very worried about you."

"My papa thinks he knows everything. I'm old enough to do what I want to."

"Old enough to run off with a no-good killer and thief like Javier Cortina?" the judge asked.

"Those are all lies."

"What about this woman's white horses?" the judge asked. "Javier stole them from her."

"Javier bought those horses on the American side of the river."

"Javier is a liar. How many of my horses does he have?" Kizzy's voice grew louder and as harsh as the judge's.

"Two. Juan's horse went lame this morning, and we had to leave it behind," the girl said with tears flooding her eyes again. "That's why Javier had to leave me for a while. He went to get a horse for me."

"And he couldn't have sent his man to go get one,

or left him here with you while he did?" the judge asked.

"He said that you would be coming, and that you would have the Rangers with you." When the girl mentioned the Texas Rangers, her mouth shaped the words like a bad taste came with them. "And Father will be coming, and he swore to me that he would have his men kill Javier if he ever talked to me again."

"Well, too bad Javier isn't still here," the judge said. "Your daddy won't be too far behind us."

"I won't go with him. Not Papa."

Newt straightened in the doorway. "No, you won't be going with your papa, yet. You're coming with us."

"I won't."

"Bring her along," Newt said. "We'll put her on the spare horse."

"What do we want with her?" Kizzy asked. "Her father should be along by nightfall."

Newt started out of the church, but paused and turned back to Kizzy. "Him showing up is the reason I want to keep her, and besides we can't leave her alone with that war party nearby."

"You'll be as much a kidnapper as Cortina in Don Alvarez's opinion if you don't wait for him with her," Kizzy said. "And my brother is at his mercy. Don't you forget that for an instant."

Newt went outside.

The judge chuckled. "Gypsy woman, you don't understand one thing about this situation, do you? Your brother is one of the reasons the Widowmaker is going to hold on to the girl. That, and looking out for his own neck."

"What do you mean?"

"What's to force Alvarez to keep his word about

your brother? What's to keep Alvarez from killing that big lummox out there that you've been mooning over the instant we hand over the girl?"

"I think Don Alvarez will keep his word," Kizzy said. "And he still needs your help to catch Cortina."

"He doesn't need our help anymore. We were just jokers in the deck, and a little insurance to run Cortina down. Alvarez will know it's only a horse race to the river now, and any value we once had went out the window when we got this close to the border."

"I don't believe he is that kind of man."

"Are you willing to risk your brother's life, and the Widowmaker's, on that? I'll tell you one thing: Don Alvarez is a man used to getting his own way, and he's touchy proud."

Kizzy stared out the window, rubbing her temples with her fingertips and thinking. She only wanted her brother free and their horses back. How did things become so tangled?

"My papa will have you all dragged behind a horse when he finds out how you have treated me," the Alvarez girl said.

"Old Gabriel here might have something to say about that." The judge patted his sawed-off shotgun. "And I wouldn't want to be your daddy if he thinks tying a rope on that man outside is going to be easy. The Widowmaker doesn't suffer fools gladly."

They marched the Alvarez girl outside, and Newt was already bringing over the black draft horse. He gestured for her to mount it.

"You can't make me," the girl said. "I won't."

"You will, or I'll pick you up and put you on it," Newt said.

The girl was stubborn, but she saw that he meant

what he said and took the rein he offered. "A lady only rides sidesaddle, and I want a different horse."

"A lady doesn't elope with bandits," Newt said. "Get up on that horse."

"Turn your heads while I mount. I'll have to lift my dress."

Newt shook his head. "And have you spur off? Get on the horse."

The girl hesitated, and that was all it took for Newt to grab her around the waist and pitch her up on the horse. The girl landed belly down on the saddle with a grunt and her butt stuck up in the air. She quickly righted herself and got a leg over the black. She cursed Newt more in Spanish while she adjusted her dress as best she could.

"Let's ride." Newt went to his own horse and mounted.

The judge and Kizzy quickly followed his example, and the four of them left the ghost town at a trot. The Alvarez girl was crying again and trying to hold them up, but the judge rode behind her and kept her horse moving ahead of him.

The trail led them out of the meadow and wound through a stand of spruce up the steep, rocky side of a ridge. The late-afternoon sun was sitting on top of the mountain, hitting them right in the face. They were to the top of the ridge when Don Alvarez's men rode into the meadow.

"*Hombre!*" one of the vaqueros shouted up to them.

Newt rode back to sit his horse beside his companions. The vaqueros had stopped their horses near the beaver pond, at least four hundred yards away as the crow flew, and several hundred feet below their position on the ridge.

"*Hombre!*" the vaquero shouted again with his voice ringing off the mountainside.

"I see a couple of those rurales down there with them," the judge said. "Apparently the Apaches didn't get them all."

Newt counted fifteen men, and he tried to make out Don Alvarez among them.

"Bring my daughter down to us!" Alvarez rode forward of his men.

Newt glanced at the red dress the Alvarez girl was wearing and knew how her father had spotted her so easily. That red dress and Kizzy's white horse stuck out like a sore thumb.

"We could leave her here for them," the judge said. "It will take them a while to get up here."

"I don't relish losing my leverage," Newt answered. "There's no witnesses up here, and Alvarez can do whatever he wants to us."

"To you, you mean," Kizzy said. "What about Fonzo? You made a deal with Don Alvarez. Turn her over as a show of good faith."

The Alvarez girl tried to charge her horse down the ridge, but the judge grabbed one of her bridle reins. She raised one leg and kicked at him, but he warded it off and doubled her horse around.

"I'm going to laugh when Papa has you beaten for what you have done to me," she said.

Newt took another look at the girl's battered nose. All he needed was for Alvarez to have one more thing to hold against him.

"Send Consuela down to me," Don Alvarez shouted at them again.

"So that's your name, girl," the judge said.

The Alvarez girl only glared back at him.

"Send someone back to get the boy," Newt shouted down the mountain. He wasn't sure Don Alvarez could understand him, so he shouted it again, like an echo.

There was no answer. And the don rode back to his men for a discussion.

Newt dismounted and took the Sharps buffalo rifle from under his stirrup leather. He walked to a pile of rocks overlooking where the trail dropped off down to the meadow below.

"What are you doing?" Kizzy asked. "Are you crazy enough to think you can fight them all off?"

Newt knelt on one knee behind the rocks, craning his neck over them to see down the ridge. "You bring the boy and meet us in Las Boquillas. We'll trade there."

Still, nothing came back from the men below. The four of them waited anxiously for something to give in their favor.

"Do you think he heard me?" Newt asked.

"He heard you," the judge said. "He's weighing his options, or figuring out how he can get around us."

"You are afraid of Papa, like you are afraid of Javier," the Alvarez girl said.

Newt lowered the falling block on the Sharps enough to see that it was loaded. He had only two rounds left for it, one in the chamber and one in his pocket. The vaqueros were riding toward the ridge. He shouldered the rifle and found Don Alvarez in the rifle scope.

"You can't be serious," Kizzy said.

"We've got the high ground," the judge said. "But there's a lot of them."

Newt lowered the Sharps, resting its butt on his upraised thigh with the barrel pointing at the sky. The boom of the gun startled their horses when he pulled the trigger.

"What the hell was that for?" the judge said when he got his gray back under control.

"I'm giving them something to think about." Newt motioned down the ridge where the vaqueros had stopped. "They'll think twice before they come up here now."

"That trail isn't the only way up here," the judge said.

"It's the quickest and easiest way," Newt replied. "It'll buy us some time."

"Are you thinking what I'm thinking?" the judge asked.

Newt started breaking off little limbs from the surrounding trees and picking up whatever dead branches, handfuls of dry grass, and deadfall material he could find on the ground. The judge dismounted and helped him. They piled their gatherings on the ground barely out of sight from where the trail down the ridge fell away.

"What are you doing?" Kizzy asked.

"Building a fire," Newt answered.

"You can't be intending to camp here."

Newt ignored her and soon had a fire going. He laid the green spruce boughs over it so that it put off plenty of smoke.

"That ought to do it," he said.

"Do what?" Kizzy asked.

Newt rose from the fire and held out a hand. "Give me that funny hat of yours."

Kizzy hesitated.

"Give me your hat. It's twice as big as the rest of ours, and should be easy to see for anyone coming up the trail."

She took off her hat, and he carried it to where he had left the Sharps on the rock pile. The trail below where he stood was relatively open to the meadow below, with only rocks, low brush, and a few scattered trees. He laid the Sharps on the rock pile with its barrel pointing down at the trail. Then he laid the hat on top of its action.

"A man down there might take that for someone covering the trail," Newt said.

"Might work if they don't get too close, or if one of them doesn't have a set of binoculars or a spyglass," the judge answered.

"Ought to buy us some time, anyway." Newt went to his horse and mounted. "We'll have to ride hard."

"My brother will die if you leave with the girl," Kizzy said.

Newt turned his horse so that he could face her. "We'll trade for your brother at Las Boquillas."

"It's a man's life you're gambling with. My brother's." She yanked her right-hand pistol from its holster and leveled it on Newt.

He glanced at the pistol and then returned his gaze to meet her eye to eye. "If we take the girl down there to him, there's nothing to stop him from letting those rurales have your brother or stretching my neck because he wants to think I killed his son."

"The rurales listen to him."

"What if he only made a deal with those rurales to hold off on tending to your brother until he saw if we could catch Cortina? A man like this Alvarez wouldn't like owing any favors to the likes of those rurales, and asking them to free your brother would be a favor that he would have to repay some day. Have you thought about that?"

"I've considered it, but what other choice do we have?"

"We run for Las Boquillas. We get Cortina, we trade him and the girl for your brother, and then we dash over the river," Newt said. "Don Alvarez won't follow us far into Texas."

"You don't know he won't follow us."

"He won't cross into Texas," the judge said. "At least I don't think so. He may be a rich man down here, but he got into some trouble north of the river when he was young, and there are people in Texas liable to remember him."

Newt turned his horse and started across the ridge top, headed north. Kizzy raised her pistol to shoulder height. "You stop."

The judge rode past her, leading the Alvarez girl's horse. Kizzy swung her gun on him.

"Stop!" The pistol in Kizzy's hand trembled.

"The problem with guns isn't always hitting what you're aiming at," the judge said over his shoulder as he left her. "Sometimes it's pulling the trigger in the first place."

"You can't do this."

"Ain't like this in your Wild West show, is it?" the judge said as he rode over the ridge top and dropped out of sight on the far side.

Kizzy took one last look at the meadow behind them. Don Alvarez and his vaqueros were still bunched up and looking up at the smoke from their campfire rising into the sky. She spurred her horse after her companions, her hair flying behind her as her horse clattered through the rocks at a run.

# Chapter Thirty-two

Two hours after they left the ridge above the church they found the other bandit who had ridden off with Cortina. He was lying dead on the side of the trail. A big-bore bullet had taken one side of his face off, and what the Apaches had done to the rest of him was an ugly thing.

There was no sign of Cortina, so they left the dead bandit behind and moved on. Nearing sunset, the trail dropped to lower country, leaving the pine, fir, and spruce forests behind for grassy, open ridges and mesa tops dotted with stunted oak trees. To the north, far away in the hazy distance, they could see the canyon of the Rio Grande, and across it the Big Bend country of Texas.

They paused often to check their back trail, but there was no sign of Don Alvarez's vaqueros, although they knew they were coming. It was only a matter of time, and delaying the inevitable.

And often they stopped for Newt or the judge to ride ahead to scout likely ambush sites where the Apaches might lie in wait for them. The Alvarez girl had grown silent, her chin resting on her chest, staring at nothing but her horse's neck and refusing to look at any of them or take a drink from a canteen when offered.

They soon found another of Kizzy's white horses atop a high, windblown mesa. It was lying on its side with strips of meat cut out of its loin and one hind-quarter. Kizzy dismounted and knelt over the dead horse with a hand on its neck.

"Her name was Sheba," Kizzy said. "She was the fastest and the sweetest of them."

"Apaches are partial to horsemeat," the judge said. "Only thing they like better is mule."

Kizzy glanced at the judge with tears streaming down her cheeks, but he either ignored her or didn't notice.

"An Apache can get anywhere he wants on foot," the judge continued. "Your common Apache, he don't love horses the way, say, a Comanche does. He'll steal him one and ride it to death if he's pressured. He'll stop and eat it and wait until he can steal him another one. Any kind of Injun will eat horse in starving times, but Apaches, they like it."

"Would you shut up?" Kizzy asked with a quaver in her voice.

Newt came riding back from where he had gone on a little ways to scout the trail ahead. He glanced at the dead horse. "Looks like Cortina got away from them."

"Looks like it," the judge said. "Those Apaches stopped long enough to cut off some supper for later tonight, and then went on after him."

Newt dismounted and stood beside Kizzy. The Apaches had tossed the dead horse's saddle aside to get at the cuts of meat they wanted. The saddlebags were already open where the war party had gone through them, but Newt checked them anyway. There was nothing to be found.

"All you care about is your gold," Kizzy said. "You don't care anything about my brother or our horses."

Newt remounted and sat quietly with a calm, unreadable expression on his face. After a while he said, "Are you coming?"

She rubbed a strand of the dead mare's mane hair between her fingers while she looked at the trail behind them. Newt's saddle creaked when his horse shifted its stance, and she could hear the judge bite the end off a cigar and spit it on the ground. A gust of hot wind picked up and rustled through the brown grass.

The whole country was dry and dead, like some desiccated corpse refusing to rot. Everything was dead or about to be dead. Waiting for the worst to come, like she and Fonzo were, and not a thing anyone could do about it.

"We'd best be moving," Newt said.

She left the dead mare and got back on Herod.

"Apaches don't have any use for a white horse," the judge said. "Too easy to spot for a sneaky fighter riding through this kind of country."

"Don't you say another word," Kizzy said to the judge. "Not another word."

They rode away and left the dead mare behind, the trail taking them off the foot of the mountains and down into a scrubland valley snaking its way through flat-topped mesas and the knife-edged mountains to the east. The trail was scarred with the barefoot pony tracks of the war party, and occasionally intermixed with them were the shod tracks of the horse Cortina rode.

Behind them, miles away and still high up in the mountains, they could see something else moving. None of them mentioned it for a long while, but they all knew it was Don Alvarez coming with his vaqueros.

The judge finally stopped his horse at the end of their line and studied the ant-sized dots on the mountainside that were vaqueros. "Do you think he sent anyone back after the boy?"

"We'll know before tomorrow's over," Newt said. "Maybe sooner if we don't pick up the pace."

Close on to sunset, they came to a point where the trail passed through a narrow defile between two mesas. The Circle Dot horse stopped at the mouth of the pass without Newt asking him to. The gelding stood with his nostrils flared and his ears erect and alert. Newt thought for an instant that the horse was going to nicker.

"Acts like he smells or sees other horses," the judge said.

Newt studied the high walls to either side of the pass. The sides of the mesas were littered with tumbled rock and a million places for someone to hide.

"Good place for an ambush," the judge said.

"We don't have time to find a way around."

"Could be you're overly cautious," the judge said. "That war party is apt to be hot on Cortina's trail and don't even know we exist."

"I'm supposing they heard my gunshot back on that ridge," Newt said. "A gunshot carries a long way."

"You thinking on making a run through there?"

"Looks like it's a short run, and then the country opens up again."

The judge grunted. "There's no such thing as a short run if there are Apaches up on the sides of those mesas shooting at us."

Newt nodded. "We've got the women to think of."

"Cortina's going to gain on us if we leave the trail and find a way around."

"How many of them do you think there are?" Newt asked. "The Apaches, I mean."

The judge shrugged. "Can't tell. Not many. Maybe five or six, but that's plenty. Worst damn fighters you've ever seen. They can kill you seven ways from Sunday, and you not so much as see them until it's too late."

Newt looked at Kizzy and the Alvarez girl, and then at all of their horses. They had watered the horses a few hours back when still in the high mountains, and despite the miles, the animals looked in good shape. Kizzy, too, looked fit, if gone unusually quiet since they had found the dead mare, but the Alvarez girl looked all used up.

It didn't matter. They had no choice but to move ahead.

"When I say *run*, we run," Newt said to all of them. "Could be I'm worried over nothing, but if I was an Apache I would be waiting up there in the rocks on either side of the trail."

Kizzy studied the pass with fear, but the Alvarez girl didn't look up at him. The judge was getting his shotgun ready and methodically chewing on the stub of the unlit cigar in one corner of his mouth. Newt propped the Winchester up on his right thigh and led them into the defile.

"Gonna be hard for me to fight and hold on to this

girl's horse," the judge said, all the while keeping his eyes on the sides of the trail above them.

Newt slowed his own horse until the judge and the Alvarez girl caught up to him. Without stopping, he took the girl's rein from the judge and handed it to her to mate with the other rein.

"You'll keep up with us if you know what's good for you," Newt said to her.

"She knows what Apaches are and what they do," the judge said. "There isn't a Mexican in these parts that don't have nightmares about Apaches."

The Alvarez girl looked from one to another of them and then to the sides of the mesas above them with her eyes big and full of fear. She nodded at Newt. "I will run when you tell me to."

Newt took them fifty yards into the pass. The trail dipped down ahead of them, and then climbed again near the far end, where it looked like open country again.

"You keep an eye on that side, and I'll watch this 'un," Newt said to the judge.

They hadn't gone a few more walking strides when Newt thought he saw movement up in the rocks to his left. It could have been some animal, a bird, or maybe nothing but his imagination and his nerves working on him, but he put his heels to the Circle Dot horse anyway.

"Run!"

All four of their horses bolted forward, and they ran abreast of each other with the white dog racing to one side of them with its tongue flopping out of one side of its mouth. The Circle Dot horse hadn't taken three strides before a bullet skimmed by them and whined off the rocks on the other side of the trail.

Other guns boomed from above and from both sides of them. An arrow thudded into the judge's saddle swells, stuck there, quivering from the impact like a rattlesnake's shaking tail.

Newt couldn't find a target. The horse beneath him was rising and falling and ducking around rocks and brush, and he couldn't have hit anything if he saw it. Kizzy was bent low over her horse's neck, and it was easy to see that white horse of hers, Herod, could outrun any of them.

The Alvarez girl had fallen a little behind, the draft horse being slow and plodding. Newt slowed up enough to slap her horse hard across the top of its hips with his rifle barrel. Another bullet kicked up dirt and gravel just beyond them.

There was no way they were going to make it. It was too far. The instant Newt thought that, the Alvarez girl's horse stumbled, and he saw the red splotch of blood and gore where some Apache's bullet had passed through its flanks. He hit the wounded animal again on the top of the hips with his rifle, and it charged on, laboring but still running.

The judge's shotgun boomed, and Newt couldn't tell if he had seen an Apache to shoot at, or if he was only firing to be firing. Newt twisted in the saddle and saw the Apaches they had left behind clambering down through the rocks, clutching bows and arrows, or their rifles smoking as they shot at the fleeing group.

In the instant before they cleared the pass, two more horseback Apaches broke from a little side canyon, leading more horses for the other warriors. Newt snapped a one-handed shot at them with his Winchester, but knew he didn't hit anywhere close to them. He fanned the Alvarez girl's horse with his hat. The judge and Kizzy were pulling away from them.

A half mile past the ambush site, the girl's wounded horse faltered and broke to trot. In a few more steps it stopped completely. Its knees buckled and it fell to the ground with the girl barely getting out of the saddle before it did. Newt was reaching to pull her up with him when Kizzy and the judge rode back to him.

Newt dismounted and handed one of his reins to the girl. "Take my horse, and I'll see if I can hold them off."

The girl took the rein, but Kizzy rode between them, knocking the rein out of her hand. She lifted a foot from her stirrup, and the Alvarez girl quickly climbed up behind her.

"You'll need your horse," Kizzy said.

"I'll see if I can slow them down," Newt said.

"Don't wait too long," Kizzy answered.

Newt slapped her horse with his hat and sent it fleeing away. The judge held his gray in place for an instant longer and then spurred off after the two women, leaving Newt alone.

There was no time to think on good-byes, for Newt spotted the Apaches coming at a run toward him. There were five of them. Newt quickly lay across the dead horse's shoulder with his Winchester resting on it. The horse on its side made a solid barricade and a good gun rest.

The Apaches were still better than a hundred yards away, but caught in the wide open. Newt found the first one in his sights and squeezed the trigger. The Winchester bucked against his shoulder, and the Apache he had fired at veered wide, wounded, or simply taking a more evasive course. Twice more, he fired, levering a new round home in the chamber and taking hasty aim. They were moving fast, and difficult targets. His second shot was a clean miss, but the third one struck the lead Apache's horse and tumbled it end over end. Two of the Apaches turned around and fled the other way, shouting at him, while the rest of them dismounted around their fallen friend. Newt could see the Apaches' horses, but he couldn't see where the warriors had taken cover in the grass and low scrub brush.

He took longer aiming that time and calmly shot the Apaches' horses in succession, one after another of them going down to the Winchester's big .45-caliber bullets. He thumbed fresh cartridges from the bandolier across his chest into the side gate of the rifle while he grimaced at the downed horses. Rising to his feet, he took one last look in the direction of the Apaches. A white streak appeared headed toward him. It was Kizzy's dog, running like its tail was on fire. A bullet passed near Newt as he was mounting, and he put the Circle Dot horse to a run in the direction the judge and the women had gone. The dog pulled alongside him. Of all of them, the dog seemed to live the only charmed life.

A couple of more shots came his way from the Apaches hiding in the grass, but he was soon out of range. After another mile run, he pulled up the winded horse to a walk. The judge and the women were nowhere in sight, and there was no sign of the Apaches following him on foot or otherwise. He took up his canteen, intending only to wash the dust from his mouth, but was shocked to find how thirsty he was. He drank half of what was left in the canteen, and let more of it slosh over his face. Nearly dying was thirsty work.

He stoppered the canteen and hung it from his saddle horn, twisting often in his saddle to check his back trail. After a short spell, he put the Circle Dot horse to a lope, his attention to the north. Somewhere up there was Las Boquillas, and maybe Cortina would be there.

# Chapter Thirty-three

He caught up to the judge and the women several hours after dark. He almost rode by them, but Kizzy's dog darted away into the night as if he had found something. And then he caught the silhouette of their horses skylined by the moonlight on top of a low hill. They had made no fire for fear of pursuit.

"Thought you were a goner for sure," the judge said.

"It was touch and go there for a moment," Newt replied.

"We ain't lost those Apaches," the judge said. "Not by a long shot. They know they have us outnumbered, and that we're only two men with a couple of women."

"If they're coming, they're coming slower than before. I shot all of their horses but two that turned tail on me and ran off."

"That'll help."

"We'll get a little rest, then we'll move on." Newt dismounted.

"Thank you for what you did back there. You risked your life for us." It was Kizzy's voice, and after a moment he recognized her shadowed shape standing very near to him.

"Are you all right?"

"I'm fine."

"What about my papa? Won't he come through those Indians?" It was the Alvarez girl who spoke then, and her voice sounded as tired as Newt felt.

"He's got enough men that such a little war party probably won't bother him."

Newt jerked his saddle off the Circle Dot horse and let it fall to the ground with a thump. He hadn't caught more than a couple of hours' sleep in almost two days. He slipped the bridle off the horse and replaced it with a rope around its throatlatch so that it could pick at whatever nearby grass it could find.

"Las Boquillas shouldn't be far away," the judge said. "Never came at it from this direction, but it shouldn't be too far."

"Give me a couple of hours of sleep." Newt didn't untie his blanket, and simply lay down with his head resting on the saddle.

"Do you think Don Alvarez sent men back for my brother?" Kizzy asked.

Newt didn't answer her.

"Is he asleep?" she finally asked.

"That he is. I think the Widowmaker is all tuckered out," the judge said.

"I can't believe he stayed behind for us. I was wrong about him."

"Ain't you learned that he's a fool for any kind of a fight? That don't make him a good man."

"I think he is. Maybe he doesn't know it, but he is."

\* \* \*

They rode into the village of Las Boquillas a little before daylight the next morning. The only one stirring in the village was a small boy who met them on the road, taking a herd of goats out to graze for the day.

The village was no more than a score of adobe and picket houses set on a low rise a couple of hundred yards above a shallow, rocky shoal on the river where the canyon walls petered out and allowed for a crossing. Newt led them in the gray morning light to a picket corral at the first home they came to, and dismounted with the fence hiding them from anyone like the goat herder who stirred so early in the morning.

Newt left his companions and walked to the corner of the corral, looking down the road where it passed through the rest of the settlement. It was still dark enough that the village was nothing but shadows and silhouettes, and he had a hard time making anything out.

The judge came to join him and took a seat with his back to the fence. "There's a tavern at the far end, overlooking the river. Used to be a trading post, but the most recent owner has a few rooms to let out in the back of it. See anything down there?"

"I don't see any horses out in front of it, if I'm looking at the right building."

"Henry O'Malley owns that tavern. He's an Irishman that deserted from the army during the war down here back in '47. That old crippled devil is a has-been horse thief and outlaw himself, and the kind to be friends with Cortina."

Newt squatted down at the fence corner to wait for better light. "Cortina might already be across the river."

"If he's holed up in O'Malley's, there's liable to be more of his kind in there with him. Nobody comes here unless they're out of options, or on the run from something."

"Soon as the sun comes up, we go looking for him."

The judge produced a bottle and uncorked it and took a drink.

"Where did you get that?" Newt asked.

"Had it in my saddlebags. Want a pull? There ain't much left."

Newt took the bottle and turned it up. It was tequila, and bad tequila at that. He grimaced at the bite of the liquor and then took another swig of it before passing it back to the judge.

"Didn't know you were a drinking man," the judge said.

"I try to stay away from it most times."

"I've found that work like this is easier when you're drinking."

"You mean killing."

"I mean anything that's hard. You either drink until you're mean enough to do what has to be done, or you drink afterward to drown your guilty conscience." The judge sloshed the contents of his bottle around and listened to the sound to gauge how much was left.

Newt leaned around the corner of the corral again and scanned the settlement. There was nothing else moving.

"Boy, you're good at this stuff. Comes easy to you."

"You think I like this?"

"I didn't say you liked it. I said it was easy for you. You ought to quit trying to be such a do-gooder. Do you think that Gypsy girl yonder is going to be so thankful to you for saving her brother that she crawls in the sack with you? Stick to your talents, son."

"And what are my talents?"

"Mayhem and destruction. It ain't much, but there are few that are really good at it."

"I'm not who you think I am."

"You're exactly what I thought you were when I first laid eyes on you. You're a fighter, plain and simple. Maybe when this is over you ought to go back to boxing, or become a bounty hunter or detective, or maybe I could put in a word for you with the Rangers. Leave the easy living for the soft folks."

The judge turned the bottle up and finished it in one long pull before he pitched it in the weeds. "Did I ever tell you about a man I once knew? His name was Kirker, and he made his living hunting down Apaches and selling their scalps to the Mexican government. Not the nicest fellow you ever met, but crazy brave and never met no kind of trouble he thought he couldn't handle. He rode a one-eyed horse and had a half-breed Comanche tracker that stood seven foot tall and could smell an Apache a mile away if the wind was right. I mind the time when old Kirker was . . ."

"It will be daylight soon." Newt cut the judge off before he could go farther with one of his outlandish tales. He wiped his mouth with the back of his hand, but the taste of the tequila wouldn't go away. He hated the taste, but he would have taken another drink if there were any left. The judge was right about that, if nothing else. Liquor made some things easier. And knowing that Cortina might be close by had his nerves on end, and the judge's constant chatter didn't help things.

"That's fine if you don't want to hear the rest of my

story. Just fine," the judge said. "How long are we going to wait? I never could stand waiting, especially with no one to swap yarns with. You want me to scout around and see what I can find?"

Newt would have preferred that the judge stay put, but then he would have to listen to more of his talk. "If you do, stay out of sight as best you can. Cortina will spook easy if he's around."

The judge went to his horse and took his scatter-gun off his saddle horn. He stuffed his vest pocket full of shotgun shells from his sack, and then went around the backside of the corral, hugging close to the fence.

When he was gone Newt went to where the women were and found the Alvarez girl had lain down by the fence and was fast asleep. Kizzy sat close to her, holding their horses and petting her dog, who lay alongside her.

"When it gets good and daylight, I'm going to go look for Cortina. Would you watch over the girl while I'm gone?"

"I will."

"If something happens to me and the judge, you hole up here and wait for Don Alvarez. Have him take you back to Zaragoza with him."

"Okay."

Newt tried to think of something else to say, but everything he thought of seemed trivial or awkward.

"Do you think you'll find the rest of your gold?" she asked.

"I doubt it. I told myself I came down here after it, but that never was all of it."

"You came down here to kill him."

He nodded. "I did."

"I thought I wanted to kill him for stealing our

horses, but all I want now is to get Fonzo back and forget this ever happened," she said. "I want to go somewhere so far away that I can forget everything."

"It will all be over before long, one way or another. If Cortina isn't here, we're going to have to see if Alvarez will trade his daughter for your brother."

"You sound so calm about it."

"It is what it is."

"After Papa died all I could think about was how bad we had it, and wished I could snap my fingers and everything would be like it had been. Nothing was good enough, and everything I thought I wanted I couldn't have."

"And you found it can be a lot worse."

"Yes," she answered. "Don't you go down there after Cortina. Let him go. We'll trade her for Fonzo like you said. If Don Alvarez has any intentions to treat my brother fairly, it has nothing to do with whether or not you catch or kill Cortina for him."

"No, I've got it to do."

"Is it worth getting killed? The only way to deal with men like Cortina is to stoop to their level. Is it worth that? What about your talk of starting a wagon shop? You said you wanted to be someone different."

"In time."

"How old are you?"

Her question threw him off guard. "I'll be thirty-two come next month."

"Somehow I thought you were older."

"I feel older. Lord, I do."

"I don't mean so much that you look older, it's that you seem so sure of yourself."

"I'm not sure of anything. I haven't done one thing

since I left home that didn't feel like I was gambling for stakes I couldn't afford."

"Thank you for what you've done for me and my brother. If I never said it, I'm saying it now. Not many would have gone out of their way for a couple of Gypsies."

"You're the first Gypsies I ever met."

"We're not so bad, are we?"

He cradled the Winchester in the crook of one elbow and gauged the light spilling over the mountains to the east, anxious to be doing something. Anything. She stood beside him, and he took the Circle Dot horse's reins from her. Before he could go, she stopped him with a hand laid lightly on his forearm. When he looked down at her she tiptoed and kissed him lightly on the cheek. Before he could adjust she went to the far side of the other horses and left him alone.

He led his horse onto the road and started through the village without mounting. A light burned here and there in a window, and a woman passed by him carrying a load of laundry in the direction of the river. She stayed wide of him, casting nervous looks back at him as she passed.

The tavern at the far end of the village was seventy-five yards up the road, and made of adobe with the rafter poles protruding through the front wall. Smooth, peeled cottonwood posts held up a porch roof across the entire front of it, and two hitching rails were in front of the porch. There wasn't a horse tied to either of them. It was likely that Cortina had his horse corralled for the night if he was anywhere around. Newt paused in the middle of the dusty road that served as a street, looking for another set of corrals or a barn. Maybe the first thing to do was to put Cortina afoot.

"*Buenos días,*" somebody called out from inside the tavern.

Newt had heard that voice only one time, but he recognized it. He stopped in the street with his Winchester held before him in two hands.

"You took a long time coming," Cortina called to him.

Newt guessed that Cortina was looking out of one of the tavern's windows or standing back in the shadows of the front door. Newt felt like easy pickings standing in the middle of the street like he was, and started walking at an angle to the nearest house on the same side of the road as the tavern.

"Why don't you hurry, gringo? You have come a long ways to find me," Cortina said.

Newt reached the house and hugged close to the wall in the shadows, still trying to locate Cortina's position.

"Come on, gringo." Cortina's voice was louder. "What do you think, Miguelito? The Widowmaker, I think he is scared."

Another man laughed on the opposite side of the street, somewhere behind what looked like a chicken house and pen. "I don't think he likes us."

Newt wondered where the judge was, and he wondered how many more might be inside the tavern with Cortina. Miguelito hadn't been with Cortina on the trail from Zaragoza, so they must have made arrangements to meet at the crossing.

The rising sun had slowly spread across the street and spilled onto the tavern's porch. He thought he saw a trail of cigarette smoke wafting from one window.

He heard Miguelito move behind the chicken pen, and the rattle of his spurs. To Newt's left there was a gap between the house he stood against, and the little yard fence surrounding the next house. He stepped into the alley, pulling his horse with him. A large prickly pear plant had grown up at the corner of the cedar stay and wire fence, and he peered through it at the chicken pen across the street. The tavern was out of his line of sight.

"Come on, Widowmaker, if you want to play," Cortina called out again. "I think I will shoot a little straighter this time."

If he went up the street they were going to have him in a cross fire and he wouldn't stand a chance. And he wasn't sure that there wasn't a third man who had yet to speak up. Cortina had survived too long to chatter so and to be foolish enough to show all the aces he had up his sleeve.

Newt draped the rein he was holding over the Circle Dot horse's neck with the other one, and slapped the horse on the rump with the flat of his hand. It took only two steps and then looked back at him. He hit it again and took off his hat and waved it. The horse took two more trotting steps and then slowed to a walk and continued down the middle of the street.

"Good horse," Newt whispered to himself. "You keep right on going."

The village was so quiet that Newt could plainly hear the creaking of his saddle and the dull hoof sounds of his horse's hooves on the street. He waited to make sure the horse was going to keep walking toward the tavern, and then ducked down the fence between the houses until he reached the back of

them. There was a goat pen between where he was
and the rear of the tavern, and he put a hand on top
of it and vaulted into it. He crossed the pen keeping
low, and easing through the bleating goats. When he
reached the far side he rested his rifle on the top of
the fence and studied the back of the tavern. There
was a horse corral and a lean-to, brush-roofed shed
behind it, and two unsaddled horses stood under the
shed. Through a gap between the side of the tavern
and the blacksmith shed next to it, he could see a
little patch of the street. The Circle Dot horse was
standing there.

Newt vaulted the fence again and ran to the corner
of the horse corral. It was made of stacked stone, little
more than waist high. He stopped again with his rifle
resting on its top and aimed at the back door to the
tavern.

"Ah, gringo, I never thought you were so tricky."
Cortina sounded like he was still at the front of the
tavern. "Did you think I would shoot at your horse?"

Newt found the gate to the horse pen and swung
it open. He backed into the corral, keeping an eye on
the door to the tavern while he got behind the loose
horses, intending on driving them out the open gate.
He was almost there when a bullet struck one of the
shed posts next to his head.

His ears were still echoing with the sound of the
shot, and he was slapping at the sting of splinters and
grit hitting the side of his face and dropping to the
ground when a second shot smacked into the rock
fence behind him. The horses milled around him,
and he used the cover of them bolting out the gate
to rise to his knees. He didn't know where the gunman
was, but the first thing he saw was that the back door

to the tavern was cracked open. He worked the lever on the Winchester as fast as he could, sending two rounds into the doorway and another one into the single window next to the door. He rose and ran to his left and went over the rock fence in a long dive, rolling and scrambling back against it for cover as soon as he hit the ground on the other side.

Another gun boomed somewhere on the street, and it sounded like the judge's shotgun. A different gun cracked, and then the shotgun again.

He took off his hat and eased it above the fence, but whoever was in the back of the tavern was too smart to fall for such a trick. On his belly, he crawled to the corner of the corral. The last thing he wanted was to peep his head around that corner, and he couldn't make himself do it. Never lead with your head, was a thing any fighter should live by. He got his legs under him and stood quickly and glanced at the back door to the tavern before he dropped behind the fence again.

In that brief glance, he thought he saw an arm stretched out through the open door. He chanced another look, this time with his Winchester taking quick aim. It was a white shirtsleeve that he had seen, and whoever was wearing that shirt looked to have taken one of his bullets. He started around the corner of the horse corral without dropping his aim on the doorway. A few steps closer and he saw the pistol lying in the dirt off the end of that dead man's hand.

The body was blocking the door from swinging inward, and he placed a hand against it and shoved. It opened enough to barely give him room to pass through. He glanced down at the dead man, but it wasn't anyone he recognized—just an old face missing teeth and staring up at him with a leering death grin. It was probably the tavern keeper that the judge had spoken of.

Newt shoved the barrel of his Winchester into the crack in the open door and let it lead the way. He was only partway inside when a gun roared and a bullet struck the forearm of the rifle, knocking it from his hands. Two more bullets splintered the door, and he ducked out of the way and hugged against the outside wall with his back to it. He could hear Cortina laughing inside.

"Come on, *cabrón*. Here I am."

Newt slid the Smith .44 from its holster and circled the building, approaching one corner of the front porch. When he reached the street, he glanced across it at the chicken pen where Miguelito had hidden.

"You out there, Judge?" he called out.

"I'm still alive and kicking," the judge called out from somewhere behind the chicken pen. "I put some lead in Miguelito."

Newt craned his neck around the corner of the tavern and chanced a glance down the front porch. The instant he did it one of the front window shutters was knocked open, and Cortina fired off two shots at the sound of the judge's voice.

"You come for me if you want me, Bean!" Cortina's voice had lost all its mocking calm. "I kill you if you do!"

"You come out, Javier," the judge called back.

"I don't think so, Bean." Cortina fired twice more.

Newt could see the end of Cortina's pistol protruding outside the window and the blossom of flame each time he fired. He snapped a quick shot at the window, but the angle was too sharp. His bullet splintered the window frame and brought on a round of cursing from Cortina.

"We'll smoke you out if we have to," the judge shouted.

"You do what you must. I'm in no hurry."

"Keep an eye on the back side," the judge called across the street to Newt.

"I already turned his horses loose," Newt answered.

"Listen to me, Cortina," the judge said. "Don Alvarez is going to be here before long. You know what he'll do to you. You come with me and I'll see to it that you get a fair trial."

"Trial for what?"

"For burglary and theft and anything else I can find on you in the state of Texas."

"What, because I stole your jaguar hide?"

"Nobody steals from me."

"You are nothing." There was a period of silence before Cortina spoke again. "No, I tell you how it's going to be. I stay here, and if I see you I will put a bullet in your *cabeza*."

"Suit yourself. Old Don Alvarez will be along, and you'll wish you had surrendered when you had the chance."

Newt could hear Cortina moving around and could tell that the man had changed positions to the window on the far side of the front door. He took the opportunity to step up onto the porch, and peered into the open window Cortina had just vacated. He could see only a slice of the gloomy room inside, and he waited with his pistol ready for Cortina to come into sight.

And then he heard the horse inside the tavern, its hooves loud on the floor. The double doors of the tavern were painted a bright green, with huge wrought-iron straps to reinforce them, and no doubt barred from the inside with more such blacksmith work from back in the days when the place had been a trading post. Both doors were made to swing to the outside, and to prop open on warm days.

Newt had taken only one step toward them when both doors burst open, the near one crashing into him and knocking him backward. Cortina charged out of the doorway on the back of a white horse, ducked in the saddle to avoid the porch roof over his head, and with a pistol blazing in his fist. He didn't know Newt was nearby, and focused his aim on the judge's position.

The judge's shotgun boomed again, and Newt could hear the buckshot rattling off the tavern front as Cortina's horse leapt high into the air off the porch and landed in the street. The bandit's move was so bold and unexpected that Newt barely had time to right himself and snap off a single shot from his Smith. Before he knew it, Cortina was racing away toward the river.

Newt holstered the Smith and ran for the Circle Dot horse. The judge was hobbling across the street toward him, shoving two more shells down the barrels of his shotgun. There was blood all over his lower right leg.

Newt swung into the saddle and slapped the Circle Dot horse across one hip with his hat. The horse squatted for an instant on its hindquarters and exploded forward in a dead run like he was shot out of a cannon.

It was two hundred yards to the river, and Cortina was already splashing across the other side by the time

Newt rode into sight of him. The bandit spurred his horse up a break in the side of the escarpment on the Texas side of the river, raising a trail of white dust up the steep slope. A bullet splashed in the water next to Newt, as he charged the Circle Dot horse into the shallows. He was almost across the river when he looked up and saw Cortina on the rise above him with his pistol aimed down at him.

# Chapter Thirty-four

Kizzy flinched when she heard the sound of the first gunshots. The Alvarez girl at her feet yawned and rubbed sleepily at her eyes with doubled fists. Kizzy listened to the men shouting back and forth down the street, and went to the horses and checked their saddles and tightened their cinches.

"What are you doing?" The Alvarez girl had come fully awake, and there was the hint of panic in her voice.

"We might need to run."

The Alvarez girl rose to her feet. She recognized Cortina's voice calling out to the judge and tried to run toward him. Kizzy caught her by the wrist and jerked her back. The girl swung wildly and clawed at Kizzy's face. Kizzy pivoted and swung her by the arm against the fence. A gush of air went out of the girl's lungs at the impact, and that gave Kizzy time to kick her ankles from under her. The girl landed on her rump.

"You stay put." Kizzy shook her fist in front of the girl's face.

"Javier will kill your men, and then he will come for me."

"You little fool."

Kizzy shushed her and listened to the fight going on up the street. The gunfire had gone quiet. After a while she heard a horse coming her way. She couldn't see anything of the village beyond her position, for the high fence blocked her view. All she could see was the road leaving the village to the south. Maybe it was Newt or the judge coming back for them.

When the horse was near she could make out bits of it through the cracks in the picket fence. It was a white horse.

She drew her right-hand pistol and backed nearer to the Alvarez girl. A man appeared around the fence corner. He was riding Solomon, and there was blood all over the bandit's right side, from his thigh to the side of his face.

He saw her and turned his horse out of the road and came toward her at a walk. He held a pistol dangling at the end of his wounded arm, and he rode slumped and weary in the saddle. She recognized the fat bandit as the one Cortina had called Miguelito, and she wondered if the leer he gave her was meant to be a smile.

"You, me. We meet again," Miguelito said in bad English.

Kizzy raised her Colt to shoulder level and pointed it at him.

He stopped the horse. His breathing was heavy and ragged. He looked down at the Alvarez girl and then back at Kizzy. "You come with me."

"Go away," Kizzy said.

He studied the pistol she held, still smiling as if the weapon were a toy and she were a small child offering it to him. "You shoot good, *chica*. But can you shoot men?"

"Leave now, or I will kill you."

Miguelito shook his head somberly. "I don't think so. You no have the guts to kill me."

"I said for you to leave."

"Javier, he stingy with the women. He have this Consuela, but he don't share her with us. Now, maybe, I have two señoritas, and I don't share with him."

The Alvarez girl dug her heels into the sand and shoved herself against the fence, looking up at the bandit with loathing and fear, as if she already knew things about him.

Kizzy stared down the top of her Colt, sighting it on the bandit's forehead. She tried every way possible to force her finger to pull the trigger, but she couldn't do it.

Miguelito laughed at her. "You gonna make me some good loving. You drop that *pistola* and get on your horse."

Again she told herself to shoot him then and there. He was no better than a mad animal that needed to be put down.

His pistol rose slowly at the end of his bloody arm. "Put your *pistola* down."

She dropped the Colt Lightning and it clattered on the ground.

"See, not so hard," he said. "Now get on your horses."

Kizzy helped the Alvarez girl to her feet and they walked to the horses tied to the fence. The Alvarez girl looked back at Miguelito.

"We can't go with him," she said. "He tried to buy me from Javier."

"She can't help you. She's too scared," Miguelito said. "I told Javier we should have taught her a lesson at Piedras Negras, but those rurales interrupted us. Now I have time. She gonna love me now. You both gonna love me. When I get tired of you I'm going to sell you to the Indios."

Kizzy turned and faced him, and the Alvarez girl fell at her feet, crying and clutching the fence as if she couldn't be pried away from it.

Kizzy stepped away from her horse. "You go on before the Widowmaker comes back."

"The Widowmaker? He don't scare me." He nodded down at his bloody wounds. "I've been shot many times, but no bullet can kill me."

"I won't go."

"Then I shoot you and take Consuela." Miguelito's aim had sagged due to his wounded and weakened arm, but he started to raise the pistol again, still smiling like a madman.

Kizzy's left-hand Colt jumped from its holster and she shot him between the eyes. He tottered in the saddle with his head tilted backward and his arms hung limply at his sides, like something impossibly balanced and teetering at the whim of a breeze. The startled horse beneath him took an unsure step forward, and he fell from the saddle, dead.

Kizzy caught the horse's bridle, hugging it to her and staring at the dead bandit. She had practiced drawing and firing her pistols thousands of times, shooting at glass balls, tin cans, and paper targets. But never at a living thing. Never at a man. She wasn't a killer, yet now she was. It was more horrible than she ever imagined it. She holstered her pistol, stooped to pick up her other, and forced the Alvarez girl to stand, all the while avoiding looking at Miguelito's body.

"I can't believe you killed him," the Alvarez girl said.

"Come on. Newt and the judge might need our help."

Kizzy put her up on the horse Miguelito had been riding. The gelding was the one the Grey family called Mithridates, slightly smaller than the others and the least steady, but her father's personal favorite.

She mounted Herod, and the Alvarez girl followed her onto the street. She could see the judge standing ahead of them on the street, looking at something in the direction of the river.

# Chapter Thirty-five

Cortina fled across the desert, and Newt followed him. The white horse Cortina rode was faster than the Circle Dot horse, and during the first half hour, Newt lost sight of anything but his occasional dust trail or glimpses of him in the distance. Cortina seemed willing to risk running his horse to death in an all-out attempt to leave Newt behind in an initial sprint. But the Circle Dot horse was tough. His hooves hammered on in a steady rhythm, through the tortured windings of the canyons, beneath the high, eroded mountains streaked with chalk and bloodred smears, and across the scrub-dotted desert basins with the fine dust of the land adhering to his dark, sweaty hide, and the laboring of his lungs and the pound of his heart like a steam engine piston chugging away.

The sun moved toward high noon, and the air burned like the insides of an oven, until heat waves danced everywhere you looked. By that time, the chase had changed into less of a mad dash and more of a long, grueling test of endurance. Cortina alternated his pace between a trot and a long lope.

Newt's mind was lost to anything but the thought of the man and horse ahead of him, and even if he wasn't gaining on them, the distance between them was remaining the same. Once, on a long stretch across a valley floor that went for miles, he could plainly see Cortina trotting a mile ahead of him, like a ghost shimmering tantalizingly out of reach, and perhaps not a real thing at all.

Cortina then took to the roughest country, perhaps hoping that the fear of him waiting somewhere in ambush would cause Newt to hesitate and fall behind, or perhaps seeking a way to lose him. But Newt came on, paying little heed to places where Cortina might waylay him, and risking everything to bring it all to an end. Occasionally, he stopped to give the Circle Dot horse a drink from his canteen—little handfuls poured into his palm, or to wipe its nostrils clean with a cool, damp rag. He sipped sparingly from the canteen himself, knowing the horse needed the water most. And then the canteen was empty.

When the sun was tilting over in the furnace sky, Newt followed a set of white-scarred hoof marks on the face of a red rock slope. The Circle Dot horse was heaving and lathered by the time they reached the top of the climb, and Newt slid from the saddle. His legs were rubbery after so long in the saddle, and he leaned against the blowing horse.

He took the saddle from the horse and left it behind to lighten the animal's load. It had come to the point where every pound mattered, and he was a big man.

He rode bareback off the little mountain and down into the maze of buttes and tabletop mesas stretching miles before him. A half hour later, and the Circle Dot horse couldn't be kicked into anything faster than a walk. The calves of Newt's pants legs were soaked in horse sweat, and the sweat salt running off his brow stung his eyes. As it was, it took him a bit to recognize the white horse lying in the mouth of a canyon only a few yards ahead of him.

The horse wasn't dead, but it wasn't far from it. Its rib cage rose and fell slowly, and it lay with its neck outstretched on the ground and the one eye he could see was closed. It was so dehydrated that there wasn't a wet spot on its hide, even lying in the full sun. When the horse breathed he could hear the raspy roaring from its windpipe and lungs. Even if it lived, it would never be worth riding again. It was wind-broken and perhaps foundered. He pulled his pistol and shot the horse between the eyes, rather than let it suffer any longer. The gunshot echoed off the badlands, dying away in the far distance.

He rode on, more carefully now, and came to a narrow canyon, more a crack in the side of a low, bald mountain, breaking it into two fingerlike buttes. The way up the slash was choked in places with scattered brush and littered with slabs of stone slid down from above. He left the Circle Dot horse at the foot of the slide and went forward on foot, climbing or crawling when and where he had to. The top of the mountain and the head of the little canyon loomed hundreds of feet above him.

Sweating and cursing under his breath, he eventually found where the rains from an occasional thunderstorm had worn a smooth trough into a long sheet of solid sandstone at the bottom of the canyon. Giant boulders had come to rest on its surface, and he picked his way through them. The sun in the west was shining right in his eyes, and he squinted at the heights above him, searching for Cortina.

"Here I am," Cortina called to him softly.

Cortina stood above him near the head of the canyon, atop one of those big slabs of stone only thirty yards away. He stood with his legs wide apart, and with the hot wind blowing across the desert lifting the flaps of his open wildcat vest. In the instant Newt looked up at him, Cortina's pistol was already roaring.

Cortina was fast on the trigger, but he was too angry and wild in his urgency to put Newt down. As it was, his first bullet spanged off the rock to one side of Newt, and seeing that he had missed, he cursed in Spanish.

Newt dodged a step to the right, and his hand went to the butt of the Smith while he was still on the move. A second shot stung him with rock fragments, but by then the Smith was already lifting to shoulder level. Newt couldn't recall drawing his gun, and it seemed to do so on its own, as if it were a live thing with a deadly will of its own.

A third shot from Cortina went wilder than the previous two, and Newt forced himself to hold steady and to lock the soles of his boots into the smooth stone beneath his feet, as if he were an indomitable thing as steady and immovable as those giant slabs of stone around him. He was sure he was going to die, but he intended to take Cortina with him. One shot might be all he was going to get, and come hell or high water, he was going to make that one shot count.

He turned slightly sideways with his right shoulder turned to Cortina and the Smith held at the end of his arm like a duelist or some target shooter, instead of a man in a frantic, deadly fight to the death. His eyes watered and strained against the sun burning before him atop the mountain. The long barrel of the Smith shifted ever so slightly and the front sight found the bandit outlined and skylined with the sun behind him, like a glowing shadow drawn on a canvas of sunlit, blazing sky.

The Smith bucked hard in his hand, and Cortina hunched over as if punched in the guts. Newt waited for his recoiling pistol to fall back on target again and drove a second shot into Cortina. Cortina's body sagged, and his pistol clattered on the rocks below him. He remained standing, for only a brief instant, teetering and staggering slowly at the edge of the boulder top. Another gust of wind blew up from the valley floor and Cortina reeled before it, until he finally toppled headfirst off his perch.

Newt climbed up to his body, the Smith held ready for another shot. But there was no need to shoot again. His first bullet had punched into Cortina right above his gun belt, and the second one had hit him dead center in the breastbone. Beneath Cortina's body, blood was sleeping slowly out onto the rocks, as if the stone itself were bleeding. And Cortina stared up at him, his eyes wide open, yet not seeming to recognize Newt standing there. Newt had heard tales of bold bandits dying with reckless smiles on their faces, at least that was the way the newspapers always wrote about such men's demises. But there was nothing but pain and hard living on Cortina's face. He let out one more sigh and then he was dead.

Newt fell to a sitting position beside the bandit, wrists resting on his upraised knees, and looking down the mountain. In time, he searched Cortina's body and found a single gold ingot in the bandit's vest pocket. He hefted the gold trinket in his palm and stared off the mountain once more, thinking about what he needed to do, and knowing that no good man could do such a thing at all.

He waited until the cool of darkness before he came down the canyon. He found the Circle Dot horse waiting for him and led it back to where the body of the dead white horse lay. He took Cortina's saddle, and when he was through cinching it on the Circle Dot horse, he tied Cortina's spotted vest behind it. The other thing he carried, he put in the saddlebags.

# Chapter Thirty-six

The judge and the women were waiting for him when he crossed the Rio Grande again and rode back into Las Boquillas a day later. They stood on the porch of O'Malley's tavern, watching him ride down the street, with Kizzy shading her eyes to better make him out. The judge was sitting in a chair with his bandaged leg propped up on a nail keg and his shotgun laid across his lap. Down at the far end of the village, at least twenty horses were tied in front of a house, and several of Don Alvarez's vaqueros loitered about, watching him. None of the village's regular inhabitants were to be seen anywhere, as if they knew the trouble coming and weren't about to be caught on the streets.

Newt dismounted wearily and untied the spotted vest and his saddlebags. He pitched the vest to the judge and set the saddlebags on the porch. He led the Circle Dot horse to the back of the tavern and turned it in the corral and forked it some hay from the stack there. When he came back to the porch he was carrying his

Winchester, and he took up his saddlebags and went inside without a word. Kizzy followed him.

The Alvarez girl was seated in the back of the room at a round table. There was a long bar to the left of the door, and he went to it first and took down a bottle of tequila from the wall behind it. He carried the bottle to the table and set the saddlebags in the middle of it with a thump. He laid his Winchester beside it and took a seat beside the Alvarez girl, facing the front door. His hand rubbed absentmindedly at the splintered forearm stock of the rifle, where the tavernkeeper had shot it from his hand the day before.

"Don Alvarez is here." Kizzy took a seat on a bar stool.

"Saw him." Newt cocked the Winchester and adjusted how it lay on the table, pointing the barrel toward the door. He opened the bottle and took a long pull of tequila.

"He's got Fonzo with him," she added.

Newt took another pull of tequila. "Go tell him to come down here."

She rose and went to the front door, pausing there as if she had something to say, but had thought better of it. She passed out the door, and the judge hobbled into the vacant space, his injured leg giving him trouble. He had split his right pants leg well past his knee, cut a chunk out of his boot top to shorten it, and wrapped the injured calf in some kind of filthy rag for a bandage. He glanced at the saddlebags on the table while he took a seat on one of the bar stools with his back to the bar and facing Newt to one side and out of the way of the open door.

"What happened to your leg?" Newt asked.

"Miguelito got in a lucky shot and clipped my calf."

"Are you up for another fight?"

The judge slapped his bandaged leg. "Right as rain. The wound's too far from my heart to kill me, and too far from my pecker to worry me."

Newt took another drink.

"Alvarez has got us cornered," the judge said. "He ain't moved a muscle since he got here or threatened us, but we've been under siege since you left. I think he's been waiting to see if you would come back."

Newt nodded. "We knew he was coming."

"He'll be coming all right, and he ain't gonna come down here alone."

"Let him bring whoever he wants."

A fly buzzed around the room, and Newt swatted at it when it landed on the mouth of his tequila bottle. He stared at the open door with bloodshot eyes and waited.

"I take it you caught Cortina, or did he get away?" The judge asked.

"I caught him."

"What did you do with him?"

"I'm guessing the buzzards are at him by now."

The judge made a low whistle. "You're one hard, wicked, mean son of a bitch, Widowmaker. Knew that when I first laid eyes on you."

Newt gave the judge a nasty look, as if daring him to call him by that name again, but Kizzy came back before the judge could say anything else. She immediately ducked to the opposite side of the room from the bar, taking a stand in a corner. Newt could hear the sound of boots and spurs on the porch, and Don Alvarez and three of his vaqueros came into the room behind her. They stopped inside the door, three-wide and shoulder to shoulder. Beyond them, through the open doorway, Newt could see more men sitting their horses in the street. He also noticed that the don was wearing a pistol.

"I've come for my daughter," Don Alvarez said.

"Papa!" The Alvarez girl started to get up.

"Where's the boy?" Newt reached out and took hold of the Alvarez girl's arm with his left hand to keep her in her chair. His right hand rested on the Winchester.

Don Alvarez glanced at Newt's Winchester, and then at the judge and the shotgun he was holding. "I have him outside."

"Bring him in here," Newt said. "That's the only way this works."

"You are a vile man, indeed, if you would hurt a woman."

"You play nice, and she won't get hurt. Start shooting at us and she's just as liable to get hit as we are." Newt turned the bottle up and watched the don's reaction while his throat worked down another big swallow of the Mexican firewater.

"Señor Bean," the don said quietly. "We had an agreement."

While the judge gave the don an uncertain look, Newt let go of the girl and reached forward slowly across the table. One of the vaqueros beside the don eased his hand toward his holstered pistol. Newt ignored him and unfastened one of the saddlebags. He reached inside and took out Cortina's head, dragging it out by the hair. He turned it so that it faced Don Alvarez, and then leaned against his chair back.

"There's my end of the bargain," he said with his pointer finger tapping the Winchester's receiver with a nervous tic. "Now bring in the boy."

Kizzy gasped at the sight of Cortina's head, and the Alvarez girl started crying again.

"You animal!" the Alvarez girl screamed.

Don Alvarez stared unflinching at the grisly trophy staring back at him. "Señor Bean, are you a man of your word?"

The judge lifted his shotgun, first pointing it at Don Alvarez and then slowly shifting his aim until the double bores of it covered Newt. "Sorry."

"I shouldn't have expected any less from you," Newt said.

"A man has to look out for himself," the judge replied. "And you ain't given me much choice."

"What was the deal? Don Alvarez lets you ride if you held me for him?"

"That, and I get to take Cortina with me." The judge made a small movement with the end of his shotgun to gesture at Cortina's head on the table. "There's a lot less of him left than I was planning on, but I reckon I can make do with what's left."

Newt took up the tequila again, had another drink, and then used the butt end of the bottle to shove Cortina's head off the table. It hit the floor and rolled a few feet toward the judge. "Take it, and be damned."

Don Alvarez glanced at Kizzy in the corner. "There is no need to risk the women. This thing is between us. Take your hand off the Winchester and let my daughter go. This circus woman can go, too. Do that, and I promise you that your death will be quick."

"You bring the boy. Now." Newt sat the bottle on the tabletop and eased his left hand to his lap.

"Easy there," the judge said, shoving his shotgun forward. "You got me feeling twitchy, and old Gabriel here has a hair trigger."

"Do you think you can take us all?" the don asked.

"No, but I'm going to take you with me." Newt's voice lowered to barely more than a whisper. "That's all that matters. I die, but I'm going to get you first."

Whisper or not, Don Alvarez heard him plainly. "I think you are bluffing."

"Try me. What have I got to lose?"

Don Alvarez studied Newt's face and then the Winchester pointed at his belly with Newt's hand on it. A dry, bitter chuckle escaped his throat.

"Bring the Gypsy boy," he said to one of the vaqueros with him.

All three of the nervous vaqueros gave Don Alvarez reluctant looks until he gave another order in rapid-fire Spanish, ending the argument.

"*Sí, mi jefe*," one of the vaqueros said, heading out the door.

"Judge, you better put down that shotgun or use it. You pointing that thing at me is beginning to grate on me," Newt said without taking his eyes from Don Alvarez.

The judge lowered the shotgun and let down the hammers. He slumped on the bar stool and wiped the sweat from his forehead with the bandanna around his neck. "You crazy fool."

The same vaquero who had gone out the door came back inside, shoving Fonzo in front of him. Fonzo looked no worse for the wear and, in fact, looked in better shape than he had when Newt last saw him in the Zaragoza jail. His bruises had faded to yellow, and someone had stitched up the bad cut on his face. He saw Kizzy standing in the corner and went to her. The two of them embraced, whispering things to each other.

"Consuela, come here." Don Alvarez ignored the family reunion going on in the corner of the room and held out his hand to his daughter.

The girl started to rise.

"You stay right there." Newt's voice was hard and low.

"You said you wanted a trade," Don Alvarez said with his voice as flat and hard as Newt's had been.

"You get the girl when we're across the river."

"Come to me, Consuela."

"No harm will come to your daughter. I'll turn her loose on the other side of the river. Everybody wins."

The Alvarez girl looked from one of them to another, wanting to get up out of her chair, but unsure and afraid. One of the vaqueros leaned close to Don Alvarez and whispered something in Spanish.

"You tell these men with you to keep their hands away from their pistols, or I'm going to blow a big, wide hole in you," Newt said.

Don Alvarez's jaw trembled ever so slightly, his nostrils flaring. He spun and marched out the door without looking back, his vaqueros backing out of the room, guarding him.

"You just got us all killed," the judge said when they were gone.

"Give me that shotgun." Newt stood so fast that his chair rattled and skidded across the floor behind him. He held out his left hand for the judge's gun, his right hand still on the Winchester on the table.

"You've got to understand the predicament I was in," the judge said.

"Give me the shotgun."

"I'll be damned if I'll be shot with my own gun."

"I ought to shoot you, but I need you to get across the river."

The judge pitched the shotgun to him, and Newt caught it one-handed. He noticed that the judge's hand had inched up near the rusty Colt in his waistband while he was busy catching the flying gun. He broke the shotgun open and pulled out the two brass cartridges, then snapped the breeches closed and tossed the gun back to the judge. The judge fumbled it and almost dropped it, so great was his surprise.

"What good is an unloaded gun?" the judge asked.

"You're going to keep it against this girl's head when we leave here," Newt said. "The don won't know it's unloaded, and you won't get nervous and accidentally shoot her."

"What if I need it to shoot someone else? Alvarez ain't going to let us ride out of here."

"I don't aim to be the one you shoot."

"I wasn't ever going to shoot you. I was biding my time until I saw how you wanted to play things."

Newt ignored him and looked at Kizzy. Fonzo had his arm around her shoulders, and she was staring at Cortina's head on the floor and then at Newt with horror and revulsion on her face. She looked out the window when he tried to meet her gaze.

"Miss Grey, I need you to go out and saddle the horses. Fonzo, you cover her from the back door."

Kizzy didn't move.

"I need you to get the horses now. Bring them around to the porch."

Fonzo gently moved her out of her tracks. The two of them headed for the back door, with Kizzy once more staring at Newt like he was a thing she had never seen before. Newt held out the Winchester to Fonzo when they were beside him, and Fonzo took the rifle without speaking.

"Those vaqueros are going to shoot you the instant you step out the front door," the judge said. "They're going to bust you up like a kid's piñata."

"Maybe not," Newt said. "You're going to go outside first with the girl."

"Why do I have to go out first? This is your idea."

Newt took another swallow of tequila, staring at the distorted image of the judge through the bottle's amber contents. He threw the half-empty bottle across the room, and it busted against the far wall.

"We could wait for dark," the judge said.

Newt eased to one of the front windows, staying well to one side of it. He glanced out onto the street and noted the vaqueros taking positions among the houses across from the tavern.

"Alvarez ain't going to let you do this," the judge said. "Can't you see that?"

Newt shifted quickly to the other side of the window and saw that three of the vaqueros were sitting their horses in the middle of the road between the village and the river crossing.

Kizzy soon came around the corner of the tavern, leading the horses. She seemed oblivious to the attention on her from Don Alvarez's men.

"Where'd she get the other white horse?" Newt asked.

"She killed Miguelito," the judge answered. "Drew on him and shot him stone-cold dead."

Fonzo came up behind them. His face was pale and he held the Winchester awkwardly.

"Stiffen up, boy," Newt said. "Go out there and get on your horse."

"What if they snatch the Gypsies? You'd be back to square one." The judge looked out the window at the vaqueros and grimaced. "I feel like I'm in a coffin already."

Fonzo and Kizzy mounted, and Kizzy held the other three horses by their reins. Her face was strained and pale, but she seemed determined.

The judge retrieved Newt's saddlebags and picked up Cortina's head and stuffed it in them, turning his head away and trying not to look directly at the thing.

Newt frowned when he saw what the judge had done, but didn't say anything about it. He took one more look out the window and then started across the room toward the Alvarez girl. "Time to go. Judge, you put her up in the saddle in front of you."

The Alvarez girl tried to balk when Newt took her by one arm, digging her heels into the floor and leaning back. He snatched her to her feet and passed her to the judge. The judge gave him one last, doubtful look, hung the saddlebags over his shoulder, and then eared back both shotgun hammers and placed the barrel muzzles against the back of her head.

"Move along, girl. Don't cause me any trouble and you'll be fine," the judge said.

The judge went out the front door with the Alvarez girl preceding him on shaky legs. She walked slowly, not out of fear of an unloaded shotgun, but because she, like the rest of them, knew there was a good chance that the vaqueros would start shooting. If you played out the scene ten thousand times, Newt's plan never worked. None of them had any faith that a bloodbath wasn't about to begin.

The judge kept his shotgun pressed against her body when she mounted his gray, but it was more difficult to keep her covered while he climbed up behind her, especially with his gimpy leg. Kizzy side-passed her horse against his without being asked to and pulled a pistol and held it on the girl while the judge laid the saddlebags across the gray's neck in front of the saddle and somehow managed to get up on the horse behind the girl. Kizzy didn't look Newt's way when he stepped out on the porch, and turned her attention to the river.

The short walk across the porch and down two steps to his horse felt like a long journey, with every one of Don Alvarez's men watching him with guns pointed his way. He swung into the saddle on the Circle Dot horse and turned toward the river. Don Alvarez was standing in the road waiting, and behind him were those three vaqueros, sitting their horses in a line with their rifles propped on their thighs.

Newt rode the Circle Dot horse right at him, with his Smith holstered on his hip and both his hands resting nonchalantly on his saddle horn. The don drew his own pistol and pointed it at Newt.

# Chapter Thirty-seven

The judge rode up beside Newt and pressed the shotgun into the Alvarez girl's rib cage hard enough that it made her cry out. Don Alvarez hesitated and his pistol aim wavered, his hand suddenly growing unsteady. Newt and the judge kept riding at him, with Kizzy and Fonzo close behind them.

"You stop." Don Alvarez's voice was shaky and a tear rolled down his leathery cheek.

Newt and the judge split off when they reached him, enough so that they passed to either side of him, and Newt so close that his stirrup brushed against him. Don Alvarez lowered his gun and his shoulders sagged and his chin dropped. The vaqueros called out to him, but he did not answer them. Then they parted slightly and let the group ride on past.

Newt led them toward the river, keeping his horse to a walk. Behind them, Kizzy's white dog growled at the vaqueros while it stopped to hike its leg and urinate on a cactus before loping off after Kizzy. A dust devil danced crazily in the windswept street.

"He's never going to let us cross," the judge said as

their horses entered the shallow water. "Damned but I hate to take it in the back."

Newt's expression never changed, and they splashed their horses into the river shoal. When they climbed up the low bank on the Texas side, Kizzy stopped long enough to look back. The vaqueros had come down to the Mexican side of the river, but the don was still standing in the street where he had been before, watching them.

The trail up out of the river breaks climbed through a notch in the tableland above, and they were all over the top and out of sight of the vaqueros below before Newt stopped his horse.

"Let her go," he said to the judge.

The judge dismounted and helped the Alvarez girl down. She took a deep breath and tried to wipe the tear-streaked grime from her face and combed her fingers through her hair.

"Ma'am, I'm sorry we had to do it this way," Newt said. "Go back to your pa."

The girl smoothed the front of her dress and turned and started on her way down to the river. They watched her disappear over the lip of the descent, and when she was gone they started northward.

"Think we ought to set a faster pace?" the judge asked. "Soon as they see that girl free of us, those vaqueros are liable to come after us."

"Let 'em come," Newt said.

And yet, the vaqueros didn't come. It was someone else entirely that blocked their course, some three or for miles later. Newt pulled them up and stared back at the four Texas Rangers sitting their horses in the trail. They were the very same Rangers he had met in Langtry.

"Sergeant, you boys sure could've showed up sooner, and I wouldn't have complained a lick," the judge said.

"We've been patrolling the river like you asked. Got two more men at Del Rio watching things there," the tallest of the Rangers said. "We've been stuck in this hellhole of a country for days, so you ought not complain about the favor we done you."

"Who are these men?" Fonzo asked.

The sergeant tapped the badge on his vest. "We're the law hereabouts, son."

"I guess you didn't find Cortina," one of the other Rangers said.

"Oh, he's a hard one to catch," the judge answered before any of the others could.

Newt glanced at the judge with a curious expression, but didn't say anything.

"Too bad," the sergeant said. "That's some kind of reward they've got out for him."

"Reward?" Kizzy asked.

The judge gave her his most sheepish grin and avoided looking Newt's way.

"The governor of Texas put five hundred dollars on Cortina's head, and the railroad put another five hundred on him, dead or alive," the sergeant answered.

"Is that a fact?" Newt's attention was solely on the judge.

"It is, indeed," the sergeant said. "Cortina and his bunch robbed a mail car outside of Fort Worth three months ago and killed the express agent."

"And how long has that reward been out?" Newt asked.

"Since about a month after the robbery."

The judge eased his horse forward. "Now see here. Let me explain."

"I ought to have shot you back there," Newt said. "I don't suppose you were planning on telling me about this reward?"

The judge spurred his horse toward the Rangers. "Get 'im, boys!"

The Rangers didn't move. When the judge reached them and turned his horse around, the sergeant pointed at Newt.

"We don't have any papers on him," the sergeant said.

"What about the murder of Amos Redding?" the judge said. "He's wearing Amos's gun and hat."

The sergeant shook his head. "We sent a man up to Fort Stockton. Seems like the Widowmaker here was telling the truth. Cortina killed Amos somewhere north of the fort, and the way that post commander told it, the Widowmaker brought Matilda to the fort and then saw her on her way to El Paso with a wagon train of freighters."

Newt relaxed slightly. "I thought there for a minute that I was going to have trouble with you Rangers, and I have enough trouble to do me for a while."

The sergeant pointed in the direction of the river. "Y'all have trouble over there?"

The four of them looked at one another and shrugged. Newt managed a weary smile and said, "Not much."

"Who are these two with you?" The sergeant was talking about Kizzy and Fonzo.

"Why, they're good friends of mine," the judge said. "That boy in the tall hat is Fonzo the Great, and she's his sister, Buckshot Annie, late of the Incredible Grey Family Circus. Ain't you ever heard of them?"

The Rangers led the way north, as they knew the country. Before long, the judge's horse fell back behind the rest, and Newt reined up and slowed until the judge rode alongside him.

"How come you didn't tell those Rangers what you've got in those saddlebags?" Newt asked.

The judge scratched at his whiskers as if he were in deep thought. "Could be they would hit me up for a share of the reward. Money doesn't grow on trees, you know, and a thousand dollars is a hefty sum."

"Speaking of that reward, how are you intending on splitting it with me?"

"How's fifty-fifty suit you?"

"How about sixty-forty, since I was the one that got Cortina?"

"You're a bald-faced highwayman if you think I would go for that."

Newt patted the Smith on his hip. "Sixty-forty, and maybe I could forget about how you tried to double-cross me back there with Don Alvarez."

"There's no way I'm going to be able to keep those Rangers in the dark, and I'll have to give them a cut out of my share, like it or not."

"You poor thing. Have we got a deal? I'm still of a mind to shoot your sorry ass."

The judge nodded slowly. "What's a hard case like you gonna do with six hundred dollars? You'll just drink it up in some dive or spend it on a spree. You ought to think on going partners with me. Invest your money, you know, and let it work for you."

"That'll be the day."

The judge pulled a cigar out of his vest and spent three matches trying to get it lit. When it was finally going, he shifted it to one corner of his mouth and said around it, "I never should have let you talk me into going to Mexico."

# Chapter Thirty-eight

**T**hey waited on the porch of the depot house at Langtry, Texas. Fonzo was helping load the horses into a stock car, and Newt and Kizzy were alone for the moment. She stood with her arms folded across her chest and her back to him on the edge of the decking next to the train. She had long since changed out of her circus costume, and she looked like someone else altogether in her new yellow dress and the prim little bonnet on her head. She looked like any other woman, but he knew she wasn't. A traveling valise lay at her feet.

"You haven't said a word to me since we left Las Boquillas," Newt said.

"I don't have anything to say to you," she answered, still not looking at him.

He stepped beside her. "Yes, you do. Say what you've got to say."

She turned to him. "You cut off that man's head. What kind of man can do that?"

"Don't make it sound like I enjoyed it," he said.

"And you couldn't have brought Don Alvarez the body?"

"My horse was worn out and half-dead, and barely in shape to carry me. You wanted your brother to live, didn't you?"

"Yes, more than anything. But I couldn't have done what you did."

He looked away. "I've always been able to do the hard things."

"Where will you go now?" She turned her back on him again.

"I'm still thinking on it. What about you? What's waiting for you in San Antonio?"

"The newspapers say Bill Cody's company is in Chicago. I'm going to send him a wire, and if he will still honor the offer he made us a year ago, we're going on to join his show."

"That sounds like a good plan."

"You ought to go back East, too," she said. "This wild country isn't good for you."

"I'll get by."

"I won't forget what you've done for me and Fonzo."

"You don't owe me anything."

"I do."

"What is it you said about folks like me? Outsiders? *Gadje?* You go on about your business and forget about the likes of me."

She turned back to him with her eyes wet and un-blinking. "Talk your tough talk, Widowmaker Jones. Go ahead, I don't care. You are not Roma, but you aren't *gadje*, either. You're a violent man, but I think you are my friend. I haven't had many friends."

Newt was about to say something else, but the judge walked up. He looked at the white horses Fonzo was helping the train crew load. "Miss Grey, I'm plumb sorry you didn't get all your horses back. What kind of a circus act are you going to have with only two horses?"

Kizzy looked at Newt instead of the judge when she answered. "I'll get by."

The judge tipped his hat to her. "I must say, for a Gypsy girl, you aren't half-bad."

She took up her valise and put a foot on the steps to the passenger car before she hesitated. "For a crooked old judge, you aren't so bad yourself."

The judge handed Newt a beer while they watched her go inside the passenger car. Newt was surprised how cold the beer was, and the judge noticed his expression.

"Bought a load of ice off the train this morning."

Newt hesitated to take a drink of the beer. "How much is this costing me? Last time I had a beer in your place, it cost me plenty."

The judge laughed. "This one is on the house."

"So long, Judge."

The judge squinted at him. "What are you going to do in San Antonio?"

"Never been there, and thought I would see the sights."

"You don't have a clue, do you? You're only going along to see that Gypsy girl on her way, aren't you?"

"Maybe."

"You remember my offer. I can put in a good word for you with the Rangers."

"Thanks, but I believe I'll pass."

"You were a sentimental fool to give those circus kids your share of the reward," the judge said. "You

ain't ever going to have two dollars to rub together if
you keep giving your money away."

Newt took up his bedroll and then he looked to
make sure the Circle Dot horse had been loaded in
the stock car before he went up the steps into the passenger car. Fonzo was going to ride with the horses,
but Kizzy sat on a bench seat alone near the rear of
the car. When Newt reached her, she made room so
that he could slide past her and sit beside her next
to the window. Neither of them said a word.

The window beside Newt was open and he looked
down the street at the hanging pole that the judge
had put up for Cortina. The judge was still on the
depot porch talking to two new arrivals to the town.

"New to the West, are you?" The judge had his arms
on both of the men's shoulders, guiding them toward
his saloon. "Well, I've got a sight for you. For a dollar,
you can look at the head of Javier Cortina, the
wickedest bandit that ever drew a breath. While you
look, I'll tell you the story of how I ran him down."

The train started forward with a hiss of steam.
Snippets of the judge's conversation drifted to Newt
as if in a dream.

"Yes, sir, that's me, the law west of the Pecos . . . law
and order every time, that's what I say . . . Cortina
wasn't the kind to be taken alive . . . I gunned him
down with old Gabriel . . . You bet you can hold that
shotgun. Old Cortina was tough, but he weren't no
match for . . ."

The judge's voice trailed off as Langtry disappeared in the window, and Newt watched the West
Texas scenery roll past with his mind still on the hanging pole.

# Chapter Thirty-nine

The miles passed behind beneath them with the clickety-clack of the train's wheels passing along the rails. Newt leaned his head against the window, trying to lose himself in the rocking of the coach, and trying to shut out the sound of the drunken man in the bowler hat near the front of the car. That very fellow was up in the center aisle, talking as loudly as he had been for most of the trip and bragging about everything he could think of. Several newspapermen near the man seemed to be hanging on his every word as if he were some kind of celebrity. The little Yankee beside him was trying to calm him down, but he was having none of it, and soaking up the attention.

"If you weren't such a wormy little fellow, I would paste you a good one on the ear," the drunk said to the farmer sitting next to where he stood, and the same farmer who he imagined had done him some offense.

The drunk was a big man. A little shy of six feet tall, but broad shouldered and deep in the chest, with a thick neck and the sense about him that he was as strong as an ox. He backed up to give the farmer he was bullying the room to stand, and handed his bowler hat to the little Yankee behind him, still trying to calm him down.

The bully ran a hand over his close-cropped head, twisted one end of his pointed, handlebar mustache, and assumed a boxing stance with his fists held forward before him, as if he were posing for a photograph.

"Get up and fight, or show all these people what a coward you are," he said to the farmer.

The farmer was half his size, and obviously wanting no part of a brawl with a man sure to hurt him badly. The farmer's wife clutched his arm.

"I never said you weren't good," the farmer pleaded. "I just said I thought Jem Mace was better than you back in his prime."

The bully turned enough so that he could see the newspapermen behind him, and so that they could hear him plainly. His clipped Boston accent was slurred from the booze. "A Brit best me? Why, you un-patriotic little sack of bones. There's not a man in the world that can lick me. I'm twenty-seven and oh, with the gloves or without."

Newt only wanted to sleep, but he couldn't ignore the noise anymore. He'd seen that kind before—braggarts who turned mean when in their cups, and the kind that tried to make themselves seem bigger than they really were by picking on those weaker than them.

"Stupid drunk," Newt said.

A man across the aisle set aside the notebook he was writing in and snorted. "That stupid drunk is

John L. Sullivan, bare-knuckle champion of the world. Why don't you go say that to his face?"

"So that's the Boston Strong Boy himself, is it?" Newt said. "What's he doing on a train in Texas?"

"Where have you been the last year and a half? Don't you read the papers?" the same man asked. "Sullivan is touring the country. He'll fight any man for four rounds, and two hundred and fifty dollars to anyone that can beat him."

"Hmm."

"Eight good fighters have tried so far, and none of them have come close. For God's sake, he knocked out Paddy Ryan in Mississippi two years ago, and Paddy was as tough as they come."

"You some kind of reporter?" Newt asked.

"*Galveston Daily News.* Sullivan is on his way to our fair city for an exhibition match." The reporter reached across the aisle for a handshake.

Newt ignored the offered hand. Sullivan wouldn't give up on egging the farmer into a fight, and he slapped the little farmer hard enough that the sound of it carried through the car. He made another of his ribald jokes, and some of those watching him laughed nervously.

"Newt, don't you do what you're thinking," Kizzy said. "You don't have to be that way."

Newt rose and slid past her to get to the center aisle. He glanced at Sullivan and then back at her. "You look away, Miss Grey. Don't pay me any attention at all."

"Don't . . ." she started.

"What was it the judge said? A man should stick to his talents?" Newt unbuckled his gun belt and handed it to the reporter he had been talking to, at the same time giving her a smile.

While the reporter was still trying to figure out why Newt had given him his gun, Newt started down the aisle. The little Yankee trying to get Sullivan to quit picking on the farmer noticed him coming.

"You aren't an officer of the law, are you?" The little Yankee tried to block Newt's way.

"No." Newt looked over the man at Sullivan.

"Please pay Mr. Sullivan no mind," the little man said. "I'm afraid he isn't himself today."

"Get out of the way."

"I'm his fight promoter. I can get you his autograph."

Newt shoved the promoter into his seat and went past him. Sullivan still had his back turned to Newt and was too intent on the farmer to hear his approach. Newt cleared his throat and reached out and tapped him on the shoulder. Sullivan turned on him slowly, his drunken, stubborn face sizing Newt up.

"What do you want, you big bastard?" Sullivan asked.

"Leave that man alone."

"This ought to be good," one of the reporters said. Several of the other reporters and those in Sullivan's entourage climbed over the back of their seats to give the two combatants room.

"And who the hell are you?" Sullivan asked, shoving one fat pointer finger in front of Newt's nose.

Newt slapped the hand away and threw a short, straight right into Sullivan's cheek. The boxer staggered back two steps and fell to the floor, and the train grew as quiet as a church.

"Widowmaker Jones, at your service," Newt said, backing off and looking down at Sullivan.

Sullivan groaned, and for a moment it looked as if he were down for good.

"Look at that," one of the passengers exclaimed. "He knocked the champ down with one lick."

But Sullivan wasn't out. He groaned again and took hold of a seat back and slowly pulled himself to his feet. There was blood on his cheekbone, and a nasty snarl on his face. He lunged off-balance and clipped Newt with a hard left hook, falling again in the process.

The blow staggered Newt to one side and back three rows, but he caught himself against a bench. The passenger car swung dizzily before him, and he tasted his own blood.

"Knock him out, Champ!" one of the crowd shouted. "Give 'im the what for!"

"I'll bet you five dollars Sullivan puts him down in the first thirty seconds," another voice said.

"What kind of fool do you think I am?" the first voice replied. "Look at the scars on that fellow. He's a born loser if I ever saw one."

"I'll take that bet," Kizzy said, quieting the room again.

Newt turned and saw her standing in the aisle at the far end of the car. Those cat eyes of her were wet again, and he wasn't sure if it was resignation or worry that he read on her face. She was truly beautiful, and not a woman easy to forget.

He gave her one slow nod of his chin and then turned and wiped the blood from his mouth and flexed his fists. A smirk of a smile revealed a broken tooth. "Just like old times."

Sullivan shuffled forward, crouched with his fists cocked and loaded. "You better fight hard, cowboy, or I'm going to beat you within an inch of your life."

The crooked, chip-toothed smile spread across Newt's busted lips again, and he laughed bitterly and quietly. "I wouldn't have it any other way."

# Connect with Us

Visit us online at
**KensingtonBooks.com**
to read more from your favorite authors, see books
by series, view reading group guides, and more.

for sneak peeks, chances to win books and prize packs,
and to share your thoughts with other readers.

**facebook.com/kensingtonpublishing
twitter.com/kensingtonbooks**

## Tell us what you think!

To share your thoughts, submit a review,
or sign up for our eNewsletters, please visit:
**KensingtonBooks.com/TellUs.**